BOUND BY
A CHILD

BY
KATHERINE GARBERA

MILLS & BOON

Published in Great Britain 2014
by Mills & Boon, an imprint of Harlequin (UK) Limited,
Eton House, 18-24 Paradise Road, Richmond, Surrey, TW9 1SR

© 2014 Katherine Garbera

ISBN: 978 0 263 91458 0

51-0214

Printed and bound in Spain
by Blackprint CPI, Barcelona

Katherine Garbera is a *USA TODAY* bestselling author of more than forty books who has always believed in happy endings. She lives in England with her husband, children and their pampered pet, Godiva. Visit Katherine on the web at www.katherinegarbera.com, or catch up with her on Facebook and Twitter.

Huge thanks to all of the readers
who chat with me on my Facebook page,
especially Danny Bruggemann, Jean Gordon,
Barbara Padlo, Angie Floris Thompson and Amelia
Hernanadez, who suggested names
for the hurricane in this book. I ended up choosing
Pandora since it sort of fitted my story. :-)

Plus a shout-out to my UK writing buddies
Celia Anderson and Lucy Felthouse.
Thanks for talking books, hotties and UK phrases
with me. Writing is a hard, lonely job
and I have to thank my darling husband
and kiddos for their support. And as always
thanks to my editor, Charles, for his insight.

One

Allan McKinney might look like a Hollywood hottie with his lean, made-for-sin body, neatly styled dark brown hair and piercing silver eyes that could make a woman forget to think. But Jessi Chandler knew he was the devil in disguise.

He was the bad guy and always had been. More tempting than sin itself as he rode in at the last minute to ruin everything. Knowing him the way she did, she couldn't imagine he had come to her table in the corner of Little Bar here in the Wilshire/La Brea area of Los Angeles for any other reason than to crow about his latest victory.

It had been only three weeks since he and his vengeful cousins at Playtone Games had taken over her family's company, Infinity Games, bringing their longtime rivalry to a vicious climax.

She'd just come from a meeting at Playtone Games where she'd made a proposal to try to save her job. The most humiliating thing about this merger was having to grovel in front of Allan. She was a damned fine director of marketing, but instead of being able to continue in her role and just get on with the work that needed to be done, she had to trek into the city from Malibu once a week and prove to the Montrose cousins that she was earning her paycheck.

He slid into the booth across from her, his long legs brushing against hers. He acted as if he owned this place and the world. There was something about his arrogance that had always made her want to take him down a notch or two.

It was 5:00 p.m., and the bar was just beginning to get busy with the after-work crowd. She was anonymous here and could just let her guard down for a minute, but now that Allan was sitting across from her, messing with her mojo, that wasn't going to happen.

"Are you here to rub it in?" she asked at last. It fit with the man she believed him to be and with the little competition they'd had going since the moment they'd met. "Seems like a Montrose-McKinney thing to do."

Her father had been adamant about staying away from Thomas Montrose's grandsons due to the bad blood between their families. She got that, but even before the takeover, she'd had no choice but to deal with Allan when her best friend, Patti, had fallen in love with and married his best friend.

"Not quite. I'm here to make you an offer," he said, signaling the waitress and ordering a Glenlivet neat.

"Thanks, but I don't need your kind of help," she said. She'd probably find herself out of a job quicker with him on her side.

He ran his hand over the top of his short hair, narrowed his eyes and looked at her in a way that made her sit up straighter in her chair. "Do you get off on pushing me to the edge?"

"Sort of," she said. She did take a certain joy in sparring with him. And she kept score of who won and who lost.

"Why?" he asked, pulling out his iPhone and setting it on the table next to him. He glanced down at the screen and then brought his electric gaze back to her.

"Concentrating on your phone and not on the person you're with is one reason," she answered. It irked her when anyone did that, but bothered her even more when the person was Allan. "Besides, I like getting to see the chinks in your perfect facade when you can't hide the real Allan."

The waitress delivered his drink. He leaned forward on his elbows. The woman was thin and pretty and wore a pair of large black glasses that were clearly a personality statement and went well with her pixie haircut. Allan smiled at her, and the waitress blushed, which made Jessi roll her eyes.

"What did I do to make you so adversarial toward me?" he asked, turning back to her as the waitress left.

"Why do you care?"

"I'm tired of always arguing with you. In fact, that brings me back to my reason for tracking you down," he said.

"What reason?"

"I'd like to buy you out. Your shares in Infinity Games are now worth a lot of money, and we both know you don't want to work for my cousin Kell or me. I'll make you a fair offer."

She sat there in shock as his words sank in. Did he think her family heritage meant so little to her? When she thought of how her dad and grandfather had always been so busy at work that they'd never been around...

well, hell, no, she wasn't selling. Especially not to a Montrose heir. "Never. I'd give them away before I sold to you."

He shrugged. "I just thought I'd save all of us a lot of frustration. You don't seem to be really interested in working for the merged company."

"I'm not selling," she said one more time, just in case he had any illusion that she was going to walk away easily. "I'm planning to keep my job and make you and your cousins eat your words."

"What words?"

"That Emma and I are expendable. Don't deny that you believe it."

She and her older sister still had to prove themselves if they wanted to keep their jobs. Sure, they were shareholders, so they'd always have an ownership stake in the company, but their actual jobs were on the line. Their younger sister, Cari, had already jumped through hoops for the Montrose cousins and had ended up keeping her position and falling in love with one of them.

Declan Montrose was now engaged to her, though three months ago he'd arrived at Infinity Games to manage the merger of the two companies, which meant he was there to fire the Chandler sisters. But Cari had turned the tables on him, revealing that he was the father of her eighteen-month-old son as a result of a brief affair they'd had. This had been a big surprise to everyone on both sides of the merger. It had been an interesting time, to say the least, but in the end she and Dec had fallen in love and Cari had managed to save her job at the newly merged Playtone-Infinity Games.

"I wasn't going to deny it," Allan said. "The situation with both you and Emma is different than the one with

Cari. When she approached Dec and I with her ideas for saving the staff at Infinity Games she was happy to listen to our ideas, as well."

His words hurt; Jessi wasn't going to lie about that. But Cari was known for being the caring sister, and Jessi, well, she'd always been the rebel, the ballbuster. But that didn't mean she was emotionless. She wanted to see her family's legacy in video games continue; after all, Gregory Chandler had been a pioneer in the industry in the seventies and eighties. "I have a few ideas that I've been working on."

"Share them with me," Allan invited, glancing again at his phone.

"Why?" she asked.

"To see if you're sincere about wanting to keep your position. No more lame ideas like sending out Infinity-Playtone game characters to make appearances at malls. You're head of marketing and we expect more than that."

"It wasn't—" she said, but in her heart she knew it sort of was. She didn't want Playtone-Infinity to be successful so she'd…shot herself in the foot. "Okay, maybe it was a little lame."

"What else do you have in mind? You're too smart not to have something big," he said, staring at her with that intense gaze of his.

"Was that actually a compliment?"

"Don't act so surprised. You're very good at your job and we both know you know it. Talk to me, Jessi."

She hesitated. She *was* good, and she wasn't ever as tentative as she felt right now. It was just that she'd been beaten and felt like it today. "I don't… What can you do?"

"Decide if it's worth my time to help you," he said at last.

"Why?"

"Our best friends are married and we're their daughter's godparents. I can't just let Kell fire you without at least making some sort of effort to help," he said. "Patti and John would never forgive me."

"Then why offer to buy me out?"

"It would solve the problem and we'd both be able to walk away from this."

"It would," Jessi said. "But that's not happening."

She rubbed the back of her neck. She didn't like anything about this merger but she also didn't relish the idea of being fired. "I'm one person who wouldn't be swayed by your bank account."

He shrugged off her comment and for a moment looked pensive.

"It bothers you that I sent the jet to pick you and Patti up that first time we met, doesn't it?" he asked, leaning back and glancing at his iPhone, but quickly looking back at Jessi, which earned him a few more points toward being a good guy.

She took a swallow of her gin and tonic. "Yes. It felt like you were trying too hard. I mean, offering your private jet to fly us to Paris…that was showing off."

"Maybe I just wanted Patti to have a proposal she'd always remember. You and I both know that John doesn't earn what I earn. I was just helping my friend out."

"I know. It was romantic. I admit I didn't behave as well as I could have…. I guess I can be a bit of a brat."

"Well, you certainly were that weekend," he said,

leaning in so that she caught a whiff of his spicy aftershave.

She closed her eyes for a minute and acknowledged that if she didn't keep Allan in the adversary category, there was a part of her that would be attracted to him. He was the only person—man or woman—she'd ever met whom she could go head-to-head with and still talk to the next day. He understood that winning was important to her and didn't get mad when she won. He just got even, which, to be fair, appealed to her as much as it irritated her.

"But that's in the past. Let's work together. I think you and Emma probably have a lot to contribute to the newly merged company."

"Probably? Jeez, that sounds encouraging," she said, taking another sip of her drink.

"I'm trying here," he said.

"Well, I've got a few feelers out in the movie industry. There are three new action movies coming next summer that I think are good matches for the type of games that we develop, which might be enough lead time to get a really good game out." Given that the merged company was not only a prime video game developer for consoles like Xbox and PlayStation, but also had a thriving app business for smartphones and tablets, making games with movie tie-ins was a naturally good idea. Infinity Games had never pursued this line of business before, but since the takeover, Jessi and her sisters had been thinking outside the box.

"That's a great idea. I have some contacts in that area if you'd like me to use them," Allan offered.

"Really?"

"Yes," he said. "It's in my best interest to help you."

"Is it?"

"I'm the CFO, Jessi. Anything that affects the bottom line concerns me."

"Of course it does," she said.

She was torn. A part of her wanted to accept his help, but this was Allan McKinney, and she didn't trust him. It wasn't just that he'd thrown around his money as if the stuff grew on trees; it was also that she hadn't been able to find out much about him from her private investigator, whom she'd hired to check out John when Patti had first met him. What the detective had turned up about Allan…well, frankly, it had all seemed too good to be true.

No one had the kind of happy, pampered existence the P.I. had found when he dug into Allan's past. It was too clean, too…perfect. There was something he'd been hiding, but none of that had mattered at the time, since John McCoy was the main subject of the investigation and he'd turned out to be a good guy.

Maybe Jessi should ask Orly, her P.I., to start digging again. When it came to Allan, there had been too few leads and many closed doors the first time around. Given what had happened with Playtone and Infinity, and that she'd recently had Allan's cousin Dec investigated, too, maybe it was time to ask Orly to find out what more he could about Allan.

"Sure, I'd love your help," she said.

"You sound sarcastic," Allan commented, glancing down at his mobile phone yet again.

"It's the best I can do," she said.

"Excuse me for a moment. I keep getting a call from a number I don't know," he told her.

He picked up his phone and answered. After a moment, his brow furrowed, and he hunched back in his chair. "Oh, God, no," he muttered.

"What?" she asked. She grabbed her Kate Spade bag and started to slide off the bench, until Allan grabbed her hand.

She shook her head but waited as he listened, and then his face went ashen. He turned away from her.

"How?" he asked, his voice gruff.

She could only stare at him as he shook his head and rasped, "The baby?" After a pause he murmured, "Okay, I will be there on Friday." He disconnected the call and turned to her. "John and Patti are dead."

Jessi wanted to believe he was lying, but his face was pale and there was none of that arrogant charm she always associated with him. She pulled her phone out and saw that she, too, had received several calls from an unknown number.

"I can't believe it. Are you sure?"

He gave her a look that was so lost and wounded, she knew the truth.

"No," she said, wrapping her arm around her waist. *God, no.*

Allan was shaken to his core. He'd lost his parents at a rather young age, which was part of the reason he and John had bonded, but this was…wrong. It was just wrong that someone so young and with so much to live for had died.

Jessi's hands were shaking, and he glanced over at her, only to find everything he was feeling inside was there on her face. The woman who always looked so tough and in control was suddenly small and fragile.

He got up and moved around to her side, putting his

arm around her shoulder and drawing her into the curve of his body. She resisted for the merest of seconds before she turned her face into his chest, and he felt the humid warmth of her tears as they soaked into his shirt.

She was silent as she cried, which was nothing more than he'd expect from someone as in control as Jessi always was. By focusing on her pain and her tears he was able to bury his own feelings. A world without his best friend wasn't one he wanted to dwell on. John balanced him out. Reminded Allan of all the reasons why life was good. But now—

"How?" she asked, pushing back from him and grabbing a cocktail napkin to wipe her face and then blow her nose.

Her face was splotchy, red from the tears, and she took a shuddering breath as she tried to speak again. The tears were at odds with her rebel-without-a-care look. She wore her version of business attire, a short black skirt that ended at her thighs, a tight green jacket that had bright shiny zippers and a little shell camisole that revealed the upper curves of her breasts and her tattoo.

His chest was too tight for words. He didn't really know how to talk through the grief. But as he stared into those warm brown eyes of Jessi's—one of the very first things he'd noticed about her when they'd met—he realized that he could do this. He would pull himself together and do this for her.

"Car accident," he said.

"John is an excellent driver, as is Patti—oh, God, is Hannah okay?"

"Yes. She wasn't with them. Another driver hit them

head-on as they were coming home from a Chamber of Commerce meeting."

Allan was John's next-of-kin contact, which was why he'd gotten the call. "Let's get out of here."

She nodded. He could tell she was in no shape to drive, and steered her toward his Jaguar XF. She got into the passenger seat and then slumped forward, putting her hands over her face as her shoulders shook.

Never in his life had Allan felt this powerless, and he hated it. He stood outside the car and tipped his head back, staring up into the fading fall sunset. He felt tears burning in his own eyes and used his thumbs to press them back. He pushed hard on his eye sockets until he was able to staunch the flow, and then walked around the car and got inside.

Jessi sat there silently next to him, looking over at him with those wet, wounded eyes, and for the first time he saw the woman beneath the brashness. He saw someone who needed him.

"What is Hannah going to do? Patti's mom has Alzheimer's and there's no other close family."

"I don't know," he admitted. "John has some family but not really anyone close. Just a couple of cousins. We'll figure it out."

"Together," she said, meeting his gaze. "Oh, God. I can't believe I just said that."

"Me, either. But it only makes sense now."

"It does. Plus John and Patti would want us to do it together," Jessi said.

"Yes, they would," he said.

The little girl would never know her parents, but Allan decided he'd do everything in his power to ensure that she wouldn't grow up alone.

He took Jessi's hand in his. "Let's call their attorney back and find out the answers we both need."

She linked her fingers with his as he made the call and waited to be connected.

When he was put through, he said, "This is Allan McKinney again. You and I were just discussing John McCoy. Do you mind if I put you on speaker? I'm with Jessi Chandler. She is Hannah's other godparent."

"Not at all." Allan put the phone on speaker. "Go ahead."

"This is Reggie Blythe, Ms. Chandler. I'm the attorney for the McCoys."

"Hello, Mr. Blythe. What can you tell us?"

"Please call me Reggie. I don't have all the details as to what happened, but John and Patti were on their way back from a Chamber of Commerce dinner and were involved in a fatal accident. Miss Hannah was at home with a sitter—" they heard the rustling of papers "—Emily Duchamp. Emily has agreed to stay overnight with the baby. Hannah will be placed in a temporary foster situation in the morning."

Jessi's grip on Allan tightened. "Patti would hate that. Is there any way you can keep Hannah in her home?"

"Actually, as cogodparents, you have certain rights, but you will need to get here as soon as possible to avoid her being placed in the state's care."

State care. Allan knew that John never would have wanted Hannah to end up there. And there was no need for it. Didn't John have distant cousins and a great-aunt on his dad's side? "I believe John had a cousin who lives nearby."

"I don't think it's best to go into this over the phone. When can you both get to North Carolina?"

"As soon as humanly possible."

"Good," Reggie said. "I'll be in my office all day tomorrow. Please let me know when you two will get here."

"Oh, we're not together," Jessi said.

"Aren't you? You called me together, and given the terms of the will—never mind. We will sort it all out when you get to my office," Reggie said.

"Why did you think we were together?" Allan asked.

"John and Patti indicated in their will that they wanted guardianship to be given to the two of you."

"We figured as much," Jessi said. "We can come up with some sort of schedule."

"In the eyes of the courts," Reggie said, "the best arrangement is to provide a stable home for the child. But again, we can talk more about this when you get here."

When Allan disconnected the call, he dropped Jessi's hand, and she looked at him as if he'd grown two heads. "We fight all the time."

"We do," he said, before turning away and trying to think. It was almost too much to process.

His best friend was dead. Allan was a committed bachelor who had been named coguardian of a tiny baby with the one woman on the planet who aggravated him the most. He looked at her again. She seemed as upset by the tragedy as he was. But he knew they'd both do whatever they could to make the situation work. It didn't matter that they were enemies; from this moment forward they were bound together by baby Hannah.

"You and me…" she said.

"And baby makes three."

Two

Allan dropped Jessi off at her place in Echo Park. She looked small and lost and so unlike the indomitable woman he usually knew her to be that he didn't know how to handle her.

She didn't turn and wave as she entered her house, and he hadn't expected her to. He knew in time she'd get back to herself, but then he wondered if that were true. How could either of them ever be the same again?

Traffic was heavy, and it took him forty minutes to get to his home in Beverly Hills. He'd purchased the mansion after Playtone had made him a millionaire. John had actually helped him build the pergola and brick backyard eating area and barbecue. As he pulled into his circle drive, he was haunted by memories of his friend on his last visit to California.

Allan dropped his head forward on the steering wheel, but tears didn't come. Inside, he was cold and felt alone. And he realized that the last person he cared about was gone. He'd loved his parents, really loved them. They'd been a close family unit—just the three of them. Allan's grandfather had disowned his daughter when she'd refused to marry a wealthy heir he'd picked out for her, intending to funnel that money into his revenge against the Chandlers. It had only been after his grandfather's death when Kell had come to Allan and invited him to be a part of Playtone that he'd joined the company and put his penchant for managing money to good use.

She'd married instead for love, and they'd lived a quiet little life in the Temecula Valley—two hours away from Los Angeles, but really a world apart.

Allan heard a rap on the window of his Jaguar XF and looked up to see his butler, Michael Fawkes, standing there. The fifty-seven-year-old former middleweight boxer had been in his employ since he'd inked his first multimillion-dollar deal for Playtone. Fawkes was a great guy and looked a little bit like Mickey Rourke.

"Are you okay, sir?"

Allan took his keys from the ignition and climbed out of the car. "Yes, Fawkes, I am. But John McCoy was killed in a car accident. I'm leaving tomorrow to fly to the Outer Banks to help make funeral arrangements and see to his daughter."

"My condolences, sir. I liked Mr. McCoy," Fawkes said.

"Everyone liked him," Allan said.

"Shall I accompany you?" Fawkes asked.

"Yes. I need you to make sure we have accommodation in Hatteras. I think we should be able to stay at the B and B that John and Patti own...owned," he said, turning away from Fawkes. "Give me a minute."

Jessi would probably have a hard time booking a flight to North Carolina at this hour, and it wasn't a big town they were flying into. For a moment he rejected the idea of making an offer to let her fly with him. But then he knew he had to at least reach out to her. She was truly the only other person who felt the way he did right now.

As much as she irritated him, and though it irked him to admit it, he needed her. She made him feel as if he wasn't dealing with John's death alone.

"Please include Ms. Chandler in our arrangements," Allan said.

"Really?" Fawkes asked in a surprised tone of voice. Jessi did her best to rattle the butler whenever they came into contact.

"Yes. I was with her when she got the news. She's as affected by this as we both are."

Allan pulled his iPhone out of his pocket and texted her.

I'm taking the jet to North Carolina in the morning. Want a lift?

Jessi's response was immediate. Thanks. I'd appreciate that. Are you leaving tonight? I've made arrangements with the funeral home to talk about Patti's service in the morning. If we go tonight I can talk to them in person.

I had thought to leave tomorrow but given that we are going to lose three hours perhaps tonight is best.

I thought so.

Can you be packed and ready in two hours?

Of course. TTYL

"Very well, sir. I shall make all the arrangements," Fawkes said when he learned of the plan. "When are we leaving?"

"Two hours," Allan said.

He left his assistant and headed to his den, where he poured himself a stiff Scotch and then went over to his recliner to call his cousins. But there was a knock on the door before he could dial.

"Come in," he called.

Kell and Dec entered the room. They looked somber, and he realized that though John was his best friend, both his cousins had counted John as their friend, as well.

"We came as soon as we heard," Dec said. He stood in the doorway looking awkward.

"Thanks. I'm leaving tonight. I don't expect the trip to take more than a week. Jessi is coming with me, Kell. I think we might have to adjust some of her deadlines," Allan said. Even if she was his most irritating adversary, he had to help her out now. He'd seen her broken and he shared her pain.

"We can discuss business later. When will the funeral be?"

"I don't know. I have to talk to the funeral home once we get to North Carolina. John only had a few distant cousins. I won't know what kind of arrangements they might have already made until I'm on the ground there. I might end up in charge of the planning. And then there is Patti to consider. I know that Jessi is arranging her service."

"Just let us know and we'll fly out for it," Dec said. "Do you need anything?"

He shook his head. What could he say? For once he was at a loss for words. "I've got this," he finally said.

"Of course you do, but he was our friend, too," Dec said. Allan saw a quiet understanding in his cousin's eyes as he looked over at him.

Falling in love had changed the other man. He wasn't as distant as he'd always been.

"I don't know how else to handle this except to plan and take control," Allan admitted.

"That's the only way," Kell said. "We'll leave you to it."

Dec glanced quickly at him again as he followed Kell out. When his cousins were gone, Allan fell back on the large, battered brown sofa that didn't quite fit with the decor in the elegant and luxuriously appointed room. The couch had major sentimental value—John and Allan had purchased this piece at a garage sale for their first college apartment.

He put the heels of his hands over his eyes, pushing as hard as he could until he saw stars and there were no more tears.

"Another Scotch, sir?"

Allan dropped his hands and glanced up at his butler. Fawkes was standing there with a glass in one hand. "No. I'm going to pack and then get ready to head to the airport."

"Yes, sir," Fawkes said. "I have already arranged the accommodations. I've been tracking the weather, as well.... There might be a situation."

"What kind of situation?"

"Tropical storm in the Atlantic, but it's not predicted to head toward North Carolina. Just keeping my eye on it."

"Thanks, Fawkes."

Allan walked away and forced his mind to the task at hand. There was no reason why he couldn't get through his best friend's death the way he handled everything else. He'd manage and take control of the situation.

For once, Jessi's sharp tongue was dulled by Allan's generous offer to let her ride on his jet to the Outer Banks with him. Or maybe it was all the talk of funerals making her numb. As soon as she finished texting, she turned to put her phone on the hall table and found herself staring at a photo of Patti on the wall.

Jessi's heart hurt and she started to cry. She missed Patti. She missed the talks they wouldn't have. She longed to be able to pick up the phone and call her again. But that couldn't happen.

She sank to the floor, wrapped her arms around her waist and just sat there, trying to pretend that the news wasn't true. She didn't want to imagine her world without Patti. Granted, she had her sisters, but Patti was the person who knew her best. They'd gotten into trouble together since the second grade. What was she going to do now?

There was a knock on the door and she stared at it before forcing herself to her feet and wiping her face on her sleeve. Then she took a quick look at herself in the mirror.

Pitiful. Suck it, up, Jess. No one likes a crybaby.

"Coming," she called, but took a moment to wipe off the smudges that the combination of her tears and her heavy eyeliner had made on her face.

"We came as soon as we heard," Emma said when Jessi answered the ringing doorbell. Their youngest sister was there, too. Both women had their children with them. Emma's three-year-old Sam was holding his mother's hand, and twenty-one-month-old D.J. was sleeping quietly in Cari's arms.

"I didn't think you guys would get here so fast," Jessi said.

"Dec heard about it from Allan," Cari said, crossing the threshold and giving Jessi a one-armed hug. Jessi wrapped her own arms around her sister and nephew and held them close. Emma shut the door and joined the group hug.

Jessi felt the sting of tears once more, but choked them back. Though it was okay to let loose with her sisters, she didn't want to start crying again. Tears weren't going to bring Patti and John back. Tears weren't going to do anything helpful.

"What can we do?" Emma asked.

"I'm not sure. The funeral will have to be arranged, and then there is Hannah.…"

"What about her?"

"Allan and I are her godparents. I agreed to it because Patti asked. But I'm not good with babies. You both know this. I'm just—" Jessi abruptly stopped talking. She wasn't going to admit to her sisters that she had no idea what to do next. For only the second time in her life she was lost. Lost. It was a place she'd vowed to never let herself be again.

Emma wrapped her arms around her again and for a minute Jessi was seven and her big sister's hug could fix all her problems. She hugged her sister back and took comfort from her before gathering herself and stepping away.

"I'm okay."

Cari looked skeptical, but was too nice to say anything. Emma just watched her, and finally Jessi turned on her heel and walked toward her bedroom. She could tell one of her sisters was following her, but didn't turn around to see who. If it was Cari, that would be fine. Cari would just accept whatever Jessi said and leave it be. But Em. Em had seen her share of heartbreak and had dealt with grief when she'd lost her young husband. Emma would be harder to keep her true feelings from.

"What bag are you taking?" Cari asked as she entered the bedroom without D.J.

Jessi breathed a sigh of relief and pretended it wasn't tinged with disappointment. She could have used a little of Emma's meddling right now. Something to rebel against instead of Cari's kindness.

"I don't know how long we'll be gone," Jessi said. "I need to leave some notes for my assistant, Marcel. My job is still on the line."

"Even Kell can't be that heartless. He'll give you some more time," Cari said. "I'll talk to him about it."

She nodded at her sister, but at this moment was too numb to get worked up about it. Patti was dead. That dominated every thought Jessi had.

"How about if I pack for you," Cari said. "You go talk to Marcel. Get everything sorted out before you leave."

"Thanks, Cari."

Her pretty blonde sister looked as if she was going to cry. For a minute, as Jessi gazed at her, with her neat preppy skirt, her tucked-in blouse and her hair in that high ponytail, she envied her. Cari had seen some rough times—giving birth to her son on her own after the father had abandoned her—but she'd found her own strength. That was what Jessi needed right now.

Work wasn't a solace for her the way that it had been for Emma when her husband died. And Jessi's personal life… Well, without Patti she didn't know what she was going to do.

She left her bedroom without another word, avoiding the living room, where she heard Emma talking to Sam and D.J. After listening a moment, Jessi made her way to her home office.

It was decorated with sleek modern furniture in bright primary colors. She sat down on her desk chair and opened her laptop to start sending emails.

As her system loaded messages and sorted them into different folders, she noticed the file labeled Patti had a new message. For some reason it hadn't downloaded to her phone, maybe because she'd turned off email during her meeting at the Playtone offices earlier in the day. As she reached for her phone and adjusted the settings, she started to cry. This would be the last message from Patti.

Jessi looked back at her laptop screen and hovered the cursor over the folder, afraid to open it. But after taking a deep breath, she clicked her mouse and read the email.

Can't wait to see you in two weeks. Here's a quick picture of Hannah. She's teething and that means her first tooth! And you, dear godmother, have to buy her a pair of shoes—according to my great-aunt Berthe. Hope everything is ok at work. I just know that you will figure it all out. Call me later.
Take care,
Patti

A photo of Hannah's little face filled the bottom of the screen. She had her fist in her mouth, there was a drool on her lips and she looked out from the picture with Patti's eyes. Jessi's heart clenched and her stomach roiled as she realized that her dear friend wasn't going to see that first tooth come in.

Since her door was closed and no one could witness it, she leaned her head on the desk and let herself cry.

As the plane lifted off, Allan watched Jessi put her earbuds in and turn away from him toward the window. To say that she wasn't herself was an absolute understatement. The woman who'd always irritated him was positively subdued. A shadow of her normal self. He saw her wipe away a tear in the reflection from the glass.

He knew it was none of his business. He owed Jessi next to nothing, and she was entitled to her grief. In fact, he understood completely how she felt, but a part of him wanted to needle her. Wanted to jar her and force her out of her funk so she could irritate him and he'd be able to forget. The last thing he wanted to do was spend a cross-country flight with his own thoughts.

Not right now when he was wondering why a confirmed bachelor was still alive and a family man with everything to live for was dead. God knew that Allan wasn't religious, and something like this just reinforced his belief that there definitely wasn't a higher force in the world. There was no fairness to John dying when he had so much to live for.

Allan looked around the cabin. He'd bought the G6 jet when Playtone had signed their first multibillion-dollar contract, and he didn't regret it. If there was one thing he prized in this life it was his own comfort. The cream-colored leather chairs had more than enough

room for him to stretch out his six-foot, five-inch frame.
He did so now, deliberately knocking over Jessi's ex-
pensive-looking leather bag in the process.

She glanced at him with one eyebrow arched and
picked up the bag without removing her earbuds. She
leaned her head back against the seat and a lock of her
short ebony hair slid down over her eye. He had touched
her hair once. It was cool and soft. He'd tangled his hand
in it as he'd kissed her at John and Patti's wedding, behind the balustrade, out of the way of prying eyes.

Like everything between the two of them, he'd meant
the kiss to be a game of one-upmanship, to shock her,
but it hadn't worked. It had rocked *him* to his founda-
tions, because there'd been a spark of something more
in that one kiss. How was it that his archnemesis could
turn him on like no other woman could?

He nudged her bag and she took her earbuds off as
she turned to him and stared. Her gaze was glacial, as
if he wasn't worth her attention.

"What's your problem?" she asked.

"Can't get comfortable," he said.

She glanced around at the six other empty seats before turning her chocolate-brown eyes back at him. "Really? Looks like you could stretch out and not bother me
if you wanted to. So I ask again, what's your problem?"

"Maybe I want to bother you."

"Of course you do. What's the matter, Allan, finally
found the one thing your money can't buy?" she asked.

"And what would that be?" he retorted. In his experience there wasn't much money couldn't afford
him. Granted, it wasn't going to bring John back, but
there was nothing that could stop death. And hadn't he

learned that at an early age, anyway, when his mother had been the victim of a botched surgery?

"Peace of mind," Jessi said, swiveling her chair to face him and leaning forward so that the material of her blouse gaped and afforded him a glimpse of her cleavage.

She said something else, but all he could concentrate on was her body. Though she dressed in that funky style of hers she always looked well put together and feminine. And he couldn't help but recall the way she'd felt in his arms at John and Patti's wedding.

Dammit, man, enough. She's the enemy and it's just grief making her seem irresistible.

"I'll grant you that. Though I do find that my peace of mind is enhanced by the things I buy," he said.

"Me, too," she admitted.

"What do you want to buy right now?" he asked. He had already decided to order himself a Harley-Davidson, which he and John had been talking about buying when they turned thirty-five. Now that John was gone, Allan wasn't going to wait any longer. Life was too short.

"Nothing," she said. "I usually splurge on travel, and Patti was my…" She turned her chair to face forward.

"Not talking about her isn't going to make your grief any easier," he said softly.

She shrugged. "You're right. Maybe tomorrow I'll be able to think about this rationally, but tonight…I can't."

"Why?"

She turned to give him one of her you're-an-idiot-glares. "Seriously?"

"I don't want to sit in silence for the next few hours.

I keep thinking about John and Patti and how the last time I saw them both…"

"Me, too," Jessi said. "I can't stop. I remember how you and I were fighting, and Patti asked me to try to get along."

She stopped talking and turned away again to wipe a tear from her eye.

"John said the same thing to me. He even went so far as to mention that you weren't too bad," Allan said.

She shook her head. "I liked him. He was good for Patti and he loved her, you know?"

"He certainly seemed to." John had spent a lot of time talking about Patti, and Allan believed his friend loved her. But Allan had never experienced any emotions like that so it was a little hard to believe love existed.

"Seemed to? Don't you believe he loved her?" Jessi asked.

"I think he thought he did. But I'm not sure that love is real. I think it's something we all come up with to assure ourselves we're not alone."

She turned in her seat and arched both eyebrows as she leaned forward. "Even you can't be that cynical."

He shrugged. He didn't get the love thing between a man and a woman. He'd seen people do a lot of things out of "love" and not one of them had been altruistic or all that great. And his own experiences with the emotion had been haphazard at best.

Especially since he'd become a very wealthy man. Women seemed to fall for him instantly, and as Jessi would be the first to point out, he wasn't that charming. It made it very hard to trust them. But to be honest he'd always had trust issues. How could you believe in love when so many people did things for love that weren't all that nice?

"But you're always dating," she said. "Why do that if you don't believe in love and finding the one to spend the rest of your life with?"

"Sex," he said bluntly.

"How clichéd," she replied. "And typically male."

"Like your attitude isn't typically female? It's true I like women for sex. And companionship. I enjoy having them around, but love? That's never entered into the picture," he said.

"Maybe because you'd have to put someone else first," she suggested.

"I'm capable of doing that," he said, thinking of his friendship with John, but also his relationship with his cousins. He would go to them in the middle of the night if they called. Hence this cross-country red-eye to settle John's affairs. "What about you? You don't really strike me as a romantic."

"I'm not," she said. "But I do believe in love. I've got the heartbreak to prove that falling in love is real."

"Who broke your heart?" he asked. It was the first time in the five years he'd known her that she'd admitted to anything this personal. And he found himself unable to look away. Unable to stop the tide of emotions running through him as he stared at her. Who had hurt her and why did it suddenly matter to him?

"Some dick," she said.

He almost smiled because she sounded more angry than brokenhearted. "Tell me more."

"That's none of your business, Allan. Just trust me. If you ever let yourself be real instead of throwing around money and buying yourself trophy girlfriends, you'd find love."

He doubted it. "You think so? Is that how it happened for you?"

"Nah, I was too young and thought lust was love," she said. "Happy?"

"Not really," he said. "If you haven't experienced real love why are you so convinced it exists?"

"John and Patti. I've never met two people more in love. And as much as it pains me to admit it, your cousin Dec seems to be in love with my sister."

"They are borderline cutesy with all that hand-holding and kissing."

And just like that, she'd turned the tables and made him realize the truth of what she was saying. John was one of the few people he'd genuinely cared for, but they'd been friends for a long time, way before Allan had made his fortune and started running with the moneyed crowd. He didn't want to admit that maybe Jessi was right, but a part of him knew she was.

Three

She'd turned away after that conversation and he'd let her. Really talking about love with Allan wasn't something Jessi was truly interested in. The music on her iPod wasn't loud or angry—in fact, she was listening to the boy band 'N Sync. She and Patti had listened to their music endlessly when they were teens, and now the songs brought her some comfort. However, when "Bye Bye Bye" almost made her cry, she pulled her earbuds out of her ears and turned her attention to Allan.

He was restlessly pacing the length of the cabin and talking on the phone. She thought she heard him saying something about Jack White. She currently had a lead on the famous Hollywood director-producer and was trying to book a meeting with him later this month to discuss developing some of his summer blockbusters into games. It would be a coup if she could do a deal with Jack, and it would guarantee her job at Playtone-Infinity.

Allan glanced over and caught her staring.

"I'll have to call you back when we land."

He disconnected the call and pocketed his iPhone.

"We're playing for the same team now," she said. "You don't have to hide your business."

"You're on probation," he reminded her. "I'm not sure you'll make it past the ninety days."

"Really? I'm pretty sure I will. Have you ever known me to fail?"

He turned the leather chair in front of her to face her, and fell down into it. "Not without a hell of a fight."

She smiled. It almost felt like old times. They were finally finding their way back to their normal bickering, but she had the feeling they were both playing a role. Hell, she was. She was trying to be "normal" when everything inside of her was chaos.

"True dat."

"With all that's going on, we haven't had a chance to talk about my offer to buy you out," he reminded her. "I'm still willing to do that."

"I thought we'd already taken care of that. My answer remains no. I'm sorry if I've given you the impression that I'm someone who walks away from a difficult situation."

"Okay, okay. So what are you going to do to convince the Playtone board of directors to keep you on?"

Aside from doing a deal with Jack White, which was a long shot, she had no idea. Her plans for her future at the merged company were vague. It wasn't like her to be so wishy-washy, but she was tired of the entire family feud thing and was beginning to wonder if she even liked video games. She'd never admit that particular fact to a living soul. There were parts of the company that she loved, but right now she couldn't name them. There had been so much contention lately with the Montrose heirs that she hadn't been able to enjoy going to work.

"I am working on a push for Cari's holiday game. It will launch in two weeks' time and my team is working to make sure it's a hit."

Her sister and the development team had come up with an idea for a game app for the holidays that enabled players to decorate houses and Christmas trees, and then post screen shots to the online game center to try to get the most votes for their decor. The leaderboard was updated every day. The project had used existing assets at the company, so had a really low cost, and Emma believed it was that kind of out-of-the-box thinking that had saved Cari's job. It wasn't that there weren't other holiday apps; it was more the fact that Infinity Games had never done one before and that practically every component of the game was pure profit.

"That's good, but it won't be enough to save your job," he said.

She wished there was something easy or magical she could do to get herself out of this situation. But it was hard enough to be in this position, let alone having to come up with something so revolutionary it would impress the board at Playtone. It was going to take a lot to do that. Kell, Dec and Allan hated her grandfather and Infinity Games for what they'd done to old Thomas Montrose, and they wanted her to fail.

She held back a sigh—she'd never let Allan see that kind of weakness from her. "I'm not about to let you win. I don't care if I have to work 24/7 when we get back from taking care of this business on the East Coast. That's what I'll do."

He gave her that cocky half grin of his. "I expected a fight. Glad to hear you will be delivering one."

"Really?"

"Yes," he said. "I like our skirmishes."

"Is that all our encounters are to you?" she asked, thinking of that one kiss they'd shared. There was something weird about kissing your enemy and finding some attraction there.

"Are you asking about the night of Patti and John's wedding?"

"Yes. Seemed like we weren't at war that night."

"Well, we were, but we got distracted," he said.

"Until someone prettier came along," she said, remembering watching another bridesmaid, Camille Bolls, walk out of Allan's hotel room the morning after.

He shook his head. "There is no one who can compare to you."

"Ah, I've looked in the mirror. I'm not a classic beauty," Jessi admitted. And clearly not his type. It didn't bother her. Really, it didn't. She had chosen her look a long time ago and had done it deliberately. Most people saw her modern punk exterior and decided she was hard as nails. Exactly what she'd intended when she'd had her nose pierced and a small tattoo done on her collarbone near the hollow of her throat. It was discreet and could be covered with the collar of most blouses.

"No, but there is still…something about you that makes it hard to look away," he said.

"You must have an iron will because you don't have any problems doing it," she said.

He leaned forward, his arms resting on his knees and his expression more sincere than she'd seen in a while. "That's because I'm not a sap. I know better than to let you think there is anything between us. You'd use it, and me, to get whatever you wanted."

She shrugged. It would be nice to believe she had that kind of power over him. "Good thing I stopped believing in fairy tales a long time ago."

"Sometimes I don't know whether to arm wrestle you or kiss you."

"Kiss me? That didn't really get us anywhere the last time," she said.

"I was hesitant because of business complications, but now Playtone has the upper hand with Infinity and there is nothing stopping me from taking what I want."

"Except me," she said softly.

She looked over at him to gauge his reaction, and it was clear that he took it as a challenge. Suddenly, she was able to let herself forget about everything else that had happened today. Forget about the mess that her life was at this moment and remember that Allan McKinney was the one man who'd always been a worthy opponent.

"Except you," he said, "But I have a feeling you want to know if that one kiss was a fluke, as well."

"I have a feeling you're nothing but ego," she countered, refusing to let him see that she was intrigued. She'd never admit it out loud, but she'd had more than one hot fantasy about him.

She didn't really want to do this now, didn't want to have some kind of intense physical attraction to Allan McKinney. But there was no denying that she'd thought about that embrace more times than she'd wanted to over the past year and a half. She'd thought about *him* more than she'd wanted to. And those thoughts hadn't always involved fantasies of seeing him roasted over a pit.

She had to admit that in her musings he was usually shirtless, and most times they were both overheated. But that was her secret desire, and no way was she letting anything like that out in the open.

She looked so determined and at the same time so adorable.... What was wrong with him? Had he really become so bored with life that the only time he felt truly engaged was when he was going toe-to-toe with this woman? He could deny it all he wanted, but he knew the truth. There was something about Jessi that turned him on.

They were alone in the jet and would be for the entirety of the flight. Fawkes rode up front in the cockpit and functioned as copilot.

Allan had thought of Jessi as steel-hearted before today. She'd always seemed sort of a ballbuster until he'd seen the cracks and chinks in her tough-girl facade. Even when she'd hired that P.I. to investigate John before he'd married Patti, Allan hadn't realized that she'd done it because of her deep emotional attachments, not just to be a bitch. Because she cared about her friend... maybe even loved her. He'd never suspected that the woman who needled him the way she did could be as soft as he was beginning to suspect she was.

"I think I might be able to persuade you to come around to my way of thinking about sex instead of love," he said. He needed to change the dynamic between them. Get them back to the familiar footing they'd always been on.

"That's putting a lot of pressure on your charm and sex appeal," she said with a wry grin.

"Trying to take potshots at my ego?" He put his hand over his heart. "Hoping to see if you can deflate me?"

"Sort of. Is it working?"

"Nah, I still know I'm all that and a bag of dough-nuts," he said.

She laughed, but it sounded a little forced to him, and he realized she was on edge, too. Maybe because she'd felt something for him that one night, or maybe it still had to do with John's and Patti's deaths. Allan had no idea, and if he were honest, he didn't care at this moment. Thinking about Jessi, sparring with her, kept him from remembering his best friend was dead.

"You're some piece of work," she said. "Let's see what you're bringing to the game, big boy. How are you going to tempt me?"

"I thought I'd make it into a challenge," he said.

"What kind?"

She seemed intrigued, and he had to wonder if maybe she needed a distraction, the way he did. They'd always made bets over outrageous things and always honored them. In fact, if she weren't so…well, if she weren't *Jessi,* he'd actually like her. But she was Jessi. A Chan-dler. A prickly, ornery woman with as much cuddliness as a porcupine.

"One you won't want to lose," he said.

"I'm listening."

"I'm betting that you're attracted to me and that you can't control yourself better than I can when we put each other to the test," he said. It was a calculated risk. A chance to prove to himself that his iron willpower over his body and his sexual prowess were still intact. Because there was something very different about Jessi, something that he didn't entirely know how to deal with.

"I know I can," she said. "So what's in it for me?"

He thought about it for a few long minutes, shifting back in the chair. Just thinking of kissing her made him stir, so he stretched his long legs out in front of him to relieve the pressure on his groin.

"If you win I'll help you keep your job at the newly merged Playtone-Infinity Games," he said.

A light went out of her eyes and he saw her nibble on her lower lip. He didn't know what he'd said to cause that reaction, and made a mental note to pursue the question at another time.

"And if you win?" she asked.

"You let me buy you out," he said. "You walk away from gaming a wealthy woman."

"If you agree to help me, can you guarantee that I won't be axed?" she asked. "Because I don't think Kell is going to be that impressed with you saying that you lost a kissing contest with me and that's why you have to keep me on."

"Oh, Jess, I'm not going to lose," Allan said. "But if I do, I will help you by making my network of contacts available to you. I have a feeling that with those connections you'd be unstoppable."

"Why not just do that anyway?" she asked.

"We're enemies, remember? From the first moment we met you knew I was a Montrose cousin and I knew you were a Chandler sister."

"True. The family feud will always be there, won't it? Even though Cari and Dec have a son and are planning to get married…there's still bad blood between our families in your eyes."

"It's hard to just dismiss it," he said. "So do we have a deal?"

She crossed her arms under her breasts while she leaned back in her chair, then crossed her slim legs. She wore boots that would look ridiculous on anyone else, combat boots with a thick, three-inch heel that gave her added height. Tight-fitting leather pants and a loose, sheer black blouse completed the outfit. But it wasn't inappropriate, given that it was Jessi. He could tell by her all-black outfit that she was mourning.

"All I have to do to win is make sure you are more affected by one kiss than I am?" she asked.

"That's it. Keep in mind in certain circles I'm known as—"

"The man with a big mouth and bigger ego?" she taunted.

"You're going down, Chandler," he said.

"Only if I agree to your deal. And given how hard you're pushing for me to accept it, I'd say I'm destined to win."

"There was something destined to happen," he said, leaning forward in his chair and putting his hands on the armrests on either side of her. "Stop baiting me and make your choice."

"Am I baiting you?" she asked, shifting closer to him and tilting her head to one side as she stared at his mouth.

"You know you are," he said, trying to ignore the tingling of his lips. He was in control here.

"Well, then I guess I'm going to have to accept your wager. Prepare to lose, McKinney," she said.

Jessi came over to him and straddled his lap. Slowly, she eased forward and brought her mouth down on his. Her only thought was to do this and win, and then she'd focus on keeping her job. But the moment her mouth met his something changed.

It had been easy to tell herself that her memory of

what had happened between them at the wedding wasn't accurate, or that everything had been due to the champagne she'd drunk that night. But now, in the cold reality at thirty-five thousand feet in the air, there was no denying that the attraction she felt for him was real.

His mouth was firm against hers and his lips were soft. He was letting her be the aggressor, and she took full advantage of that, running her tongue over the seam where his lips met. He tasted minty and fresh, and she pulled back, but felt his hand on her head, keeping her in place.

His tongue traced her lips, as well, and she wondered if he'd like the flavor of her strawberry lip gloss or if it would be too sweet for him. But he didn't say anything, only kept coming back to taste more of it and of her.

She opened her mouth and felt the brush of his tongue over hers. She wanted to moan, but kept that sound locked away. She struggled to remember she was competing here. And suddenly it seemed stupid to her that the first man she'd kissed in a long time—and wanted to keep on kissing—was playing a game with her.

She closed her eyes and let herself experience the embrace of a man who made her want to forget she was a Chandler, and just enjoy being a woman.

His mouth was warm, and he tasted good. So good she never wanted the kiss to end. She shifted to get closer to him, but he kept the distance between them and she realized she was in danger of losing this bet. She hadn't anticipated having to fight her own urges while she kissed him.

She tried to think of Allan, tried to stem the need welling up inside her to feel his solid chest pressed against hers. Tried to forget that she'd seen him shirt-less enough times to know that he had solid pecs and a well-developed six-pack. Tried to forget that the man was seriously ripped.

She was losing it and losing the challenge. But then she felt the barest movement of his fingers against her neck. The tracing of a pattern that sent shivers down her spine and electric tingles through her entire body. *Dammit,* she thought, as every nerve ending started to pulse in time with her heartbeat.

She reached for his head. Tunneled her fingers through his thick hair and pulled him closer. She thrust her tongue deep into his mouth and forced him to take her. Reminded him that she was in control of this de-sire and this embrace.

But then he answered back and she was once again adrift. Forced to forget about wagers and feuds and every single thing except the way his mouth felt against hers and the way he made her wish this kiss would never end.

She rubbed her thumb against the base of his neck in a small circle and felt his heartbeat quicken. She took her time spreading her fingers out and enjoying the feel of his scalp under her hand, until she shifted forward and forced his head to the side, where she could take more control of their embrace.

But it was no longer about power or winning. Now she was kissing him because the taste of him was ad-dictive. She'd never forget this one moment for years to come; she knew it with bone-deep certainty. The way he felt with just her hands in his hair and her lips on his. The way his tongue felt deep in her mouth as the smell of his aftershave surrounded her.

The dreams and desires she'd forced aside for too long came rushing up to her and she saw a chance to have everything she'd ever wanted. A man who could make her feel real desire and an out to walk away from the gaming world once and for all. All she'd have to do was give up everything she'd made herself into as an adult.

She'd have to lose to Allan. She'd have to show him that she could be vulnerable, and she'd have to admit it all out loud.

She sucked his lower lip into her mouth and bit down, and then rubbed her tongue over it to soothe it. She didn't think she could do that. But when she felt his hands tightening in her hair for a moment and a low groan issued from the back of his throat, she realized she might not have to.

He pulled his mouth from hers. She opened her eyes to look up into his intense gaze, and shook from what she saw there. He might want to pretend that she was nothing more than an old enemy to him, but the truth was there in those dilated pupils and in the flush across his cheekbones.

She almost cursed out loud as she realized there was no winner in this. No outcome that could be decided other than the truth. She was attracted to him. And though she'd hoped that maybe kissing him would distract her from the lonely feeling in her soul, it hadn't worked. In fact, she really wanted to just curl up next to him and forget about challenges and the world outside, and take some comfort in his arms.

If he hadn't made this a contest and if she'd been a different sort of woman—the kind who was okay being emotional and needy—then she'd be able to just rest her head on his shoulder and admit that she hadn't ever felt this scared and alone before.

"So…" he said. "That was more than I expected."

"Me, too," she admitted. "I guess we underestimated how much we'd enjoy each other."

"I sure did. Tonight especially, I…I enjoyed kissing you, Jessi."

"Me, too, Allan. I don't think you're my archnemesis anymore."

"That's good. So what are we going to do about this? Is it just grief? Did we turn to each other because our friends are gone?"

She shrugged. A part of her wanted to say yes and make this about the tragedy that had brought them both together. But she knew that would be a lie. And lying even to herself was something she didn't like to do.

"I really don't know," she admitted.

"Me, either. I have always been able to… Never mind. The real question is what are we going to do about it?"

She didn't have an answer. There wasn't a clear solution. He had surprised her and made her realize that there was more to this man than she'd previously thought. Because if he'd been all ego, then he would have swaggered away from her. But he was sitting across from her, looking just as perplexed as she was.

Four

It was humid and breezy as they stepped off the plane at the Dare County Airport in Manteo, North Carolina. Unlike the Los Angeles area, where everything was either developed or part of the desert, North Carolina—and especially the Outer Banks—was made up of small villages surrounded by state-owned land that had been preserved to keep this part of the world wild.

As the breeze flattened her shirt to her breasts, Allan was transfixed for a second by the sheer beauty of Jessi. Who'd have guessed that she would be a femme fatale without even trying? He fiddled with the strap on his overnight bag to distract himself.

But there was no distraction from Jessi. Her perfume danced on the wind and wrapped around his senses as he stood there in the eerie predawn light.

"Thanks for the lift," she said in that smart-ass way of hers that signaled the truce they'd sort of reached on the plane was over.

"You're welcome. It was an enjoyable flight," he said.

"Whatever. I figured I'd stay at Patti and John's bed-and-breakfast until we go home," she said.

"Fawkes has taken care of all the arrangements. The staff has canceled new arrivals, and when I spoke to the caretaker, he said there were only two couples left at the resort and that they would be leaving today."

"I guess that's one less thing to worry about," she said. "I'm more than ready to talk to their attorney and do whatever we need to do. Patti's mother isn't going to be much help...since she's ill."

Allan understood that Patti's mom, Amelia Pearson, was in the second stage of Alzheimer's-related dementia, but John had told him to keep it quiet, since Patti hadn't wanted anyone to know. He saw how thinking about Amelia's condition affected Jessi. Her shoulders were stooped for a second and he imagined it was from the burden of knowing that your best friend's own mother might not be able to mourn her.

"As soon as we see the attorney this morning we'll know more," he said. It wasn't something he was looking forward to, but at least Allan already knew a lot about John's wishes for the future. His friend had always been very loquacious and liked to share his dreams once he'd met and married Patti.

"I don't get why they wanted to live here," Jessi said. She glanced around the small airport. "I mean, it's nice enough to get away from the bustle of L.A. once in a while, but all the time? I don't think I could do it," she said. "It's going to take us over an hour to get to their place on Hatteras."

"I know, and my cell phone signal stinks. I think Kell is probably going to disown me if I don't check in, and I've only got one bar," Allan said.

Jessi pulled her iPhone out of her pocket and glanced

at the screen. "I've got almost two bars...want to use mine?"

He looked at her. As an olive branch gesture it was almost remarkable. She'd never offered him anything before. He tucked that fact away in the back of his mind to analyze later as he nodded at her.

"I have his number preprogrammed. He's listed under Darth Sucks-A-Lot," Jessi said as she handed the phone over.

Allan turned away to keep her from seeing the smile that spread across his face. He couldn't wait to tell Dec, who would think Jessi's tag for Kell was funny. "Don't let him see that. He hates *Star Wars*."

"Who hates *Star Wars?* Just another thing that proves your cousin is an alien cyborg," Jessi said. "Do you need privacy to talk to him?"

"Yes, if you don't mind."

"No problem. I'll go check with Fawkes about the car."

"Sounds good. Will you need to call your sisters?" he asked.

"Not at this time of the night. They both have little kids and will probably be sleeping," she said. "Are you sure Kell will be up at 4:00 a.m.?"

"Yes. He only needs four hours of sleep a night. Plus he'll be waiting for me to check in," Allan said.

"Of course, since he's some kind of future-engineered, high-performing robot," she said, walking away.

Allan watched her leave, as he had many times before, but now he noticed how her entire body moved. The swish of her hips in those skintight leather pants, the way the heels on her boots canted her hips forward and made her legs seem miles long. The way the tail of her blousy shirt curved around her ass.

He appreciated her as a woman, and despite how chaotic things were inside him right now, watching her walk was like a balm. It reminded him that he was still alive.

He hit the auto dial for Kell and waited three rings until his cousin picked up.

"Montrose here."

"It's Allan."

"What number are you calling me from?" he asked. "I had this down as someone else's."

"It's Jessi's phone. Mine isn't working right and I couldn't get a signal, but hers did. I wanted to check in and see if I missed anything last night."

"Not much. I sent you an email that details everything I need done today. Will you have reception later?" Kell asked.

Allan felt as if he had to defend the fact that the cell towers in this part of the world weren't thick on the ground. But he knew Kell wasn't irritated with him per se, but more with anything that interrupted the normal flow of business. "I don't know. John has Wi-Fi at his place so once I get there we should be good to go. I'm going to be busy this morning with the attorney and the funeral arrangements, but I'll get everything back to you today."

"That's what I was hoping you'd say. It's not much, but I need you to run some figures on a pro forma that Emma submitted. Also, I've talked to Dec, and unless Jessi pulls out something spectacular we're in favor of offering her a package and cutting her from the company. I need you to work on that today."

"Can't you cut me a little slack? I get that this is business, but we're dealing with the loss of our best friends," he said.

There was silence on the other end of the phone, and Allan wondered if he'd pushed Kell too far.

"You're right. I can give you both a few extra days. How are you holding up?"

"Fine," Allan said. "You know me."

"I do, which is why I don't buy that B.S. answer. You and John were like brothers."

"It's hard, Kell," Allan said. "But I can't talk about it."

"Fair enough. I'm here if you need me," he stated.

Allan knew that his older cousin would be there for him. Despite how cold he seemed in the office and how single-minded he could be in his quest for revenge against the Chandlers, Kell had a very strong sense of loyalty to both his cousins.

"I'll call when I know something more. I'm going to have to reboot my phone, so until I notify you, call me on this number."

He clicked off and thought about his cousin's hard-line attitude. Kell was determined to let Jessi go, and there was nothing Allan could do to save her. And a part of him was very glad about that, because she was the kind of complication he didn't need in his life for the long term, even though he knew that she was in it for the foreseeable future.

The Land Rover Fawkes had arranged for them to use was a new model. It was spacious and comfortable and had four-wheel drive, something that seemed important out here in the wilderness of North Carolina.

Fawkes had stowed their bags in the back of the vehicle and then opened the door to the backseat for Jessi. She stood for a minute as the warm breeze stirred around her. The sun was rising and for a minute she enjoyed the view of the sun coming up over the ocean instead of her normal view of it sinking down into it.

"Thanks," she said, climbing in.

"You're welcome, Ms. Jessi."

"You can just call me Jessi, you know."

"Very well," Fawkes said.

Allan didn't say anything as he got into the passenger seat in the front, which suited Jessi just fine. She put her earbuds in her ears and pretended to disappear. She loved the fact that it was acceptable by society to do so, even though a part of her felt a bit rude. But right now she couldn't talk to anyone.

She didn't want to talk to anyone. Being here made Patti's death more real. Jessi watched as they left the small barrier island where the airport was located and crossed the bridge to another small strip of land. The Outer Banks were really just tiny bits of land that barely kept the sea at bay.

Once again she pondered Patti's choice in making her home here on the edge of the wilderness. It was pretty, though, she thought, as the sun continued to rise over the ocean. They turned right at Whale Bone Junction Information Station and followed NC 12 south, crossing the Oregon Inlet Bridge. She took her earbuds out when Allan gestured toward her.

"Yes?"

"Seems like the end of the world, doesn't it?" he asked.

She nodded, a bit unnerved that they were thinking

along the same lines. Was it also occurring to him that if Patti and John hadn't moved out here maybe they'd still be alive?

"I think that's why Patti liked it," she said at last, unwilling to voice her real thoughts.

"I agree. No rat race here. Especially now that it's the off-season," Allan said. "Fawkes was just mentioning that the man at the desk in the airport warned him that that tropical storm in the Atlantic is now predicted to strengthen into a hurricane, and one of the projected paths has it coming straight toward Hatteras, where the B and B is located."

"Really?"

"Yes, ma'am—Jessi," Fawkes said. "I didn't think it would be a concern, but seeing these roads, I thought it best to mention it. Any kind of surge in the tide would wipe some of this out."

"I agree," Allan said. "Fawkes is going to keep an eye on the situation while we're taking care of the funerals and other arrangements. But if need be we should be ready for a quick escape."

"I always am," Jessi said.

"That's right, you are," he agreed. "So am I. But escaping a tricky personal situation and escaping Mother Nature are two different things."

She nodded. She put her earbuds back in as the conversation lagged. She was listening to Pink's latest and enjoying the mix of raw emotion and anger that Pink was always able to capture in her songs.

Twenty or so minutes into their drive, she noticed skid marks on the road. She pulled her earbuds from her ears as Fawkes slowed the Land Rover to a stop.

"Is this…?"

"I think so," Allan said, opening his door before Fawkes had the car in Park.

Jessi sat where she was, looking at the crushed grass, the wreckage from the other car and the remains of Patti's sweet little Miata, which still was there. Upside down and impossibly mangled.

Her heart started beating fast, and in her mind she heard screams. But she knew that was only her imagination. She got out of the vehicle and walked over to the side of the road. This was it, she thought.

Oh, God. This was it. This was how Patti and John had died, and it was worse than anything Jessi could have pictured in her head.

Car accident. Those words could mean anything, and the reality was so much harder to stomach than anything she'd imagined.

Staring at the wreckage, she heard the far-off sound of someone sobbing, and realized it was her. She turned away, not wanting Allan or even Fawkes to see her like this. But then she felt a hand on her shoulder.

When she turned back around, she didn't look up, but just moved forward, wrapping her arms around Allan's waist and burying her face in his chest. He held her tightly as she let loose the emotions she'd tried so unsuccessfully to tamp down.

She wanted to pretend that none of this had happened. But she had never been one for running away from the truth. And in this moment she knew she no longer could keep alive the very small hope that the authorities here had gotten it wrong. That Patti and John were still somehow alive.

No one had walked away from this scene. She knew it and accepted it. But the pain of losing her friend felt fresh and new, and so sharp that she couldn't breathe. Allan's hands moved up and down her back and she felt him shudder in her arms. Tipping her head back, she looked at the underside of his stubbled jaw.

When she noticed a thin line of tears running down his neck, she turned her head into the curve of his shoulder and held him as tightly as he held her.

She'd always seen him as her enemy. Even the ride out here and that kiss they'd shared on the plane hadn't really changed her perception—not at a gut-deep level. But in this moment, as she held on to the only other person in the world who understood her grief, she realized that he'd ceased being her rival.

Somehow in the past twenty-four hours he'd started to become simply Allan. Her Allan.

It was safe to assume he'd never felt this way before, and if he was completely honest, he never wanted to feel this way again. Losing John was making Allan question so many things, but most importantly, as he held Jessi in his arms, he wondered why he'd waited until his friend was gone to finally listen to him.

John had claimed from the beginning that he'd observed Allan and Jessi checking each other out when they thought no one was looking. And now, holding her in his arms, letting the tears he couldn't contain fall, Allan admitted that once again his friend had been right.

He felt a heavy hand on his shoulder and knew that Fawkes had joined them. The three of them, who'd never gotten along, were now united in grief.

And Allan had to wonder how much of what he felt at this moment was simply the need to feel the loss. The need to ensure that the empty part of his soul was filled with something…someone. He didn't want to be alone and didn't want to lose the memories he had of John, and whether he liked it or not…well, right now he'd be lying if he said he didn't like the fact that Jessi was here with him. She was the one he wanted to be with.

"I didn't think I'd fall apart like that," she said.

Pulling away, Fawkes walked closer to the wreckage, leaving the two of them alone. The breeze off the Atlantic was warm and strong, and for a minute Allan wished it could carry them away from here.

But that was only because he had no idea how to handle his grief. He turned his head away from Jessi and wiped his eyes before turning back.

"I saw you cry," she said, her tone kind and the look in her eyes one of the softest he'd ever seen. Her short punky hair was flying about in the wind, and her eye makeup had run from her tears, leaving dark tracks down her face.

"I saw *you* cry," he said, trying hard for a teasing note he just didn't feel.

"I guess we're even then," she said at last. "You know what?"

"What?" he asked. He wasn't sure he wanted to keep talking when every word she said made him feel raw and exposed.

"I'd be happy to lose to you now if it meant Patti and John were still here."

One of the things Allan had always respected about Jessi was her honesty, even when it would serve her better to lie. At first he'd thought her bluntness was just another tool she used to keep him disarmed, but then he'd realized that she had no barriers.

It had been his first clue that the girl who looked as if she'd take on hell with a bucket of water was actually vulnerable. He didn't need to be reminded of that right now. He needed her fierce and prickly, needed her to be his enemy. But he feared that ship had sailed. He was never going to look at Jessi the same way again.

"Me, too," he admitted.

"What the hell happened out here?" Jessi asked. "I know they were hit and then drove into the tree, but really, who would be driving that fast on this kind of road?"

"An idiot," Allan said. Inside, he felt some of that rage, as well. But his modus operandi was to channel it into graciousness and fake ennui. "I hope I never meet the guy," he added.

"Same here. I don't think it would be easy to have to see the person who caused this and… It would just be too much, you know?"

"I do know," he said as she looked up at him with that gaze of hers that cut through a man and made him feel he was completely exposed from the inside out. God, Allan hated that. He didn't want Jessi to see him—really see him.

She started laughing, and he glanced at her to see if she was okay or if she was truly losing it.

She shook her head. "Sorry. I was just thinking that we're finally getting along. Patti would be giving me an I-told-you-so look if she were alive at this moment."

"John would, too," Allan said. He couldn't count the number of times his buddy had taken him to one side and asked him to give Jessi a chance. To stop baiting Patti's best friend and just let her into that protected inner circle of trust that Allan fiercely guarded.

"Why didn't we?" she asked. "Why didn't we do this before they were gone? They were our dearest friends. All they wanted was for us to get along, and we could never be anything but enemies."

"We are 'enemies' because there's something very similar in both of us, and we were raised to distrust each other's families. We like to win, we like to protect our friends, and mostly, we don't like it when anyone notices that we aren't invincible," he said.

She crossed her arms over her chest, and then with a sigh uncrossed them and turned to face him. "I don't want to admit this, but there is a small kernel of truth in what you just said."

He felt the band of tension inside of him loosen.

"I was right?" he asked. Those were words he'd been positive that Jessi Chandler would never utter in his presence.

"Don't let it go to your head," she said, putting her arms around her waist and turning to walk back toward the Land Rover. "I'm pretty sure that it won't happen again."

For the first time since he'd gotten the awful news that John was dead, Allan felt something. He wanted to pretend it was lust, because just looking at Jessi made him want her. Or maybe he could explain it away as shared grief. But the truth of the matter was much harder to accept.

He liked her. He liked being with her. And he'd have to say, in all honesty, that he wanted this new feeling to grow.

Five

Jessi sat next to Allan in the attorney's office, trying to let the newest shock sink in.

Reggie Blythe was a tall, thin African American man who looked to be in his mid-fifties. He had a little gray at his temples and a wiry look that said he spent more time at work than at home. Jessi thought that his office had a charming Old South feel to it, but freely admitted to herself that the impression came from images she'd seen in Hollywood movies.

She felt nervous and unsure. She didn't know how to handle this meeting or Allan.

Actually, it was only Allan who was shaking her up right now. She could handle attorneys. But Allan was something else.

Reggie had been giving them a rundown on John and Patti's will and their hopes for Hannah's upbringing. But Jessi was busy looking at Allan and remembering that moment when they'd stopped by the accident scene and he'd held her in his arms. He had just offered comfort, and been so damned human that she'd had to rethink everything.

Not just what she'd thought about him, but also what she'd always believed about herself.

"I don't understand. Is that even legal?" Allan asked.

Damn. She needed to pay better attention. What had he said?

"It's highly unusual for joint custody to be given to two people who aren't married, but it's not illegal," Reggie said.

"Why would they do this?" Jessi asked. It was slowly sinking in that Patti and John had left custody of Hannah to her and Allan, even though they'd known that she and Allan didn't really like each other.

"I suspect they didn't anticipate dying so young," Reggie said with a wry note in his voice. "Also that they wanted to ensure Hannah had influences from both sides of her parents' lives."

"Of course. Where is Hannah now?" Allan asked.

"She's in state custody now. We couldn't keep her with her babysitter, but we'll be turning her over to you both as soon as this meeting is finished," Reggie said, glancing at his watch.

"And that's it? We can just go back to L.A.?" Jessi asked.

"No. A judge will be reviewing the case, and once you are both approved as joint guardians, then you can return to California. Patti and John have already paid me to serve as your legal counsel in the proceedings, unless you have objections and would like your own attorney."

"What if one of us isn't interested in being a guardian?" Allan asked.

"Is that the case?" Reggie asked, his kind brown eyes meeting Allan's gaze first before shifting to Jessi.

Allan didn't say anything else. Jessi was worried. She knew nothing about raising a baby—in fact, she'd already decided she wasn't ever having kids. But this was Patti's final request, and she found that she couldn't deny her friend.

"Can we have a moment alone to discuss this?" Jessi asked.

"Of course. You may use my office," he said, getting up to leave the room. When the door closed behind him she turned to Allan.

He stood and paced to the window, pausing with the sun behind him, which made it very difficult for her to see his expression. He didn't seem like the Allan who'd held her so tenderly and shared her grief. He seemed like the old Allan, maneuvering around while trying to figure out the best position to be in.

She didn't like it. Which man was the real one? She wanted him to be…something she suspected he couldn't be. But maybe she should give him the benefit of the doubt. He was in the same situation she was. Just as blown away by the fact that they were going to be raising a little girl.

Or were they? Would he stand by her and help her or was she going to be doing this on her own?

"Do you not want to be a guardian?" she asked bluntly.

"Of course I do. She's John's daughter and he was closer to me than a brother. I only voiced that option in case you wanted an out but were too timid to ask," he said.

"Are you kidding me? I don't do timid," she said. "You know that. So what's this all about?"

Allan walked toward her. As he moved closer, she

could see for the first time since she'd met him a very sincere look on his face. He wasn't doing the fake charming thing or acting as if he could buy his way out of this.

"I don't walk away from commitments," he said. "John and Patti must have had their reasons for appointing both of us. I don't know what they were, but today I started to see a glimpse of it. I'm just not sure if you did."

"I did," she admitted. "But is this real?"

"We won't know until we get Hannah and return to the West Coast."

"I agree. I can't say no to this," Jessi said.

"Me, either."

The atmosphere in the room was becoming too heavy, the situation too real, and she didn't like it. She needed time to process the fact that Allan was going to be in her life for the rest of it. She started doing the logistics. "So what are we going to do?" she asked. "I mean, from a practical standpoint. I live in Malibu."

"I'm in Beverly Hills," Allan said.

"Well, we can hand her off to each other at work," Jessi said. "I'm not as familiar with the Playtone Games campus, but if we use the facility at Infinity, they have a first-rate day care center where Hannah can stay during our working hours. Then we can divide up her nights."

"I like that plan, but we should have a contingency in case your probation doesn't work out," Allan said.

She made a face at him. Of course he'd bring that up. "I'm not going to lose my job. I've already told you I have some new ideas."

"I'm just saying we should figure out some more options," he said. "I like to plan for every eventuality."

She wondered if she'd ever really know what he was thinking. Then she shook her head. She had other things to worry about than that. Hannah, her future, dealing with Allan every day from now on. It was a big responsibility and one Jessi wouldn't shirk. She'd figure out a way to make this work.

"I guess it's decided then," she said.

"Yes, I'll go and get Reggie."

She sat back in the leather chair and tried to relax, but she couldn't. Every time she thought she'd adjusted to losing Patti there was something new that surprised her. Jessi ran her hands through her short hair and realized it was getting easier to think about her friend being gone. Not *easier;* that wasn't the right word. She just could do it without crying, which was a relief.

She'd always hated the fact that she couldn't control her tears. In general, she didn't cry unless she was mad, but this kind of grief, well, she supposed there was only one way for it to be expressed.

She heard the door open and turned to see Allan striding in with Reggie. Allan was a bit taller than the attorney and had his head bent to listen intently to what Reggie was saying. For all the world they looked as if they'd known each other for years. Typical of Allan, she thought. The man never met a stranger.

"Allan has told me the good news that you both will share guardianship. I can't tell you how happy that would have made Patti and John. They were adamant that they wanted their best friends to raise their daughter," Reggie said.

"Well, we really want to honor their wishes," Jessi answered.

"Good. I've got some paperwork for you to fill out,

and then I'll drive you over to get Hannah. The authority from the state wants to check you both out and ask you a few questions before she's released to you temporarily. I've already got a call in to the judge's office for scheduling."

"How long do you think this entire process will take?" Allan asked. "I'm— We're both needed back in L.A."

"I don't think it will take too long—maybe a week to ten days."

A week was definitely too long to Jessi's way of thinking. Hell, the plane flight with Allan had seemed endless. Sure, she knew there was no speeding this type of thing up, and there shouldn't be. She wanted the state officials to do their job and ensure that Hannah was going to be well cared for.

But staying in Hatteras with the man who was turning out to be her Achilles' heel didn't sound ideal. And she needed to think of the future. When it was just her it wouldn't have mattered if she lost her job at Playtone-Infinity Games. But now that she was going to be an example to Hannah…

Dammit, Jessi was going to have to rethink everything she'd thought she knew about herself, and reorder her priorities for Hannah's sake.

And that meant trying to get along with Mr. Allan McKinney, not liking him more than she already did, and most importantly, staying out of his bed.

When Reggie drove them to the foster home where Hannah was being kept, Jessi realized she was glad they'd gotten to Hatteras when they did. The home was nice enough from the outside, but the people inside were strangers to the baby girl. The sooner she was set up in a more permanent custody arrangement, the better.

"Hi there, I'm Di, and this my husband, Mick. We own a local restaurant and knew John and Patti," the foster mother said as they entered the house.

"This is Allan McKinney and Jessi Chandler, Hannah's guardians," Reggie replied.

"I'll go get her," Di said, as Mick led them into the living room.

Jessi was too nervous to really pay attention to the conversation. Inside, she was a quivering mess, because she knew next to nothing about babies. She always avoided holding her sisters' kids because she was afraid of dropping them or breaking them in some way. And she hadn't held Hannah for more than five minutes in her short life. Jessi figured she didn't have a maternal bone in her body. "Here she is," Di said, returning with a sleepy-looking Hannah.

Jessi went over and held her arms out, and Di handed her the baby. Jessi felt awkward and unsure until she looked down into those eyes that were so similar to Patti's.

This was Patti's daughter, Jessi thought. She held her closer and had a moment's horror as she realized she was about to start crying. She tried to turn away, but then Allan was there by her side. He didn't say anything, just wrapped his arm around her and looked over her shoulder at the baby.

Jessi didn't feel as overwhelmed when he was touching her. She wasn't alone. It didn't matter that there were still big issues between the two of them; they were united in this and right now that was all that mattered.

"I guess John and Patti's instincts were correct,"

Reggie said. "You two are going to make good guardians of their little girl."

"We will do our best," Allan said, looking Jessi straight in the eye.

It felt as if he was making a promise to her, and she couldn't help but feel as if together they would make this work. But she wondered how her sisters and his cousins would react to the news that she and Allan were going to be raising a child together.

She felt a twinge as she imagined the look on Darth-Sucks-A-Lot's face when he heard that another one of his cousins was so closely involved with a Chandler sister. But that little bit of mirth didn't change the fact that she and Allan were going to have to figure out how to be friends, because they were going to be the closest thing to parents that Hannah had.

"We can't screw this up," Jessi said.

"We won't," Allan answered. "We both are very good at making things happen the way we want them to."

Allan poured himself two fingers of Scotch and put his feet up on the railing as the sun set over Pamlico Sound. He was making promises he had no business making, he thought. But being here in John's old home, he found it hard not to feel the man he was in L.A. slipping away. The water was still and calm, and there was a soothing element to sitting here and forgetting about the long forty-eight hours he'd just lived through. Today had seemed endless, and he was more than ready for it to be over.

They'd finished making the funeral arrangements. In the end it had made more sense to have a joint ceremony, and Jessi had been very efficient at managing the little details.

Seeing that side of her had made him realize why she was so good at her job. He'd seen the reports on the interviews that Dec had conducted with the employees at Infinity Games. They'd all said that Jessi was singularly organized and always successfully launched their games.

Allan rubbed the back of his neck. He was square in the middle of it right now. Kell's hatred… Was it really just Kell who resented the Chandlers anymore? Allan knew that he'd started out with just as much anger toward them, but right now it was hard not to see the Chandlers, especially Jessi, as real people.

People who weren't part of the long-ago feud.

Jessi had volunteered to give little Hannah a bath after dinner, and he'd let her. He knew that she was tired, too, and maybe he should have been gentlemanly and stepped in to do it, but he wasn't ready to deal with a child yet.

He decided to text his cousin Dec, who was the father of a toddler himself. Of course, Dec had just met his son for the first time a few months earlier, but that made his perspective perfect for Allan. He needed some info, and quick, if he was going to do what he always did—make life look effortless. Because the baby was already throwing him off.

She'd cried and then spit up on his shirt, and he hadn't been too successful at diaper changing, either. He'd have to fix this situation. He didn't allow anything to get the better of him and he certainly didn't intend to start now.

He'd managed to reboot his phone so that he had cell coverage now. He messaged Dec.

Help. How do you deal with a baby?

The phone immediately rang and he answered it. "McKinney here."

"I love it. The great Allan McKinney doesn't know what to do," Dec said.

"I doubt you knew what to do the first time you held D.J."

"True. I didn't. Do you want me to ask Cari for advice?"

"No. Don't you dare. Just wanted to know how you handled it when you met D.J."

"I was afraid I'd break him. I kind of held him at arm's length. But then after I started spending time with him, I realized two things—one, it didn't matter what I said if I talked in a quiet, kind tone, and two, everyone screws up with kids. Even Cari, though she'll deny it."

"Thanks for that. Hannah's a little girl, Dec. I don't know anything about girls. I mean, we were all boys...."

Dec laughed. "You seem to do okay with women."

"Hannah's not a woman. This is different. I can't be charming or do all the things I know women expect a man to do. I have to be—"

"Real," Dec said. "It's that way with D.J. for me. I can't just phone it in. Kids require more. Hannah's a baby, and she's new to this situation just like you are. You'll figure it out."

"I hope so. I've downloaded a few books about child rearing on my Kindle app. But I needed to talk to someone who's actually done this."

"Well, that's all I got without asking my woman," Dec said.

"I'd rather you didn't, since she'd probably tell her sister," Allan said.

"How's that situation?"

He had no idea how to answer his cousin. The truth was, Jessi irritated him more now than she had two days ago. But she also fascinated him more. And he was obsessed with her, spending his time thinking about how soft her skin was and how much he liked her perfume.

Finally, he just said, "Good. We're both making the best of it. The funeral is going to be in four days' time. Are you coming? I can send the jet back for you."

"Yes. That would be great. I know that Cari and Emma are both interested in attending. Kell doesn't want to travel with them. In fact, he said he might not come at all."

"I'm worried about him. He has too much hatred toward the Chandlers," Allan said.

"Me, too. But what can we do? Hey, do you want to go with me when the Lakers play the Mavs in two weeks? Cari has to work," Dec asked.

Allan smiled to himself. He and Dec had grown closer since Dec had come back from Australia and found himself a family.

"Love to. Later, dude."

"Later," Dec said, disconnecting the call.

Allan skimmed the first book he'd downloaded on his phone, and felt a lot better about the next few days than he had before. After a while, he put his Scotch aside and got up to go find Jessi.

He wasn't too confident that their child-sharing plan was going to be successful. Even though Hannah was tiny she seemed to require a lot of attention, and two heads were better than one.

He wondered… Should he suggest that the three of them live together? It might cause less disruption for Hannah and help them both out. But he didn't know if his self-control was up to having Jessi in the same house. Already just the thought of her sleeping down the hall was enough to make him contemplate things he knew he shouldn't.

He heard the sound of singing and went to investigate. As he got closer, he realized that Jessi was singing Pink's "Blow Me" to Hannah as she dressed the baby.

Not exactly Brahms, he thought as he stood in the door of the nursery. But he saw that Hannah seemed to like it; she was slapping her hands and staring up at Jessi.

When Jessi finished singing the song, she said, "That was Pink. Your mom and I saw her in concert about eight times. For a while we both had our hair cut real short like Pink's. And your mom…"

All of a sudden Jessi's voice broke and she leaned in close, lifting Hannah off the changing table and into her arms, burying her head on top of the baby's. Allan started to back away. This moment was between the two of them, and he knew he'd be intruding.

Suddenly, that song seemed entirely right for her to sing to the baby. It was something that Patti and Jessi had shared. This was why their friends had named them coguardians. So that their daughter would never forget either one of them.

It also underscored why Jessi and Allan couldn't live together, ever. The more times he saw her looking like a real woman—not a punk pain-in-his-ass, but a real human being—the harder it would be for him to help Kell fire her.

And he knew that he was going to have to do that. His cousin had better appreciate the situation that Allan was in right now. It was hard enough to fire someone he knew casually. But to do it to a woman he was starting to like and respect and—ah, hell—really care for... There was no way he was going to be able to do it and not lose a little part of himself.

<u>Six</u>

Jessi had thought everything was going well with Hannah until she and Allan were watching *The Daily Show* and the baby started crying. Jessi tried to comfort the little girl, but nothing seemed to work. Singing had calmed Hannah down earlier, but no way was she going to sing in front of Allan.

"Your turn," she said, picking the baby up and taking her over to Allan.

"Gladly. Why don't you go and get yourself a drink?" he suggested.

Though she'd been planning to do just that, she decided not to. She didn't want to let the dynamic between the two of them change now. It would be too easy to fall into the pattern of roommates…and much more. And she'd already promised herself that what had happened on the flight out here wouldn't happen again.

Kissing him had been a mistake, and given that they were now alone together, with Fawkes mostly out of the way in the guest quarters, she had to be especially careful to keep her sexual urges firmly under control. But

even though she had about a million other things on her
mind, the images of kissing Allan kept cropping up.

Right now she hoped that Hannah would settle down
and go to sleep early, because tomorrow they had a lot
of stuff to do, including going to visit Hannah's grandmother. It was a visit that Jessi wasn't looking forward
to, but she knew it had to be done.

She had talked privately to Reggie Blythe and knew
that the care home had been notified of Patti's death.
But Jessi wouldn't feel right unless she went and visited Amelia herself.

She noticed that Allan was walking around the room
with Hannah. The little girl had her binky in her mouth
and was now sleeping. Jessi told herself it was just be-
ginner's luck, but a part of her was jealous that he'd been
able to get the baby to sleep when she hadn't.

"I'll go put her down," he said in a very quiet voice.

She nodded.

As soon as he left the room she stretched her legs
out on the couch, put her head back against the armrest
and stared at the ceiling. They were in the back of the
bed-and-breakfast in the suite of rooms that John and
Patti had lived in. It was small compared to her place
in Malibu, but so homey. Everywhere Jessi looked she
saw her friend's touch, and it made her miss Patti that
much more.

She rubbed her forehead, thinking that she'd better
get started on a decent marketing plan tonight. She'd
already had one email from Kell telling her that her
deadlines for delivering her items hadn't been changed.

She felt torn. It went against her nature to back down,
but this time she just didn't feel like the fight was worth
it. Even Allan, who didn't hate her as much as Kell did,

had intimated that she was probably not going to be keeping her role at the end of her probationary period. Should she put in the effort?

It was just one more thing she had to contemplate. A part of her liked the thought of her, Allan and Hannah all spending the day in the same place. And that made Jessi contemplate a future for herself that she'd never wanted. For a minute she felt like a little girl. The little girl she'd been before reality had intruded and taught her that things like perfect families didn't happen all the time the way they did in TV sitcoms.

She was okay with that. She prided herself on being a realist, but now that she'd had a glimpse of domesticity she'd be lying if she said she didn't want it for herself. A part of her did want to be part of a family unit.

But that was a pipe dream, probably brought on by Patti's death. Hell, it wasn't even Jessi's dream. She'd never wanted a husband to tell her what to do, the way her father had dominated her mother's life and her choices. Never wanted a child who could be used as a pawn in that relationship.

She sat up and leaned forward, putting her elbows on her knees. She had to fight for her job at the newly merged Playtone-Infinity Games. And then she had to do her best to raise Hannah to be strong, but also open to love, the way Patti had been. Jessi sensed that had been why her friend had wanted her to be coguardian. Because Allan would never let the little girl want for anything material. But there were things a man—a father—wouldn't understand about a daughter.

"Are you sure you don't want a drink? I'm getting myself one," Allan said from the doorway. He'd changed out of his suit and had on a pair of basketball shorts that rode low on his hips and a loose-fitting Lakers tank top.

She couldn't speak as she stared at his chest. He was lean and tan—not like some gym-crazed guy, just fit. Damn, she didn't need a reminder of just how good-looking he was. Or how much she still wanted him.

She had to ignore her baser instincts....

"Do you want a drink?" he repeated.

"Yes, please," she said at last, and then realized it had to have been obvious to him that she'd been staring at him. "Are you getting them?"

"I was planning on it," Allan said.

"I wasn't sure you could function without your butler, and since Fawkes is staying in the guest quarters…"

"I think I can manage to get us both a beer. Then I'm hoping to catch a little of the Lakers game," he said. "Want to watch it with me?"

"Yes, but I have work to do. And you mentioned giving me some contacts," she said.

"I believe our contest ended in a draw."

"It did. But Kell isn't budging on his deadlines and I could really use some help."

"I'll email the information over to you," he said. "But I'd rather you stay and watch the game with me."

"Why?" she asked. "I know you don't think I can pull it off, but I'm intent on saving my job."

"I'm sure you'll do it. I've seen you in action before. But for tonight I'd rather just enjoy some time with the one person who must feel the emptiness in this room as keenly as I do."

Jessi swallowed hard, surprised he'd mentioned what they'd both been avoiding: that without John and Patti, being here felt wrong somehow.

* * *

"I've got an idea," Allan said as he came back into the room with two beers.

"For what?"

"To distract us," he said.

"We need distracting?"

"I do, Jess. I'm on the edge here and I don't like it."

"What don't you like?" she asked, in that way of hers that made him want to just bare his soul and stop pretending that he wasn't attracted to her.

No matter what had happened in the past two days, she'd made adjustments and seemed to be dealing with everything okay. And he wanted to know how she did it. On the outside, sure, he looked like a guy who was holding it together, but on the inside…he was a hot mess. And he hated that.

Emotions made a man sloppy, and made Allan in particular realize how often he'd pushed them aside to keep focused on the path ahead. But being here in John's living room with his baby sleeping down the hall, and knowing that he was going to be raising her with this woman had shaken him to his core.

"Emotions," he admitted. "I need something to take my mind off things."

"And the basketball game can't do that?"

"Not when you are sitting there looking sexy," he said.

"I look sexy?" she asked. "I'm wearing a button-down shirt and a denim skirt. Not exactly femme fatale gear."

"It is on you," he said. "All evening long I've been sitting here watching you and thinking about that kiss on the plane. The one we both meant to be a competition that turned into something else entirely."

Suddenly, she didn't look smug or aloof. She looked intrigued and vulnerable. The way he felt inside.

"So what's your solution?"

"The way I see it," he said, moving into the room and handing her the beer he'd poured for her, "we've got two choices."

"Two?" she asked, and he noticed that when he sat down right next to her on the couch, she didn't scoot over. In fact, she sort of leaned a little bit toward him.

He nodded and took a sip of his beer before he said, "We could always ignore this and hope that it goes away. But to be honest, I'm not that good at ignoring a beautiful woman."

"Don't lie to me," she said.

"I'm not."

"Really? I know I'm not beautiful," she declared. "I'm cute and sexy, but beautiful—not so much."

"We'll have to agree to disagree on this," he said. He didn't know how she defined beauty, but for him she was the embodiment of everything female. She was strong enough to know who she was, bold enough to go after what she wanted, and also smart enough to admit when she needed someone. Earlier, she'd needed him, and that had awakened something inside Allan that he didn't know how to control.

"You were saying?"

"We can either ignore the attraction between us or face it, decide to have an affair and see where it leads," he said.

"Are you trying to shock me?" she asked.

"Nah, I do say things sometimes to throw you off.

Mainly to see if you react. But seriously, those are our only choices, ya know?"

"Ignoring it doesn't seem like it's going to work," she said slowly. "Right now you are the only person I can turn to. And I haven't been able to stop thinking about that kiss, either."

"What have you been thinking?" he asked.

She tipped her head to the side and took a slow sip of her beer. "Are you sure you want me to be honest?"

"Hell, yeah. I'm laying it all on the line here," he said.

"I liked it better when you were just my enemy…that douche, Allan. I don't want to think of you as the guy who makes me hot and wet."

Her words were evocative and made him harden in his pants. He wanted to say screw it, then take her hand and lead her to the bedroom. But what he wanted was physical, not emotional.

Liar, he thought. But he really wanted to keep the two things separate if he could.

And he wanted to keep her hot and wet.

"You said be honest," she said. "Did I shock you?"

"A little, but I shouldn't be. You've never been shy about speaking your mind."

"True. Plus I wanted to see if you were as horny as I am."

"Stop. We can't have a logical discussion if you keep talking like that."

"Why not?"

"Keep pushing me, Jessi, and I'll prove to you that you've barely seen hot and wet."

"I'm tempted to," she said.

"Why?"

"If I keep pushing and you react, then neither of us is responsible. We can blame hormones."

"But neither of us would believe that," he said, watching as she took another delicate sip of her beer.

She tossed her head and then leaned forward to set her glass on the coffee table. "I'm tempted, Allan. But I can't do it. Emma would kill me if I hooked up with you and screwed up something at Infinity for her."

"This has nothing to do with our families."

"Sure, we can say that now, but we both know it would impact them," she said. "Emma is already struggling, and with Dec and Cari…it just makes things difficult at times."

Allan understood what she meant. Kell was difficult. He still hated the Chandlers. Allan had been trying to stay neutral as Dec tried to influence them to go easier on the Chandler sisters.

"So we're still at a crossroads," he said. He'd always been very good at reading people, but Jessi had never been easy for him. Yet he had a hunch that giving in to the attraction might be a solution for them. But it would mean mixing together the two separate areas of his life, something he'd never done before. And it would mean showing Jessi a part of himself he preferred to keep private. Yet at the same time it could be the answer to this entire sexual tension thing that was going on between them.

"I'm okay with ignoring it until we get back from North Carolina, but I don't know how successful I'll be. I'm not handling Patti's death as well as I wish I was. I can't be philosophical about it."

"I'm not handling it well, either," he said, still searching for the words that would give them both what they needed. "That's why I brought this up."

He put his free hand on the back of the sofa and touched the skin at the base of her neck. Jessi flinched, spilling some of her beer on him. Her eyes were glassy and he didn't have to be Sherlock Holmes to guess that thinking of Patti was going to make her cry.

"Sorry about that," she said.

"Sorry is not enough," he said.

"It's not? That was just a drop of beer."

He arched one eyebrow at her. And she reached for his thigh, rubbing her finger over the spot the beer had left.

"What do you think I should do about it?" she asked.

"Clean it up," he said.

She leaned back and crossed her arms over her chest. "You surprise me, Allan. You know I'm not the type of woman to take orders from a man."

He shouldn't be surprised. Jessi had been making him uncomfortable since they met. Unlike most of the women he dealt with, she hadn't been wowed by his charm or money. He'd put that down to their family rivalry, but it was more than that.

"There is a lot about me you don't know," he said at last. "And I think there's a lot about you I haven't seen yet, either. I'm willing to bet that you take orders when it suits you."

"Maybe. It depends on the man," she said in that quiet way of hers, watching him with that gaze that was almost too serious. She shook her head and he thought that would be the end of it.

"I'm the right man," he said. "And I'm waiting."

* * *

Jessi hated to admit it, but she was intrigued. He was flirting around with something that had always been a secret fantasy of hers. She was so bold in life that most men expected her to be the aggressor once they got to the bedroom. But Allan didn't.

She wondered if she could actually do it, even though the thought of giving over control of her body to a man had always been a turn-on. She wasn't sure that giving up control to Allan was something she could embrace, but she'd always been a never-say-never type girl. "I don't know. I'm leaning more toward just handing you a towel and letting you dry your shorts," she said.

He shrugged, and she watched his body movements with different eyes now. What did it say about the out-wardly effusive man that he liked his sex controlled and with limits? She didn't want to know. Really, she didn't. She liked keeping Allan in the jerk category. It made life easier when he didn't seem multidimensional. She could just not like him and move on.

But now…now he was starting to seem human and real to her. She groaned.

"What?" he asked. "What are you afraid of?"

"Not you," she said hastily, and then realized she probably had given away the fact that he did unnerve her. "I don't want to make things awkward between us."

"When hasn't it been?" he asked. "Listen, we're at-tracted to each other whether we like it or not. Our lives are forcing us to be with each other. So we can either let this thing control us or—"

"We can control it," she said. She leaned back on the cushions of the couch and looked at him. Taking her time and letting her gaze start at his feet and move slowly up to his waist and his chest, to his face.

He was good-looking but he wasn't classically handsome. Though there was something in the blunt cut of his lips that made it hard for her not to lick her own at the thought of his mouth against hers again.

He sat there, all arrogant male, and then did the one thing that tipped things in his favor. He held his hand out to her.

He hesitated for a second and then closed the gap between them. He took the back of her head in his hand, his grip on her firm but not forceful, and brought his mouth down hard on hers.

If their last kiss was exploratory and new, this one was about domination, and left no doubts in her. He wanted her. She knew that whether she wanted to admit it or not, she was going to end up in Allan's bed.

Allan McKinney. *Dammit,* she thought. *Why him?* Why did he have to be the man to make her feel like this?

But then she stopped thinking as his mouth moved over hers. His tongue plunged deep inside and she shifted, trying to get closer to him. She opened her mouth wider and sucked on his tongue, but that still didn't bring the relief she sought. She tried to lean in closer to him. Wanted to feel his body wrapped around hers, but he lifted his head and eased away from her.

His lips were swollen and wet from kissing her, his face flushed with desire. His silver eyes narrowed as his kept his gaze fixed on her, and she shivered with awareness, but also anticipation.

She did want what he was offering. The attraction to him was more powerful than she wanted it to be, but she wasn't about to lie to herself. It existed and she wasn't going to be happy until she had him in her bed.

She leaned toward him, but he held up a hand to stop her. "No. That was just a sample of what I can offer you, but there is no halfway. If you want this take my hand."

She wasn't entirely clear what he was offering, but at this point, with her pulse racing and every nerve in her body crying out for more, she really wasn't going to turn away. If one kiss could do that to her…she had to find out what else was in store.

It had been too long since she'd had really good sex. The trouble with the takeover and her general dissatisfaction with her career had conspired to keep her from focusing on her needs. And now Allan was offering her a solution to that situation.

She lifted her hand and saw how small it looked when he clasped it in his. His nails were square and blunt, his fingers large, his palm warm. There was strength and control in his grasp.

She nibbled at her bottom lip as he drew her close, until barely an inch of space separated them. He put his forefinger under her chin and tipped her head back, making her look up at him. He didn't say anything, just let his gaze move over her face.

She noticed he paused as he took in the small diamond in the side of her nose, and then his hand moved down her neck to trace the pattern of her tattoo. The small raven was her reminder not to let herself be swept away, and for the first time since she'd made the decision to get the tattoo, at age eighteen, she realized she was in very real danger of not heeding its warning.

Seven

Jessi felt small under his hands. He used his touch on her back to turn her and draw her toward him.

Seeming eager for his kiss, she lifted her face toward his, so he nipped her lower lip. Her tongue darted out and tangled with his, and he hardened.

He pulled her onto his lap. He took her hands and held them loosely behind her back, in the grip of one of his. She raised an eyebrow at him.

"We can't both be in control," he said.

"Why not?"

"That's not how I like things," he said. Then he brought his free hand up between them and ran his finger down the length of her neck. He liked touching her. Her skin was soft and the scent of it…peaches on a summer day.

"This doesn't work for me," she said. "I want to touch you. I don't want to be at your mercy."

"You already are," he said with confidence. She wasn't trying to get her hands free. She was sitting there waiting to see what he'd do next. He reached for the tasseled gold cord holding the decorative curtain in place and used it to bind her hands together behind her back. The cord was thick and didn't have much give. When he was done tying it, he reached for the buttons that ran down the front of her shirt.

She watched him with an unreadable gaze, but her breathing became more rapid, pushing her breasts against the fabric of her shirt. As the cloth fell away to reveal her cleavage, he paused to take a deep breath and admire her.

She was small but not tiny, her breasts full and suited to her frame. She wore a plain cotton bra, which surprised him. For a minute he'd expected a corset or something else punk. But he realized that the inner woman was very different from the outer one.

He ran his finger along the top curve of her breasts. "Do you like this?"

She shrugged, which pushed her breasts forward, and he reached beneath the fabric of her bra to caress one nipple. "It's different. There is something tantalizing about watching your reaction to my body."

"What do you see?"

"That you like touching me," she said. "You also like just looking at me. When you think I'm not watching, your eyes narrow and you stare at my breasts. What are you thinking?"

"I'm wondering what you'll look like naked."

"Why not find out?" she asked.

"I intend to, but in my own time," he said. Caressing her narrow waist, he ran his finger around her belly button. She shivered, and her stomach clenched. She liked being touched as much as he needed to touch her.

He reached behind her and undid the clasp of her bra and then pulled the straps forward on her arms until the fabric fell away, framing her breasts. Her nipples were a rosy-pink color and he cupped both breasts in his hands, rubbing his palm over them until they were hard. He leaned in to delicately lick at first one and then the other.

Jessi's hips moved against his erection, and he shifted his legs to get into a more comfortable position.

"Untie me," she said.

"Are you uncomfortable?" he asked.

"No," she said. "But my shirt is open…."

"I will untie you if you insist, but I like you this way and I think you do, as well," he said.

He leaned down to capture one nipple in his mouth. He suckled her and ran his tongue around it before biting lightly. "I like you this way!" he repeated

"I'm still deciding if I like you or not," she said.

Inside, he smiled. He wasn't too sure how much longer he could wait, but the knife's edge of anticipation made him feel…alive. And he knew that he'd keep this going for as long as he could.

He dipped his finger into his beer and rubbed it against her nipple, watching it tighten, before licking her slowly and then moving up her chest to taste her mouth with long, slow kisses. The saltiness of the beer and the taste of Jessi blended together, and he felt something clench deep inside him.

He was about to give in to the desire, free himself and take her. He knew it was time, knew he was hanging on to control by a thread. So he reached behind her to undo her hands and then set her next to him on the couch, tipping his head back to stare at the ceiling.

Jessi had never felt so sexually charged or as unnerved as she did at this moment. And she didn't like it. In fact, she'd rather just have a quickie than this.

The true problem was that it felt as if he was playing mind games. Her body was so turned on, but Allan was just sitting there, looking cool as could be. It was like their kiss on the airplane. A test to see who could hide their reactions the longest.

Right now she felt like the loser. Except…well not entirely. "I'm not sure this is the wisest bargain I've ever entered into with you."

He gave her one of his wry, knowing looks, and she shivered a little as she realized that he wasn't as unaffected as he wanted to be by their exchange.

"Nothing involving the opposite sex ever is," he said.

"Is that your motto?"

"No, actually, it was Grandfather's. But I have to admit the old bastard was right."

"What was he like?" Jessi asked to distract herself. She didn't really know that much about old Thomas Montrose. Unlike Allan and his cousins, who'd been taught to see the Chandlers as the enemy, she and her sisters hadn't really been raised to hate the Montrose family. As a matter of fact, a portrait of old Thomas had hung in the lobby of Infinity Games for as long as she could remember.

"He was bitter and thought only of revenge. That kind of attitude really taints a man's perspective."

"Yours?" she asked. As they talked, she almost forgot that her shirt was unbuttoned and her breasts were exposed, that there was nothing normal about the conversation they were having.

"No, Kell's. I don't think he's ever going to accept Cari as part of the merged company, and he really doesn't want you or Emma to come on board."

"What about you?" she asked.

"I'd rather buy you out, as well. But it's really hard to think about that stuff when you're sitting here like this," he admitted.

She breathed a little easier at his admission. "For me, too. But I'm sort of getting used to it."

"You are?"

"Now that I know it's distracting you," she said with a smile. Patti had always said there was more to Allan than the antagonist she knew.

"Still feel like backing down?" he asked.

"Never. I'm wondering if you are interested in me or if this is all a game to you?"

He stood up and took her wrist, drawing her hand to his crotch. "What do you think?"

She ran her palm over the heavy ridge of his erection. She stroked him through his shorts, wondering what he'd feel like naked in her grip. She used her forefinger to trace the line of his erection and heard his quick intake of breath.

She took hold of the waistband of his shorts and tugged it down slightly. But then stopped.

"What are you waiting for?" he asked.

"I thought you liked taking things slow," she said.

"Only if you are under me...taking me," he answered. She felt herself moisten and realized that this had long ago ceased being a game. Allan was the one man who could make her feel this way right now. She wasn't entirely sure she liked it, but she knew she wasn't going to walk away from him.

Their lives were entwined now and it was silly to pretend that they weren't.

"That doesn't sound like it's completely by the rules," she said.

"Nothing with you ever is," he said, picking her up in his arms and walking toward the bedroom at the back of the house.

She wrapped her arm around his shoulders and studied his face as he moved. There was a flush to his skin, which she put down to desire. There was a birthmark behind his left ear that she'd never noticed before. She traced the small kidney-shaped mark with her finger and he shivered and turned to face her, his silver eyes intense and sexual.

He definitely wasn't in the mood for games now and she was glad. She'd never been the kind of woman who liked to play around in the bedroom. She tried very hard not to equate sex with emotion, and instead tried in her own way to keep the two things separate, since she'd learned early in her dating life that most men did that.

"I like the way your hands feel on me," he said.

"Good, because I plan to put them all over you," she said.

He set her down on her feet next to the bed, put the baby monitor on the dresser and nudged the door closed with his hip. He kept his hands on her waist and they both just stood there for a long moment. In her mind this was the quiet before the storm. The moment when they both waited to see who would break first.

He lifted his hand and she felt his touch on her tattoo once again. He traced the shape of the raven over and over, and she felt shivers of intense pleasure move down her body from that one point of contact. She stood there watching the intensity on his face as he touched her.

It would be impossible to ever believe after this moment that she left him unaffected. She saw the proof of how much she turned him on in the narrowing of his eyes as he lowered his head toward hers, then felt it in the heat of his kiss.

His mouth moved over hers with surety and strength. He claimed her in that kiss. This was not the same way he'd teased and tempted from the first moment that they'd met. Now he was intent on leaving his mark on her, and as she reached for him and tried to draw their bodies together, she admitted to herself that she wanted nothing more than this.

For this moment it was enough to have him physically. She understood this wasn't her wisest decision and that there would be consequences, but she just didn't care.

She wanted him and she was determined to have him. She sucked his tongue deeper into her mouth, and as he held her by the waist with one hand to keep her from brushing her aching breasts against his chest, she reached between their bodies and stroked his erection.

His other hand moved from her neck, tracing a path straight down her ribs to her belly button. She'd had it pierced a few years ago, but had let the hole close up. Feeling the way he toyed with her navel made her wish she still had the piercing. His touch seemed too knowing and too intense for her, and she shifted a little, pulling her head back to look at him.

His eyes were half-closed, but she still felt the intensity of his gaze. He pushed her backward until her thighs hit the edge of the bed, and she sat down. He smiled at her as he pushed her shirt down her shoulders and off. She shrugged out of her bra and reached for his shorts. She didn't want to be the only one exposed.

She felt vulnerable and needed to keep the scales balanced between the two of them. If it had been any other man she would have changed positions, pushed him down on the bed and taken control. But with Allan everything was different—and it always had been.

In a moment of clarity, she admitted that from the first moment they'd met she'd felt a zing of attraction.

He grasped her hands to keep her from taking off his shorts. "Not yet."

"Yes," she said.

"No. Put your hands on the bed by your hips," he ordered. His voice was forceful and commanding, sending a pulse of liquid heat straight through her loins. She almost did it, but then stopped herself.

"You're not in charge anymore," she said.

"Oh, I think I am," he said, kneeling down and bringing her hands together behind her back. His face was close to her breasts, and she couldn't help arching her spine and thrusting them forward. He dropped soft kisses along the pale white globes and then tongued his way around the areolas.

She shuddered and shivered, shifting on the bed to try to relieve the ache between her legs. She parted her thighs, and he maneuvered himself forward between them. She felt completely dominated by him physically. He held her hands behind her, forcing her thighs apart with his body as he buried his head between her breasts.

Though she was clearly not in a position of power, his shuddering breath and the way he held her let her know that he was enthralled with her. Her body, which had never seemed to her to be the ideal of beauty, made her proud now. That she could literally bring this strong, domineering man to his knees made her sit a little taller.

She leaned forward and rested her head on top of his, rubbing her cheek against the thickness of his hair as he suckled one of her nipples. She stretched her legs farther apart and then canted her hips forward until she rubbed her center over his erection.

He lifted his head and shifted his body back from hers. Still holding her wrists with one hand, he pushed her skirt to her waist, and she felt him pause as he realized she wore thigh-high hose. He groaned. And then stood up, drawing her to her feet with him.

"Indulge me?" he asked.

"How?" she asked.

"Take off everything," he said.

"What are you going to take off?"

"Nothing."

"That hardly seems fair."

"Sex isn't about fair, it's about what turns us on. And I have a feeling that having me fully dressed while you're bare naked will be a big turn-on for you," he said.

He was right, but that didn't mean she would admit it. It scared her a little how well he seemed to know what she wanted sexually. "I'll do it, but only if you take your shirt off."

"Done," he said, quickly pulling the tank top over his head and then moving to sit in the armchair next to the bed.

He had a lean chest, his well-defined pecs covered with a light dusting of hair. She liked the way he looked, and stood there for a minute drinking him in.

Slowly, keeping her gaze on his, she reached for the zipper at the back of her skirt and tugged it down.

"Is this what you wanted?" she asked.

The skirt slipped lower on her hips, but she kept her stance wide enough that it didn't fall all the way off. Then, when she'd made him wait long enough, she shook her hips and slowly let the skirt fall to the floor.

"Pick up your skirt," he said, not answering her question.

She turned away from him and slowly bent down, watching him over her shoulder as she did so. His eyes narrowed as she reached for the garment and slowly picked it up before tossing it on the bed next to her bra and her shirt.

She shivered a little at the look in his eyes. She slowly pushed her panties down her legs and once again bent to remove them over her boots. He was suddenly there behind her, his hands on her waist and his body bent over hers. She felt the heat of his erection against her buttocks as he pulled her back into the cradle of his hips.

She put her hand out for balance as he rubbed himself against her. He was long and thick and hot. She felt branded by him, and empty as she waited for him to enter her. She was wet and had never been more willing for sex. Ready for him to take her. *And like this,* she thought. She didn't want to have to guard her reactions. She just wanted to let go and enjoy this without worrying if she seemed too vulnerable.

He leaned over her and whispered dark, sexy words into her ear, things that made her even wetter. He told her what he was going to do to her and how deep he was going to take her. She canted her hips back and rubbed herself against him. He took her hands in his and guided them to the footboard, and with their hands joined, she felt him shifting behind her and the tip of him poised to enter him.

"Dammit, give me a second," he said.

He turned away, and she stayed exactly where she was as she heard him open his shaving kit on the nightstand. She glanced over at him to see him opening a condom and putting it on. Later, it would bother her that he had planned for sex, but right now she was grateful.

He was back behind her again, his palms on her waist and his mouth on the back of her neck. He nibbled his way down her spine as he held her still. His hands shifted up to cup her breasts, his fingers pinching lightly at her nipples as he positioned himself behind her again. She felt him shifting between her legs, and one hand lowered to her feminine mound. His finger circled her clit, rubbing lightly. She shifted her hips and moved to where she needed his touch. Then he pulled his hand away, after tapping her lightly with one finger, which made her moan out loud.

She felt him at her entrance again. He teased her with the tip of his erection, and she enjoyed the sensation of his body pressed to hers for a little while, but then the wanting was too much. She arched her back and tried to take him into her body. But he shifted away from her, and she moaned again.

Then he leaned over her, whispering into her ear, "Do you want me?"

"Yes," she said, hating the breathy quality of her own voice. "Dammit, Allan, I need you now. Enough of the games."

"But waiting is the best part," he said, rubbing himself over her again.

"Taking is the best part," she countered.

She heard him groan, and then he plunged into her body in one long, hard stroke that sent the first shivers of orgasm through her. But then he stopped and when she tried to take in more of him, or force him to move, he didn't. He just stayed buried in her body as he kissed her neck and caressed her skin.

But it was too much. She needed him slamming into her and driving her over the edge. She didn't like the feathery sensations that were making the hairs on the back of her neck stand up and shivers course through her.

"Enough waiting," she said. "Take me."

"Not yet." It sounded as if he spoke through gritted teeth.

She tightened herself around him and heard him groan yet again, and then he started moving. His hips rocked with so much force that each thrust drove her forward. She held on tighter to the footboard as he continued moving in and out of her body. Oh, he felt good, she thought as he reached the right spot inside her.

She arched her back to take more of him and keep him hitting her in that delicious spot, as she was so desperate to get to her climax. His breath was hot against her neck and his body warm and sweaty as he moved faster and faster, until she felt the first pulse of her own orgasm. Then he called her name and thrust into her hard for three long strokes, before leaning forward and resting his head between her shoulder blades.

He dropped a kiss on her skin, one so gentle and

tender it made her heart clench. He was supposed to be the arrogant playboy. He wasn't supposed to kiss her like that. He wasn't supposed to be gentle with her. He was supposed to be…well, the Allan she'd always thought him to be.

She shook her head and tried to pretend this orgasm was like any other she'd had, but she knew it was different. She wanted to be a guy about it. To just make some sort of remark about scratching an itch, though inside she knew that this had changed everything between them.

She hated that very fact. Why was it that Allan McKinney, the man she'd always thought of as the devil incarnate, had just made her come harder than anyone else? Or actually made sex seem fun and—

He pulled out of her body, interrupting her thoughts. Unsure what to say, she stood up and looked over at him. They'd just been closer than she'd ever thought they would be, but they were still enemies, she figured. Nothing had changed, yet at the same time everything had.

Allan cursed under his breath and then drew her into his arms, pushing her head down on his shoulder as he hugged her close.

"What are you doing?" she asked.

"Hiding," he said.

"What are you hiding from?"

"You," he said. "You have a way of looking at me that makes me feel like I don't measure up."

His words were a tonic for her weary soul and she struggled to let herself take them at face value. She refused to believe that he'd glimpsed her vulnerability, but at the same time she knew he had, and that there was no way she was going to be able to keep fighting with him and pretending that she loathed him.

The truth was finally forced into the light, she thought. Allan McKinney wasn't her bitter enemy, he was a man. A man she found sexy as hell—and that unnerved her more than she wanted to admit.

Eight

Jessi was jerked awake by the sound of a baby crying. She lay in bed in Allan's arms, not recognizing the strange room for a split second, before she jumped to her feet, grabbed the closest piece of clothing she could find—Allan's shirt—and pulled it on as she ran through the door down the hall to the nursery. Allan was hot on her heels, pulling on his shorts.

They both continued into the nursery, where in the glow of the soft night-light they found Hannah on her back, crying. All her limbs where flailing as she sobbed for all she was worth. They both reached for the baby, but Allan let Jessi pick her up.

She cradled little Hannah against her chest and looked helplessly up at him. "What do you think she needs?"

"I think she might need a bottle. I'll go and warm up the formula while you change her diaper," Allan said.

He left before she could respond. She carried the baby to the table and changed her wet diaper. It bothered Jessi a little that Allan was right. He was probably

spot-on about the bottle, too. How was it that he knew
more about kids than she did?

She knew he hadn't visited their friends since Hannah was born. They'd both flown out to be there for
the birth—and they'd kind of called a truce that day,
as well. She remembered how they'd looked at each
other in the hospital waiting room when they'd gotten the news about Hannah. They'd almost hugged, but
then John was standing there and it had just seemed so
awkward.

But for a few moments when they'd been focused
on John and Patti, they had sort of gotten along. And
then there was little Hannah to hold. And their friends
to congratulate.

Hannah was still crying now, and Jessi leaned over
the baby. She hummed a tune she'd heard playing earlier on the mobile over Hannah's crib, and then slowly
sang words she made up.

"Stop crying, little Hannah. Soon Allan will bring
your bottle and you'll go to sleep."

"Here it is," Allan said as he rushed back into the
room. "I checked the temperature of the formula on my
wrist so I know it's safe for her."

"Great thinking," Jessi said. "I didn't consider that
it might be too hot."

He shrugged. "I'm thorough like that. Do you want
to feed her or do you want me to?"

"You can do it," she told him.

He came over and scooped the baby up, placing the
bottle in her mouth. He stood there next to Jessi while
the baby drank eagerly. She brought her little hands up
and touched Allan's finger as he held it.

Both adults stared down at Hannah, and Jessi for

her part again felt the heavy loss of John and Patti. "I wonder how often they both stood here like this?" she murmured.

"I was thinking the same thing," Allan said. "It's a sin that we're here and they aren't."

She agreed. Not that she wanted to be dead, but it made no sense that John and Patti had been killed when they had so much to live for. Jessi reached down and touched Hannah's cheek as her little eyes drifted closed, even while she kept drinking her bottle.

"She's so sweet," Jessi said softly. "I'm never going to let anything happen to her."

"Me, either," Allan stated.

She glanced over and noted that he was looking at Hannah as intensely as she was. "You really mean that."

"Of course I do. I gave my word to take care of her," he said.

"Sometimes girls need things that men don't under-stand," Jessi commented.

He glanced back at her, and she realized too late that she'd revealed something she hadn't intended. "Is that why you're so prickly?"

She smiled a little at the way he said it. "I'm not. I simply get that no one is going to fight my battles for me. At least not the ones that matter to me. And I'm going to make sure that little Hannah here knows she's always got me in her corner. No matter what."

"What battle did you have to fight for yourself?" Allan asked.

"All of them," she said. "But then I'm a bit argumen-tative, as I'm sure you've noticed."

"With your dad?" he pressed.

"And Granddad. They both had certain ideas about

how a Chandler woman should behave and what she should do."

"Go into gaming and ruin all the Montrose men?" Allan suggested.

Jessi thought about it and wondered if that was the motivation behind her grandfather's desire for her to be so proper. But in the end her family just hadn't worried too much about Thomas Montrose or his heirs. "We didn't really talk about your family that much."

Allan's face tightened. "My grandfather was road-kill to yours, and he never looked back to see the consequences, did he?"

Jessi had never thought of the ousting of Thomas Montrose from the gaming company he'd cofounded with her grandfather that way before, but she could see a certain truth to what Allan said. Gregory Chandler had really cared about only one person and that had been himself. Something he'd passed along to her father.

"Grandfather really wasn't very good at relating to people," Jessi said. "I guess you could say the same about me."

"Nah." Allan walked over to the crib to put the sleeping Hannah down. Jessi joined him as he removed the bottle, and they both sort of held their breath to see if she'd stay asleep.

She did.

Allan looked up at Jessi and smiled, and she smiled back. They had averted a middle-of-the-night crisis. When they got out into the hallway, she started to walk back to her room, but Allan stopped her with a hand on her elbow.

"You're nothing like your grandfather," he said.

"How do you know?"

"By all reports he was a driven man who cared about nothing but the bottom line. Who thought that the people who worked for him were nothing but cogs that kept the machine going. But you aren't like that, Jess. You care about the people around you—I've seen you passionately defend them."

"Yes, you have. I'm amazed John could forgive me for what I did. I did have the best of intentions when I hired that P.I. to investigate his past," Jessi said, trying not to feel all bubbly and warm inside that Allan had called her Jess, an intimate nickname that only her true friends ever used. Maybe it meant nothing, though. It probably was just a slip of the tongue.

"John told me that he couldn't do anything other than forgive you, because you'd been the one to keep Patti safe until he could find her and take over the job. And he said if he'd been anything other than honest with Patti, he wouldn't have deserved to marry her."

"He was truly a great man. Patti was lucky to have fallen in love with him." Jessi felt a lump of emotion in her throat and turned away, but Allan noticed and drew her into his arms, hugging her close. And for the first time since she'd known him she felt a moment's peace in his presence as he eased the ache in her heart.

Allan loosely held the bottle in one hand as he hugged Jessi with his other arm. No matter how hard he tried, it was impossible to keep his distance. They kept having little moments like this one where he couldn't help but see her as a woman. Not his enemy. Not the granddaughter of a man who'd ruined his grandfather's life. Just a girl who'd been wounded, as well.

This was dangerous, he thought. Sex was one thing,

but emotions... He couldn't allow himself to start caring for her. That was when he'd lose the steely grip he'd always had on his control. And he couldn't do that.

Not just because of the situation with Kell and work, but also because of Hannah. If he and Jessi had an affair that involved more than sex, it would end. Everything did. Allan knew this to be the one certainty of his life. And then they'd have to see each other at every important event in Hannah's life.

It would be difficult. More difficult than when their best friends had married and he and Jessi couldn't stand each other. He knew this, yet he also loved the smell of her perfume as she was nestled against his chest. With her head pressed over his heart, for this one second it was easy to forget she was Jessi. Yet at the same time he knew exactly who she was. It was that juxtaposition that made the moment that much more untenable for him. Made it that much harder to drop his arm and move away—something he knew he should do.

Yet he didn't do it. Instead, he let the bottle drop to the floor, so he could wrap both arms around her as she tipped her head back and looked up at him. He saw the same questions in her eyes that were echoing inside him. This was a mistake; they both knew it, yet couldn't stop.

He closed his eyes, trying to remember all the reasons why he needed to let her go, and then he felt the one thing that made it impossible: her lips brushing lightly against his.

"Thanks for being almost human," she said, so softly he had to strain to hear her.

"You're welcome," he said with a chuckle as he opened his eyes and looked at her.

Her gray eyes were cloudy, and for a minute he almost wished he was a different kind of man. One who would know how to soothe the savageness he saw there.

Despite that knowledge of his shortcomings, he hugged her close. "I'm always that way."

She shook her head and put her hand on his shoulder, just a soft light touch as she stayed on her tiptoes, staring into his eyes. He knew she was searching for something—probably answers to the questions that lingered in her own mind—but he had no idea if she'd find them. He wasn't even sure he knew what the answers were.

She opened her mouth, and he put his fingers over her lips. "Don't. We're not going to change this."

She nodded and took his hand in hers and turned to lead him down the hallway in the direction of the room she was using. He followed her even though he knew it wasn't smart. This wasn't a controlled sexual encounter. She was emotional, and he'd be lying if he said he wasn't, too. He already knew there was something else going on inside him. Maybe it was just losing his best friend. Maybe it was—

Who cared? He wasn't going to deny himself Jessi, and he'd figure out everything else later.

She paused on the threshold of her room, turning back to look over her shoulder at him. He realized how irresistible she was with her spiky pixie haircut and that oversize T-shirt that fell to the tops of her thighs.

"Dammit, woman, you're sexy as hell," he said, tracing the hem of the shirt.

"I'm not wearing silk or lace," she said.

"That's probably part of the reason why I find you so hot," he admitted. "It's my shirt."

"This doesn't change anything," she said a warning in her voice.

It changed everything, and she knew it. But by denying it, she was sending him a message that tomorrow they'd be back to acting like the only reason why they were together was because of the their friends' deaths. But last night had changed all that. And there was no going back, no matter what she said now.

He just nodded and picked her up, carrying her into the bedroom and dropping her in the center of the bed. She bounced lightly and arched one eyebrow at him.

"That's not very smooth," she said.

"I'm not smooth or romantic. You know that," he said. He needed to make sure she understood who he was. At heart, he wasn't polished or sophisticated. It didn't matter that he had money and could buy whatever and whoever he wanted. He needed Jessi to understand that growing up in the shadow of hatred had forged him into the kind of man who wasn't gentlemanly. He was a man who'd fought for everything he had, and he doubted if there was a force on earth that could change him.

Not even Jessi Chandler, with her spicy-hot kisses, smooth, pale thighs or strong arms that pulled him closer to her. He knew that she was running from something and using him, but that suited him just fine, because it made it easier to lie to himself and pretend he was using her, too.

Jessi had given in a long time ago to the fact that she often did things that others might deem stupid, such as what she was about to do tonight. But this behavior made her feel alive and distracted her from things that really scared her.

Like how tender Allan had looked holding little Hannah.

Jessi wanted that image out of her head. She wanted him to be a quick lay, and as he stood next to the bed, shoving his shorts down his legs, the last thing she was thinking of was sappy emotional stuff.

She hadn't gotten a chance to really see him when they'd had sex earlier, and as he started to move over her, with one knee on the bed, she reached out to touch his thigh.

She traced the hard muscles with her fingertip, trying to concentrate on that instead of his sex, which jutted toward her. But when she turned her head to look at it, she drew in her breath at the size of him. A shiver of sexual desire coursed through her, making every nerve ending come to attention.

She lifted her hand and wrapped it around the length of his shaft, stroking him up and down until he moved forward to straddle her waist. Then she let go of his sex and raised her hands to his chest.

He was warm, and the light dusting of hair there tickled her fingers as she caressed him. His hands were busy finding the hem of her shirt and tugging it up over her head. He tossed it aside and then looked down at her. He didn't say anything, but leaned forward and slowly swept his hands over her torso to her waist and then lower to her hips, where he squeezed her and held on to her as he rolled to his side and kept her there, pressed against him.

They were both completely naked, and she didn't want to admit it, but they felt right pressed together.

Their bodies just naturally fit, as if they were meant for each other.

He thrust one thigh between her legs and used his hands on her hips to draw her forward. As the ridge of his shaft rubbed all along her feminine core, she shuddered.

She tipped her head back, and he lowered his mouth to hers as she did so. His kisses were long and languid and left no room for thoughts of anything but where his next touch would fall on her body and how long she could wait before she reached between them and forced him to enter her.

She swept her hand down his back. It was wide and smooth, and when she reached lower to cup his buttocks and draw him forward, he groaned her name. She flexed her fingers, letting him feel the bite of her nails as she rocked her hips against him.

He shuddered in her arms, and she felt a wave of feminine power washing over her. She exploited it, claimed it as her own by pushing him onto his back and climbing onto his lap, lifting her mouth from his.

He smiled up at her in an expression she'd never seen on his face before. Then his hands were on her breasts as she shifted until the tip of his erection was at the entrance of her body. It was the feel of his naked flesh that jarred her and made her realize she was about to have unprotected sex with him.

She cursed and drew back.

"What's wrong? Oh, the condom."

"I don't have any," she said.

"I do. But I don't want to leave your bed," he said.

She understood that, and she'd always lived with no regrets. But the impact of the past few hours and realizing that she wasn't ready to have a child with this man made her extra cautious. "Well, you're going to have to."

He sighed and rolled out from underneath her. He returned in a quick second with the condom already in place. He climbed into bed and drew her back over his lap. He didn't say anything, just tangled his hands in her short hair and drew her mouth down to his for a passionate kiss that left no doubt that he was still very much turned on.

She put her hands on his shoulders and watched him carefully as she lowered herself onto his shaft and took him completely. His eyes were closed and his neck arched back, and she leaned forward, drawing his head to hers and thrusting her tongue into his mouth as she rode him.

His hands caressed her back, cupping her butt and urging her to quicken her pace, and she did, driving them both toward climax, which she reached instantly. She felt him keep thrusting inside her, and he tore his mouth from hers and leaned down to catch her nipple in his mouth, sucking strongly on it until his hips jerked upward. He gripped her hips, drawing her down hard as he groaned her name.

He turned his face to the side, and she collapsed against him as he held her to his chest, rubbing his palms up and down her back.

She wanted to pretend that nothing had changed, just as she'd said earlier. But as she lay there in his arms and felt the fingers of sleep drawing her in, she realized that everything had changed. She was no longer sure that running away from her emotions was a viable option, because somehow when she hadn't been expecting it, Allan had slipped past her guard.

Nine

Allan woke up with the sun streaming in the windows of an empty bedroom. He knew where he was and remembered clearly holding Jessi in his arms through the night. But she was nowhere to be found this morning.

Neither was Hannah, he discovered after he put on his basketball shorts and checked the nursery. A quick trip to the kitchen revealed Fawkes sipping coffee and doing the *USA TODAY* crossword puzzle on his iPad.

"Good morning, sir. Would you like breakfast?" the butler asked. "Ms. Jessi left a note for you. It's on the counter."

"Coffee's fine," Allan said, waving to Fawkes to keep his seat while he poured his own coffee, which he drank black. "I need to go to John's office this morning and also speak to the funeral home to make sure we're all set for Saturday."

"I have the car ready to go. Ms. Jessi asked me to pick her up at Hatteras Island Care Home at noon. Will that accommodate your plans?" Fawkes asked.

Allan nodded. Well, that explained where Jessi was.

She must have taken Hannah to see her grandmother. "I'm going to shower and then we can leave."

"Yes, sir."

Allan took the note and his coffee mug back to the bedroom he was using. He settled onto the edge of his bed and unfolded the piece of paper.

Allan,
I took Hannah to visit Amelia at the Hatteras Group Care Home. I'm not sure she'll recognize us, but I wanted to go and chat with her to see if I could make her understand Patti is gone. I hope you don't mind, but I asked Fawkes to drive us there and pick us up. The man was just sitting around waiting for you to wake up.

The letter was signed with a big *J*.

Just as he'd expected, there was nothing about last night. Underneath their obvious differences, they were very similar, he thought as he gathered his clothes and showered and shaved. They both ignored anything that might make them seem weak. And emotions were definitely something that could do that.

He checked his email and saw that Jessi had been busy sending in a revised promotion plan. He'd been cc'd on one of the exchanges between her and Kell that mentioned three meetings she'd set up via Skype to talk to a production company in Hollywood who were producing a new movie franchise based on a string of very popular books. She'd also managed to arrange a meeting with Jack White, one of the hottest producer-directors in town.

He admired her initiative and wondered when she'd

had time to do all that work. While he'd been sleeping? It bothered him that she might have seen him so relaxed in her arms. Because he knew that it had been a long time since he'd felt that laid-back and had slept so soundly.

He pushed that thought to the back of his mind and instead read the emails that Kell had sent privately to Dec and him.

If she can pull this off we will have to reevaluate our plan to end her employment. Keep me posted, Allan. I need to know about all developments.

Kell didn't seem happy, but at the end of the day he was a fair man, and if Jessi met the terms they'd laid out for her, then Kell would honor his end of the bargain. Allan emailed his cousins back and then got down to business, really analyzing Jessi's plan. He saw that she'd obviously given it some thought. It was almost as if someone different had come up with the plan compared to her offering of a few days ago.

The other proposal had shown someone who didn't really care, but this new plan had innovation and real drive behind it. He'd be lying if he said he wasn't impressed. What had made her change her mind?

And it was clear to him that something had. But he didn't have time to dwell on it. Instead, he left for John's storage unit in town to start sorting through a lifetime's worth of stuff his friend had kept there. John and Patti had left behind high-powered careers to open the bed-and-breakfast, Patti as a highly sought after interior designer and John as a corporate lawyer.

When Allan got to the facility and started sorting

through boxes from his friend's life and career, he realized that he finally got why John had left it all behind.

If his friend had still been living in L.A. and hadn't married Patti, these boxes would be all that he'd left behind. Things that had been generated by long hours spent working for someone else. A life lived on someone else's terms.

Mostly it was John's private notes on his clients. Stuff that wasn't part of his official work files. Things about their habits and how they liked to have their paperwork prepared.

Allan shook his head, surprised that John's death was making him reevaluate his own life and choices. But there was one key difference between his friend and him, and that was Patti. John had found his soul mate, a woman who shared his vision of the future and what life should look like. Allan hadn't found anyone like that and doubted he ever would.

He liked being just a little bit selfish and answering to no one save himself when he wanted to do something. It was an attitude he doubted he'd ever lose.

He rubbed the back of his neck as he got a text message from Fawkes informing him that he was going to have to leave to go and pick up Jessi and Hannah. Suddenly, Allan didn't want to keep sorting through files. He wanted to see Jessi and ascertain for himself if she had changed.

There was something different about her note and emails from this morning, and he was curious as to what it was. He told himself it was important that he figure it out so he could advise Kell and keep Playtone Games on top, but he knew that wasn't the only reason he wanted to see her.

He missed her. He hated that he'd woken up alone, and he wanted to see if she was running from him. It could be construed as cowardly, but to him it had seemed as if Jessi had beat a strategic retreat to regroup and refocus.

He wondered why she'd done it. One thing was certain—if it was a calculated move, she'd been successful, because all he'd done this morning was think about her.

Jessi had been running on adrenaline and nerves all morning.

The house where Amelia lived looked from the outside like another bed-and-breakfast, but as soon as she stepped inside, the smell of antiseptic let her know it was a nursing home.

"Hello," the duty nurse said in greeting as she came inside.

Jessi carefully shifted Hannah so she could reach out to shake the nurse's hand. "Hi, I'm Jessi Chandler. Patti McCoy was my best friend and I'm here with her daughter, Hannah, to visit Amelia Pearson."

"Have a seat over there and I'll call for Sophie, Mrs. Pearson's care nurse."

Jessi took a seat and five minutes later a woman wearing crepe-soled shoes and a floral dress came over to her. "Hi, I'm Sophie. I understand you're here to see Mrs. Pearson."

"Yes. Would that be okay?"

"Let's go into my office and talk. There are some things you should know. Who is this little cutie?"

"This is Hannah. She's Amelia's granddaughter," Jessi said.

Hannah made a sweet little coo as Sophie tickled

her chin. Then the nurse led the way into her office. "Please have a seat."

Jessi did. "I don't want to create a problem, but I would feel better if I could talk to Amelia myself and make sure she understands about Patti."

"We've already let Mrs. Pearson know about her daughter's death."

"I figured you had, but I wouldn't feel right if I didn't talk to her myself."

"She's having a good day, so I think we can arrange it. The most important thing for you to do is not agitate her. I'm going to give you a pamphlet to read over while I go and see if she'd like to have visitors."

Jessi read the pamphlet and felt a knot tighten in the pit of her stomach. It made her sad to think that the woman who'd always been so kind to her and treated her like a second daughter was lost in a world that was so confusing.

"Okay, we're all set. She remembers you and is looking forward to talking to you," Sophie said.

"Great," Jessi said, following the nurse into the solarium, where Mrs. Pearson was already seated in a fan-backed rattan chair.

"Jessi. How wonderful to see you," Amelia said as soon as she walked in. The older woman stood up to hug her.

"Look at this baby. Is it yours?" Amelia asked.

"No, she's Patti's daughter," Jessi said, careful to keep her tone quiet and calm, as the brochure had recommended.

Sophie stood in the corner observing them, which made the situation all the more surreal.

"May I hold your baby?" Amelia asked.

Sophie nodded, so Jessi got up and handed the baby to her grandmother. What was truly surprising was how she reached for Hannah and then held the baby so tenderly.

Jessi took her iPhone out of her pocket while Amelia was staring down at the baby and talking to herself, and after making sure it was on silent, took a quick picture, knowing that Hannah might want to see this someday.

Jessi carefully sat back down, and Amelia looked over at her. "Patti is the best baby. Her father's gone a lot but she never fusses."

Jessi glanced over at Sophie in confusion, but then remembered how the brochure had said to restate facts but not to argue. "Patti was a great a baby. This is her daughter, Hannah. She's a little bit of a stinker sometimes, but also a great baby."

"Hannah? My best friend growing up was Anna. I haven't talked to her in years," Amelia said.

"That happens as we get older," Jessi said. "You know Patti was my best friend, right?"

"Yes, I do. Patti is so lucky to have found you as her friend. I remember the first time you came to our home, when you two were in elementary school. You'd been in a fight."

Jessi nodded. She'd been a mess back then. She'd been defending Cari from some boys who used to pull on her long blond ringlets. Jessi had torn her shirt and knew she'd get in trouble at home if she came in looking like that, so Patti had brought her to her house instead. "You were very kind to me, Mrs. Pearson. You fixed my blouse and gave me cookies and promised not to tell my dad I'd been in a fight."

"Well, I could see you needed some love."

Jessi swallowed hard. She had just needed to feel accepted for herself instead of always being the middle Chandler girl, part of a unit instead of an individual. And Patti's mom had done just that.

"Patti is sleeping a lot today. She won't sleep tonight," Amelia said.

"It's okay if *Hannah* sleeps a lot, Amelia. I'm sure she'll sleep tonight."

"No, she won't," Amelia said. "Derek will be mad if the baby cries at night. He needs his sleep."

"It's okay. This is Hannah, not Patti," Jessi said again, seeing Sophie move quickly toward them as Amelia started shaking Hannah.

Jessi jumped up and took Hannah from her grandmother as the baby started crying. Sophie rushed over and tried to calm Amelia, who was now agitated by the baby's cries. Jessi tucked little Hannah against her shoulder and rubbed her back, trying to soothe her.

"It's okay, Amelia," the care nurse was saying. "Ms. Chandler, why don't you step outside? One of the staff will take you to see the doctor on duty."

Jessi went into the hall and found a nurse waiting there, along with two technicians, who went into the solarium to help subdue Amelia. Jessi's heart ached as she watched the woman who'd once taken such good care of her falling to pieces.

Hannah was still crying, and Jessi reached into the Vera Bradley diaper bag and found her pacifier, which the baby latched on to as soon as it was in her mouth.

"I think I'd better have a doctor check Hannah out. Amelia shook her," Jessi said to the nurse.

"I'll take you to him. Are you okay?"

"Yes. But I didn't get to tell her that Patti is dead. I don't think she understands that."

"We've informed her, and her care nurse will keep reminding her of those things when it's needed."

Jessi knew there was nothing more she could do. But seeing Mrs. Pearson in such a state made her glad her own mother's struggle with cancer had ended quickly. Jessi would have hated to see her suffering the way Amelia was.

The doctor on duty was a GP.

"I'm Dr. Gold," he said when he entered. "I heard you had a little incident?"

"Yes," Jessi said. "Hannah was shaken and I just want to make sure she's okay."

"I can check her out. Put her on the bed over there, but keep holding her little hands."

He examined Hannah, making comments to the baby as he worked. Then he looked over at Jessi. "She's going to be just fine."

"Thank you, Doctor."

Jessi had already texted Fawkes to come and pick them up, but he wasn't there when she stepped out into the sunny October day. She tipped her face to the sun and held the baby.

When the car pulled up about five minutes later, she almost groaned as she noted that Fawkes wasn't at the wheel. It was Allan. He got out and pushed his sunglasses up on his head.

"You okay?"

"Yes. Amelia had an episode, so we had to end our visit early," Jessi said. She couldn't recount any more of it since she was still shaken by what had happened.

"What kind of episode?" Allan asked, opening the door to the backseat and reaching for Hannah.

Jessi passed the baby to him and noticed that he dropped a quick kiss on her forehead before putting her into the car seat, fastening her in and then tucking her stuffed frog next to her cheek.

"What kind of episode, Jessi?" Allan asked again as he closed the door.

Jessi realized she'd been staring at him. She didn't like that he kept her off-kilter all the time lately. She mentally gave herself a slap, the type Cher gave herself in *Moonstruck,* and told herself to snap out of it.

"She was worried the baby was sleeping too much and shook her awake. Then she got really agitated when I took the baby and Hannah kept crying. I had to leave so the nurse and some technicians could calm her down," Jessi said.

"She shook Hannah?" Allan asked.

"Yes, but the doctor on duty checked her out, and she's fine. I also was informed before I left that Amelia has been sedated and is sleeping now."

Allan held her door open for her, and Jessi seated herself. She watched him walk around to the driver's side and get behind the wheel. He started the engine and then turned to her.

"It had to be difficult to see that happening with Patti's mom."

"It was, but it just underscored that we're all the family Hannah has now. Amelia will never be a grandmother to her," Jessi said.

"We'll be good to Hannah," Allan said. "Together we will make sure she has all the family she needs."

He'd made them a team, a family, and Jessi didn't

know what to say. She was silent as he drove down the little two-lane road back to the bed-and-breakfast. She really didn't know how she felt about being linked to Allan McKinney for the rest of her life. The part that was upsetting was that it didn't bother her as much as she would have thought it should.

While Jessi put Hannah down for a nap, Allan took some iced tea that Fawkes had made to the porch and then quickly read another chapter in one of the baby care books he'd downloaded to his phone.

"Whatcha reading?" Jessi asked as she came and sat next to him on one of the large pine rockers.

"Uh, nothing," he said. "I saw your aggressive plan to win over some business with the producer Jack White."

"I know it's bold, but, hey, that's my style. He was more than happy to take the appointment when I appealed to his sense of fairness."

"How did you do that?"

"I simply reminded him that at one time he was making small, independent films and he'd had to rely on bigger names to help him along. One of them was my grandfather, who invested a lot of money in what he called *Project 17* back then."

"I didn't know your grandfather did that," Allan said. The Montroses had focused a lot of time on studying the ins and outs of Gregory Chandler's business, but only his gaming stuff. Allan supposed his grandfather hadn't been interested in anything but that. However, this was key information they should have had.

"Well, he did. *Project 17* went on to become his first blockbuster, *Cowboys from Space*...so I appealed to his sense of fair play and asked for a meeting."

"And you got it. I like that you didn't hesitate to go after it, but I'm curious about something," Allan said. He glanced over at her. She was wearing a pair of white shorts that hit her midthigh and a sleeveless top that was fitted over her breasts and then fell loosely around her stomach. She'd put on a denim jacket to combat the breeze. Her sandals had a slight heel. For once, she didn't look all rocker chick, but instead looked like any other woman on the island.

He felt as if something was changing in Jessi and he wondered what, exactly, it was and how he could use it to his own advantage. Because no matter what changed, his reflex was to assume that they were still at war and always would be. Or were they? Had last night changed her enough to call a real truce?

He had woken up with the feeling that something was different in himself, but then when he'd found her gone… Dammit, he hated when he got petty, but had just realized he was bothered by the fact that she'd left him alone in her bed.

"What?"

"Well, two things," he said.

She arched her eyebrows and gave him a look that said to get on with it. He realized she hadn't changed as much as he'd previously thought and wondered again if the change was in him and not her. He hoped not.

"What caused your new attitude toward Playtone-Infinity Games? Don't deny something has changed— last week you didn't use your old contact with Jack White. So why now?" he asked.

"Hannah," she said. "I'm going to be her mother figure now, and I know that kids get a lot more from what we do than from what we say we do. So if I told her to always do her best, no matter what the situation, but she knew that I'd sort of phoned it in at the end and let myself be fired…well, I just don't want her thinking that."

"How would she ever know about this? She's only three months old," Allan said, pushing his sunglasses up on his forehead and turning to face Jessi.

"I figured you'd mention it. I just didn't want it to be an issue. What was your second question?" she asked, leaning back in the chair and looking out toward the Pamlico Sound.

"I'm not ready to let you change the conversation," he said.

"Too bad," she replied. "Do you have another question or not?"

"Actually, I do. Why didn't you wake me up this morning?"

She sat up slowly, nibbling her bottom lip for a second before she seemed to realize what she was doing. She straightened her shoulders and looked at him. "You don't seem like the type of guy who wants a clingy woman, and goodness knows I don't cling."

"Liar," he said. He could hear the bravado and the challenge in her voice.

"Why did you come to my bed last night?" she asked. "And don't say it was just physical."

Allan knew there were two ways he could play this. One was blustery and posturing, and the other was… honest.

He reached out and took her hand in his. "Because I couldn't help myself. I don't know what it is about you, Jessi Chandler, but you always cause me to act in a way… Let's just say you make me forget myself."

"I do? I don't believe that," she said. "I think you get

a wild feeling and just can't resist following it to see what happens."

"I'm not that unpredictable," he said. "Most of the time when it comes to you I just won't back down, because I know you'd see it as a sign of weakness. And like you said earlier, actions speak way louder than words."

"I never see you as weak," she admitted, her voice a little bit softer, all that challenge and bravado ebbing away.

But it wasn't entirely gone, and he realized then something about Jessi that had been abundantly clear from the first moment he'd met her, even though he'd never taken notice of it before. She was always on the edge and ready to jump off. And now he had to decide if he was going to let go and watch or join her for the crazy ride.

Ten

They fell into a sort of rhythm over the days after the funeral. Kell hadn't come but Dec, Cari and Emma all had. It was very somber, and she had been glad to have her sisters there, but their stay had been too brief—they flew in and out on the same day.

She'd hoped that Reggie would have the custody all wrapped up so they could go back to L.A. by now, but the judge didn't move quickly. And then there was the storm in the Atlantic to contend with. First the predictions had the storm going toward Florida, and then into the Gulf of Mexico, but it had stalled out and now a stronger storm was taking its place, this one aiming straight for the Atlantic Seaboard.

Focusing on hurricane preparedness gave Jessi an excuse not to dwell on Allan. Which was difficult, because the last thing she wanted was for any of this to start to feel normal. But that was exactly what had happened. Worst of all, she couldn't wait to wake up each morning and have coffee with Allan while Fawkes did his crossword and baby Hannah drank her bottle.

He was quiet in the morning until he'd had his first

cup of coffee, which had surprised her because he was so chatty the rest of the time. And Fawkes had thawed toward her. If she had to pinpoint the moment when it had happened, she thought it was at the funeral, when she'd wrapped her arm around Allan's shoulders to keep him from breaking down. She didn't like to remember that moment when he'd seemed all too human and vulnerable.

But that time had passed and she was well aware that they were existing in a sort of vacuum as they waited for the custody of Hannah to be approved, and they wrapped up the rest of Patti and John's business matters. Fall seemed just around the corner. Jessi had even surprised herself by buying a tiny Halloween costume for Hannah to wear—an Elvis wig and leather jacket, which she thought would crack Allan up.

They had become that family unit she'd sort of been afraid of, and yet at the same time they hadn't. There was a tension between the two of them that couldn't be explained away. And no matter how nice it was to sit quietly in the kitchen in the morning, usually the rest of the day would reinforce in one way or another that they were still members of two different families embroiled in a feud.

It looked as if Jessi wouldn't be able to get back to L.A. for the meeting with Jack White, and Kell wasn't budging on his timeline. For an entire day she'd debated returning and giving up her rights to Hannah, but in the end she realized she'd only decided to try to keep her job at the merged company for Hannah's sake, so it made no sense to sacrifice her.

On Tuesday morning, Allan and Jessi were sitting at the kitchen table with Hannah and Fawkes, settling into their usual routine, when Allan asked, "Why are you staring at me?"

"I'm still marveling at the fact that you can be quiet for more than a second," Jessi said. "Every morning it's like discovering a new treasure."

He lowered his eyebrows, but didn't say anything, just took another sip of his coffee and went back to reading the *Wall Street Journal* on his iPad. Or at least that's what she thought he was reading, until Hannah slammed down her bottle and formula splattered across the table and onto the tablet. Jessi grabbed a towel and leaned over to wipe it off, noticing in the process that he was reading a book.

"You rat," she said.

"What?"

"*Baby 411!* That's what you've been reading every morning? No wonder you're so much better with Hannah than I am."

"I'll take Miss Hannah into the other room," Fawkes said as he got her out of her baby seat.

"Why?" Allan asked.

"She shouldn't hear you two fighting," he said as he walked away.

"Are we going to be fighting?" Allan asked when they were alone.

"I don't want to, but honestly, why would you go behind my back like that?" Jessi said. "I wondered why you knew what to do, but I figured you were going on gut instinct like me. Is being able to best me so important to you?"

"I don't like to lose," he said with a shrug, putting the cover over his iPad before standing up and taking his mug over to the Keurig machine. He made himself another cup of coffee as she watched him.

"I thought things were changing between us, but you're still the same," she said as he leaned back against the kitchen counter.

He stared down into his cup before putting it down. "I'm not the same. I downloaded the book because I knew nothing and was totally afraid I'd do something wrong. I can't be in a situation without knowing as much as I can about it."

"Why not just say that? Or suggest I read up on baby care? Clearly, I'm not a natural mother," Jessi said.

"Jess, you are wonderful with Hannah. Even when you screw up, you course correct and make it into something that is okay."

"Still, I wish you'd said something."

"If I had suggested you read a book on baby care you would have exploded and told me not to boss you around," he said.

"True. But I thought you were just supersmart when it came to kids," she said. "I'm kind of glad you're not. I was beginning to think you really were the superman you believe yourself to be."

"Ah, now you see the chinks in my armor? I suspect you knew they were there from the first moment we met," he said.

She thought back to that day. She'd never in her life been so scared. Her best friend had found her soul mate, and Jessi had known that she and Patti would never be as close again. And then there was sexy Allan acting all chummy with Patti and John. Jessi had heard of him before because of their family history, but hadn't expected him to be this obnoxious. She'd felt isolated… left out again, and it hurt.

"Only once you started talking," she said.

He threw his head back and laughed. "You're a pain in the ass. You know that, right?"

"I try. So what's that book say about when she can have real food?" Jessi asked, because she'd rather talk about the baby than about him and her. It had been so hard to keep her distance for the past week, but she'd done it because she already liked Allan too much, and allowing the physical bond between them to get any stronger would only lead her down the path to love.

And that frightened her more than anything else she'd experienced in her entire life. She just didn't think she was ready to give over her heart and her happiness to a man who kept so much of himself hidden.

"Let me look," he said.

She watched him for a minute and then realized what she was doing. "I'll go get Fawkes and Hannah."

She left the room without looking back.

Allan didn't dwell on feelings; he'd never been that comfortable with emotion. And nothing that he'd experienced since he'd arrived on Hatteras had changed his mind. Emotions were uncomfortable and created a lot of stress. The more he cared for Hannah and Jessi, the more he worried about them. Over the past few days he'd tried a couple times to lure Jessi back to bed, but she'd resisted, and frankly, he thought that was for the best.

What he needed was to get back to L.A. so he could have a little distance from Jessi. In terms of finalizing custody of Hannah, he was rattling cages, but he had no connections in North Carolina, and the local judge wasn't going to be rushed. Even though Patti and John had asked in their will that Jessi and he become guardians, the state wouldn't simply give the baby over to them without paperwork and visits. They'd had two in-home visits, and Reggie was doing all he could to speed the process along, but Allan was ready to get back to California.

He wanted life to return to normal. He'd never admit it aloud, but he was starting to like the routine of living with Jessi. Hannah was the sweetest thing, too, and he felt safe admitting that he loved that little baby as if she was his own daughter. But there was something almost surreal about sharing that bond with Jessi.

She'd changed since they'd been here. Her rocker chick clothes had given way to a wardrobe of casual jeans and blousy shirts. He realized she'd brought them with her, so she must have just been wearing her badass clothes to rile him.

Which she had. And that was part of the problem between the two of them. She was fire where he was concerned, and though he knew he'd get burned, he kept moving closer to her. In fact, he didn't mind being singed by her heat.

"Allan, you better come in here," Jessi called from the living room.

He went into the other room and saw that she was sitting on the floor playing with Hannah, while Fawkes sat in one of the armchairs. But they were both watching the television.

"What's up?"

"Hurricane warning. One of the tracking models has it heading straight for us."

"Great. I'm going to call Reggie and see if this will finally convince the judge to move on the custody ruling," Allan said.

"Let's switch over to the Weather Channel and see what it means for us. I think that the models are often unpredictable," Jessi said.

"Even if the Weather Channel has a different prediction, we don't want to take any chances," Allan said. "We both want to get back home, right, Jessi?"

She nodded, but there was something in her expression that made him wonder for a moment if she might not be in that big a hurry. But he doubted it. She had her own life, and the other night she herself had said that it would be easier with Hannah once they got back into their own routines.

He left her with Fawkes and walked back to his room to make the call. Allan sat on the edge of his bed and pondered whether he should try to convince Jessi to sell the bed-and-breakfast. He didn't think they were going to be able to manage it from across the country.

"Reggie Blythe." The attorney answered his phone on the second ring.

"Reggie, this is Allan McKinney. We just saw the weather bulletin about the possible hurricane. Any chance this will help the judge hurry his decision?"

"I was thinking along the same lines and already sent my secretary over to see if we can get on the docket for today or tomorrow. You and Jessi will need to leave the island if there is an evacuation."

"Really?"

"Yes, it's illegal for a nonresident to stay on Hatteras if that happens," Reggie said. "I think maybe the weather is going to work in your favor."

"I hope so. We want the right decision for Hannah, but we're also ready to get back home. Hannah needs to start adjusting to her new environment."

"I agree. I'll let you know as soon as we hear something more," Reggie said.

"One more thing," Allan said. "What does John and Patti's will say about the bed-and-breakfast? Does it have to be held for Hannah until she comes of age? Can Jessi and I sell it and put the money aside for her?"

"I'll look into it, but I do know that John hoped you'd keep the place open," Reggie said.

"That's all well and good, but neither Jessi nor I know a thing about running a hotel. I'm just trying to figure out what makes sense," Allan said. "I want to honor John's wishes…."

"I'll see what I can come up with. I might be able to find a caretaker for the property who can be paid out of the profits until Hannah is of age," Reggie suggested.

"That might work. Let me know if I can help in any way."

"I will."

He ended the call and then dialed Kell's number.

"What's up, Allan?"

"It looks like the hurricane in the Atlantic is headed straight for us," he said.

His cousin gave a mirthless laugh. "Seems like Jessi is never going to get back to L.A."

"It actually might speed up our leaving the island. We are using it as a reason to force the judge to make a decision. I just wanted to keep you posted."

"Thanks," Kell said.

"Kell?"

"Yeah?"

"Why do you hate Jessi so much?" Allan asked. It was one thing to have been upset about what happened with the past generation, and he knew that Jessi could be irritating, but he had no idea why his cousin didn't like her.

"Because she's a Chandler. I don't know her personally," Kell said.

"She's a great woman, Kell. Talented and dedicated to the company—"

"Don't tell me you've fallen for her. You hate her. You said she's a pain in the ass," Kell said.

"I did, didn't I." But he finally realized that "hating" Jessi had been a self-defense maneuver to protect himself, because she was too easy to respect and like and fall for.

"Yes. So don't desert me," his cousin declared. "I have to listen to Dec telling me how great all the Chandlers are every time we get together."

"I won't. I'm still staunchly a Montrose heir."

"Good to hear it," Kell said and ended the call.

Fawkes went out for supplies, and Jessi called a local handyman to see if he could come and make the bed-and-breakfast hurricane-ready. He was listed in the notebook where Patti had kept all the local services she used, including housekeeping and lawn maintenance.

"I'll be there as soon as we know it's headed this way," James the handyman said. "I know that property well, since it was in my family before the McCoys purchased it."

"Have you considered acting as a caretaker here?" Jessi asked, remembering that Allan had floated that as a possibility.

"Perhaps. I have my own business now and I'd have to ask the wife," he said. "She gets mighty pissed if I don't run things past her first."

Jessi smiled to herself. "How long have you been married?"

"Twenty years. Still feels like we just got back from our honeymoon," he said.

She smiled to herself. Happy couples made her feel better about the possibilities. And then she realized that for the first time she wasn't thinking of love and togetherness in vague terms, but specifically in terms of herself and Hannah and Allan.

His faults still loomed in the back of her mind, and she knew he hadn't said a word about them dating when they returned to California, but a part of her knew things had changed between them.

She thought back to this morning in the kitchen, when he'd admitted, well, that he was human. That he had flaws and that he didn't want her to see them. It was enough to fan the flames of the secret desire in her heart. She wasn't entirely sure when something as ill-advised as falling for Allan had started to be…well, something she wanted.

She liked that her heart raced every time he entered a room or that she got a little thrill from flirting with him and teasing him. True, she'd been cautious and tried to keep him at arm's length, but a part of her was very sure that Allan and she were…what?

Even to herself she couldn't admit it. Even in her own head she was afraid to let it be true.

She was falling in love with Allan.

Hannah made her little gurgling noises, and Jessi smiled over at the tiny baby. She scooped her up and held her in her arms, leaning close to take a deep breath of the fresh clean baby smell.

"You did good, Patti," she said out loud. She hadn't let herself hold Hannah or even talk to Patti about the baby much when her friend had been alive. Jessi had always thought she'd lived her life on her terms—no fears, no regrets—but now she realized how paralyzing that lie and the fear underlying it had been. It had been strong enough to make her miss out on sharing this joy with Patti because she'd been terrified of even holding the newborn.

Her entire self-view shifted in that instant, and Jessi understood that she'd been cowardly her entire life. Being here with Hannah was making it crystal clear how much she'd missed by keeping everyone at bay. Instead of facing the things that scared her, she'd fought with them, told herself she didn't need them and walked away.

She'd done it this morning in the kitchen. When her gut had told her to move toward Allan she'd backed away.

Hannah was starting to get sleepy, her little eyes drifting closed, and for a moment Jessi debated sitting on the porch and just holding the little girl. But then she decided she wanted to get some work done.

She took Hannah upstairs, stopping under the picture of Patti and John that Allan had hung above the crib. It had just appeared there two days ago. And when she'd asked him about it, he said that he didn't want her to forget their faces.

It had been a sweet sentiment, but then he'd spoiled the moment by making a pass at her. Now that she thought back on it, Jessi realized that Allan ran from emotion the same way she did.

Maybe that meant that he was starting to care for her. She put Hannah in her crib and sat down in the rocking chair to think. Was she going to keep running away from life or was she going to be the woman she'd always believed herself to be and face the thing that scared her the most?

Ironically, it was Allan. She'd fought with him and dared him and taunted him since the moment they'd met, and it was only now that she could recognize she'd done all of those things to keep herself from falling for him. And they hadn't exactly been successful. There had always been a part of her that had wanted to see him again.

She pushed herself up from the chair, resolute in her conviction that she wasn't going to run anymore.

Walking down the hallway to his bedroom, she paused on the threshold as she realized he was on the phone. She didn't want to eavesdrop, but heard him say that he was still a true Montrose heir.

Jessi knew better than to listen at doors, but she couldn't deny what she'd overheard. It was a fierce reminder of something that she already knew. No matter how he acted when he was here, he was still her... frenemy.

Eleven

She started for the stairs, but then remembered her new promise to herself. No more running away.

Resolutely, she strode back to Allan's room and found him still sitting on the edge of the bed, looking contemplative.

"So you're a staunch Montrose heir?" she asked.

"That's not exactly news," he said, tossing his phone on the bed and standing up. "Why were you eavesdropping?"

"Sorry. I didn't mean to. I kind of thought we'd changed in our attitudes toward each other…well, at least I know that I have. I no longer view you as one of those nasty Montroses."

She put her hands on her hips and looked at him, daring him to lie to her.

"You're right. We have changed toward each other. But at the end of the day we're still business rivals— no, that's the wrong word. But things aren't going to magically fix themselves. I know you're working hard to change Kell's image of you, but it's still down to financial gain as far as he's concerned," Allan said.

What exactly was he saying? "You're not being very clear. Even if I get Jack White to agree to a deal, the money won't come in this quarter or probably even the next. Is all that work for nothing? Because I'm fine with not keeping that meeting and letting you guys go hang," she said.

"That's not what I was saying. Potential profit will satisfy the terms of your probation," Allan said. "Why are you being so argumentative?"

"You shook me. I've just been thinking about my life and myself, and I made some discoveries I didn't necessarily find comfortable. But I was thinking you and me—we'd both… Never mind. I just sound like some sappy schoolgirl."

"You are the furthest thing from sappy I've ever met. Finish your thought," he said, closing the gap between them and touching her chin. "I like you when you are at your most honest."

"I like that quality in you as well, but I don't get to see that guy as often as I'd like."

He dropped his hand and thrust it through his thick hair. "What do you want me to say? I learned early on that when you care for someone they have power over you."

"Do I have power over you?" She felt a shot of pure adrenaline as she asked the question that had been burning in the back of her mind since that kiss they'd shared on his plane. Living so openly and so honestly gave her a rush of excitement, but she also saw the potential for a lot of pain.

"You know you do," he said. "All week I've been trying to get you back into my bed, but you keep pushing me away. Why is that? Do I have some sort of power over *you*?"

He wanted to keep things even and she couldn't blame him, but with her new knowledge she realized that if she was truly living bold and large she couldn't hedge her bets or hesitate. She had to go all-in.

"Yes, you do," she said quietly. "And it's not just about sex, but influences every corner of my life. I really hope that I'm not just making you into the man I want you to be, because you are becoming very important to me."

Allan looked at her in shock. She saw the fear in his eyes—or at least that's what she hoped it was, because otherwise it might be pity.

Oh, please don't let it be pity.

He stepped back from her, turned away and walked over to the window that overlooked the garden in the backyard.

"I don't know what to say to that," he said after a few minutes had passed.

"It's not that hard," she said softly. "If you're honest with yourself you know exactly what to say, and if you're brave enough you'll be able to say it."

She heard the dare in her words and decided she was okay with that. She couldn't completely change her attitude in one day. And if he was man enough to be with her, man enough to actually be there for her as she really hoped he would, then he'd have to be as honest with her as she'd been with him.

"I... You want something from me that I've given no one else, not even my parents or my best friend," Allan said, still not facing her.

She saw the proud set of his shoulders and thought

that he'd never be able to say the words she desperately wanted to hear. She hesitated and wondered if him saying them made a difference to what she was already feeling, and knew that it didn't.

Her heart sped up as she walked over and put her arms around him, linking them together over his chest as she rested her head between his shoulder blades. He was tense for a few seconds, but then brought his hand up to cover hers. He didn't say another word, and neither did she.

For this moment it was enough. She didn't need to hear the words from him, but the small knot in the pit of her stomach warned that she would need to sooner or later, and she only hoped that he'd be able to give them to her when it was time.

He turned in her embrace and stepped away from her, and that tiny knot grew as she realized that her gamble hadn't paid off. Allan wasn't the man she thought he was. She'd taken a chance on love and in the end it would have been better if she'd simply kept running from the emotion, because it seemed it wasn't for her.

"We've got a lot to do," he said at last.

"Of course," she replied, swallowing hard. "I've called a handyman to come and make the house hurricane-ready. He's waiting until the final warnings are issued. Also, he might be interested in applying to be the caretaker here."

Allan nodded.

Jessi turned and walked out the door, hoping he'd call her back and pretending she wasn't disappointed when he didn't.

Allan almost wished he was a different type of man. The kind of guy who'd run after Jessi and bring her back. But he wasn't. And he knew he couldn't be. He'd seen his father devote himself solely to one person's happiness, and in the end that devotion had killed him. His dad hadn't been able to live without his mom.

He knew that women often thought that was romantic or sweet, but he'd seen the other side of it. How his father wouldn't leave the house for days while his mom was on business trips. His dad had a career of his own, but had been crippled by loneliness when his mother had traveled out of town. And then there was the almost manic way he'd act when she was back. He'd never let her leave his sight. That kind of dependence on someone was something Allan vowed to never experience.

He had promised himself a long time ago that he'd never let any woman have that control over him. And if he was being completely honest with himself he'd have to admit that Jessi was already starting to make him feel a little like that. He refused to let it go further.

If he hurt her feelings now, he was sorry, but he knew that in the end no woman could live with that kind of obsessive love. He wasn't guessing or speculating; his mother had told him that when she'd left their family home to go back to her own father. It was just an odd twist of fate that she'd died in a car crash on her way there.

Allan rubbed the back of his neck. Damn, he never thought about those two—his parents, who had been so doomed in love. He had plenty of other things to occupy his mind. The hurricane brewing out in the Atlantic. Finding a caretaker for this place. Raising baby Hannah. And what to do about Jessi.

There was no way that he could force her from his thoughts. And part of him feared that he might be just like his dad, because the past few days had proved how much he really enjoyed being in her company. Every morning he got out of bed a little more easily than he ever had before, and actually looked forward to sitting in the quiet kitchen with her across the table from him.

There was something about her that called to him, and no matter what he said or how he acted toward her, he couldn't change that. So that made priority number one getting off Hatteras Island and keeping Jessi from satisfying the objectives in her probation. He wanted her to fail—needed her to.

Somehow the thought of seeing her every day at work and in his personal life was too…tempting. And he didn't like it. He'd always known that he wasn't good at personal relationships but he hadn't understood until this moment the real reason.

He didn't like the vulnerability that came with letting someone past his guard. Not just anyone—Jessi. She made him feel weak and unsure because he needed her and that wasn't acceptable.

But he knew he wouldn't be able to force her hand or to *make* her fail. He just had to hope that she ran out of time. It seemed unlikely, given the type of woman she was.

And that made him realize that he also had to decide if he was going to keep his guardianship of Hannah. Maybe he should let that go, as well…though John wouldn't have liked that.

In fact, if his friend were here right now he'd probably punch Allan in the shoulder and tell him to stop acting like an ass.

He paused in front of the mirror and stared at himself. He looked nothing like his father, but that didn't stop him from following in his footsteps where obsession was concerned. His grandfather, too, had been obsessed—with business. Allan didn't want to be like either of the main male influences in his life.

Was it impossible for him not to be like them? It seemed that obsessive personality trait ran deep. He knew from his own rigid attempts at control that he had somehow mastered it after all these years, until Jessi.

She threatened him. Threatened his sanity and his control and his core belief in himself. And now she wanted him to... What exactly did she want? He both admired and envied that she was able to be transparent and come to him and ask how he felt.

He knew that took more courage than he had. Because even though she'd sort of said what she was feeling toward him, he still couldn't bring himself to let her know what she meant to him.

He didn't care if that made him a coward—sure, he'd have kicked anyone's ass who said he was one, but he couldn't deny it to himself. It didn't change anything. He wouldn't let it.

But the words felt hollow and empty as he went downstairs and saw Jessi in the backyard, talking to the handyman and then working beside him to gather up loose articles in the yard.

She wore a pair of ridiculously high heels, skintight jeans and a white tank top paired with a black leather vest. She was back to her rocker chick clothing. He took a deep breath, acknowledging to himself that he was glad.

This was the Jessi he knew how to handle. He could challenge her and bet with her and probably even take her to his bed. She was the woman who gave as good as she got, and never let him forget it.

But another part of him was sad. He realized he'd missed a chance with Jessi. A chance to really know her and maybe find some sort of happiness.

Who was he kidding? He'd never really be happy. Not with Jessi Chandler. Not just because of the Chandler connection, but also because she did challenge him and dare him, and she'd never have settled for only half of what he was. She'd never have accepted the small bit of himself he'd have felt comfortable giving her, and a part of him was glad.

Because the way he felt about her, he wanted her to have it all. All the happiness and love that she deserved. And he knew he wasn't the man to give it to her.

With the hurricane warning slowly turning into a real threat, James had suggested they go ahead and do a few preventive things, such as get anything loose in the yard stored. And since it was either work with her hands or choke Allan, Jessi decided to dig in and help. She had the baby monitor speaker attached to her hip as she worked, putting away hoses and chairs and piling up loose tree limbs.

She could see as she puttered about the yard why her friend had enjoyed this pace after years of working eighteen-hour days and striving so hard to make her business a success. Jessi was glad that Patti had decided to sell her interior design company and come down here to the Outer Banks. The past two years were probably some of the happiest of her friend's life.

"Want some help?" Allan asked, coming up behind her.
"No."

"Jessi—"

"I'm mad at you. I'm not going to pretend we're okay or anything like that. You might want to go and talk to James and see if he needs your help," she said. There was one thing about being so honest, and that was that she felt freer than she had in a long time. She sort of liked it.

"No."

"What do you mean, no?"

"Just what I said. You changed the rules on me in one second and expected me to keep up with whatever was going on inside of you. That's not fair. Just this morning in the kitchen you walked away instead of staying," he reminded her. "I'm trying to catch up, Jessi. But I'm a guy. And these are emotions, and I'm not even going to pretend that I will ever be comfortable with them. Yes, I have them. No, I never want to talk about them."

She stopped what she was doing and looked up at him. He had his sunglasses on so it was hard to tell if he was sincere. But his words made a lot of sense to her. She had made a radical change of heart and she'd wanted him to immediately catch up to her. In fact, she wondered if she'd been a little bit cowardly by trying to force him to. His reaction had given her the freedom to feel superior and also the safety to back away again.

"I just have no idea what to do with you."

"Me, either," he admitted. "I guess for once we're both in the same place."

"We're always in the same place when we are warring, and I liked that for a long time," she admitted. "But now I want something else. And it scares me because you're still you."

"Yes, I am. But I'll let you in on a little secret…. You

scare me, too. I have no idea how I came to be in this position," Allan said. "I don't like it. I'm going to do everything I can to figure out how to get us back to where I feel comfortable. And it's not because I don't care."

She took his hand and led him from the yard up to the back porch, where they were hidden from the view of the handyman. "I want to know two things…first, where do you feel most comfortable with me, and second, how much do you care?"

"Right here," he said, pulling her into his arms and bringing his mouth down on hers.

It had been too long since they'd kissed and since she'd really held him in her arms. That one-sided hug upstairs hadn't done anything for her. But in his embrace she thought she heard all the things that he couldn't or wouldn't say out loud to her. And it was enough.

She saw this as a first step to something new and exciting. Something worth the scary knot that she felt in her stomach when she looked into the future and thought she saw Allan by her side. It wasn't anything concrete, but she felt as if it was the start of something.

"Uh…excuse me," James said in a gruff voice. "I don't mean to interrupt."

Allan slowly let his arms fall from her, and turned to face the other man. He was about six feet tall, and weathered from a life spent outdoors. His face had sun and laugh lines on it and he wore his faded jeans and work shirt well, as if he was very comfortable with the man he was.

"Yes?" Allan asked.

"There's been a weather update and the storm is confirmed to be heading straight for us. Landfall is in less than four hours. I'm going to go and get the storm shutters to cover the windows. You two should make plans to head off island."

"I'm not sure we can," Allan said. "Until we hear from our attorney."

"I'll get Hannah ready," Jessi said. "And then call Reggie. I also read some stuff on hurricane preparedness, and I've bought water and some nonperishables at the grocery store. Is there anything else I should do, James?"

"Fill the bathtubs with water in case something happens to contaminate the local supply. Also gather a radio, flashlights, candles and that sort of stuff all in one room. I'd pick one without windows."

"Okay," Allan said. "Do you need my help?"

"Yes," James said. "We have to secure everything in the yard and get the windows covered."

Allan squeezed Jessi's hand before he walked away, and she watched him go with a smile in her heart. It didn't matter that a big hurricane—Hurricane Pandora, it was now officially called—was heading straight toward them. Sure, she was scared, but having Allan there to help her reassured her a little because he wasn't the type of person to just sit passively by. She knew there was still so much that had to be settled and figured out between them. But for the first time in her life she had someone by her side.

A man she could count on. It was something that she'd never guessed she'd find. That the man was Allan McKinney was even more surprising, but there it was.

She gathered all the supplies that James had listed, as well as enough diapers for a week, and put them in the small study at the back of the house. The room had bookcases on all the walls and no windows.

She piled up pillows and blankets and a spare bassinet she'd found in Patti's closet for Hannah to sleep in. Then she called the attorney.

"Reggie Blythe's office, this is Reggie," he said.

"It's Jessi Chandler. I was hoping to find out if you'd had an update from the judge," she replied. "We've been told we're going to have to leave the island."

"As I mentioned to Allan, you can't leave with Hannah. It's not allowed until we get the paperwork. The farthest you could go would be to a hotel farther inland—is that what you both want? You can leave her with her foster family, or if you want, stay with her, I'll bring over the notice from the judge so that the police don't try to clear you off. I'm afraid all the judicial offices are sort of shut down while everyone prepares for this storm."

"Should we be scared? Should we go inland?" Jessi asked. "I don't know what to expect."

"I'd stay here. That bed-and-breakfast has weathered many late-season hurricanes. You'll be fine as long as you follow instructions and do what you're told. Do you have enough water and food for a few days?"

"I think so." She thought of the stocked cupboard and cases of water and soda she'd purchased. How much food would they need?

"I'll stop by to check on you," Reggie said.

"That would be nice, but only if you have time. We sort of have a handyman helping us out."

"Very well. I'll call as soon as I hear something from the judge."

Jessi busied herself getting ready for the hurricane

and tried to ignore the storm inside her as she adjusted to everything that was happening. Not the least of which were her feelings for Allan, and that they were all each other had in the coming storm.

She was scared by that, because if she took this gamble with her heart and it didn't pay off, she had the feeling she'd never again take a chance on loving a man.

Twelve

Allan sent Fawkes off island as Hurricane Pandora came toward them. The bed-and-breakfast was secured and they'd done everything possible to get prepared. Now all they could do was wait.

Reggie had finally gotten the judge to sign the papers that gave guardianship to both Jessi and Allan, but it had been too late to leave Hatteras when that happened. The rains had already started falling heavily and the road leading off the island was washed out.

Now they were sitting tensely in the study with a transistor radio on, because the electricity had gone out. They had flashlights and water. For a long time Allan pretended to be reading on his iPad, but the sound of the wind whipping through the yard and the harrowing noise of tree branches scraping against the house distracted him.

Jessi sat on the floor next to a sleeping Hannah.

"I don't like this," she said at last. "It sounds creepy outside and it's so dark and gloomy in here. Distract me, Allan."

"How am I supposed to do that?"

"I don't know. Tell me something about you that no one else knows."

"Okay, and then you'll tell me something?" he asked.

"Sure. Anything is better than listening to the storm," she said.

He got off the couch and came and sat on the floor next to her. "What do you want to know?"

"Tell me about your first kiss," she said. "Ballsy guy like you, it was probably remarkable."

He shook his head. "It was awkward. One of those moments in middle school when I thought I knew everything. It was at Amy Collins's thirteenth birthday party. It was a boy-girl party—a big deal. Her parents were trying to be cool, so they left us all alone in the converted third-floor game room. Jose kept watch at the door while we played spin the bottle, and I got to kiss the birthday girl.

"We went behind a bookcase that held DVDs and stared at each other. Finally, I leaned in and kissed her. Sort of missed her mouth and ended up kissing her cheek and then her mouth. It was over really quickly and both of us looked at each other, wondering if that was it."

Jessi smiled. "My first kiss was sort of like that, too. At a birthday party. Tons of other kids around. Patti liked this boy in our class, but he wasn't about to make a move, so I organized a game of truth or dare, intending to help Patti get her kiss. But instead I got dared to kiss Bobby and I did it. It wasn't bad. A bit like yours, where we sort of smashed mouths and then backed away. Isn't it funny, that age? I felt so ready to be a grown-up, but after that kiss I knew I'd end up waiting before I tried it again. It was scary, letting a boy that close to me."

"I bet. Boys have cooties at that age," Allan said. He had felt energized by the closeness with Amy that day and had become determined to get another kiss, which he had. But as he looked over at Jessi and the sleeping Hannah, he felt differently. "I definitely am not going to be the 'cool' dad where Hannah is concerned. I know how boys are and will keep my eye on anyone that gets too close to her."

Jessi laughed. "Good. You protect her and I'll teach her how to protect herself, in case one slips by us."

"Deal," Allan said.

"Did we just agree on something?" she asked with a smirk.

"No, you're mistaken.... I was about to ask about your tattoo. When did you get it and why?" He liked the intimacy created by the storm raging outside and the quiet ambient light inside. For this moment they were the only two people in the world, and that suited him.

"I got it when I turned eighteen. My parents wouldn't allow me to have one, but on my second day at the University of Texas in Austin I went and had it done anyway. I wanted something to commemorate the fact that I was on my own, free and flying toward the future."

"Why did you get it here?" he asked, touching her collarbone. He liked touching her and used the tattoo as an excuse to do it now.

"I wanted to see it every time I looked in the mirror so I'd remember the promises I made to myself."

"What promises?" he asked.

"That's another question," she said. "And it's my turn to ask."

"I'll tell you whatever you want to know," he said. "Just tell me what promise you made to yourself."

She stared at him for long moments and then shifted up on her knees and leaned forward so that barely an inch separated them. "I promised myself I'd never again let someone make me be something I'm not."

"You certainly have lived up to that," he said.

"It hasn't always been easy. You make it hard for me," she said quietly.

"Good, because you're always keeping me off my guard," he said. "Every time I think I've figured out how to deal with you something changes."

"Ha."

"Ha?"

"That's just a nice way of saying you can't manipulate me," she said.

"Perhaps. But I've discovered I'm not a big fan of manipulating you," he said. It hadn't taken him long to figure out that he wanted the real responses from Jessi instead of the bad-girl attitude she gave everyone else. "What's your question for me?"

She glanced over at Hannah and then moved a little bit closer to him. "Will you answer me truthfully?"

"Yes," he said.

"Then my question is this, Allan McKinney. How long are you going to keep pretending that everything in your world hasn't been changed by the past two weeks?" she asked.

It was a gutsy question and left no doubt as to what she really needed from him. He put his hands on her hips and drew her closer.

But she stopped him with a hand on his chest. "No funny business. I want your answer."

But funny business was the only answer he had. He wasn't going to confess his feelings, which he'd thought he'd made plain to her earlier in the day. Instead, he tangled his fingers in the back of her hair and drew her forward, kissing her with all the emotion that was pent up inside of him.

He cared for this complicated woman who had the ability to make him feel things—things he didn't want to feel. And he wasn't about to let her have the upper hand now.

Something hit the side of the house hard and they pulled back from each other, startled by the sound.

"What was that?" she asked, moving to pick up Hannah.

"I'll go and check," he said. It was impossible to really see through the windows, which had been boarded up, but he knew there was a tiny window near the front door that they had only taped. The handyman had told him the tape would keep the window in one piece, preventing it from shattering if it blew out of the frame.

When Allan got to the front hallway and looked through the window, he saw that a large tree limb had fallen on the front porch. He took a step back as the wind continued whipping branches and other debris down the street

"Are we going to be okay?" Jessi asked from down the hallway, where she held Hannah in her arms.

"Yes," he said. Suddenly, his determination not to show how much she meant to him seemed stupid. Their best friends' death had proved how short life could be, and the storm raging outside seemed a reminder to him to grab on to what was important to him while he still could.

He walked to her and wrapped an arm around her shoulders, leading her into the living room, where he pushed a love seat into the corner, away from the windows, and then gestured for Jessi to sit down. She did, and he settled next to her, wrapping his arm around her and pulling her and Hannah back against his chest.

"I'm not going to let anything hurt you or the baby. I'm going to protect you both," he said. And he repeated that vow inside himself, knowing it was one he'd never break.

"I'm scared," Jessi said. "This storm isn't something I know how to deal with. Plus it lasts so long, not like earthquakes."

"Spoken like a true Californian," he said. "I feel the same way. Give me an earthquake over this any day."

The storm seemed to be getting more intense, and he held her closer, wrapping his arms around both her and Hannah, until he heard Jessi mumbling something under her breath.

"What's that you said?" he asked.

"I'm praying," she said, tipping her head back to make eye contact. "Usually I'm not spiritual at all, but if anything makes me believe in a higher power it's this kind of storm."

"It makes me reprioritize my life, too. Family hasn't really mattered—"

"Yeah, right. You do everything with your cousins," she said.

"That's true, but our bond feels more like one brothers have. We've always been united with a common goal, and no matter what you think, our 'family' has had some problems over the years," Allan said. He'd never wanted to be tied to his cousins other than through the business. But they were friends and they'd shared the bitterness of their grandfather's goals for so long they couldn't be anything else. "What I was trying to say is that I always liked my money and my expensive adult toys, but being here with you and Hannah has made me realize that I can enjoy the quiet things, as well."

"Facing death makes you more accepting of certain things," Jessi murmured.

"Indeed," Allan said.

Jessi went back to her quiet prayers, and he held her and Hannah in his arms, watching over these two females who'd become so important to him in such a short time. He didn't know if these feelings would last beyond the storm or even beyond the time here in North Carolina. But he did know that they were very real and he liked them. He didn't have to talk about it to anyone, and as the storm raged outside, his feelings finally settled down inside.

He didn't need to know anything else at this moment.

"You're quiet," Jessi said.

"Just thinking," he said.

"About?"

"Stuff," he said.

"Stuff…what's that mean? Something weighty or something naughty? I can tell it's a subject you don't want to talk about," she said.

"Then why are you asking me about it?"

"Because I'm nosy and I like needling you."

"You certainly do a very good job of it," he said.

"Thanks."

He squeezed her and dropped a quick kiss on her neck, biting the spot just next to her tattoo. "Keep it up and I might have to give you what you're asking for."

"And that would be?" she asked in that cheeky tone of hers.

"Something naughty," he said.

"I like you when you're naughty," she responded.

"I like you that way, too," he said.

He leaned in close and whispered exactly what it was he would do to her, in detail. He could tell she was interested by the way she settled back against him. He kept talking, seducing her with his words.

He felt a little sad as he realized he'd never met another woman who suited his many sides and his many moods. Jessi's sexual drive was as fierce as his. Her loyalty to her sisters and her company was as laudable as his was. Her closely guarded emotions were hard to ascertain and made her as vulnerable as his did. And he didn't mind right now. At the moment that seemed exactly as it should be.

The worst of the winds seemed to pass a little after midnight, and they decided to sleep in the study with Hannah. The radio was still on and every once in a while they heard something else fly around in the yard. Jessi was feeling so much at this moment that she feared she was going to implode. She was worried and scared, and it seemed her awakening a day ago was timely, because this storm just reinforced that she wanted to live her life and stop being scared of things.

She needed to be more honest with the people who mattered to her, and she vowed once the storm was over she would do just that.

Allan made a quick trip through the house to check on the storm as she got Hannah into bed.

"Jess, come here," he called to her.

She walked down the hall to where he stood at the entrance, where that small window gave them a glimpse of the street and the world in the eye of the storm. He wrapped his arm around her and pointed outside.

"This reminds me that no matter how much research I do there are always going to be situations where I'm not in control," he said.

"It makes me feel small," she said. "And as you saw earlier, makes me believe in God."

"Did you make a bargain with Him?" Allan asked.

She turned in his arms. The faded scent of his aftershave, a fragrance she associated only with him, assailed her senses. "I did."

"I did, too," he said, surprising her.

"What'd you ask for?"

"I told God that if he got us through this then I'd stop…running from life, and give happiness a real shot."

Jessi narrowed her eyes as she watched him. "I don't believe that. Sounds a little too pat."

"Now you're judging what I asked for?" he demanded.

"It's like saying you wanted money when you already have enough," she said. "You haven't run from anything in your life. You stay in place and manipulate everything around you."

He tipped his head to the side and studied her. "You're right, but inside I run away and lock myself in a place where I don't have to engage. You said pretty much that very thing to me earlier."

"Fair enough. I shouldn't have judged. You just always seem so strong and so brave it's hard to think of you as someone who would run from trouble," she said.

"You seem to be the exact same way," he commented.

"You couldn't be further from the truth," she said. "And I promised God that if he kept us all safe I'd be better."

"Better?"

"Yes," she said, "Nicer to my sisters and to you and your cousins. I'd stop being afraid for Hannah and embrace loving her, even though I know that I can't always keep her safe."

Allan didn't say anything, just pulled her close and hugged her so tightly she couldn't breathe. She hugged him back with the same strength. Then she tipped her head up so she could see his face, and the expression on it made her breath catch in her throat.

He'd said earlier that he couldn't express his emotions, but right now there was something stark and raw in his eyes that she couldn't describe as anything other than love. And it awakened that same well of feeling inside her.

"Allan—"

He kissed her, his mouth moving over hers with purpose and she knew that he couldn't talk about whatever was in his heart. But for her it was enough that she'd seen in his eyes the emotions she'd been afraid to admit she wanted from him.

His hands moved over her body, not in a calculated seduction, but in a frenzied burst of passion, and it awakened the exact same frenetic desire in her. She quickly freed his sex from his pants, and he fumbled with her zipper. For the first time since they'd become intimate partners he wasn't smoothly seductive, and that rawness turned her on like nothing else could.

He lifted her and her pants fell to the floor and she shimmied out of her panties before he lifted her again. "Wrap your legs around me."

She did as he asked and felt the world spin as he turned them so her back was against the wall. His mouth captured hers, his tongue plunging deep as he thrust heavily into her. She clenched down hard on him, holding tight to his shoulders with her arms, and his waist with her legs.

He pulled his mouth from hers and kissed his way down the column of her neck, stopping at her tattoo—a spot that she was slowly coming to understand he loved. He laved it with his tongue and then leaned down to kiss and suck there.

Thought left her and instinct took over. With each thrust of his body he drove her closer to her orgasm and made his way deeper into her soul.

There was nothing of the Allan she'd come to expect in this fast coupling. When he lifted his head from her neck, she stared into his silver eyes and watched his pupils dilate as the first wave of her own climax washed over her.

Her orgasm seemed to trigger his and he started thrusting even harder, driving them both to the brink and then over it again as he spilled his seed inside her. It was warm and filled her with his essence.

She didn't even mind that they'd forgotten to use protection. It would have been an intrusion in this moment when their souls had united and their hearts had taken small steps toward each other.

It was not a moment she could regret, because for the first time in her life she felt as if she'd found a man she could depend on. And she was so glad it was Allan McKinney.

Thirteen

The next afternoon, once the winds had subsided, Jessi was glad to get out of the house and away from Allan for a few moments. Neither of them had spoken about what had happened in the hallway or afterward, when he'd carried her back into the living room and they'd fallen asleep in each other's arms, watching over Hannah.

Now that the storm had passed, she knew that everything was going to change. They were cleared to leave Hatteras, and Fawkes was on his way back to the island to help them make arrangements to return to L.A.

She stared outside at the sand that had been pushed up onto the street and into the front yard and the water that hadn't subsided with the tide. It was hard to imagine this place ever getting back to normal.

Downed branches and debris were strewn everywhere she looked. She remembered that howling wind and driving rain and wanted to keep Hannah as far away from this area as she could.

The hurricane had been big and scary. The only thing that had made it tolerable had been Allan, and Jessi was afraid that she was really relying too much on him. He was the man who didn't believe in love. He was the son of her family's sworn rivals. And he was truly the only one that she wanted.

Jessi was surprised when her phone started ringing. The cell towers must already be working again.

"Jess—thank God. Are you okay?" Cari asked when Jessi answered the call. "I've been dialing your number every half hour trying to get you."

She could imagine her younger sister carefully watching the clock and making sure she didn't miss a chance to call. "I'm okay. Allan is assessing the damage, but I think we made it through without too much."

"What was it like?" Cari asked.

"Intense. Loud and scary," Jessi said. "I wouldn't want to go through one again. We can't even drive on the main road. We have to walk everywhere."

"You won't have to once you come home. You're staying here, right?" her sister asked.

"Of course. Why wouldn't I?"

"I didn't know if you'd decided you'd had enough with the gaming world and wanted a change."

"No. My life is there. And I am working toward my objectives to satisfy my probation. I'm pretty sure I'll be joining you on the safe list soon," Jessi said. There was no way that securing a big money deal with a Hollywood producer wouldn't save her, and she had managed to reschedule the meeting with Jack White before the full force of the hurricane hit.

"Emma said you're on the cut list. Something about missing a deadline yesterday," Cari told her.

"What are you talking about? There was a hurricane and all the communications were down on the island. Hell, the entire southern Atlantic Seaboard was cut off," Jessi said.

"I know. Believe me, I think it's ridiculous and I've already raised my objection. If Kell doesn't back down I'm going to take it to the board."

"Fat lot of good that will do you," Jessi said. "I'm sure…I'll figure it out. Rest assured, I'm going to be back home to stay."

"Good. I miss you. And I really want to get to know little Hannah. She is so cute," Cari said. "Are you adjusting to being a mommy?"

"No," Jessi said bluntly. "I love her and I am doing stuff for her like I should, but it doesn't feel natural to me. I still hesitate before I do everything. I'm afraid I'll screw up."

"That's just part of being a parent," Cari said. "We all get overwhelmed sometimes.

"Emma doesn't feel like that," Jessi said.

"Emma's not human. She's a perfect oldest child who exists solely to make us feel inadequate," Cari said with a laugh.

"It seems that way sometimes," Jessi agreed, glancing at herself in the mirror. She had on a pair of artfully faded designer jeans with rips in the knees, and a silk blouse that she'd tied at her left hip. She'd put the combat boots on because walking in debris was going to be tricky.

As she glanced at her own reflection she admitted to herself she hardly looked like a mom. But inside she felt fiercely protective of Hannah, and she knew that moms came in all kinds of packages.

"Thanks for calling, Cari," she said.

"I love you, Jessi. I miss you and I was very worried about you."

"We were safe from the hurricane. I think this house has been standing for a long time, and John made sure to keep it up-to-date regarding hurricane codes."

"That's not why I was worried. You haven't been yourself lately. You've been a lot...harder than normal."

Harder. She knew what her sister meant and it just reinforced what she'd discovered recently: that no matter how well she thought she was doing at making the world think she was doing okay, she wasn't fooling anyone. "Life's been tough lately."

"Yes, it has," Cari agreed. "Doesn't seem fair that Grandfather sowed all this bad karma and we're the ones who are reaping it."

"No, it doesn't," Jessi said. "But no one ever said life was fair."

"It should be," Cari insisted. "We will do our best to make sure it is. I'm going to camp out in Kell's office until he agrees to take your name off the cut list."

"Thanks, little sis, but that's not for you to do. I already have a meeting scheduled that will change his mind. It's funny to me that a big-shot Hollywood producer understood that I had to reschedule due to Mother Nature, but the CEO of a gaming company couldn't," Jessi said.

"Kell hates us more than a normal person should," Cari said. "He's not all bad, though. He is nice to D.J."

"He's probably secretly brainwashing him to hate us," Jessi said.

"Jess—that's not true. I've got to go. I have a meeting in a few minutes. Love you."

"Love you, too," Jessi said, disconnecting the call.

She couldn't believe that Kell was being so stubborn about that timeline he'd developed. Did he really hate her so much? She'd hardly met the man. Was he that bitter just because of her last name?

She wasn't too worried, though. She'd win Jack White over, and surely after all they'd been through together Allan would be on her side. He had some sway over his cousin. She knew that and expected him to use it to help her.

And the two of them had a new bond. One that was stronger than ever. She felt confident that the man she'd spent the past tense night with was on her side. She knew she'd seen love in his eyes, and there was no way that someone who was in love would let his partner be hurt.

Partner… That almost sounded scarier than being in love. Was Allan her partner now? Did they have a true bond that would make them both stronger? Or was she kidding herself again? All her doubts made her feel small and insecure, and she wasn't going to give in to them. She couldn't.

She had to believe in Allan and in herself.

Allan had never seen this many downed limbs or this much standing water. It was the first time he'd seen damage like this. He'd grown up with mudslides and fires, but this was different. And the storm last night had been so loud…so intense. They were lucky the bed-and-breakfast was still standing.

He continued walking around the yard and searching for damage. He felt glad that now that the storm was over, he could get out of North Carolina. Frankly, he was ready to get away from Jessi.

Last night had been intense. He'd never been more alive, never felt every sense come awake like that. But this morning, with the sun shining down from the clear blue sky, he felt too exposed. Too vulnerable to the one person in the world he needed to be the strongest around.

He looked down at Hannah as she kicked her arms and legs in the carrier he was using to keep her with him as he surveyed the land. She seemed in good spirits this morning, and he had to admit the baby was a joy.

But at the same time he was always a little scared to let himself care for her. If things got sour between Jessi and him, one of them was going to have to give up their rights to the baby. Him, he thought. It was the perfect out. An easy way to hide from the emotions he felt toward both of them. He wasn't sure he could handle being that vulnerable. Both of them made him weak.

And though the judge had granted guardianship to both of them, in the back of his mind Allan was braced for the moment when he might lose Hannah. Lose them both.

If his life had followed one pattern, it was that no one he cared about stayed around forever. His mom had left; his dad had followed by taking his own life. His grandfather had been distant; Allan had never been close to the bitter old man. He was close to his cousins, but they all lived their own lives and went their own way.

Better that he make the break now before he let them both any deeper into his life and his heart.

And then there was John. John was probably the final blow, in that he was the one person who'd known Allan best. The one person he'd trusted to have his back. And now he was gone.

Why then would this little girl be any different? Or for that matter, Jessi? They'd both tried to make the situation between them into one that they could live with, but they both knew they were too different.

Last night, with a storm raging outside and that feeling that the world was just the three of them, it had made sense to let his guard down and make love to Jessi. Really make love. They'd had sex prior to that, but last night he'd felt as if he could almost let the full force of his emotions free. And now today…that seemed stupid.

It seemed like the move of a man who didn't know how to control himself or his own future. And that was a mistake. He just wished he had a solid plan for fixing the situation.

He was going to have to handle things carefully or he'd leave himself open to a lot of hurt and pain from Jessi. And a part of him almost believed he might deserve that. A part of him last night had been swept away by things…dreams that he knew he'd never really attain. They weren't things he really wanted, no matter how much he thought he might have in that moment.

"Looks like the bed-and-breakfast weathered the storm pretty well," James said, coming up to him. The handyman had called earlier to say he'd come by and help take down the storm shutters.

"It did. This building is certainly sturdy," Allan said.

"Yes, it is. John did a lot of work on it before Patti came down here. That man just wanted to keep her safe," James said.

"There are no guarantees in life," Allan stated.

"That's true enough. I've been meaning to talk to you about something that Jessi mentioned," James said.

"Yes?"

"You still looking for a caretaker to keep the inn open?"

"Yes, we are. I've asked Reggie Blythe, the McCoys' attorney, to help in the search," Allan said.

"Well, I talked to the wife and we'd like a chance at the job," James said.

Allan liked the idea of James and his wife taking over the inn until Hannah was old enough to decide what she wanted to do with it. "I'll tell Reggie, and then we can get him to draw up a contract and all that."

"Sounds good," the handyman said.

"Allan?" Jessi called from the front porch. She sounded troubled. "Can I talk to you?"

"Go on then," James told him. "I can get the storm shutters down by myself and store them."

"Thanks," Allan said.

"No problem," he replied.

Allan walked toward the house and noticed that Hannah waved her arms as they got closer. He wondered if she recognized Jessi. The book had said that she should start doing so at this age.

"What's up?"

"Um…your cousin still has me on the cut list, supposedly because I missed a deadline yesterday."

"I haven't had a chance to talk to him," Allan said. "The lines have been down all morning. Do you have a signal on your cell?"

"Yes. Cari called me," Jessi said. "So you don't know anything about this?"

"No, I don't," Allan said. He was angry on her behalf, until he realized that if he played this on Kell's side Jessi would back away from him. He'd be left alone, but it might be better given the fact that he couldn't see a way for them to really move forward from this, except as coguardians of the child and nothing more.

He wasn't prepared to let Jessi be his heart and soul every day for the rest of his life. He wasn't sure he could exist, feeling that insecure and vulnerable. As James had just said, no matter how much a man tried to protect the ones he loved, somehow when fate wanted them, they'd always be taken.

"Let's go inside and discuss this," Allan said. He walked past her, taking Hannah from the carrier he wore and transferring her to his arms. For a moment Jessi just watched him and tried to keep herself from feeling so in love with him. He was all the things she'd hoped to find in a man, but had never wanted to admit she'd been searching for.

He handed Hannah to her while he took off the carrier, and then went into the kitchen to wash his hands and pour himself some sweet tea.

She followed him and watched, waiting for him to call Kell. But it soon became apparent he wasn't going to.

"Aren't you going to call your cousin and chew his ass out for not taking me off the cut list?" Jessi said when he went to pour himself a second glass of sweet tea.

"No. Listen, Jessi, I understand your point, but Kell has one, as well. In business there are deadlines and they have to be met. That's how successful companies stay successful."

"I'm not saying I shouldn't have to meet the objectives laid out for me, but when there's a hurricane I think even Kell Montrose will have to admit it's impossible to do business."

"Yeah, but Kell won't."

"What about you, Allan? Will you?"

"Will I what?"

"Back me up. Support me. That's what I really need from you in this," Jessi said. She went to the fridge as Hannah started to get a little fussy and took out a bottle she'd prepared earlier. After heating it up, she gave it to the baby and stared at Allan, waiting to hear what he had to say.

But Allan was simply standing there, watching her.

"You're a good mother," he said.

"Thank you, Allan. I really did need to hear that," she said. "I'm learning, but I'm nowhere near where I need to be, and I don't want to talk about mothering right now. I'm still trying to figure out if you're in my corner or not. I thought we had each other's backs last night in the storm...."

Allan scrubbed his hand over his face and turned his back to her, putting his palms on the countertop in front of him and lowering his head. She wasn't asking much from him, so couldn't really understand his reaction.

"I just want to know you're on my side," she said again, and then realized that his continued silence was his answer. "You're not, are you?"

"I am just saying that, legally, Kell's not in the wrong here."

"We're not talking about Kell. We're talking about you and me. And if you feel what I do, then the answer is simple. You should want what's best for me. Even though you are being a complete ass right now I still care for you, Allan. I'd still defend you."

"That's good to know. I've never had you in my corner," he said.

She literally started shaking as his words sank in. Anger swept over her and she was livid. "I can't believe you're going to be flip about this. The last few weeks have been intense. They've changed my life and made me see things in a completely new way.

"I thought last night when we talked we shared something deep and meaningful, and yet right now you're acting like nothing has changed at all between us," she said.

She had to put Hannah in her baby chair with her bottle, because she didn't feel steady as her emotions got the better of her.

He turned back around to face her, but quickly averted his eyes. "Calm down," he said.

"Don't say that to me," she retorted. "I am calm. I just need answers from you."

"Well, I don't know what to say. Our time together has been intense, but it's not real. We both know that our lives are in California, and no matter what I might say to the contrary we are too different from each other to have a relationship. These days have been great and I'll treasure them always, but this has no meaning in our real lives. No matter how much I want to pretend otherwise."

"Pretend?" she repeated. She let his words sink in for a moment and then shook her head. "Last night I thought I saw the real man. The man behind the big gestures and the witty banter. Last night I had a glimpse of a man who was strong not by waving around his money or whisking people to places they've never visited, but with the quiet strength to know that all he needed was the right people by his side."

"There is an element of truth to that," he admitted. "I do lo—care for you. It's just that we've been living under a very intense set of circumstances. This isn't real. I can't pretend it is and neither can you."

"We weren't pretending last night. Or at least I wasn't," she said.

"Last night we thought we'd die in the house. Today…"

"Today you are showing yourself to be the man I guess you are, Allan. You're a coward. I never thought you'd be so shady. No matter how much we butted heads I always had a sort of grudging respect for you. The way you cared about John and your cousins, I thought you were a man with a heart. A man who would be worthy of not only my admiration, but also my love. Yet I see now that you're nothing but a hollow shell of a man."

"Is that all?" he asked, crossing his arms over his chest.

"Yes, it is," she said. "I'm taking Hannah back home as soon as I can get off the island. We'll work out a visitation schedule through our lawyers."

Still she hesitated, waiting to see if he'd stop her from leaving, and maybe ask her to stay. But he didn't. Instead, he just nodded at her.

"That makes sense. I'm going to stay here and settle things with the insurance company. Luckily, there wasn't as much storm damage as there could have been. I'll contact you when I'm back in California. Unless you have any objections, I've decided to hire James as the caretaker for the bed-and-breakfast."

She shook her head. "You really are all about yourself, aren't you? I thought I got a glimpse of a man who wasn't so shallow, but it seems I was wrong."

Picking up Hannah, she left the kitchen and her broken heart behind. She'd known from the moment they'd met that he wasn't all he pretended to be. But a part of her had hoped she was wrong, and she was really upset at herself for believing in the illusion of Allan McKinney.

Fourteen

Jessi didn't have any time to sleep after she got back to California. Her sisters met her at LAX and they went straight to her house. As they sat on the patio catching up, Jessi started to have a new vision of herself rising out of the ashes of her humiliating confession to Allan.

"Can one of you watch Hannah for me this afternoon?" she asked.

"Of course," Cari said. "Why?"

"I've got that meeting with Jack White, and even though the Montrose cousins are busy acting like I've shirked my responsibilities, I'm going to go through with it and deliver what I said I would."

"I'll go with you," Emma said.

"Why?"

"Because you'll need someone to make sure the financials make sense. Kell will crucify you if they aren't solid. It's your deal. I'll just be there to verify things," her big sister said.

"Thanks," Jessi replied, going back to staring out at the Pacific. It was a beautifully sunny day here, and on the outside, it seemed as if nothing had changed. But inside she was aching. Aching for Allan, which made her angrier than she'd expected. She had to admit that it was anger and hurt that were really driving her right now. She wanted to do what she could to prove to herself to the Montrose heirs, but most especially to Allan, who'd been too much of a coward—

Stop it, she reminded herself. She wasn't going to let herself go down that path again.

"Tell us more about what happened in North Carolina," Cari said.

"There's not much more to say," Jessi answered. "It was tough dealing with Patti's funeral and checking in on her mom. And then that hurricane…I don't think I ever want to experience anything like that again."

"What about Allan? Did something happen between the two of you?"

"No," she said.

"Liar," Emma declared. "You look like Cari did when she was pretending that Dec was nothing to her or D.J. You can't fool us. What really happened with Allan?"

Jessi looked over at her big sister and suddenly felt as if she were eight again. Back then, she might have been the one to defend Cari, but Emma had always been the one who defended Jessi. "I fell for him, but he didn't feel the same. I screwed up and now I'm just trying to survive."

"Oh, sweetie," Cari said.

Emma got up, came around to where Jessi sat and wrapped her arms around her.

"Love sucks." Jessi sighed.

"Yes, it does," she agreed.

Emma's husband had been killed in a car crash. He'd

been a Formula One driver and had been ripped from Emma's life while she'd been pregnant with their son.

"It's worse for you," Jessi said. "I'm just being a baby."

"It's not worse for either of us. When you fall in love with someone and they aren't in your life anymore, whether they are deceased or not it hurts. And you just have to learn to move on from it," Emma said.

"How, Emmy? How am I supposed to do that? I've never let myself care about a man like this. I've always kept it light."

"It's different for each of us," she murmured. "I kept Helio's obituary on my nightstand and reread it any time I thought I'd just imagined that he was gone."

Jessi hugged her sister back. Emma always seemed so strong that it was shocking to hear how vulnerable she had been.

"What changed for you?" Cari asked. "Why did you let Allan in?"

"I didn't mean to. I guess I could blame it on Hannah, but the truth is, I've been restless for a while. The Playtone takeover made me realize how life was changing and so were my priorities. But honestly, I didn't mean to fall for Allan. He's good-looking and all that, but he can be an ass."

"You would know better than either of us," Cari said. "He's always been pretty nice to me."

Emma glared at Cari.

"I still hate him for what he did to you, Jess."

Jessi had to smile at her sisters rallying around her. And it drove home something that she'd been completely unaware of her entire life. She'd thought she was the rebel and the loner, but she'd overlooked the fact that her sisters always had her back. It didn't matter if they held a differing opinion on things or if they were fighting about something else—when the chips were down they were always by her side.

"Thanks, girls," she said, smiling at both of them. In the corner on a blanket she heard Sam talking quietly to his little cousins. She reflected on how two years ago there had been only the three Chandler sisters, but now there was a future generation. Jessi needed no further proof that life just kept moving on no matter how much you felt like checking out from it.

"You're welcome. But what did we do?" Cari asked with a smile. Her youngest sister had such a good, open heart that Jessi had thought she was weak at times. But the past few weeks had changed that, and now Jessi understood the true strength that came from loving someone. Hannah had shown her that, and even though she hated to admit it, so had Allan.

"You just reminded me that I'm not alone. And that no matter how many times I might have thought I was, you were both always here for me." Jessi stopped herself before she turned truly sappy and way too emotional. But after all those years of thinking she wasn't a good Chandler girl like Emma and Cari, she finally accepted that that was exactly who she was.

"Of course we were," Emma said. "We're sisters and blood is thicker than water."

"And more trustworthy than men," Jessi said.

She saw the doubt in Cari's eyes, but her youngest sister was in the first throes of a new love.

"You're the exception that proves the rule," Emma said to Cari.

"I don't want to be. I want you each to find a man

who loves you as much as Dec loves me, a man who makes you happy."

Jessi wished she could believe there was a man like that out there waiting for her, but she knew there wasn't. She was fickle in her emotions, and as Emma had said, getting over loving someone was hard. Jessi had the feeling she might never truly stop loving Allan, or being mad at him for not loving her back.

Allan looked around the boardroom at his cousins, but didn't join them in their small talk about the NBA scores. He had never felt emptier than he had since Jessi walked out of his life. And it was his own fault. He'd let her go. Hell, he had encouraged her to leave, thinking that if it was a clean break it would be easier. But he'd been wrong.

He'd never in all his days felt such pain as he did when he woke up every morning alone. He'd been avoiding her ever since he got back to L.A. because a few days earlier he needed to find out if he'd been successful in cleansing her from his soul.

God, he was starting to sound pathetic even to himself. He just knew that he missed her. He didn't want to, but there it was. And the fact that he was going to be able to see her today was the only thing that had made him come into the office. He'd been working from home, getting scruffier by the day and turning into a miserable hermit.

Next week he'd have Hannah with him for the first time since his return, and even that hadn't been enough to stir him from his malaise.

"Allan?"

"Hmm?"

"Snap out of it," Kell said. "I don't know what happened to you in North Carolina, but you've been acting strange since you got back, and I need you sharp and on the ball. I think Jessi is up to something. She was vague when she asked for this meeting, but determined that we all be here."

"She was pissed off the last time I saw her. I'm not sure why she wanted us all here," Allan said, and then thought about it long and hard. So much had changed since the hurricane almost a month ago. It felt as if a lifetime had passed them both by, and now he was faced with a new life. One in which Jessi wasn't his enemy, but was his—what? The answer eluded him and he knew today he had to figure it out. "I bet she's done something to prove us wrong, Kell. She's a fighter and we both backed her into a corner. She's coming out swinging."

"You think so?" Dec asked. The other cousin stood by the window looking out at the sunny October day.

"I know so," Allan said. For the first time since she'd walked out of his life he realized he felt a charge of energy coming back through him. He'd missed her more than he wanted to admit, but he also missed sparring with her. There was so much to Jessi that he had needed, and he'd let her go. "I was a fool."

"Probably," Dec said. "Your name is mud at my house."

"Cari hates me?" Allan asked. She was the sweetest of the three sisters, and he hadn't thought she was capable of disliking anyone.

"I don't think she has it in her to hate. But she's very mad at you and said she pities you."

Nice. Jessi's sisters probably knew all about him.

Knew that he'd been afraid to take a chance on loving her.

"What the hell happened down there?" Kell asked.

"We got close," Allan said.

"Close? Did you fall for her?"

"Obviously," Allan said. "But you don't have to worry about that. I backed you and stayed true to my roots as a Montrose heir."

At what cost? he asked himself. He'd known all along that he was just using Kell and the family feud as an excuse to keep her at arm's length, and now he knew he'd acted like a fool. He had wanted Jessi from the first moment they'd met. It was ridiculous to pretend now that he hadn't.

"Thanks for your loyalty," Kell said. "I know I've made things difficult for both of you."

"You have, but we started this journey together," Allan said. "I'm not cut out to share my life with someone. Not even a woman like Jessi."

"I don't know about that. Our fathers weren't exactly solid examples of how to love a woman and be happy," Dec said.

There was a knock at the door. "Can we continue this conversation later?" Kell asked irritably.

"Come in," Allan called out.

The door opened, and Jessi walked in, but Allan hardly recognized her. Her normally spikey hair was tamed into a sedate style and she wore a suit. A gray-and-cream-checked business suit that made it seem to him as if all the light had gone out of his Jessi. She wore proper makeup, too—no outrageous cat eyes or bright purple lipstick. She was subdued.

He'd done this to her, he thought. He'd killed that rebellious light inside of her with his words on Hatteras. By saying that what they'd experienced together was fueled by circumstance instead of real emotion.

Suddenly, all his fears disappeared, as he acknowledged to himself that she was *his* Jessi. And he wasn't a coward as she'd said. He didn't run away from something he wanted; he claimed it, and he intended to claim her. He tried to catch her eye, but she refused to look his way.

But as the meeting went on and she made her presentation about the deal she'd hammered out with Jack White over the past few weeks to make games out of his latest movie trilogy, Allan knew he'd lost her. She was cold and icy in the meeting room. When any of them asked a question she answered it in a calm, quiet voice and ignored him.

Allan was afraid he'd realized his mistake too late. That he'd never be able to win her back. But when she'd concluded her presentation she gave a quick peek over at him. If he'd blinked he'd have missed it, but it was enough to convince him she was still in love with him. She had to be. Jessi wasn't fickle and wouldn't be able to love lightly.

"We'll have to review this, but we'll get back to you shortly," Kell said.

"Of course," Jessi said, standing up and leaving the room without another word.

Allan reached for the folder in front of Kell, started skimming the numbers and saw that it was a solid business case. Jessi had done more than he'd dreamed she would, and he was impressed anew at her talents. She was strong and smart and sexy and a million other things that he couldn't name just then because he felt

such a strong outpouring of love for her. All he could
say was, "This is beyond what we asked of her."

"I know. I think we're going to have to offer her a
role in the newly merged company," Kell said.

"Um...would you mind doing me a favor?" Allan
asked. "I think it could take me months to win her back
without a little help from you guys."

"Just tell us what you need," Dec said.

"Am I going to have any cousins-in-law that aren't
Chandlers?" Kell asked, but there was a faint grin
around his mouth.

"No," Allan said impatiently. "Will you just tell her
that you'll have the decision for her tonight, and ask her
to return at seven?"

"Okay," Dec said, going out to talk to Jessi.

Allan was energized with a plan and knew exactly
what he had to do to win back the only woman he
wanted by his side for the rest of his life.

Jessi wasn't sure what the big deal was on the decision, or why she had to come back to the Playtone offices at seven that night, but since the Montrose heirs
held all the cards, she did as they asked.

She felt battered from seeing Allan today. She'd
thought she'd had control over her emotions. That she'd
finally gotten him out of her heart, but she knew now
that would never happen.

The love she'd hoped was temporary was starting
to feel like the real thing. And keeping a job where she
was going to be forced to see him, well, it was tempting. She hated that inside she was so weak where he
was concerned, but that was the truth of it. She liked

Allan McKinney and she wanted to see him every day even if it was just at work.

Cari was babysitting Hannah for her tonight, and when Jessi parked her BMW convertible in the parking lot she admitted to herself how hard it had been to be in the same room with Allan and not look at him this afternoon. But she was glad she'd resisted all but that one little glance, which had made her breath catch and her heart beat faster.

She wasn't any closer to falling out of love with him than she'd been on the first day she arrived back in California. In fact, if her racing heart had indicated anything this afternoon, she might be even more in love with him.

She was still mad at him, and realistic enough to know that he was never going to return her feelings, but that hadn't changed anything inside her. She had no idea how she was going to handle things next week, when she had to meet up with him to give him Hannah. Maybe she'd just send Emma with the baby instead of going herself.

Her sister would do it for her. Emma had been in full-on big-sister mode since Jessi had returned from North Carolina, and right now Jessi was wallowing in it. But that had to stop. She was hiding and letting her emotions get the better of her.

Whatever they told her tonight about her job, she was going to have to figure out how to get Allan out of her mind and out of her heart so she didn't raise Hannah to be just as pitiful when it came to love.

Jessi got out of the car and walked into the office building, expecting to find a security guard waiting for her. But instead there stood Allan.

His hair was still as thick as ever and brushed the

back of his collar now. He wore a stylishly slim-cut black suit with a narrow gray tie. But he looked tired, and for the first time since she'd known him he watched her carefully before talking.

"I guess you guys decided to fire me if you're here," she commented when he didn't say anything.

"Don't jump to conclusions," he said.

"Oh, believe me, I don't do that anymore," she stated.

He cursed under his breath.

"Do you trust me?" he asked her.

She could only stare at him, but then took a deep breath. "You want the truth?"

"Always," he said.

She nodded. "I trust you. I trust you to break my heart and to let me down."

"God, Jessi. That's not true. I never wanted to break your heart. How could I?"

She didn't answer that.

"I'm sorry," he said. "I should never have let you leave North Carolina under those circumstances, but I was afraid. You were right when you said that we'd changed in those weeks we were out there together. And the truth was I wasn't ready for us to be different. I was still dealing with the loss of my best friend and finding out that the one woman I'd always thought I hated was actually the woman I loved."

She listened to his words, hoping he was sincere, but then she remembered that Allan was always honest when he spoke. She felt a spark of hope when he closed the gap between them and went down on one knee in front of her.

"I'm begging you, Jess, please forgive me and give me another chance."

She stared down at him as a million thoughts ran through her mind, images of the two of them from the moment they'd met. There had been something between them from the very beginning, and it had taken their friends' deaths to force them both to look at each other in a different way.

"I've missed you, too. I think I got too used to our morning routines and just talking to you during the day."

"I'm sorry I didn't say something to you before. But I didn't want to admit I'd been wrong about so much."

"But you hurt me, Allan. And I'm not the kind of person who likes that emotional pain."

"I won't do it again," he vowed. "I love you, Jess. I thought if I didn't say the words then I couldn't be vulnerable to you, but that wasn't true."

She felt silly standing while he was kneeling at her feet, so she got down on her knees in front of him and wrapped her arms around his big shoulders and kissed him. "I'll give you a second chance, but if you screw up again…"

"I won't," he said, kissing her and running his hands through her hair. "Will you promise me something?"

"Maybe. Depends on what you want."

"I want you to be you. No more suits like this, okay?"

She laughed. "Okay."

They got to their feet. "I have something else to show you."

He led the way to the elevator and took her up to the boardroom where his cousins and her sisters waited. There was a banner with her name on it that said Congratulations.

"Welcome to Playtone-Infinity Games," Kell said. "You hit one out of the park for us."

"Thanks. You didn't make it easy."

"Nothing worth having ever is," Kell said.

Everyone took turns congratulating her, and Jessi felt as if she finally had something she'd always been searching for when she watched Allan take Hannah from Cari. He held the baby in one arm and her with the other. She had a man she could count on, sisters she loved and a family of her own making.

"Just one more thing," Allan said.

"What now?" Jessi asked.

He took a box from his pocket and handed it to her. "Will you marry me?"

She stared at him. Dammit, he'd surprised her and gotten the upper hand, and the grin on his face said he knew it.

"Yes, I'll marry you," she said.

* * * * *

"It'll be difficult to remain strictly professional if I have a drink with you."

"I hope not. And thank you for the compliment." He received another smile that revealed her dimple.

"C'mon. Sit with me and have a drink. If you get uncomfortable, we'll come in and have dinner. Deal?"

"Sure, Ryan." Even saying his name was as tangible as physical contact and stirred desire. He was having a volatile reaction to her and he was digging himself in deeper every second by letting her stay, by asking her to have a drink with him.

But she was damned difficult to resist.

* * *

Her Texan To Tame
is part of the Lone Star Legacy series:
These Texas billionaires are about to get richer
…in more ways than one.

HER TEXAN
TO TAME

BY
SARA ORWIG

Published in Great Britain 2014
by Mills & Boon, an imprint of Harlequin (UK) Limited,
Eton House, 18-24 Paradise Road, Richmond, Surrey, TW9 1SR

© 2014 Sara Orwig

ISBN: 978 0 263 91458 0

51-0214

Printed and bound in Spain
by Blackprint CPI, Barcelona

Sara Orwig lives in Oklahoma. She has a patient husband who will take her on research trips anywhere, from big cities to old forts. She is an avid collector of Western history books. With a master's degree in English, Sara has written historical romance, mainstream fiction and contemporary romance. Books are beloved treasures that take Sara to magical worlds, and she loves both reading and writing them.

With thanks to Stacy Boyd and Maureen Walters,
who have been so important in my life.

Always, with love to David and my family.

One

"Jeb, I'll come out and look at this tractor you want to fix, but it'll have to be later today. I have interviews this morning for a cook. In fact, the first applicant ought to be coming up the road any minute now."

Beneath a broad-brimmed black Stetson, Ryan Delaney's brown eyes gazed into the distance. Jamming his hands into his pockets, he listened for the sound of an approaching vehicle while he stood on the wraparound porch of his West Texas ranch house.

"It's kinda early for a city woman to get out here for an interview," Jeb said.

"This one wanted an early interview. She's driving in from Dallas, so she's been on the road the past three or so hours."

"Gets up early—good sign. What about her husband? What job is he interested in?"

"There is no husband."

Jeb's eyes narrowed. "I thought you had a policy with that agency that you only hire couples to work in the house."

Jeb was right, but somehow Martin Clayburne at the

agency had talked him into this interview, promising he
wouldn't regret it. Ryan figured it'd be a quick one. "I
told Martin not to send a young single woman out here.
I'm just interviewing her long enough to show her the
door. No way will I hire her."

"Well, come look at the tractor when you can. When
you see the problem, you'll agree fixing it is better than
buying a new one," Jeb said.

"I'll look, but you find out what fixing it will cost. It
might be more economical to get a new one." Ryan heard
an engine and turned to see a spiral of dust on the road
moving toward the house. He turned back to talk to his
foreman, whose wide-brimmed tan hat was pushed back
on his head, revealing neatly combed graying brown hair.
"Another thing—when will the two new mares be delivered?" Ryan asked.

"I'm picking them up tomorrow afternoon."

"Stop by the house and I'll look at them," Ryan said,
glancing at the corral and breathing a deep sigh of satis-
faction. He enjoyed ranch work more than his work at the
drilling/energy company he owned. Though he wished he
could be here all the time, he at least spent one week out
of each month here. He wanted to be a part of everything
that went on at the RD Ranch. This was the life he loved.

"They're fine horses. You'll like them." Jeb pushed
his hat farther back on his head and gazed beyond Ryan.

"My, oh, my. Would you look at that," Jeb said in a
voice filled with awe.

Ryan turned as a car sped up the drive. Staring in
surprise, he took in a shiny fire-engine-red convertible
sports car sweeping around a curve and parking a hundred yards from the porch. A blonde cut the engine and
picked up her purse.

"Holy Holstein," Jeb said. "Ry, I'm willing to bet my paycheck she can't cook toast. Not that it will matter," the foreman added.

"I'm not taking you up on that bet," Ryan answered, his gaze never leaving the red car and its driver. The door swung open and she emerged from the car. She wore a light blue summer suit with a skirt short enough to reveal long shapely legs. The matching blouse had a low-cut V-neckline.

"Make you another bet—you'll hire her whether she can cook or not."

"You'd lose that one," Ryan replied.

"Hire her anyway. I'll teach her to cook."

Ryan couldn't stop looking at the woman, but he smiled at Jeb's offer. "I'll keep that in mind. She would pretty the place up, though. I'd be shocked if she's ever had a job cooking before. She's movie-star or model material, not a cook buried on a West Texas ranch."

"I'll get out of here."

"Stay and I'll introduce you in case she's hanging out in any of the local watering holes." He glanced again at the car, which looked new and incredibly expensive, and gave voice to his thoughts. "What's she doing applying to cook when she's driving a car like that?"

"I can't imagine any possible reason," Jeb said, sounding dazed.

Ryan knew enough women to know that the clothes she wore were also expensive. As she approached the front steps, he went to meet her. Climbing the steps, she displayed more of her long legs and he couldn't keep from staring.

She smiled, flashing white, even teeth and revealing a dimple in her cheek. He walked faster and held out his hand to shake hers. The moment he made physical contact with her soft skin, a current sizzled down to his lower extremities. When he met her crystal-blue gaze, he felt as if he were sinking in a sun-dappled sea.

"Mr. Delaney, I'm Jessica Upton. I'm here to interview for the position of cook," she said in a mellow voice that he could listen to the rest of the day.

"It's nice to meet you. This is my foreman, Jeb White," he hoped he said. He was lost in her dazzling smile. He felt a slight tug and looked down to see he was still holding her hand, so he released her swiftly and reluctantly.

Jeb shook hands with her. "Real nice to meet you, Ms. Upton." Jeb turned to Ryan. "I'll be going now. See you later at the garage."

"Sure," Ryan replied without taking his eyes from Jessica. Her smile must have short-circuited his brain, because he asked, "Was your husband unable to come this morning?"

He received an even bigger smile that made him weak in the knees. Hands down, she was the most beautiful applicant he'd ever interviewed.

"There is no husband, because I'm divorced."

"But you're wearing a wedding ring," he said, noticing the wide gold band with a row of diamonds and an engagement ring that had to be four carats. Her red nails were long and well shaped, indicating the care of a professional.

"I'm not ready to date anyone," she said, losing some of her sparkle. "I thought the wedding ring might head off unwanted invitations."

He seriously doubted it would head off all of them, but he merely nodded.

"I heard about this opening from someone I know in

Dallas and I talked the agency into letting me have this interview. Please don't be angry with them. Sometimes I can be persuasive."

"Oh, yeah. I'm sure he couldn't say no." The remark came out before Ryan could stop it. Where was his professionalism? It was getting blown out of the water by someone so enticing that she dazzled him and made him feel sixteen years old again.

He should reinforce that he hired only couples and send her away now. The thought was fleeting. He wasn't going to hire her, but he did want to interview her. Heck, he wanted to date her.

"Come inside to my office."

"Here's a résumé," she said, handing him a manila folder. "I mailed a copy after I inquired about this job."

Tucking the folder beneath his arm, he held the door for her to enter. He hadn't looked at her résumé, tossing it because the agency he used handled the screening of applicants.

When she entered the house, Ryan inhaled a sweet, enticing scent. As she passed him, he couldn't help noticing the sway to her hips. He took another long look, noticing her pale blond hair, which had a slight wave and swung across her shoulders with each step she took. Her silky hair was pinned up on the sides of her head.

Wisdom told him to send her packing. She shouldn't even be here and he shouldn't be showing her to his office. She might be nothing but trouble and she didn't look as if she had ever worked for anyone a day in her life. Despite all that, he followed her inside, where she turned to look expectantly at him.

"My office is in the study down the hall. Come with me. Did you drive from Dallas this morning?"

"I stayed with friends who know you—the Jimsons. Pru and I have been friends for a long time. They told me you're looking for a cook and the agency to contact. The agency highly recommended you."

"Where's your home, Ms. Upton?"

She smiled at him. "Please, just call me Jessica. Ms. Upton sounds as if my mother is nearby."

Smiling in return, he nodded. "Sure, Jessica. You can call me Ryan."

"I grew up in Memphis, Tennessee, and that's where my family is."

"Here's the study."

He waved his arm and let her precede him into a room with dark walnut walls and a handwoven Navajo area rug with a red-and-black design on a white background. She crossed the room to stop at one of the brown leather wingback chairs facing his desk.

He turned the other leather chair slightly to face her. "Please be seated."

Sitting, he glanced briefly as she crossed those fabulous legs. Unless he stopped looking at her, he was never going to resist the temptation to hire her.

"Where have you worked before?" he asked.

"I haven't held a regular job, but I have done a lot of volunteer work for charities. I have them listed in my résumé."

He opened the folder in his lap to glance at it and was surprised by the amount of time she had given to volunteering. "You've done a lot of charity work."

"Yes."

"Why do you want this job, Ms. Upton?"

"At this point in my life, this is a perfect job. I've been through a bad divorce. An emotional one. I want to go someplace new and quiet and for the coming year do something entirely different from what I've always done."

Ryan thought about her answer. Everything in him said to get rid of her politely and quickly. If he kept her around, he would seduce her and eventually, when he was ready to say goodbye, it would be difficult. And they would say goodbye. His relationships were always over at some point. He had never had a serious relationship and this was not where or when he would start.

"You're an attractive woman who could easily find a better-paying job in a big city where there are people and lots of things to do. You came from a city. Why would you bury yourself in a low-paying job in what is almost isolation out on my ranch?"

She smiled at him as if he were a slow learner and she was trying to encourage him. "Thank you for the compliment. I'm ready to be 'buried' somewhere with peace and quiet. I'm at a crossroads in my life and I need to think about my future and recover from my past. If I take this job, I can keep busy, earn some money, be away from everyone—namely my family and my ex—who would distract me while I try to chart my future."

Logical answer, but he didn't believe her. She was too pretty to need to bury herself. Memphis was big enough for her to escape her family and her ex, and if not Memphis, a lot of other big cities. She looked like a city person, not a cook on his ranch, where she wouldn't see anyone, including him, for days on end. A small inner voice still persistently told him to get rid of her. She would never fit in as his cook and all he would get would be one headache after another.

"I have a business in Houston and am only on the ranch about a week out of every month. I pay my staff whether I'm here or not, but for a lot of the time you'd be on your own. What would you do?"

He received another dazzling smile that made him ignore the persistent inner voice that told him to end this interview.

"I'll find some way to occupy my time," she said. "That's never been a problem and it will be even less of one now that I'm older."

He looked at her résumé again and saw when she'd graduated from high school. Calculating quickly, he was surprised. She was twenty-six. From her looks, he would have guessed twenty-two.

"A year can be a long time. Way before the year is over, you may want to date again. You'll meet only a limited number of men out here."

"I can live with that," she said with a twinkle in her eyes.

"Frankly, Ms. Up—er, Jessica, I don't think—"

"Give me a chance and I promise you won't regret it."

Her silky voice wrapped around him and he guessed very few men could deny what she asked. He couldn't imagine what killed her marriage.

He returned to reading the papers she had handed him, swiftly glancing over her transcript and looking more intently at her, trying to hide his surprise.

"You have almost a straight-A average and a degree in accounting. Accounting and cooking?"

"My dad steered all of his kids toward accounting. He said we could use it in whatever we do. I don't know about that, but it was not difficult for me."

"I'm impressed," he said. "Have you cooked for anyone before? I see here you've had some courses in cooking and you attended a prestigious culinary school in Paris."

"Yes. I love to cook and I guess that helps. You let me cook something for you and you'll hire me," she said, smiling at him. "What's your favorite dish?"

He was tempted to say "blue-eyed blondes," but he knew better.

"My favorite dessert is blackberry cobbler. My favorite dinner is roast beef and mashed potatoes covered with brown gravy—pretty simple stuff. No fancy French dishes."

"Ah, you're easy," she said, smiling slightly.

He had to clamp his mouth closed to keep from answering with the first thing that came to mind. His inner self was now jumping up and down, screaming to send her on her way. "I usually hire only couples," he said. At last he had turned a corner and was heading toward turning her down.

"You won't need two cooks," she said sweetly.

"Usually the wife is the cook and the man has another area where he prefers to work—chauffeur, gardener, handyman. Once I had a husband who was cook and his wife cleaned. It might be a little awkward having a young single female for my cook. Sometimes the two of us are the only ones in the house. I have a large staff who all live on the ranch. Also, the cowboys who work for me, but they're all off doing their own thing a lot of the time."

"No problem. You came with all kinds of recommendations and references and an absolute declaration that you would be totally professional."

He wanted to lean closer, speak softly and tell her he'd been questioning his professionalism since he laid eyes on her. And then he wanted to ask her out tonight. Instead, he stared at her résumé as if he were thinking deeply about it. "You're staying in Dallas?"

"I did last night. If you aren't interested in hiring me, I'm packed now and I'll just keep driving west. I'll find work somewhere, I'm sure."

"You should go to one of the modeling agencies. You'd have far better pay and a more interesting job."

She smiled as if he had made an impossible suggestion. "Thank you. I prefer to stick to cooking. It's something that I love."

She leaned forward slightly. "If you're concerned because I'm single, I can reassure you that it will make no difference. The way I feel right now, I have no desire to get into any kind of relationship again." She paused to look down at her hands in her lap and he waited because it seemed an emotional moment for her.

"I can understand that now," he said. "But you're young, healthy. Six months from now, you may feel differently about going out. I have a bunch of single guys working for me. They're going to start asking you out."

"They'll soon see that I'm not interested and then they'll lose interest." She held up her hand. "Besides, I'm wearing a wedding ring."

"You're divorced. That word will get around. They're good guys."

She smiled, looking in control again. "Are you encouraging me to go out with some of the cowboys who work here?"

"Not at all," he said, glad she was composed again and her sparkle had returned.

"It's a needless worry about my dating. I just plain cannot yet. It's like this. You want a cook. I will be quiet and stay out of the way, and you'll like my cooking. If you don't, then that's that, but," she paused, giving him a wide-eyed look that held him immobile, "I've never had anyone dislike my cooking. I really love to cook," she said in a breathless tone of voice that made him think of hot kisses and soft curves and forget all about food.

"If you'll give me a chance, you'll be pleasantly surprised," she continued. "That's really all I want, a chance," she said, looking at him with even wider blue eyes, leaning a bit closer, close enough he could catch the scent of her perfume again. Close enough that the blue silk blouse with its low V-neckline revealed the beginning of luscious curves. Close enough that her rosebud mouth tempted him. He couldn't get his breath and he wanted to lean toward her, put his hand at the back of her head and place his mouth on hers.

Realizing how he was staring and where his thoughts were going, he straightened up.

"Ryan," she said softly, in a coaxing tone. "You did say to call you Ryan, didn't you?"

"Yes, I did," he replied, and his voice was gravelly.

"Just let me stay and cook for you today," she urged in that breathless voice that made more sweat break out on his forehead. "I'll leave shortly after dinner as soon as I've cleaned the kitchen. I'll stay out of your sight ninety percent of the time. How's that?"

He was being manipulated by a woman he had known only half an hour and who wanted a job working for him. He should end the interview, tell her goodbye and get his life back right now. Instead, he was dazzled more than ever.

"Also, I am quite well-fixed in my own right, so I'm not trying to figure a way to get your money. My father has an accounting firm, a construction company and a trucking company and owns a bank. He has three sons and two daughters, one of them being me. He is very generous with his children. Other than cooking, you'll never know I'm around."

"That, Jessica, is absolutely impossible," Ryan said, unable to hold back the words.

She laughed softly. "I'd still like a chance to cook for you."

"I already have interviews set up throughout the morning and two after lunch." He couldn't believe he was arguing with her.

"You can still do them. You might find someone you like better. Just, please," she said, getting that sultry, breathless tone again, "give me a chance. What have you got to lose?" she added, touching his arm lightly with her fingertips. The contact was electric. His body tensed and heated. He wiped his damp forehead.

The interview had lost professionalism and he had lost his wits. By now she should be driving away out of his life forever. He could not recall a single time in his adult life where he had ignored judgment and common sense and let someone else take control.

It was time to be firm, positive and polite and send her on her way. He gazed into her wide blue eyes above a faint smile, enough of a smile to reveal the dimple.

Get rid of her, his inner voice commanded. He opened his mouth to tell her why he couldn't hire her and surprised himself when he spoke.

"Jessica, you've got yourself a deal."

Two

"I really appreciate this chance you're giving me." Jessica smiled, even though she had mixed feelings. She had argued with her friend about applying for this job. She would have preferred working for a couple. An older couple or a couple with children. Not a good-looking single guy.

But when she had turned in to the ranch, it had looked like the perfect place, exactly the peaceful surroundings she wanted in order to recuperate.

Her divorce had been a bad one, emotional for both of them. Carlton had not wanted the divorce. He wanted her back—probably to soothe his wounded ego, because it certainly wasn't out of love for her. Her parents wanted her to go back to him. As for her, she wanted to get away from all of them, somewhere quiet where they couldn't bother her and she could recover and let her nerves settle.

She hadn't told Ryan Delaney about losing her baby in her second month, but that miscarriage had added to her stress and heartbreak. First finding Carlton had cheated on her from the beginning of their marriage and then losing her baby. Yes, she thought, this isolated Texas ranch, where life was quiet and laid-back, seemed the ideal spot to recuperate.

Ryan Delaney was an appealing man—that alone shook her because no male had held even a tiny degree of appeal since she had moved out and filed for divorce. How had Ryan gotten through her numbness and hurt?

Ryan's appeal was a minus in her opinion. But he was nice, so that balanced out. He had remained professional, although if she wasn't mistaken, she felt a spark between them, which was another reason to seek a job elsewhere. On the other hand, she had a job and a place to stay in a part of the world where no one should be able to find her.

Besides, Ryan had said they would see little of each other, and she was counting on that. First she had to get the job with her one chance tonight.

She sighed with anticipation and relief that was short-lived. When following him out of the office and into the hall, she noticed his broad shoulders and thick black hair neatly cut above the collar of his blue denim shirt. He fell into step beside her, making her aware of his height and even more conscious she might regret this job. When close to him, this breathless, tingly feeling was not welcome. She needed an obscure, remote place to settle and heal, but this ranch might not be the place at all. Fear nagged that she was making a big mistake.

"You have a beautiful home."

"Thanks. I love the ranch. This is my getaway. I can relax here. Have you ever been to Texas?"

"Not until now."

"Here's the kitchen," he said, leading her into a large room filled with what looked like the newest appliances. The kitchen was an instant draw as she looked at the practical arrangement, the excellent equipment and an adjoining comfortable living area. A tall woman with a thick brown braid turned from the sink and smiled at her. Dressed in a T-shirt and jeans with a yellow apron tied around her middle, she smiled. "Jessica, this is Gwen Grayson, who works for me. She's in charge of cleaning. There are two more on my cleaning staff, but Gwen is here the most. Gwen, meet Jessica, who is applying for the cooking job."

Gwen's eyes widened as she looked at Jessica. "Welcome to the ranch," she said, staring.

"Thank you," Jessica replied. "I'm glad to meet you. This is a wonderful kitchen."

"Oh, yes," Gwen said. "Everything you can possibly need."

"I'm showing Jessica around and then she's volunteered to fix lunch and dinner, so you can go on with whatever else you want to do," Ryan said to Gwen.

"I'll be happy to do lunch," she said.

"I appreciate that, but I want to do this," Jessica said, smiling at Gwen, who smiled in return and shrugged.

"Ask me if you want some help."

Jessica nodded. "Thank you. I will."

"I'll show Jessica where she'll stay and she'll be back," Ryan said, taking her arm lightly and turning her. His touch ignited a sizzle. He released her. As she turned with him, she glanced at the bar with high stools dividing it from a connected room that held a fireplace, a pool table, and a big-screen television.

To one side of the kitchen a door stood open on a walk-in pantry that was neatly filled with supplies. At the end of the pantry was another freezer.

"This kitchen is wonderful but big enough you could cook for a U.S. Army base," she said.

"You'll only have to cook for me and any company I have. Also my house staff, which is Gwen, Paolina and Chiara, who clean, and Enrique and Dusty, who are maintenance. I doubt if you will see any of them except Gwen. Paolina and Chiara are off this month. Enrique and Dusty are maintenance for all the buildings. When they're working here, they eat here. Gwen's been filling in until I hire a cook, but she has a full-time job cleaning. I told you, I'm not here much of the time and when I am, I'm usually alone. Mainly, you'll just cook for me."

The idea made Jessica's insides flutter and she wondered how much just the two of them would be together.

"If you need help finding things, let me know. Especially this first day," he added.

"I'll find everything I need, I'm sure," she said, glancing up to catch him studying her with a look that made her warm and tingly.

"One more thing—my cook does the grocery shopping. I have an account and you just charge it to the account. It's in Bywater, a nearby small town. Are you certain you would want to get out to do that task?"

"Sure."

"It's Bywater, Texas, and it's a very small town. And no, it's not by any water. I don't know why they named it that."

"I don't mind at all."

"That settles the grocery buying." He glanced around. "I usually let my cook stay in one of the houses on the ranch, but since you're single, I think you'll have more peace and quiet staying here," he said. "This way to your suite," he said, going a short distance down the back hall to enter a suite. "Look around. See if this will do. You can stay here. You'll be close to the kitchen, as well as downstairs by yourself."

She stood in the living area and could see the adjoining bedroom with French Provincial fruitwood furniture, polished hardwood floors, another large-screen television, a desk with a computer.

"This is lovely. It'll be fine," she said, turning to look into dark brown eyes that captured and held her attention again, stealing away all thoughts or conversation. The moment stretched between them.

He turned abruptly and the moment was gone, leaving her breathless and with a racing heart. Declining the job to go elsewhere was the sensible thing to do. But right now she was too busy trying to get her breath and regain her composure.

"Give me the key to your car and I'll bring in your things," Ryan said in a deeper, huskier voice. Was he having a reaction as much as she was? Warning signals were flying like sparks from an exploding firecracker, yet she didn't want to turn down the chance for the job.

She motioned toward the door. "I'll go, too. I can carry something."

"While you're here, you can keep your car in the garage."

"Thank you."

When they reached her car, he removed two bags and shouldered a carry-on.

Gathering her laptop, a shoulder bag and another small bag, she followed him back to the house, where he set things down in her new suite.

"Have some more things in the trunk?"

"No."

"You're traveling light for someone moving away from home."

She shrugged. "Starting over. I don't need a lot and my folks will take care of my things. I have a small condo I leased for a year. I've already paid the rent for the year."

One corner of his mouth lifted slightly, making slight creases bracket his mouth. Once again she thought he was an incredibly handsome man, which would not make this job easy.

"Why are you smiling?"

"I suspect what you paid for that year's lease will be more than your salary here. You went to college. You have an accounting degree and you're qualified for a job that would give you a career and a good salary. Are you sure this is the choice you want to make?"

"At this time in my life, it is. My heart wouldn't be in any accounting job. I'm changing and trying to decide what I want to do the rest of my life. I want to work at something I like to do. My marriage is definitely over. I made a mistake in judgment about my ex that has shaken me."

"Well, you're following your heart, something not many of us get to do," he said, sounding slightly wistful, and she recalled what he'd said about wanting to spend more time at the ranch. "Give me your key and I'll put your car away for you," he said, holding out his hand.

She placed a key ring into his hand. "I'll wait on the porch and see where you go." As they walked through the house, she glanced at her surroundings. "Did you grow up on this ranch?"

"No. I had this house built five years ago to suit myself. Now, there's another Delaney ranch with a house that goes back generations. We lived there part of the time, but because of school and Dad's business, we lived in Dallas most of the time.

"There were quite a few of us. My brother Adam is deceased, but I have two others who live around here. Will is the next oldest brother. He's married and lives in Dallas. We have a half sister, Sophia, who is married and lives in Dallas and her husband is like another brother. Middle brother Zach has married, shocking the family because he was a world traveler. I'm the youngest. We're all in Texas."

"I come from a big family, too, as I told you. I have an older sister and three older brothers—a banker, an accountant and an attorney, all professions my father approves."

"There must be something you want to do your dad doesn't approve," Ryan guessed.

"I'd like to have my own restaurant. He would see that as a highly frivolous risk. Actually, my parents want me to be what I was—married to a highly successful man and not working outside the home, a socialite. I followed that life but spent a lot of my time volunteering, which I did enjoy."

"At least you helped others. That's good," he said, holding the door for her to step outside. She was conscious of passing close to him, constantly aware of his proximity.

"I'll be right back," he said, taking the porch steps two at a time.

She watched his long strides as he headed toward her car. Her gaze ran across his broad shoulders down to his narrow hips and long legs while her insides tightened. What would it be like to kiss him? She tried to think of another subject and get her mind off Ryan. What was it that stirred such chemistry between them?

She looked at her car and decided if this job didn't work out, she would drive back to Dallas and sell the car, then head north. Maybe Montana or Wyoming would have another isolated ranch where a family could use a cook. Or a small-town restaurant off the main highways.

Common sense still urged her to go now. There was a hot attraction between Ryan and her. The fact that he had remained professional, resisted flirting, until after the interview had not cooled the fires. She glanced at her surroundings again, the outbuildings, corral, stables, garage, wide-open spaces and, through a stand of mesquite trees, a bunkhouse. She could not imagine any of her family or her ex finding her here. So the place was perfect—except for one tall Texas rancher.

Ryan came striding back and handed the keys to her. When his fingers brushed hers, another sizzle danced in her insides. "Nice car. Want to sell it to me?"

"You'll get the first chance if I do decide to sell it. But I really like my car and I'd hate to let it go." She took a deep breath and looked toward the door. "I'd better go get accustomed to your kitchen. What would you like for lunch?"

He gazed at her a moment in silence. "Surprise me," he finally said. "I'll get ready for the next interview. I'll answer the door when she arrives."

Jessica nodded and left for her room to change clothes. She wasn't putting anything away until she was certain she had the job. She thought about his offer to buy her car. For the time being she didn't want to sell. As soon as she sold her car, it would be easier to look up records and find she had been in Texas.

She changed into jeans and a red cotton shirt, tying her hair behind her head with a red scarf. Slipping on flip-flops, she left for the kitchen. Certain Ryan was closed in his office to interview someone, she glanced down the empty hall. She hadn't heard a doorbell or anyone talking, but the house was big enough that she wouldn't hear when she was in her suite or even back in the kitchen.

The first thing she did was familiarize herself with his kitchen. It was as well stocked as a store. As she began collecting what she needed from the pantry, she heard someone in the kitchen and turned around to see Gwen.

"Ahh, you're here to fix lunch," Gwen said, smiling at Jessica. "You really don't need to, because I've been filling in. You don't actually have the job yet—right?"

"I'm trying out for the position," Jessica said. "I'm starting with lunch. He didn't say what he likes to eat, so I'm guessing. I'm going to make a pie first, for after dinner."

"He'll like that. I've never seen him turn down pie. You're trying out? He doesn't usually do that when hiring," she said, looking puzzled.

"He said he usually hires couples. I'm divorced. I sort of talked him into giving me a chance and letting me cook for him today."

"Ahh." Gwen chuckled. "Good. If you need help, I'll be happy to."

"Thank you. That's sweet, but this time I better do it all on my own since it's sort of a trial to show him what I can do."

"And you're up for this?"

"Oh, yes," she said, smiling at Gwen, who gave her a big grin.

"Good for you. Ask me if you have any questions or can't find something."

"Thanks. I will."

"My husband has worked for Mr. Ryan since he bought this ranch. After he built the house, I was hired on to clean. We live in a house here on the ranch and we like working here. So for tonight—what kind of pie are you baking?"

"I'm not baking. It's a chocolate icebox."

"Very good choice. He has a weakness for chocolate. Burgers, roasts, steaks, barbecue and just plain potatoes are his favorites. That and blueberry waffles."

"Thanks for letting me know."

"Do you really know how to cook?"

"Oh, yes," she said, smiling.

"Then you'll get hired. And you'll definitely be the prettiest cook we've ever had."

Jessica laughed with Gwen. "Thank you. And thanks for telling me what he likes."

"It's quiet here. Are you sure you want the isolation of the ranch?"

"I'm sure. I had a bad divorce and my ex didn't want me to leave. This will be a good place for me. I'll like it here," she said, thinking of Ryan's irresistible smile.

"I'll be through cleaning and out of here by four. If you need something or want help, here's my cell number," Gwen said, getting a piece of paper and jotting a number to hand to Jessica.

"Thank you. That's very nice."

"I think you'll be a good addition here. I clean upstairs today. I better get started. Oh, if you want flowers for the table, Mr. Ryan doesn't care if we pick some and bring them in for bouquets. Just watch out for rattlesnakes in the garden."

"Rattlesnakes? I think I'll skip the flowers."

When the housekeeper had left, Jessica checked and found frozen raw hamburger patties that she could cook. She found buns and all she needed. She busied herself with making the pie first and setting it in the refrigerator to chill.

When noon came, she looked around, making sure everything was ready. Thirty minutes later she still hadn't seen Ryan and she wondered if an interview was running long because he had found someone who would be more satisfactory for his cook and would have a husband to work here also.

By one she was certain that was what had happened and then she heard his boots as he approached the kitchen and stepped through the door.

Her heart missed a few beats when she smiled at him. "I'd given you up."

"Sorry, I should have let you know," he said. He filled the doorway and dominated the room. Would she ever get accustomed to him and see him as just another person? "I'll look over my notes and be back in about twenty minutes. That should give you some time."

"Sure. By then your lunch will be ready," she said, hearing the breathless sound of her voice and wondering whether he noticed it.

"Eat with me, okay? We can talk some more."

"Isn't that a little irregular?"

"Because you work for me? I don't think so and that's all that matters, unless you don't want to—"

"Oh, no. That's fine," she said, flashing a smile at him.

"Good. See you in twenty minutes," he said, and left.

Eat with me.

His request replayed in her mind. Once again this job was taking another unexpected turn. Could she continue being close to him, associating with him daily, and still stay remote and impassive around him? He had to know he was having an effect on her every time they were together. It was obvious sometimes that he felt it just as much as she.

She hurried to get his lunch, and twenty minutes later she took the hamburgers off the small grill as he came through the door.

They sat at a table overlooking the formal garden and a pond with a fountain, a waterfall and blooming lilies.

"This is a beautiful view," she said.

"Yes, it is," he said in a warm voice that held a note that caught her attention. She turned to look at him as he gazed back with a faint smile. He looked back at his plate. "This looks great and I'm hungry. It's been a long time since breakfast."

"I baked beans," she said. "I thought that might be healthier than the fries."

"You're probably right. So far, I've rejected both women I interviewed this morning. You're still at the top of the list." He took a bite of his burger.

"That's good news because I think I'll like it here. We'll see how you like my lunch and dinner. Lunch isn't really a test, because burgers are sort of always the same and very easy."

"The burger is good."

"Thank you. Are you planning on staying at the ranch for a while now or will you go back to Houston soon?"

"I'm in and out right now. I'll go to Houston later this week."

As he spoke, she gazed into his warm brown eyes. She had made such a poor judgment with her ex; was she making more poor decisions now with Ryan? He smiled and picked up his burger to take another bite.

"I'm glad to hear the job is still open," she said.

"Oh, yes. I have two interviews after lunch. I'll let you know how it goes. So far, lunch is good. The beans are great and the burger is cooked just the way I like it."

"I'm glad. Gwen told me you like burgers, but not how you like them cooked."

"You guessed well. Gwen and her husband both work here, you know."

"That's what she said." She wiped her hands on her napkin and stood up. "I have pie for dinner tonight, but I baked some cookies for now." She went inside to get a plate of chocolate-chip cookies, which she placed in front of him. He promptly held the plate out to offer her one as she sat.

"No thanks," she said. "I'm not a sweets person."

"I'll remember that," he answered, taking a cookie.

"I don't think you need to remember your cook doesn't eat sweets," she said.

"I might want to send you a present sometime and I would need to remember," he added. He still kept his voice impersonal. There was no flirting, no touch, but when she looked into his chocolate-colored eyes with those thick bedroom lashes, a current sizzled between them. The attraction was still there, like bedrock beneath a stream of polite conversation.

She drew her eyes away, focusing on the nearby fountain. She had to get her head back in the game.

"Did you go with this guy in college?"

Ryan's question drew her up short, and she realized

she must have missed something he said. "My ex?" she guessed. When he nodded, she replied, "No. He was a bit older than I am. I've known him all my life.

"I think he thought I'd be the perfect wife. That I would never find out about his affairs. And if I did, I'd go along with his infidelities." She shook her head. "I was just naive about everything. Anyway, it's over now."

"Your family is in Tennessee. Won't you go back someday?"

"Oh, my, yes. I love Tennessee with all my heart, especially Nashville. That's where I plan to live. It's close enough to my family in Memphis to be convenient but far enough that I can live my own life and I won't run into my ex often. Before I go back, though, I want to recover from the stress of the past few months."

"If peace and quiet helps you recover, you've come to the right place." With a glance at his watch, Ryan rose. "Excuse me, Jessica," he said, her name spoken by him stirring a tingle, sounding deeper, more personal than when he'd previously said it. "It's time I get back to my office and look over my notes before the next interview. Thanks for the lunch."

She couldn't help but feel disappointed that he would continue to interview applicants, so she went into work mode, gathering the dishes and bringing them inside. She turned from the sink and almost bumped into Ryan, who stood there with glasses in his hands. He steadied her, his fingers lightly on her shoulders, but the moment he touched her, she saw his eyes narrow slightly. Inhaling deeply, he released her. Her heartbeat raced and she wanted to lean closer to him.

But Ryan hurried out of the room in long strides.

Watching him, she took a deep breath. Once again

common sense said to pack and go. She was having a volatile reaction to Ryan Delaney and he had had a reaction to touching her, too. Maybe he would hire someone this afternoon and the job decision would be out of her hands.

She cleaned the dishes and then got more familiar with the kitchen, turning on an oven to start cooking a roast for dinner. She spent the afternoon laboring over dinner, checking on the roast, making rolls and mashing potatoes. Later she set the table for the evening meal and finally reached a point where she could go to her suite to get ready to be with Ryan.

After showering, she slipped into a blue sundress and sandals and brushed her hair out. By five she was back in the kitchen to finish cooking dinner. Everything was going well, which lifted her spirits. Whether she got the job or not, she was happy to discover she could turn out a lunch and dinner when the result was crucial and time was of the essence. It was dinner tonight, one good enough to get her hired, or she was out. There would be no second chance tomorrow.

As she made gravy and steamed collard greens, she couldn't squelch the nagging question: Was she more excited over the prospect of a dinner that would determine her future...or the thought of an evening with Ryan?

Three

Ryan straightened up over the tractor. "All right. Buy the parts if you think that's the way to go and you're certain you can fix it."

"I can fix it." Jeb stepped away from the tractor to walk with Ryan. "What did you do today? I see the red car is here. Am I going to teach her to cook?"

"No. Tonight is a test. She talked me into giving her a chance."

Jeb's mouth twitched. "Imagine that. I suspect she'll talk you into hiring her no matter her cooking ability."

"No. If she can't cook, she goes and she knows it. But I agreed to give her a chance and let her cook dinner tonight."

"Well, I can guess the outcome of that. As I said, I'll be happy to teach her to cook."

"Thanks for the offer. I won't forget," Ryan answered drily. "Lunch was good, a burger and beans, so maybe she can cook."

"Even a kid can cook a burger and beans. Go enjoy dinner and the evening."

"Sure, Jeb." Ryan left the foreman to head for his

house, wondering about his dinner. In spite of a good lunch, he didn't expect her to have as much success with dinner. He reminded himself that she did have some credentials in her background, though, so maybe she could really cook. Why did he doubt it?

He didn't go in through the kitchen and see her but instead went straight to his suite from a side entrance. He showered and dressed in a fresh dark brown cotton Western shirt, jeans and black boots.

While he dressed, he thought about the interviews today. None had been someone he wanted to hire, including Jessica. Jessica would be trouble at best because if she could cook beyond burgers, she had an ex-husband who wanted her back and parents who also wanted her to return. If they showed up to try to talk her into moving home, he would be involved. He was attracted to her, but he wasn't going to seriously date her or any other pretty woman. He had too much fun making friends and flirting with a passel of willing females.

Yet in spite of the complications accompanying her, he had allowed her to stay and cook as a trial run.... He didn't want to analyze that move.

No, he told himself. He had an out. If dinner was not particularly good, he would simply not hire her. He'd tell her goodbye and send her on her way.

Why did he have a funny feeling in the pit of his stomach when he thought about that? Because he was sorry for the troubles she had had.

"Yeah, right, Ryan," he said softly to his reflection in the mirror. He couldn't lie to himself. He wanted to go out with her. Sparks flew when he was with her and both of them were trying to keep their employer-employee relationship, or whatever they had, professional and unemotional. It never happened. The slightest physical contact was electrifying. He wanted a night out with her. He wanted to hold her and kiss her; he wanted to seduce her. She took his breath away with her looks.

The woman had emotional problems from her bitter divorce. She needed peace and solace—not someone hot for her.

Ryan lectured himself about his motives and tried to steel himself to get rid of her because they both would be better off. And should she persuade him to let her stay, he needed to leave her alone. Stay away from her, go back to Houston and his work and let her mend and go on her way.

Maybe he'd look her up when she got over her divorce.

On impulse he went to the phone to call his friends the Jimsons. Brad answered and Ryan talked to him briefly, checking out Jessica to learn if her friendship was what she had said and the Jimsons had recommended she come to the ranch to apply for a job as his cook.

He then spoke to Pru and after a few minutes hung up. Jessica checked out. Now it all hinged on dinner. If dinner wasn't any good, was he really going to get rid of her?

He had told Pru about the trial meal. She had laughed and said she guessed he would hire Jessica. He suspected Pru was basing that guess on Jessica's looks and his friendships with pretty ladies.

He walked downstairs and headed to the kitchen. Enticing smells of beef and hot bread lured him to the room. He heard singing and a pan clattering and water running. His pulse sped and eagerness to see Jessica gripped him.

He stopped in the doorway, his insides in a clutch while he noticed several things at once. She was not in a panic, running frantically around the kitchen trying to get dinner together. The kitchen was neat and orderly, and she had tidied up from cooking. Her pale blond hair was secured in a ponytail, tied with a scarf that matched her dress. She had her back to him while she slid a covered platter into the warming drawer in the oven. He wanted to walk up to her and slip his arms around her tiny waist, but he knew better than to do any such thing.

"It smells wonderful in here," he said in a husky voice that he couldn't change.

She turned and gave him a radiant smile that revealed her dimple. Right then he admitted to himself, cook or no cook, there was no way he could send her packing.

"Dinner is ready."

"How about a drink with me first outside? It's a beautiful evening. We could forget employer and employee for a few minutes without it hurting anything."

"That's crossing a line," she said, frowning slightly and studying him.

"Doesn't have to. We can just sit, enjoy the evening, talk a little and relax. You've been cooking in a hot kitchen."

Her frown disappeared. "Not exactly slaving over a hot stove."

"Maybe not, but this won't be disastrous and we don't have to cross a line."

"Still, I don't think you usually have drinks and dinner with your staff, do you?"

As he shook his head, he grinned. "I don't usually have a gorgeous single woman on my staff. For just a minute, can we drop being strictly professional? I don't want to upset you in any way, but you asked the question."

"It'll be a little difficult to remain strictly professional if I have a drink with you on your patio. I can't quite address you as 'Mr. Ryan' the way Gwen does either."

"I hope not. That's her doing. I've told her to call me Ryan, but she insists. Her husband calls me Ryan, but Gwen won't. I'm not going to argue the point. They've worked for me several years now, but they've also worked for my older brother Adam, so they've known me for years."

"And thank you for the compliment." He received another smile that revealed her dimple.

"C'mon. Sit with me and have a drink. If you get uncomfortable, we'll come in and have dinner. Deal?"

"Sure, Ryan." Even hearing her say his name was as tangible as physical contact and stirred desire. He was having a strong reaction to her and he was digging himself in deeper every second by letting her stay, by asking her to have a drink with him. Was he on a track to seduction and reluctant to face up to his own motives? Guilt assailed him because Jessica was emotionally vulnerable. Surely he had no intention of taking advantage of her…but she was damned difficult to resist.

"What would you like? I'll get drinks," he said, his voice going husky again, a telltale sign of his desire.

"I think I'll have iced tea. I've already made a pitcher."

"Tea for you, a cold beer for me."

"I set the table inside, but I can move things to the patio, if you prefer," she said as he got ice and then poured tea from a pitcher sitting on the counter.

"No, we'll eat indoors." Walking farther into the kitchen, he saw the table, set and ready.

"Very nice. Here's your tea," he said, handing her the drink and touching her slender fingers as she took the glass—another slight touch that heightened attraction.

He was amazed that he had such an intense reaction to so many insignificant brushes with her.

He got his beer and held the door for her to go outside. It was a cool June evening with no wind stirring. She sat facing the formal garden and he pulled a chair close to hers. The full skirt of her dress hid her legs almost to her slender ankles.

He raised his bottle to her. "Welcome to Texas. May you like your stay."

Smiling, she touched his bottle with her glass lightly and sipped her tea before setting her drink on a small table beside her chair.

"I'll admit I hope you hire me, because I think this is what I'm looking for. This is a perfect place for me to heal, to get over my divorce. If you don't hire me, though, I understand, and I'll head north, maybe to Montana or Wyoming."

"I don't think you have to plan on driving to Montana or Wyoming. We'll work out something. I talked to Brad and Pru. You come highly recommended," he said, fighting the temptation to move his chair closer. He wanted to flirt with her, ask her out, kiss her. Seduce her. Instead, he had to be polite, distant, professional. Only friendly, nothing more. He suspected she would be a daily torment working for him because he would constantly be fighting himself. Even knowing that, he couldn't turn her away. One look at her and he wanted her to stay.

"They're close friends, particularly Pru, so of course they would give me a good recommendation. The best references as far as my work will be the ones I listed and gave to you today because those are people I've worked with on volunteer projects. Those and two names I have from the cooking school I attended. I enclosed letters they've written for me."

"I haven't read all your information yet," he admitted. "When I saw you were single, I didn't think there would be a chance I would hire you."

"Thanks for giving me a chance," she said, with another dimpled smile that made him want to do anything she asked.

"You're persuasive," he said. "I doubt if many men have said no to you."

"As a matter of fact, they haven't," she said with a twinkle in her big blue eyes. "So tell me more about your family. I suppose if I work here, I'll meet them at some point."

"They're in Dallas and yes, you will. I've told you we lost Adam. He had a little girl, Caroline. Will is her guardian and Ava, Will's wife, is far more of a mother than her birth mother, who walked out on them early."

"Walked out? That's dreadful," she said, looking upset for the first time. "How could a mother walk out on her baby?"

"She never had any interest in Caroline. Still doesn't. Actually, if something were to happen to Will and Ava, I'm in the will to be appointed Will's children's guardian. I can't imagine being Daddy."

"Why not? You're kind, cheerful, intelligent."

"Thanks," he said, grinning. "Will has done a wonderful job caring for Caroline and so has Ava. She went through some tough times and Ava helped bring her out of her shell and get over her hurt."

"That's sad, for a little child to be hurt. I'm glad it's worked out for her."

"She has a little brother, Adam, now. He is a cute baby

and Caroline is a doll. Both happy, fun kids, which is the way it should be." He took a long pull from his beer, then placed it back on the table. "Where do your sister and your banker, accountant and attorney brothers live?"

"They're all in Memphis, not far from our parents. I'm the one rocking the boat. My sister and my brothers are all married—each has two kids. My sister has two boys. Each of my brothers has a son and a daughter. I have delightful nieces and nephews and I miss them a lot."

Her voice was wistful, reminding him of her loss and the fragile side to her. One more reminder to avoid flirting with her or crossing the line any more than he already had.

"Are you close with your siblings?"

"I'm close to my sister and close to my youngest brother, Jason. I guess because of our ages. He's five years older than I am. Derek is eight years older, Lydia is ten years older and Dillon is twelve years older. Dillon and I have gotten to know each other a little better since we're grown, but we're not close. What's worse, he's friends with Carlton. So is Lydia's husband, Frank."

"How did you get interested in cooking?" he asked her. He was curious about her but truthfully, he enjoyed sitting with her and wanted to keep her talking. His chair was turned enough that he could watch her, gaze into her blue eyes and get an occasional whiff of her perfume. She smelled wonderful and he could look at her all evening. He could listen to her, too. Her voice was perfect—neither too high-pitched nor too low.

"We had a woman who cooked and cleaned for us. Her name was Sandy and she would let me help when I was little and then she taught me how to do things on my own. She was a wonderful cook. People wanted to hire her away from us occasionally, but she stayed with us. I still keep up with her and go see her. She's elderly now and my dad helped her get some investments and a savings plan, so she's comfortable. Dad put a down payment on a house for her about fifteen years before she finally quit work and she paid off the mortgage before she quit. I've called her since I left home and she knows I left and will stay somewhere else for a while and she knows why. I'm really close to her. She was like another mother to me."

"That's nice you've stayed close. And nice you didn't burden her with telling her where you are, although you might be better off if someone knows."

"Oh, several people know where I am. I keep in touch with Mom. She doesn't know specifics, but she knows enough. My sister knows where I am and what I'm doing. We text daily. I have a close Memphis friend—Olivia— who knows. She won't even speak to Carlton. My parents won't bother asking her about me, because they'll know she won't tell them.

"Olivia and Carlton move in the same circles and she'll let me know when he's seeing somebody else, which he should be doing by now. Then he'll be far less interested in finding me. He knows I'm not going back. Our divorce was final a year ago. I left him five months before that." She paused and gave him a solemn look that startled him. "Before I left him, I miscarried and lost a baby. I was in the second month of pregnancy." She looked away, but not before he saw her eyes fill with tears.

"Sorry for your loss."

"Even though the doctor said I can still have babies, I can't seem to get over it," she whispered. He barely heard her and saw her hands locked together in her lap.

His sympathy went out to her. He thought of Caroline and Adam, and Zach's little girl—how adorable they were—and felt a stab of sadness for her loss. Impulsively, he reached over to pat her hands.

She wiped her eyes and inhaled, finally turning to face him as she stood.

"Thank you. I think I should go look at dinner and get it on the table. I don't want it to get dried out."

"I'll help," he said, standing with her and walking back. She was tall for a woman, but not as tall as he was.

"Please have a seat and I'll get dinner on while you finish your beer."

"I can help. Do you want more tea?"

"Yes, please," she said, hurrying to get things out. He helped and was pleasantly surprised with each dish she pulled out of the warming oven or the stove. Everything looked appetizing.

In minutes they were seated, overlooking a platter with chunks of tender beef. There was steaming brown gravy in a white gravy boat with a silver ladle. She had made fluffy mashed potatoes and steamed collard greens. She had found a jar of peppers for the greens. And they had salad plates for a tossed green salad.

The moment he took a bite of roast, there was no question she had the job. The tender meat was the best ever. So was the dark brown gravy. A timer dinged and she left to return with huge fluffy rolls that astounded him.

"I don't recall these being in my freezer."

"They weren't in your freezer. I made them today."

"You really can cook," he said, staring at her and thinking her ex had to be unhinged to treat her so badly. She was every man's dream.

"So what does that mean?" she asked, slanting him a curious look.

What it meant was that he was doomed. He had to hire her and he had to stay professional, remote, keep his hands to himself and his conversation impersonal. Now that he knew about the loss of her baby, it was even more important to leave her alone to let her heal.

"It means you have a job as my cook if you want it."

"Thank you," she said, giving him one of her radiant smiles, which turned his insides to jelly and killed all appetite for dinner. He needed to pack and get back to Houston sooner than he had planned because staying around here was going to be an incredible challenge.

"We should discuss a menu for the coming week. I don't really know what you like. What would you like in the morning?"

The answer that instantly came to mind could not be said. He could feel sweat breaking out on his forehead. She was sexy, hot, the most beautiful woman he had met, and he couldn't do one thing about it. He did not want to hurt her and she looked like the very earnest kind, not one for an affair that would be done and forgotten swiftly.

"You're talking about breakfast," he said, unable to hold back that much.

She blinked and he saw understanding dawn as her cheeks flushed. "I definitely mean breakfast," she said briskly, but there was a breathless note to her voice now that added to his climbing temperature. "Orange juice? Tomato juice? Eggs, pancakes, what?"

"I'll think about it," he said. It was impossible to decide what he wanted for breakfast. He looked down at his plate, drinking his iced tea, trying to get his thoughts elsewhere and cool down. "After dinner we'll make a grocery list and Saturday I'll go into town with you to the store."

They ate in silence while he tried to cool his libido and stop thinking about how he'd enjoy flirting with her. As he took a few tentative bites and tried to get her out of his thoughts and avoid looking at her, his appetite began to return. Jeb was going to be speechless the first time he ate her cooking.

"What kind of restaurant do you want to have?" Ryan asked, finally risking a look at her.

"Just American. That's what I know. I had it all planned. I dreamed about it during college, but then when I married I had to give it up." She took a bite of the beef, and the gravy lingered on her lip, drawing his eyes.

"Now I want to live and work in Nashville," she continued as she wiped her mouth. "That's close enough to home and family, but not too close. It gets me out of Memphis society, which is great. It gets me away from running into my ex a lot. I love Tennessee with all my heart. It's the most beautiful state—the Smoky Mountains, Chattanooga, the little towns, the cities, Nashville is wonderful with bluegrass and country music, Centennial Park, the beautiful Southern homes and gardens, the best food ever. I don't want to live anywhere else. I guess you feel that way about Texas, so you should understand."

"Actually, it's the ranch I feel that way about. This is the place where my heart is. I can't imagine leaving it. This is my idea of paradise."

"See? You wouldn't want Nashville. I wouldn't want here, not for a lifetime, but for now, this place is perfect."

"Speaking of this place and your new job—I prefer breakfast about six a.m." As he looked at the most beautiful woman he had ever seen, the moment was surreal.

Instead of flirting, laughing with her, getting closer—
what he really wanted to do—he was telling her breakfast
at 6:00 a.m. And she was nodding as if she was totally
happy with their arrangement.

"Six is fine. I'll have everything ready."

"Like I said, you can select that menu. I don't care
to plan meals." At the moment he didn't care what she
made. He was far more interested in spending time with
her than what she was going to cook for him.

"If I select the menu, that makes this job easy."

"I'm an easy guy," he answered. "I'm not a vegan, not
on a restricted diet and when I want a steak, I'll tell you
and I'll grill it. Otherwise, it's up to you."

"Fine. Just like tonight, more or less?"

"Right," he said, gazing into her wide blue eyes while
she listened. He realized he was going to feel silly eating alone with her waiting on him or hanging out in the
kitchen. "Jessica, this is a slightly different situation than
I've ever had. You're different from other cooks I've had."

She gazed solemnly at him except for a faint lift of
the corner of her mouth.

"So just plan on eating with me. Okay? I can't see myself sitting here eating alone and you waiting on me and
watching me eat," he said, voicing his thoughts.

"You don't have to eat with me. I can disappear or ignore you or whatever you want," she protested.

"I want you to eat with me," he said, complicating his
life once again. From the moment her red car had pulled
to a stop and she had stepped out, his life had been spin-
ning into a strange new orbit. Eating every meal with
her and still not flirting would be another horrendous
challenge. Right now he wanted to forget this somber
conversation and have some fun with her. And he could

well imagine there were moments when she could be a lot of fun. He ached to ask her to go dancing.

"You'll get tired of seeing me."

"Jessica, I wouldn't get tired of seeing you even if we ate every meal together until you quit this job," he said, the words tumbling out in spite of his intentions.

She laughed softly. "Yes, you will, but if that's what you want, you're the employer."

"It's not a job requirement," he answered, wondering what her feelings were. "If you don't want to, you don't have to."

"We'll start out that way. You said you're not here much of the time, so it shouldn't be a problem," she stated casually, as if the whole matter were insignificant to her and she had no physical reaction to him.

"Now, what happens when you're away? Does my job go away? Do I find another job?" she asked.

"No. I pay the people who work for me whether I'm here or not. I couldn't keep anyone if I didn't."

"Everyone else has work to do whether you're here or not. I don't. Can I help with the cleaning or something while you're away?"

"That's just the problem about having a cook. I can't think of anything else for you to do unless I have staff working here at the house. Otherwise, they eat at the bunkhouse. Gwen probably won't let you cook for her and will do her own. You ask. They'll let you know if they'll be here to eat. Gwen cleans, so I don't need you doing that unless you want to help her, but she probably won't let you help clean either. Do what you want when you have the chance."

"What about the little town where I get groceries? Is

there anything going on there where they would need a volunteer to help?"

"I'll ask around and see." Having had his fill of the meal, he sat back and put down his napkin. "That was a delicious dinner and you're a fine cook."

"Thank you," she said, smiling at him.

"C'mon. I'll show you around the house. I can give you a small map of the ranch because it can be confusing when it's all new to you. As for the house, we'll just look at the downstairs now because that's where you'll be."

When they entered the dining room, she glanced around. "This is a beautiful room. If my mother could see this, she would probably stop worrying about me. You have beautiful things," she said, looking at two tall crystal candelabra on an Edwardian buffet. The dining room table could seat twenty and she wondered when he had such elegant parties.

She wandered around the formal room, looking at beautiful china and sparkling etched crystal in his fruit-wood china cabinet.

They moved on to a large room that had to be the most occupied room next to the kitchen and the living area there.

The large family room overlooked the patio and pool. It held a big-screen television, a stone fireplace flanked by bookshelves, family pictures on the walls, comfort-able leather furniture. She circled the room and paused in front of a picture box with a large gilt frame. Inside, against black velvet, was what she guessed was an an-tique pistol. Ryan came to stand beside her.

"That's an old family heirloom. It's a Colt revolver in an antique picture box."

"My dad would be impressed by this."

"Maybe he'll see it someday."

Laughing, she shook her head. "I don't think so."

"Let's move back to the patio and watch the sun go down."

"I should go unpack," she said, her smile disappearing.

"Come sit with me. You can unpack later," he said, seeing a flicker in her eyes and realizing she was trying to avoid him. That realization might mean she was as aware of him as he was of her. The thought brought another tight clutch to his insides. Both of them were trying to remain professional. If she hadn't been so hurt, he would toss aside this determination and just have fun.

As they walked toward the patio, she stopped short. "I almost forgot. I have a chocolate icebox pie for dessert."

He inhaled. "Let's save it for later unless you want a piece now."

"Waiting is fine. You sit here on the patio and let me clear the table."

"I'll help you in a minute. I want to call Jeb first and tell him to come get some leftovers."

"You call and I'll clear," she said, going into the kitchen.

Ryan pulled out his cell phone to call, watching her as she worked.

"Jeb. We've finished dinner, but there's plenty here. Come get some leftovers and try Jessica's cooking. You can eat here at the house or take it with you. We'll be happy to have you stay."

He listened to Jeb question the "we" part. "That's right," Ryan said, trying to avoid letting Jessica know about Jeb's questions. He listened to his foreman and finally put away his phone. He went inside and gathered dishes from the table to help her. "Jeb's coming up to get dinner."

"You're close with your employees."

"I suppose I am. I've known all of them a long time." He tilted his head to study her. "You know, you're not at all like I guessed you'd be when you drove up looking for a job."

"Neither are you, Ryan. And you're not who I was hoping to find either, but I know I'm not who you hoped would apply."

He heard a knock and headed to the door to find Jeb waiting. "You must have jogged all the way here."

"Ran. I'm hungry. I'll fill my plate and take it with me."

"You can sit with us."

"Evidently you have a new cook."

"Oh, yes. Wait until you sink your teeth into the roast and the rolls she made from scratch. That's why I called you, so you can see for yourself."

"Do tell." He gave Ryan a sly smile. "This ought to be interesting in the next few weeks."

"Nothing's changed. She's still on the mend and you might as well put out the word about her."

"Already have. I figured she'd get hired whether she could boil water or not. Howdy, Ms. Upton," Jeb said as they entered the kitchen.

Jessica smiled at him. "Hi, Jeb. Unless you want me to call you Mr. White, please just call me Jessica."

"Jessica it is."

"Help yourself, Jeb. We're going to sit outside shortly. You're welcome to join us and eat out there," Ryan said.

"Thanks, but I'll head back to my house. The dogs are waiting," he said, getting a pie pan from a cabinet and helping himself. "Welcome to the ranch, Jessica. Glad to have you working here. Ryan's not always around, so if you ever need me, just call. My number is on the speed dial."

"Thanks, Jeb."

"Thanks for dinner. It smells wonderful."

"Let me cut you a piece of pie." She worked swiftly, cutting a slice and placing it on a paper plate, covering it with another to hand to him.

"You should eat here," Ryan said. "If you drop all that, you won't have dinner."

"I'm not dropping anything. Thanks, Jessica. Glad to have you with us," Jeb repeated.

Ryan followed him to the door. "Enjoy dinner. I know you will."

"I know *you* did," Jeb whispered.

Ryan got his meaning. "I have to keep reminding myself of all she's been through."

"You'll manage. Thanks for the food."

Ryan closed the door behind Jeb and returned to the kitchen to help Jessica until they had the kitchen back in order.

"You don't have to clean the kitchen with me. The cleanup is what you're paying me to do," she said, looking up at him. She stood close, so close he could see her flawless skin and long thick lashes. Her mouth was full, rosy, tempting.

"There is no way this is an ordinary employer-employee relationship. This is different and you know it. You're single. If you weren't recovering from a bad divorce and your loss, I'd want to ask you out," he admitted.

"But I am recovering from both of those things," she said softly, shaking her head. "Thanks for following my wishes. If you didn't, I couldn't stay and work here. It would probably be easier for us both if you didn't help me clean after meals."

"We'll see. I can keep my distance," he said, feeling sweat pop out on his forehead again while his insides knotted. She had as much as admitted that she was as physically attracted as he was, which was not going to help him dredge up resistance.

When they finished putting the dishes away, he turned to her. "Let's go watch the sunset. It can be pretty out here this time of year. We can sit on the screened part of the patio so bugs won't bother us," he said. "Want a drink to take out?"

"No, thank you," she replied, and walked beside him in silence.

He was aware of her at his side, her silky-looking blond hair, her enticing perfume. Frankly, it was all he could do not to groan aloud.

She sat in a chaise lounge and he pulled a chair close, turning to face her. She put her feet up on the chair and his breath caught and held as he glimpsed her long shapely legs before she covered them to midcalf with her skirt.

"It is beautiful out here."

"Yes, it is," he said, his gaze running the length of her. She slanted him a look and he turned to gaze over his yard. "I always enjoy it out here," he said, trying to get back to impersonal topics.

They sat and talked and after an hour he went inside to get her another iced tea and himself a cold beer. The sun sank and then was gone, twilight finally changing to darkness. Pool lights, torches and patio lights came on, soft lighting that still left shadows but highlighted the sparkling blue water, the fountains and the flowers.

They talked as the hours passed and finally she swung her legs off the lounge and stood. "It's late, Ryan. Six a.m. will be here soon."

"It is late. Make it seven in the morning. Neither of us will be up for six o'clock breakfast."

"Sure."

He walked her to her door, where she turned to look up at him. He knew he was too close, but he couldn't resist. "I'm glad you applied for the job and talked me into giving you a chance. You're a fine cook."

"Thanks for the job, Ryan," she said, extending her hand to shake his. The minute his hand closed around hers, he drew a deep breath. Her hand was warm and soft and he didn't want to release her.

"You're all the good things that Pru and Brad said you are," she said. Her words were breathless and he still held her hand.

He shook his head slightly. "I don't really want to have to live up to their recommendations. But I will," he added quickly, releasing her hand to move away from her. "At least, I'll try, Jessica," he said. His gaze lowered to her mouth. He couldn't kiss her, but he wanted to so badly a tremor ran through him. Her lips looked soft, full, inviting.

"Good night, Ryan. Morning will come quickly," she said breathlessly, and stepped into her suite to close the door.

He shook his head and turned away, going back to close up and turn off lights, moving automatically while his pulse raced and he ached with wanting her. Tomorrow was going to be more torment than today, yet he wanted to be with her. He had no intention of avoiding her.

He swore under his breath and headed to his room, knowing sleep would be a while coming tonight. Jessica Upton, his new cook. Beautiful, sexy, seductive—even without trying.

He groaned and raked his fingers through his hair. "Jessica," he whispered. He had never wanted a woman as much as he did her. At the same time, he had never had as much reason to leave one alone. She was on the rebound, on the mend from a terrible loss. She had a wall around her heart, and for sufficient reason. She was the type of woman who would take a relationship seriously, while he would not. He never had and he wouldn't now.

He had made a big mistake moving her into his house, but he just hadn't been able to resist.

"Jessica, I want you," he whispered in the dark.

Four

Three days later she had orange juice poured and bowls of blueberries and strawberries on the table. On the kitchen counter she had choices of cereal because Ryan seemed to prefer cereal and fruit to any other breakfast.

She heard him coming and smoothed the apron she wore around her waist over jeans and a red shirt.

When Ryan stepped into the room, her pulse skipped a beat. His hair was still slightly damp from his shower. He was freshly shaved, neat in a navy polo, jeans and his brown boots. His dark eyes met her gaze and her pulse jumped again.

Each day her responses to him grew. Most of the time Ryan resisted flirting, occasionally slipping for only a moment. He was perfect to work for, helping her to begin to recover from the ordeals she had been through.

She became instantly aware of her appearance, resisting the temptation to catch a wayward tendril of hair that had escaped her ponytail.

"Good morning," he said, walking toward her. "You've got breakfast ready, I see."

"Sort of. Do you want cereal and fruit?"

"That's perfect," he said. "Have you had breakfast?"

She shook her head. "Actually, not yet," she said, knowing she should have come down and eaten earlier.

"Great, join me. I'll pour your orange juice and coffee," he said.

Laughing, she reached to take the bottle of orange juice from his hand. "I think I'm supposed to wait on you, not you on—" The moment her hand closed over his to take the orange juice, heat flashed from the point of contact. He inhaled deeply and turned to look at her, a look that sent another shower of sparks flying.

"I'm working on the ranch today, but tomorrow I have to go into Dallas. We have a Delaney Foundation meeting. You might as well come with me to Dallas and meet my family because they'll be around and you'll hear about them and talk to them on the phone. While I'm in the meeting, you can entertain yourself, which shouldn't be too difficult in Dallas."

"Thanks," she replied, not hiding her eagerness. His quiet ranch suited her for her purposes, but the prospect of getting into Dallas was great after the past few days on his ranch. "I'd love that," she added, and he laughed.

"The ranch and all the quiet getting to you?"

She felt the heat rush to her cheeks in embarrassment. "Maybe a little," she admitted. "But I'm grateful all the time to have this job. It's perfect and the ideal place. I can relax here without worrying about my ex. It was awkward to run into him at parties and he called a lot. Anyway, Dallas sounds like a day of excitement and fun. I'll enjoy meeting your family. They sound so nice."

"They are. The entire bunch—the Delaney brothers and half sister and the spouses. You'll enjoy meeting everyone."

"I'm sure I will," she said, surprised he had asked her to go. Was he just being polite and friendly? She suspected he had not asked any of his staff to go with him before. "Thanks for including me."

"We'll fly back to the ranch late in the afternoon. Unless you want to stay and I'll take you to dinner."

The offer was such a temptation she didn't dare think it over. She had to turn him down instantly.

"Thank you, but I think I should come back here," she said, longing to toss caution aside, accept his invitation and have a wonderful evening with a sexy, exciting man.

Instead, her refusal was already spoken and now she had to live with it.

"Home it is," he said.

A date with Ryan. Dancing. She had to avoid thinking of what could have been.

Disappointment hit her like a brick to the heart.

The next morning eagerness to go to Dallas made her wake early. She dressed in the light blue cotton suit she had worn when she had come for an interview with Ryan.

She finally left her suite to meet him and found him waiting in his study. The minute she walked into the room, he stood, his gaze drifting over her with a warmth that made her tingle. Adding to her response, his appearance set her heart racing. In a dark suit, white shirt and charcoal tie, he looked more handsome than ever. He wore a fancy pair of black boots and his hair was neatly combed, although he already had wayward locks that had sprung free just above his forehead.

"You look great," he said in a husky voice.

"You look rather good yourself," she couldn't resist saying. "I'm looking forward to today."

"So am I."

"Let's go," he said, taking her arm, heightening her awareness of him.

In less than an hour they were airborne in his plush jet. She looked at the wide stretches of ranch land spread below, the feathery mesquite bent by the prevailing south winds. The occasional arroyo slashed the earth, or a dry winding creek bed cut through the endless land.

"I talked to my mother this morning and texted my sister and my friend. My mom wants me to come home. My sister and my friend are happy I've found a place and a job I like. My mom doesn't know specifically where I am, but she knows she can get in touch with me on my cell or through my sister. I don't want my parents to worry about me, but I also don't want them trying to talk me into returning home."

"You can say no to them, can't you?"

"Oh, yes, but my dad doesn't give up easily and what's worse, they will tell my ex and then he'll appear. They really like him and my mother thinks I should overlook his infidelities. I have no intention of doing any such thing. We said vows that meant something to me, even if they meant nothing to him."

Ryan gazed at her, but she was unable to read his expression. "You're saying nothing. Does that mean you agree with them?"

"Not at all. Far from it. I agree with you. You said vows that you promised to follow. No, I was just trying to imagine why they would want you with someone like that. And wondering why your ex had affairs if he had you to come home to."

She smiled at him and shrugged. "I wasn't enough for him, I guess. I don't think he really wanted to be married, but he did it because it was the thing to do. I was the right kind of wife until I walked out."

"If he ever shows up at the ranch, just let me talk to him."

"I can't imagine he will come to your ranch."

Ryan reached out and squeezed her hand. "Good. Now let's talk about something more pleasant. We're meeting my family for lunch and then you'll be on your own this afternoon. I'm having a limo meet us at the airport and you can have use of it all afternoon to shop wherever you want. I'll call when I'm finished with the meeting."

She smiled. "I can't wait to go shopping. By the way, does your family know I'm your cook?"

"Sure. That's no secret."

"How many cooks have you taken to meet them?"

"None. You're the exception in every way."

She tilted her head to study him as he gazed at her in silence. How she wished she could read his thoughts.

Finally, he clamped his jaw closed and looked away.

They spent the rest of the flight talking, until they landed in Dallas and moved to a black limo that whisked them to a country club.

As they entered a room with a large round table set for lunch, she recognized his family members from their pictures. The first man she noticed had to be a Delaney. Tall, with dark brown eyes and thick wavy black hair, he had a facial structure that bore an uncanny resemblance to Ryan's. He was with a beautiful sandy-haired blonde with gorgeous green eyes. She looked younger than him and welcoming, with an easy smile.

Ryan made the introductions. "Jessica, this is my brother Will. Will, meet Jessica Upton."

"I'm Ryan's new cook," she said, smiling as she shook

hands with Will. "I've heard all about you and I'm so happy to meet you," Jessica said.

"Happy to meet you, too, and glad you joined us for lunch," Will replied.

"I've heard about Caroline and Adam," Jessica said to them. She looked at Ava. "Any chance you have pictures?"

"Of course," Ava said, smiling and glancing at Will, who nodded. "We both do," he said with a laugh. "I'll let Ava show hers."

Ava pulled out her phone and held it so Jessica and Ryan could see a picture. Jessica felt a pang as she looked at a beautiful little black-haired girl who was smiling and holding a fuzzy white dog. For an instant she remembered her own loss and how it had hurt. "So this is Caroline. She's so pretty. Ryan said she's a little doll and he's right." Jessica's insides knotted and she had a lump in her throat. She fought the emotion. She had thought she was over all the uncontrollable tears and hurt.

"Show her Adam," Ryan said, slipping his arm casually across Jessica's shoulders.

Ava flicked the pictures and then she held out a photo of a smiling little boy with dark eyes and dark brown hair.

Getting her emotions under control, Jessica looked at the picture intently. "He's so cute."

"We think so," Ava replied happily.

Ryan dropped his arm and stepped away, saying something to Will, the two of them talking about business briefly.

"I know you have a wonderful time with them," Jessica said as Ava put away her phone.

Ryan turned to take her arm. "Y'all excuse us, please. I want to introduce Jessica to Zach and Emma. We'll see you later. Let's go meet the wanderer who likes to demolish buildings." He chuckled. "Who's all demolished now by Emma."

"Sorry if I was a little emotional with them. Sometimes it hits me about losing my baby and I'm still having difficulty accepting the loss."

"Don't worry about it. No one noticed and if they did, they would understand. That's a loss that will always be with you. Also, just remember the doctor told you that you can have more."

"If he's your brother, no one would know it. He doesn't look like you in the least," she said, looking at Zach's thick curly hair and his vivid blue eyes as they approached him. A slender redhead stood beside him. His arm was across her shoulders and Jessica assumed that was Emma Delaney, his wife.

"No, we don't look alike. The older family members all say that Zach looks like one of our grandfathers. I still am shocked by the changes in his life. Changes none of us thought he would make until he was much older. Zach is home nights now, works in an office and has made a total change in his lifestyle. That's what marriage does to a guy."

She laughed. "You sound quite against marriage."

"Nope. It just changes things. For Zach it meant monumental changes. Not so much for Will. And Garrett—he's Sophia's husband—he's changed, too. Almost as much as Zach. Garrett has switched careers. He was our financial advisor but now he makes furniture. I guess the women have changed, too. Ava's a mother of two. Emma has a baby girl now. Sophia is wrapped up in her art and she's good at it. When I get around them, I'm heartily

glad I'm still single, because they're all loaded with responsibilities."

"So says the man who runs a big company and a
ranch."

They stopped in front of a couple and Ryan greeted
them, brushing a kiss on his sister-in-law's cheek. He
made introductions: "Emma, Zach, meet my new employee, Jessica Upton. Jessica, my sister-in-law, Emma,
and my brother Zach."

Jessica smiled and greeted both but was amazed that
she faced one of Ryan's siblings, because she could not
see any resemblance.

They stood talking and finally Ryan took her arm
lightly. "Excuse us while I introduce Jessica to Sophia
and Garrett."

They moved on and Jessica glanced up at Ryan.

"You have a nice family."

Before Ryan could reply, a couple approached them.
Ryan shook hands with the man and kissed the woman.

"Sophia, I want you to meet Jessica Upton," Ryan
said. A striking black-haired woman turned brown eyes
on Jessica. Sophia wore her hair swept up on one side of
her head with a large white rose pinned in it. Her blue
dress had a low rounded neck and Jessica thought she
was a stunningly beautiful woman.

"I'm so happy to meet you," Sophia said, smiling at
Jessica. "This is my husband, Garrett Cantrell," she said,
turning to a tall ruggedly handsome man with gray eyes
and a friendly smile.

Garrett offered his hand. "I'm glad to meet you. I hear
you're from Tennessee, which is such a beautiful place."

"I think it is," Jessica replied. She talked to Garrett
about some time he'd spent in Tennessee on a summer vacation until finally it was time for lunch. She was seated

between Ryan and Emma Delaney. All of the Delaneys were friendly, as were their spouses, and she enjoyed getting to know them.

When lunch was over, they each told her goodbye but promised they would see her again, and finally Ryan walked out to the limo with her.

"I have a list where I will go. Pru has told me the best places to shop."

"I'll call you when we're out. We can eat here before we fly back so you won't have to cook tonight," he said, smiling at her. "Sure you don't want to go dancing while you're in the big city?"

"Not this time," she said, glancing around at cars passing in the parking lot and people going in and out of the sprawling clubhouse. "We'll do that another time," she said, putting him off.

"Think it over. See you later," he said, stepping back while the driver held open the limo door and she climbed inside.

As they drove away, she watched Ryan disappear back inside the club. She was still astounded by her physical reactions to him. She had thought she was completely numb where men were concerned, but with Ryan she definitely wasn't. Cooking for him, living beneath the same roof, sharing conversations with him, now meeting his family—all were moments that wove a stronger bond between them. She would have to guard her heart around him. Because she was so emotionally vulnerable right now, she didn't trust her judgment yet at all.

All she knew for certain right now was that it was going to be next to impossible to keep from falling in love with Ryan.

She had to start avoiding him more. That was her only hope.

* * *

So much for avoiding Ryan more, she thought after dinner and the flight back. It was after ten when they finally reached the ranch and he helped carry her purchases to her suite. Ryan had shed his coat and tie, rolled up his sleeves and unbuttoned the first three buttons of his shirt. He looked sexy and appealing, already testing her decision to remain aloof.

"I don't think I need to worry that you didn't have enough cash or didn't find something to buy. Looks like you bought out Dallas."

"It's not that bad. I've been limited in what I have to wear," she said.

"You look good in anything," he said, standing a few feet away from her with his hands jammed into his pockets. They stood in her bedroom and with the last statement the air became charged and she could feel the sparks dance between them. For a moment his gaze lowered to her mouth and she couldn't get her breath.

"Night, Jessica," he said, turning and leaving abruptly.

Inhaling deeply, she trailed after him to close the door to her suite.

She had to avoid him more. She had almost expected him to kiss her and she had wanted him to. She rubbed her temples with both hands and shook her head. She couldn't fall in love with Ryan. That would only compound her problems. And an affair was the last thing that she should get involved in at this point in her life. She had come here to recuperate, not to complicate her life further.

She was still telling herself that when she got up extra early the next morning so she could eat breakfast before Ryan came down.

He showed up at seven. She heard his whistling in the hall before he entered the kitchen. In jeans and a navy knit shirt, he exuded energy and cheer and the whole place seemed to brighten the moment he walked in.

"Good morning. Ah, new duds, right? I like your selections," he said, glancing over her jeans and cotton shirt. She had on the new clothes she'd bought in Dallas and had her hair in a braid that was tied with a red ribbon.

She liked his, too, but she was not going to tell him. She intended to remain impersonal and professional. "I have strawberries, blackberries, blueberries, kiwi and slices of mango. There is oatmeal and I have cheese grits."

"I'll have it all," he said, helping himself. "Sounds good. Come eat with me."

"Thank you, but I ate earlier." She turned away to set dishes in the dishwasher, so she didn't see if he had any reaction to her announcement.

"After I finish breakfast, we'll go into town to get groceries. Okay?"

"Yes, that's fine," she said without looking around. A tiny kernel of disappointment disturbed her. He hadn't seemed to have cared that she didn't eat with him. She should be glad instead of disappointed, she told herself.

She worked in the kitchen while he sat in the breakfast area reading the thick Dallas paper as he ate. When he finished, he brought his dishes to the sink to rinse. "How soon can you be ready to go?"

"About five minutes," she replied, and he smiled.

"Great. We'll go then. I'll bring my truck around."

She finished quickly and ran to her suite to get her purse. When she stepped outside, he was waiting in a shiny black pickup. She climbed in beside him and they set off toward the county highway.

"When I go to town on my own next week, should I drive my own car?" she asked him, keeping conversation work related.

"No. We have a van in the garage you can take. It will hold everything you'll need. Have you ever lived in the country or a small town?"

"Not until now."

"It's different in a lot of ways and your grocery shopping will be different."

She twisted in the seat to watch him drive. "How so?"

"The store is a social gathering place as well as a grocery. You'll meet a lot of locals."

"Sounds like fun. So far, I've liked all the locals I've met." He glanced at her and she smiled at him.

When they pulled into Bywater, Jessica felt she had gone back in time. Mulberry trees lined the sidewalks, and wood-frame houses with front porches were scattered along the wide main street. Flowers and tall yucca bloomed in front beds by porches, and an occasional baby swing hung from a tree limb. Children rode bicycles along the sidewalks with dogs trotting after them.

"There's the Bywater Hotel. It was built in 1910 and it hasn't had a whole lot of improvement since that time. Rustic is the best way to describe it," Ryan told her as they got farther along the main street.

In the next two blocks, they passed a hardware store, a dress shop, an ice-cream parlor, a restaurant and a gas station on a corner. Across the street on the corner was the grocery store, with pop machines in front along with a newspaper stand and a long bench. The door stood open, with a screen door to keep out flies. Inside, Ryan got a small cart. "Go ahead. I'll follow."

"Morning, Ryan," a woman said. "What are you doing at the grocery on Saturday morning?"

"Morning, Grace. This is my new cook, Jessica Upton. Jessica, this is Grace Parker."

By the tenth person she met, Jessica gave up trying to remember each name. Some greeted her and moved on. Most stopped to talk to her and she suspected it would be noon before they finished in the grocery. Once, she looked around and saw Ryan talking to a cluster of men.

Ryan was the tallest, easy to spot because of his height. His gaze met hers and even in the busy grocery with people and goods between them, she felt a current that held her. For an instant she was shut away in a world of their own. With an effort she turned away, moving down an aisle and checking her list.

Later, after he was back beside her, someone called Ryan's name and he turned, catching her wrist. "Meet my friends Molly and Jas Cooley. I've known both of them too long. And this is little Benny Cooley, the newest addition."

"What gorgeous big brown eyes," Jessica said, looking at Benny in his mother's arms and unable to keep from feeling another pang of longing for the baby she'd lost. "You must have a wonderful time with him."

"We do—until two a.m.," Jas said, grinning at his son. "Then he's not quite as cute as the rest of the time."

"Give us a break," Ryan teased. "At two in the morning it's Molly who's up with him. An atomic blast wouldn't wake you."

They all laughed, and Jessica realized she had come to the perfect place for a job. People were friendly, and there was little chance of seeing anyone from home or hearing from her ex. Ryan was being incredibly kind and attentive yet trying to remain professional to a degree. She was already sleeping better, feeling better about her future—even thinking about it.

As they moved away, she ran back over her grocery list. "Only a few more things. Your friends were nice and their baby is adorable."

Ryan put his arm lightly across her shoulders as she looked at a shelf of bags of beans. "You'll marry again someday and you'll have another baby. I know there will always be a place in your heart for the one you lost, but there will be more to love, Jessica."

"I hope so," she whispered, aware of her racing heartbeat, of Ryan standing so close, his arm across her shoulders, aware of the gentle note in his voice. "Right now marriage seems like an impossible thing. I don't know how long it'll be before I'll trust my own judgment again. I made a huge mistake the first time."

"Forget it and go on. You won't make a mistake the second time."

She shook her head. She didn't care to argue the point, but she doubted she'd ever have the certainty that Ryan expressed.

It was another hour before they finished and left.

"C'mon. There is a pretty good hamburger place here—not as good as yours but above average. I'll buy you a burger at the café and you can meet more locals."

She laughed. "This town is tiny, but people keep appearing as if it's ten times larger."

"It's Saturday. They come from all around here. They shop, see each other, eat in town, get supplies. Tomorrow is church and another big wave of people will fill the church for three services. Then Monday the place will be quiet and almost empty."

He held the screen door to the small café where red-and-white plastic covered the tables. As they ate thick juicy burgers, Ryan sipped his ice water and then set down the glass. "Roy, the gray-haired fellow I introduced you to, is having a cookout tonight at his place. It's casual and friendly. Want to go? Might do you good to get out and have some fun."

He asked casually, but Jessica knew she should still say no. She worried about spending the evening at any kind of party with Ryan. That would just compound the bond growing between them. But to get out and go to a party, even just a cookout… The invitation dangled like a fantastic gift. To let go and have fun for just a little while was an enormous temptation. The word *no* wouldn't come. She looked into his dark brown eyes and wanted to go more than anything else.

"I know I shouldn't, but I just can't tell you no. It's been so long since I've gone out, and I've never gone to a barn dance or a ranch cookout. Thank you," she said so softly she doubted if he heard her.

"Good. How's seven? The shindig starts earlier than that, but we don't need to go rushing over there at five when it's hot out and the sun is still blazing."

"Seven is fine," she whispered. She shouldn't even have thought about accepting. Instead, she was making plans with him and already planning what she would wear. She was thankful for the clothes she had purchased yesterday. She'd blown some of her savings on clothes, but she planned to make the money back in her job as cook at the RD Ranch.

She was going to a party with music and friendly people. She was going with Ryan. Eagerness gripped her and she couldn't keep from smiling.

All the rest of the drive back to the ranch, they talked about people she had met. Ryan helped her to try to remember them, telling her anecdotes about most of them.

Once at the ranch, he helped her shelve the groceries until she shooed him away. She knew he had things to work on and was meeting Jeb. Some things, he didn't seem to know where they should go and she took them, already getting accustomed to the kitchen and the pantry.

As the afternoon passed, her eagerness grew. Finally, she showered and dried her hair, dressing in another new pair of tight jeans and a bright red cotton top and new Western boots. She brushed out her hair, wore dangling Native American earrings she had bought during her shopping trip.

Excitement bubbled, her anticipation growing by the minute as she picked up a flat pocket purse and left to go to the study to meet Ryan.

He stood in his study with his back to the door, and her gaze ran over his broad shoulders and down to his Western boots. Tight jeans hugged his slim hips and his blue plaid Western shirt was tucked into his jeans with a wide hand-tooled leather belt circling his narrow waist. He looked fabulous. Sexy and seductive. Tonight, she told herself, she would just try to forget the past and enjoy the moment.

How could she not with this man at her side?

Five

Ryan smiled at her while his heart thudded. In tight washed jeans, a red cotton Western shirt that clung to full curves, and black boots, Jessica made his temperature climb. He was taking her to a barn dance and cookout, an evening of fun, and he had to keep his distance, resist flirting and handle her with the greatest of care.

Who was he kidding? He couldn't handle her at all. He had to back off now. But how could he when it made him hot just to look at her? Had he made a colossal mistake in inviting her to the cookout?

"Wow," he said quietly, walking toward her. "You look absolutely great."

"Thank you," she said, her smile widening until her dimple showed. His gaze lowered to her full lips and the temperature in the room became suffocating. How could he avoid thinking about luscious, soft lips and hot, wet kisses?

Lassoing his libido, he forced himself to focus. "Let's go join the party. The food should be super, although not as good as your cooking."

She laughed as he took her arm and they headed out

the back door. "My cooking, I hope, is a bit above ordinary, but it's not the greatest yet. I expect to get better with practice," she said as she walked beside him to the truck. He leaned slightly closer, inhaling her scent. She smelled enticing, a fragrance that made him want to keep her at his side all evening.

As he helped her into the truck, he looked at her shining hair and could imagine winding his fingers in it. Instead of being fun, the evening might be pure hell as he struggled to keep his hands to himself.

"Ryan, this is a whole new world for me. I've never known cowboys and been to Texas. I'm excited about tonight. It's difficult to remember you're a businessman and not a rancher all the time."

"This is what I love. I love the ranch more than anything else. I hope to retire from the business in Houston early and just be a rancher."

"Why not retire now if you love the ranch that much? You can afford to."

"I have some things to prove to myself and to my brothers. They've succeeded in the business world and I think I should. I want that company bigger before I step down. I've already expanded it from only a drilling company. Now we are exploring and have natural-gas wells. I want a well-rounded energy company. I want to know that I can do it. I know I can do the ranching."

"I suppose most of us set our own challenges," she said, looking out the window, and he realized the conversation was taking too serious a turn for her.

He caught her hand in his and changed the subject. "You'll like the dinner. They'll have all sorts of food to eat because people will bring their specialties to add to the dinner."

"Should we be bringing something?"

"I got beer and wine today when we were in the store and they loaded it into Roy's truck. I got enough for a gift from both of us."

"I could have cooked something."

"Oh, no. We're not letting everyone know what a cook you are just yet. They'll all be hovering trying to hire you away from me."

She laughed. "I think you exaggerate, but okay."

She hadn't taken her hand out of his. He shouldn't have been holding her hand, but she was warm and soft. He liked the contact, liked having her close beside him, liked knowing she would let him hold her hand. This was not the woman for him to be drawn to, but he was and had been from the first moment he saw her step out of her car. He didn't care about dinner or the party; he just wanted one dance with Jessica tonight. Whether he should or he shouldn't didn't matter. One dance couldn't hurt anything.

Jessica spent the first hour just meeting people or talking to some she remembered from the grocery store. Children had been invited and there were pony rides and games for all ages. People were as friendly as they were in Tennessee. The accent was different, but the warm smiles were the same.

Ryan stayed at her side, constantly introducing her, sometimes draping his arm casually across her shoulders. Some very beautiful women stopped to talk to him and she was aware of some curious looks from them. It was obvious he had known some of them well and whatever relationship they'd had, they had stayed friends, which didn't surprise her. Ryan was so laid-back and easygoing she couldn't imagine him having a serious commitment and she needed to remember that.

They saw Molly and Jas with Benny and within minutes they'd talked Jessica into joining Molly in the women's three-legged race.

"If we count the beat and walk in time, maybe we can keep in step," Molly suggested.

Laughing, feeling silly yet ready for the fun, Jessica agreed.

Someone shouted "Go" and they were off, laughing together as both tried to count and keep in step. To her surprise, they crossed the finish line seconds ahead of the next two. Molly lost her balance and they both went down laughing.

Ryan gave her a hand to pull her to her feet while he congratulated them.

The next game, she played an egg toss with Ryan that they lost when they were down to only three couples.

Afterward they walked away from the games. "You and Molly did that race like pros," Ryan told her. "She's a runner—or she was until Benny was born."

"I didn't know. I was running nearly every day, too, until I got pregnant and for a long time afterward. I picked it up again about four months ago, so maybe that's why we were good together." She fanned her neck with her hand. "This has been fun."

"I'm glad. I hope you worked up an appetite. You barely eat."

"I'll eat. It all smells wonderful." But Ryan was more enticing than the food. As she glanced at him, he turned to meet her gaze and an electrical charge crackled in the air. From the way he inhaled and his eyes darkened, she suspected the look they had just shared had affected him, too.

Ryan grabbed her hand and took her over to the cooking area. The smell of the cooking meat was mouthwatering and she was interested in seeing all the open pits and turning spits with slabs of meat or whole chickens. There were grills with men frying fish and tables lined with covered dishes.

When a dinner bell rang, lines formed at the long row of tables with a delectable-looking array of food.

She couldn't begin to try everything and selected a corn casserole, grilled asparagus, some steaming baked beans, grilled bass and jalapeño corn bread. She tried a tiny bowl of chili. After a thin slice of coconut cream pie, they left the picnic area. The sun had set and lights and torches burned. Games were still being played, but Ryan took her hand and headed toward the barn, from which they heard music from fiddles while someone called square dances.

"Know how to square-dance?" he asked.

"No, but I have a feeling I'm going to learn."

"That's right. Just follow me and do what they say. You'll catch on."

The barn was filled with huge fans stirring the air. While fiddlers tapped their feet and played, one man called out the dance steps. Couples danced and a big group circled the dirt floor, dancing around the barn while spectators watched from the lofts and lines formed at the soft-drink chests and the lemonade and tea fountains.

"Let's join them," Ryan said, taking her hand and pulling her with him into the circle to dance with the others. In seconds she was dancing around the barn, aware constantly of the tall cowboy at her side. She found it impossible to think of Ryan any other way except as a cowboy. Sometimes she remembered his status in the business world, his billion-dollar wealth, the power and influence he must have, but seeing him here, in his element, she forgot the other part of his life.

As she held hands with two men she didn't know and they circled the dance area, she couldn't keep from smiling. It was fun to dance, play games and turn loose of fears and responsibilities for a while. She had gotten separated from Ryan and she glanced over her shoulder at him to find him watching her. Once again they could have been shut away from the world. She felt the sparks and wondered why she had found this with him. It could lead nowhere, because this wasn't the time in her life for a love interest and this Texas cowboy wasn't the man, because someday she definitely would go home to Tennessee. She reversed directions, following the caller's instructions, and gave herself over to the thrill of the dance.

It was one in the morning when she finally told Ryan she was ready to go home. They told people goodbye, said their thanks and soon were in his truck on the way back to his ranch.

"That was so much fun tonight. Thank you for asking me. I had a wonderful time. Also, I'll never forget all the delicious food. I wish I could get that chili recipe."

"I don't know. There were about eight people who brought chili. I'll ask and see what I can find out. You could get recipes from all of them and try them. I'm glad you enjoyed yourself. I did, too."

"Now I know how to square-dance. What fun it was."

When they reached the ranch and walked inside, he turned to face her. "Let's sit outside and talk for a while.

You can sleep later in the morning. You don't need to cook on Sundays. I'll manage."

"I don't mind cooking on Sunday. I don't have any reason to take it off," she said, thinking about his invitation to sit and talk. She constantly was torn between being with him and doing the sensible thing, going on her way. It was always too enticing a prospect to spend more time with him. "I'd like to go to church in the morning, like I usually do at home. But then I'll be ready to cook."

They got drinks and sat on the patio. It was a cool evening and once again the garden lights showed off the fountains and the waterfall in the pool.

"It's an oasis out here," she breathed.

"I think so."

"You should come see Tennessee. I think it's so beautiful and the flowers are gorgeous in the spring."

"I've seen Tennessee and it is pretty. So are the ladies who live there."

She smiled at him. "Thank you, Ryan. So where's the woman in your life? I've been waiting for her to show up. I know a lot of ladies talked to you tonight."

"She hasn't shown up, I guess. There's never been any one special person for a long, meaningful relationship. Just lots of friends I have fun with."

"You don't take life or relationships too seriously, do you?"

"Life is a blast. No, I guess I don't take some things seriously, but there are a few I do. My family is important to me. As for relationships—I'm not into long-term or serious relations. Don't worry about that."

She nodded. "Tell me about the rodeos. I haven't ever been to one. What do you do?" she asked, trying to get away from being so personal.

They talked until she realized it was after three in the morning. "Ryan, I have to go in."

He stood and walked with her, switching off lights and locking the house. In the kitchen she turned to face him. Only a small light burned, which created a coziness that seemed more intimate. His prominent cheekbones were highlighted and a lock of his hair fell on his forehead. But it was his brown eyes that caught her attention and made her heart beat faster, because there was no mistaking the look in his eyes. Desire was blatant and she could barely get her breath.

When his gaze lowered to her mouth, her lips parted. He stepped closer. She should stop him, say something, move away. Instead, she was held by the expression in his eyes. She wanted his kiss as much as he wanted hers.

One kiss should not be devastating. One simple kiss wouldn't be more than what they had already done— gone to the party together, gone to town together, gone to his family's lunch before the Delaney Foundation meeting. They had been crossing the line constantly from the first and it hadn't been life changing. They were not in love, not seeking a relationship, not involved except as employer and employee. It would be just a simple goodnight kiss, something she hadn't had in over a year. What harm could that be?

Ryan stepped close and placed his hands lightly on her shoulders. "Tonight was a super night."

"It was for me, too. Thank you." Ryan held her shoulders lightly, rubbing them slowly, his hands barely touching her, yet she tingled from his touch. Her gaze lowered to his mouth. "Ryan, we shouldn't—"

"It's meaningless," he whispered. "Just a kiss after an entertaining evening together. A light, friendly kiss that ends the evening. You won't melt or fall in love and I won't either, but this is the icing on the cake for tonight and something I've wanted to do since you stepped out of your red car." One arm slipped around her waist and his focus was on her mouth.

While her heart drummed, he leaned down, his mouth covering hers. Her heart slammed against her ribs. His tongue went deep and her tongue played over his. She felt hot, light-headed, falling in a dizzying spiral. She wanted to lean away and tell him that he had been wrong. It was more than just a "friendly kiss," more than the "icing on the cake." It was the most fantastic kiss ever.

Never in her life had a kiss been like this. Her toes curled, her body heated and her heart pounded. She had been wildly in love when she had married, but kisses then had never been like this. Not once. As long as she lived, she would remember Ryan Delaney's kiss. All they had done together—the socializing, the dancing, the eating together, the games, the grocery shopping—all of it could be forgotten. But not this kiss. His kiss changed everything.

One kiss became many until she realized how long they'd been standing there. She was on fire with longing, a physical need that made her tremble.

Trying to catch her breath, she stepped away from him. His eyes were dark as midnight, intense with desire. His hand was still on her waist and his fingers tightened as he started to draw her back to him until she shook her head and moved farther away.

"Ryan, no more kisses," she whispered, staring at him. Why did his kisses make such a difference? They barely knew each other, so it wasn't because she loved him. His kisses were hot, filled with passion that melted her and set her ablaze with need. She ached right now, wanting him, wanting to kiss all night, to walk right back into his embrace.

"Good night, Ryan," she said breathlessly, and turned, blindly heading into the hall and hurrying to her suite to close the door and gasp for breath as if she had run a mile to get to her rooms.

Tomorrow she wouldn't cook for him. She'd avoid him for the day and get her emotions under control. Was she so terribly vulnerable that his kisses had set her on fire? Maybe his kisses had seemed so hot and sexy because she hadn't kissed anyone in over a year and for a long time, kisses had not been great with Carlton. No, his kisses had never been like this.

There was no reasoning away her intense reaction to Ryan. His kisses were unforgettable, the most seductive ever. She needed distance between Ryan and herself. With kisses like that, she would soon be in his bed and she would never be able to separate a physical relationship from an emotional relationship.

Was she going to have to quit this job that seemed so perfect in every other way? The isolated ranch, the friendly people, Ryan himself—all had been more than she had hoped to find. A job doing something she liked to do where she could relax and not be pulled in all directions by Carlton and her family. All changed because of a few kisses that Ryan had said would be meaningless.

Had they been meaningless to him? He hadn't looked as if they had been. He had looked as shocked as she had felt, which compounded the problem. If she had had the effect on him that he'd had on her, then it was mutual, something unique they had found only with each other, and that made kissing Ryan incredibly special.

She rubbed her temples, wishing she could take back the kisses, turn the evening back to the way it had been until that moment. Fun, a little sexy, exciting, tempting, but nothing earthshaking.

She doubted if she would sleep tonight.

Lost in her thoughts, she got ready for bed, switched off the lights and lay in the darkness thinking about Ryan and the sexiest kisses she had ever known.

Sunday morning she rose early to shower and dress in a T-shirt and jeans. She hurried to eat breakfast and then returned to her room, where she changed for church. She took the van, driving carefully, wondering if he would stop her or call her to see what she was doing and where she was going.

She wore a new white linen suit and pale yellow blouse she'd bought in Dallas. She had pale yellow high-heeled pumps. Going for a more sophisticated look, she'd put her hair up in a roll on the back of her head.

She was halfway to town when she noticed a car coming up behind her. As it got closer, it looked like Ryan's black sports car. Why would he be following her into town? He wasn't flagging her over, so she stopped glancing at it until they drove into town. Her curiosity grew. Maybe he hadn't intended for her to take the van except to go for groceries on Saturday. When she parked in the church parking lot, he pulled up beside her and climbed out.

She stepped out and her heart missed a few beats as she looked at him. Wind caught locks of his black hair, blowing them slightly. The businessman was back instead of the cowboy because he wore his charcoal suit with a white dress shirt. The French cuffs were fastened by gold cuff links. He had a red tie and his fancy black boots. She waited as he came around his car to her and she hoped when he was close, he could not hear her pounding heart.

"I don't think you're here because you want to go to church with me," she said. "Did you not want me to take the van except for groceries?"

"I don't care when you take the van. I'm here to go to church with you and whatever else you do."

"That's nice, but why? You don't need to accompany me."

"Except for at the grocery, if you start appearing in town alone, without me, you're going to have guys in the next six counties asking you out. Word will get around that the gorgeous blonde who works on the RD Ranch is divorced. If I'm at your side, they'll all stay away and lose interest because they're not taking someone else's woman, to put it plainly. If you want to maintain your quiet lifestyle at the ranch, you should keep me at your side when you're out in the local scene. In Dallas it doesn't matter. Here it does. Now, want me to go to church with you?"

"Yes, thank you. You know the people around here. It's difficult for me to imagine that I would stir that much interest or notice, but you know better."

"I sure as hell do. As gorgeous as you look, I'll bet money every cowboy in West Texas will know about you."

"Maybe I better go back to the ranch."

"Nope. Just let me take your arm so it looks as if you belong with me."

"Sure, Ryan," she said, smiling up at him as he placed her arm inside his and he held her hand. "This seems a little old-fashioned."

"It sure as hell is. Around here some things don't change much." His eyes swept her from head to toe and when they met hers, she noticed a look of approval. "Did you buy that suit in Dallas?"

"Yes, I did."

"It's gorgeous." His smile could light the nearby church on a dark night. "I'm glad I heard you drive the van away. Shall we go?"

As she climbed the steps beside him, she was aware of her arm linked with his. After the service they talked to what seemed like everyone who'd attended church. Finally, they stood by their cars.

"We can drive back to the ranch, eat in town or I can get the plane and we can fly into Dallas."

"Goodness, no. We don't need to eat in Dallas. Let's just go back to the ranch. I have religion now and I've talked to what seemed like five hundred people."

He laughed. "It wasn't that many. Ride back with me and I'll have one of the guys get the van. Someone will be going to church tonight and can pick it up. I told the secretary we're leaving it in the lot until then. They know my cars and wouldn't have paid any attention anyway."

"Thanks for joining me," she said, glancing up at him and thinking about their kisses the night before. How long before she could see him without thinking about his kisses?

As he sped back to the ranch, she looked at the countryside.

"I'll be going to Houston this week and will probably be home Saturday," he said. "I need to check on some things."

"Ryan, stop. I saw something back there."

He glanced in the rearview mirror as he slowed and

backed up. No cars were in sight for miles in either direction. "I don't see—" He stopped and adjusted the mirror. "Yes, I see a dog lying on the side of the road."

"It might have been hit. I want to find out why it won't get up."

"Let me go see. If it's hurt, it might bite." He backed up and stopped yards away to pull off the road. "I don't want to get closer, because it might scare him."

She climbed out when Ryan did. "I want to come with you," she said. "I'll be careful."

He walked slowly, talking softly. A large shaggy brown-and-white dog lay in the grass and thumped its tail as Ryan approached.

"Oh, damn," he said quietly, slowing.

"What? Ryan, there are puppies."

"Someone probably dumped them. Dammit. People leave dogs in the country, figuring someone will give them a home. We've got about ten dogs at the ranch now. I'll call the sheriff," he said, getting out his cell phone.

"Ryan, those are babies," she said. "We have to take them. Take the dog food cost out of my salary. Don't call the sheriff. I'll find homes for them somewhere."

Ryan laughed. "You can't find any home except the RD Ranch. The sheriff will take them to the vet, who will find homes for them."

"And if he doesn't? No, you let me take them. They can stay in the barn and I'll take care of them and feed them and pay for them and take them with me when I go."

"Jessica, with your looks and your red car, if you leave with—" he paused to look at the mother dog and her pups "—six dogs, you'll stand out like a circus parade."

"Ryan, these are babies," she said, petting the mother dog, who wagged her tail. "I'm not abandoning them."

Jessica yanked off her suit jacket and turned it, tying the ends of the sleeves. She handed two puppies to Ryan and then began placing the remainder in her jacket.

"Jessica, you'll ruin that white jacket. Take my suit coat," he said, juggling puppies while peeling off his jacket to hold it out.

"Of course not. I'm fine. I can get my suit cleaned. You might have to wear yours to work Monday. Carry the pups. C'mon," she said, whistling to the mother dog. She headed toward Ryan's car and glanced back to see him standing, watching her. He shook his head and followed.

She set the pups on the floor of the backseat and the mother jumped in to lie down with them.

Ryan placed his pups in with the others and in minutes they were headed toward the ranch. "Did you do this at home in Memphis?"

"Take in strays? Only a couple of times that I couldn't find a home. We had two dogs and when I divorced, my sister took them in. Sort of temporarily. I'll get them back someday, maybe, except I think her family will get so attached they'll keep them. One is a sweet little beagle and the other is a sheltie mix."

"Maybe I better do the grocery shopping. A lot of dogs are dropped off in the country."

She laughed. "You really wouldn't pass them and leave them abandoned or you wouldn't have so many at the ranch. I'll get the groceries."

"I'll ask the guys. I'm sure some of them will watch the mother dog and her pups."

"Thank you, Ryan," she said, smiling broadly at him, watching him take a deep breath and exhale.

When they turned in the drive to the ranch house, Ryan called Jeb and told him about the dogs. As soon as he finished, he glanced at her. "Don't worry about the dogs. Jeb and some guys will come get them and they'll take care of them. You don't have to."

"Thank you," she said, giving him another big smile. "That's so nice of you." She hugged his neck and released him swiftly. Once again he inhaled deeply and let out his breath. A muscle worked in his jaw and she didn't know whether he was angry, but at least he was seeing that the dogs had care and a home.

"You're a nice guy, Ryan," she said quietly, thinking he was. "If there is a vet in town, I'll pay to have shots and whatever else we need to do for the dogs when the time comes."

"You won't need to. I routinely have all our ranch animals taken care of and we'll just have them looked at with the others."

"You've had a complete turnaround about the dogs."

"I just know when I've lost a battle."

She laughed and squeezed his wrist affectionately. He was nice and if he kept up being so great, she would fall in love with him. She hadn't thought there was any possible danger of that when she had accepted the job, but now she knew better. Ryan was wonderful in too many ways.

She unbuckled her seat belt to turn and check on the dogs. She sat back and buckled again. "They're fine. This is so good. Thanks for all you've done today."

"Oh, sure. What are six more dogs at the ranch?"

When they arrived, Jeb waited along with three more cowboys. They all took puppies and Jeb gave a treat to the mother dog, who happily followed them as they headed toward the barn.

"Now your dogs have a good home."

"Will someone check on the pups? If not, I can."

"Someone will check on all of them, mother and pups. You can forget all about them because they will be fine now."

"Thank you," she said, and he nodded.

For the rest of the day, she saw little of Ryan, except for when he stopped in briefly for lunch, and she stayed in her suite a lot of the time to unpack and contact her sister and Olivia. She ate an early light dinner of greens, frozen shrimp and an apple and then returned to her suite.

The next morning she had already eaten breakfast when Ryan appeared. If he had noticed she was avoiding socializing with him, he said nothing. Wearing navy slacks and a white dress shirt, he looked dressed for an office and she guessed he would fly to Houston shortly after breakfast.

As she put dishes away after Ryan had eaten, he appeared, standing just inside the room.

"I'm leaving now. I'll be back Friday evening, but not for dinner. I'll see you Saturday morning, probably."

"Fine. I'll see you then," she said, hiding the pang she felt. Ryan was brimming with energy, full of life. It was impossible to be unaware of him when he was present. For the next week she knew she'd miss him more than she should. She turned back to her task and the next time she looked, he had gone.

She paused, staring at the empty kitchen doorway. She was going to miss him. How could he already have become a significant part of her life? She had to forget him, to stop being with him and deal with this job without Ryan making a difference.

The week was quiet, and it seemed quieter than her life had ever been. On Tuesday she drove into town and spent the morning walking and talking to people she had met. She was beginning to know some of the people and they were all friendly, welcoming. The town had a small library that was in the City Hall and Town Center, which was next to the sheriff's office and the jail. She had already met Millie Wales, who was the mayor's secretary as well as the librarian. When she entered the Town Center, she found the auburn-haired librarian piling books on a cart.

Thirty minutes later Jessica left the library with a stack of books beneath her arm.

Over the next few days she got back into exercising, working out in the gym at Ryan's ranch for thirty minutes a day to start, adding weights three days also. At least it kept her occupied.

Friday night came and she still didn't see anything of Ryan. As he'd predicted, Saturday morning as she worked in the kitchen after eating breakfast, she finally heard his boot heels in the hallway. Anticipation filled her as she gazed at the door and in seconds Ryan appeared.

The realization hit her hard: she'd missed him more than she'd ever thought possible.

Six

When he entered the kitchen, Ryan's pulse raced. He had missed Jessica, more than he should have. He had spent the week arguing with himself because he should just stay in Houston another week and keep away from the ranch. He usually spent a week out of each month there, sometimes more in the summer than the winter, but now he wanted to get back to see her.

He couldn't keep from remembering their kisses, which had caused a subtle change in their relationship. Since that time, she had avoided him far more than before. He had tried to avoid her, leaving for Houston. But the effect of her kisses hadn't diminished. He could recall them with a vivid clarity that still got him aroused.

Like everything else about her, her kiss was hot, unforgettable, opening a Pandora's box into his life. Jessica was no longer just his beautiful cook. She was the sexiest woman he had ever met and she was off-limits. He had just set himself up for all kinds of trouble. Real trouble this time. Not just skirting around being personal or flirting with her. He wanted to seduce her and he wanted to make love to her. He wanted her in his bed for days. But he would never be serious and she would be serious from the first.

He had always been able to walk away, even stay friends with the women he had had a relationship with, but he instinctively knew Jessica would not take seduction lightly. He'd never been into getting deeply entangled and he wasn't starting now.

He shook his head, trying to put memories aside. He had to stop remembering, stop dreaming about her, which he had done too much this past week, even during business meetings.

He couldn't get her out of his thoughts—beautiful, a great cook, kind and softhearted. Sexy beyond his wildest dreams. How was he going to resist her? He always reminded himself of the reason she was at his ranch. She couldn't take a casual affair. And Jessica wasn't the type to want to.

After breakfast alone, he carried his dishes and placed them in the sink. She stood with her back to him, singing lightly. Even in faded jeans and a blue knit shirt with an apron tied around her waist, she looked gorgeous.

"I'll go with you to the grocery, Jessica. I need to get some things in town."

She twisted to look over her shoulder at him. Her big blue eyes focused on him. Her full rosy lips were temptation to him. He wanted to wrap his arms around her and kiss her. "Can I get them for you?"

"I don't think so. I need to talk to Fred at the hardware store and select new shingles for an office I had built near the barn. What time will you be ready to leave?"

"I can go in about thirty minutes," she said.

"I'll meet you in the kitchen," he said, and left.

He waited the half hour and when she'd said she would

be there, she came rushing into the kitchen. When they left, he locked up and turned on the alarm.

Once they were on the road, she twisted slightly in her seat to face him.

"Tell me about your week," he said.

"I'm getting accustomed to your kitchen, which is super nice. It's a good place to work. I haven't needed any appliance that you don't have. How did you get it so well stocked?"

"At the time, Garrett was close friends with a woman who had a catering service. She came out and helped. She's gone out of the picture now. That was before he met Sophia."

"She did a good job. It's the dream kitchen."

He couldn't say why, but he was happy she approved.

"I've got to tell you my home news," she said. "When I contacted Olivia, my friend at home, I learned that Carlton is still looking for me, because he's called her. I thought he would have given up by now. I've contacted my mother and she wants me to come home. I talked to Lydia, my sister. She said my parents, my oldest brother and, of course, Carlton all want me to go back to him. They don't seem to realize marriage would never be the same as before."

"Why is your family so convinced that Carlton is the right husband for you?" He couldn't help but voice the question that had plagued him since Jessica had first told him about her unhappy marriage.

"I think it's because my parents liked to have me in their country club, their social world. My brother admired Carlton for his success and was friends with him." She waited a few seconds and added, "And Carlton…well, he probably wanted me partly for his ego and because I had been the type of wife he wanted until I discovered his infidelities."

"Is your divorce final?"

"Very final. We've been divorced a year now. Nobody in my family seems to pay any attention to that. I guess because Carlton pays little attention to it. With time he will. He'll move on."

"So your ex-husband hasn't left Memphis to search for you?"

"Not that I know about. I'd hear about it right away from my sister." Jessica shrugged her shoulders, as if to cue him that this topic of conversation was over. "That's enough of my news from home. Now here's the big news from the local scene. You know Millie Wales."

"Sure," he said, unable to keep from smiling over her big news on the local front. He couldn't imagine anything big that he wouldn't have already heard from Jeb.

"I talked to Millie and now I'm a volunteer at the library two mornings a week. I will read to the little kids. When my reading is done, I will tutor any kids in reading who need and want a tutor. If there is a big response, we'll see about adding an hour, but Millie didn't think there would be more than one or two."

"That's nice, Jessica."

"And I've started myself on an exercise plan since you have a gym here in the house, which is great. Anyway, that's my life at this point. What about you?"

"Very ordinary compared to yours. Business as usual. I'll go back to Houston this week, and then the following week, I'll be at the ranch. Jessica, I noticed a big yellow tabby at the back door this morning. Is that cat a new addition? I asked Jeb and he said we don't have a yellow tabby."

"Well, you do now. Sort of like the dog and her puppies. The tabby just appeared. She seemed to be another stray, so I've fed her and I intended to call Jeb and get her on the list for a check by the veterinarian when he comes. Ryan, just take the expenses for the animals out of my paycheck."

"At the rate you're going, you won't have a paycheck," he said, staring straight ahead. "You're mighty softhearted. But you can't leave Texas with a car filled with animals," he said, glancing at her.

She smiled at him. "I'll find people to take them. I'll ask around when I'm at the grocery. The cat's name is Sunshine. I found her on the step when the sun came up and she's got yellow fur, hence the name."

"Jessica, you've been with me almost two weeks and we now have seven more animals we're caring for. You're averaging a new animal almost every two days. At that rate, it's sort of mind-boggling." Her softheartedness was just another facet of her that he was drawn to.

She laughed and placed her fingers lightly on his wrist and he wondered if she could feel the jump in his pulse when she did. "We probably won't get another animal the whole time I'm here. You'll see. It'll all work out. Don't worry, Ryan."

Her touch sent an electric current shooting to his toes. Desire centered in him as his insides clutched. She could acquire a zoo while she stayed and he wouldn't object.

All he could think about was his plan. Tonight he planned to take her to dinner and he couldn't wait. Dinner and dancing.

They spent the morning in the grocery, meeting more people, talking to everyone. Jessica was still new in town and everyone they encountered wanted to meet and talk to her.

Because Ryan had brought coolers for the food that had to be kept cold, they loaded the groceries in his truck and then did some shopping. He went to the hardware store and Jessica went in the dress shop. When he finished, he met her there. She had a purchase under her arm. He greeted the store owner, who smiled at him.

"I've been talking to Jessica. We're glad to have her."

"I've got a very good cook now," he said, turning to Jessica to take the package she held. "I'll carry this and we can put it in the truck. Ready?"

"It was so nice to meet you, Natalie," Jessica said to the blonde owner.

When they stepped outside, Jessica walked beside him to the truck. "This is a friendly town."

"Oh, yes. And you're new, so that's interesting to one and all because they don't have a lot of changes or new people." When he shut the truck door, he asked, "How about a burger again? Want to eat here in town?"

"Sure," she answered, giving him one of her radiant smiles.

As they sat in a booth and ate their burgers, he sipped his cold drink and set the glass down. "There's a new restaurant opening in downtown Dallas that's caused a stir and is supposed to be so great. Want to eat there tonight?"

"That's a long drive to make for dinner."

"We can fly. I thought you might like to see what they're doing and how their food is. The menu isn't up on the web yet, but the people opening it have impressive backgrounds in the restaurant business. Would you like to go?"

She gazed at him solemnly for a moment and then smiled. "Thank you. I would like to see what they do."

"How about leaving at six?"

"Fine." He didn't tell her he had reservations in Dallas and had had them for a week and only gotten them because he knew one of the owners.

They ate, talked to more people and finally arrived back at the ranch midafternoon. "Jessica, you don't have to carry in all the groceries, today or any day. Call the barn or bunkhouse and the guys will come unload everything. You'll have enough work putting it all away."

As Ryan carried in groceries, she carried sacks and began putting them away. Soon he left her to her work while he checked on mail and calls.

Later, as he dressed for the evening, excitement built in him, even though he shouldn't be taking her out and he shouldn't do more than just harmless kisses again. How many times had he reminded himself to wait until more time had passed and she was over her divorce, more able to cope with dating, kisses, seduction? He should wait until she was out of his house, living elsewhere—somewhere he could have an affair and walk away when he wanted, the way he had always done.

She was beginning to focus on other things with her reading to kids and starting an exercise program and both should help her adjust and heal. He just needed to control himself until she mended a bit more. But his good intentions seemed to evaporate when he was around her.

He wore a charcoal suit, a matching tie and his boots. He was ready before she was and waited in his study, thinking about kissing her. Finally, he heard her heels clicking on the polished oak floor in the hall. She entered the room and his breath left as if an invisible fist had punched him.

In a plain sleeveless black dress with a low V-neckline, she was stunning. The dress ended just above her knees and she wore black pumps with stiletto heels. Her blond hair was held away from her forehead by a thin diamond-and-sapphire headband, and she had diamond studs in her ears.

"You're beautiful, Jessica," he said, his voice hoarse and deep as yearning enveloped him and intentions to keep his distance became nonexistent.

"Thank you," she said, smiling at him. "You look quite handsome, too. I'm looking forward to this evening."

"So am I. You'll see some Dallas nightlife," he said, knowing they had different reasons for their anticipation of the evening. Still, he avoided telling her that he had been looking forward to this night all week.

"The plane is waiting," he said, taking her arm and heading to his black sports car, which would take them to the airstrip.

All the way during the flight she was bubbly about the restaurant and what plans she had for her own, as well as the part of Nashville she wanted to be in when she opened a restaurant. He didn't care what she talked about, because he just wanted to be with her and look at her.

"It's going to be expensive, Jessica."

"I have money put away from my grandfather. I've never touched it. I have some more money I've saved. My sister says she wants to buy into it and my friend does, too. I don't think I'll have any financial problems. If it looks like a solid business, my dad will be willing to invest. He can't resist something good, but he'll wait to see. I doubt if he can imagine that I can handle the business side."

"After what you've done at the ranch, I expect you to handle the whole thing quite easily."

"Thank you for the vote of confidence. I hope some-day you'll come visit and eat in my restaurant so you can see what your former cook has done."

"I promise I'll do that," he said, smiling at her, making an effort to keep from looking at the long legs that her short dress revealed. Her eyes sparkled and her cheeks were rosy. She looked happier than ever, so maybe Texas was going to be good for her. He hoped so and he would try to squelch his impulses to flirt for this evening, but someday, sometime when she had recovered, maybe moved out, he wanted to just go out with her, flirt with her, seduce her, make love to her.

For now, though, he'd settle for less. He wanted to hold her in his arms, to dance with her and later tonight to kiss her. She had kissed him before; he thought she would again. Kisses would never hurt her. Kisses would be therapy.

He almost had to laugh out loud at himself. When had he been this foolish about a woman?

As they flew east over the flat prairie, he listened to her talk about the library and whom she had seen in town. The flight seemed to go quickly as she spoke enthusias-tically and held him in her spell. He couldn't wait to see her reaction to the restaurant.

She'd had a rough time, losing her baby and having her marriage fall apart. He wanted to see the sparkle in her eyes, to help her get over the trauma. Tonight he wanted just to have a fun time, the kind of fun they'd had at the barn dance. With every minute that passed, his anticipation of her kiss grew. Hers were the best kisses of his life. Like so much else about her, they were fantastic.

Jessica glanced around, taking in all the details. Set atop a new Dallas high-rise, the elegant restaurant had floor-to-ceiling windows that offered a panoramic view of the skyline in the setting sun. All around her the decor was black-and-white. Black carpeting and black linen tablecloths. White gardenias floating in crystal vases that were rings centered with tall candles. Even the waitstaff wore black and white. Providing the perfect soundtrack to the elegance, a man played a piano in the corner of a small dance floor.

Ryan had already ordered white wine and she saw their waiter approaching with a bottle and glasses.

When they were alone and the wine had been poured, Ryan raised his glass. "Here's to *your* restaurant. May it be as huge a success."

"Thank you," she said, smiling at him as she touched his glass lightly and then sipped the dry white wine.

"And here's to you, Ryan. May your life on the ranch always be what you hoped."

As his brown eyes held her gaze, she took a sip and her heart drummed faster than usual.

"So, Jessica, do you want a fancy place like this or something folksy and simple?"

"I want it upscale, but not to this extent. I want a family business with kids, so that automatically means far more informal than this. No dance floor, just nice. Not too folksy. I don't want peanuts on the table and shells on the floor."

"I hope no pets allowed."

"No, no four-legged animals in my restaurant." She

laughed and watched as he stood and held out his hand. "More people are dancing now. C'mon. This will be exercise and therapy."

She hadn't planned to dance with him. She hadn't even expected to find a dance floor, but now that he was holding out his hand and asking in such a casual manner, she couldn't say no. She placed her hand in his and got up, excitement fluttering in her at the thought of dancing with him.

They walked to the darkened dance floor to join half a dozen other couples for a fast number. She began to dance with Ryan, looking into his dark eyes, smiling at him, feeling good about moving around and having fun. How easy with Ryan to let go of worries and hurtful memories she had dwelled on too much for too long.

They danced two fast dances. When a ballad started, he took her hand. "Shall we go back and see if our salads have been served?"

"Sure," she replied, feeling a tiny knot of disappointment because she was having fun. But a slow dance with Ryan might be more personal than she should get, so it was just as well to go back to their table.

She had left her hand in his, aware of their holding hands, curious if he ever gave it a thought. She enjoyed being with him, probably a bit more each time she was. She couldn't get entangled with anyone yet. She didn't trust her own judgment and wondered whether she ever would again. When she had fallen for Carlton, she had been so certain he was the right man for her. She had been sure he was all the good things he seemed. She had been wrong on all counts. How could she have been so blind? She needed to keep her distance from Ryan because she was too vulnerable right now.

Their salads had been served on white china plates. Next came the main course. She had ordered grilled salmon, while Ryan had lobster.

"The lobster mashed potatoes are marvelous," she said. "This is something I should learn to cook."

"Good. I'm glad you like the dinner. I thought it might be difficult to please an excellent cook who plans to have her own restaurant."

"No, I'm sort of easy to please. Maybe there are some things I definitely do not like, but in general, I don't think I'm picky."

After dinner he asked her to dance again when a fast number played. Each time there was a change to something slow, they would sit out a few dances.

Finally, when the tempo changed to a slow song and he led her back to their table, she stopped. "Are you avoiding a slow dance with me, Ryan?"

"Of course not. I'm trying to do what I figured you wanted, but now if slow dancing suits you, I'll be more than happy to oblige," he said, looking amused. Taking her hand, he drew her into his arms to dance to an old slow song that she'd heard her parents play when she was a child.

Ryan was warm, solid, moving with her in perfect time to the music. She could dance with him without it becoming a major thing. It was just a dance at a restaurant. "Ryan, you're the best therapy possible," she said quietly. "I almost drove on and didn't go to the agency to see about working for you, but Pru really pushed me to see about the job."

"I'm glad she did. I have the best cook in all of Texas and that's saying a lot."

She laughed. "I don't think you really do. Texas has

wonderful cooks. So does Tennessee. I guess great cooks are everywhere. Dinner tonight was excellent."

"I'm glad you liked it. Since this place is new, it was a shot in the dark."

"It was very good and this is nice, Ryan."

"I think so, too," he said, looking down at her. He wrapped both arms around her waist as they danced slowly, barely moving, and her breath caught deep in her throat while her heartbeat sped. Looking into his eyes, standing so close, his arms around her, desire stirred. Ryan was bringing her out of her depression, out of being numb, out of hurt and uncertainty about her own judgment.

Was she falling in love with him?

The thought scared her because she definitely was not ready for love. Even if she were, Ryan would not be the man for her. He would never take an affair seriously enough for it to develop into a real relationship and she suspected marriage wasn't even a tiny speck on Ryan's radar. He loved the girls and they loved him—it had been obvious at the barn dance, at the grocery, at church. This rancher belonged on his ranch in Texas and she belonged home in Tennessee.

She needed to back off and keep falling in love from happening. She shouldn't have asked him to slow-dance with her.

No, Ryan was not the man for her. She wasn't happy-go-lucky like Ryan, with everyone he met a friend but none too close. She definitely planned to go home to Tennessee when a year was up.

The music ended and a fast piece started and the moment was gone. The next slow dance, when he took her hand, she tugged lightly to walk in the direction of their table.

"Maybe we should start home. It's a long way."

"That it is," he said. "I've already taken care of the check, so we can go."

He took her arm and they left, riding down in the elevator. The limo waited and they were driven to Ryan's plane, which was ready for the return flight to the ranch.

It was midnight when they entered his house. "Jessie," he said, shortening her name, something no one else had ever done, something uniquely Ryan. Her heart thudded as she turned to him. His eyes conveyed his need before he wrapped his arms around her and pulled her close and all her sensible thoughts about Ryan not being the man for her vanished. His mouth covered hers in a possessive, demanding kiss.

Her heartbeat raced as she wrapped her arms around his neck and kissed him in return. "You make me want you, Ryan," she whispered, and placed her mouth over his to kiss him again.

He released her briefly, tossing aside his suit coat and yanking loose his tie to drop it. Watching her, he reached out with care to take off her fancy headband and set it on a nearby table. He drew her back into his embrace, leaning over her and holding her close while he kissed her hard.

She wound her fingers in his hair, feeling the thick texture, pouring herself into her kiss, wanting to kiss him, wanting passion and loving and to know that she was desired by him. She wanted to give to Ryan, to shower him with kisses for bringing her out of despair, for making life fun again, for making her feel like a woman, whole and wanted.

Trying to convey those feelings, she kissed him, relishing his touch, which ignited fires and set her own desire raging.

She ran her hands over his broad shoulders, down over rock-hard biceps. Her fingers flew to the buttons of his shirt and she twisted them free, then pushed the fabric off his shoulders to run her hands over him. Yearning grew, a physical hunger, a need for Ryan, his strength, his kisses, his passion.

She felt his hands at the neckline of her dress and then he slid the zipper slowly down her back, finally, pushing the soft material off her shoulders until it fell around her ankles. While he continued kissing her, he cupped her breasts, filling his hands.

She gasped with pleasure, wanting him, needing his caresses and kisses. She ran her fingers over his muscled chest and barely noticed when he unfastened the clasp to her bra and pushed it off. A dim voice warned her to stop before she was captivated and her heart belonged to him. She paid no heed to wisdom. Instead, she followed her heart.

His thumbs drew circles, stroking her as he held her softness in his hands. She gasped again while need for more grew.

Her hand slipped to his belt to unfasten the metal buckle and then his trousers, letting them fall. He stepped out, shedding the rest of his clothes swiftly and peeling away her lacy panties until he placed his hands on her hips to hold her back and look at her slowly.

"You're beautiful, so beautiful," he whispered before pulling her into his embrace to kiss her passionately again.

With a muffled cry, she clung to him, feeling his arousal press against her, hard and thick and ready.

She ached to make love with him, to not stop to think, to just take this man with her whole being.

"Ryan," she whispered, and then his mouth covered hers again and words were gone. Still kissing her, he picked her up to carry her to her bedroom. He knelt on the mattress, placing her down, continuing to kiss her.

When he finally moved away, he shifted. Holding her ankle gently, he showered kisses along her leg, behind her knee, moving up along her thigh while her fingers twined in his hair and her breath caught with pleasure.

Next he knelt between her legs to touch and kiss her, his hands moving over her to drive her wild. Sitting up, she wrapped her arms around his neck to pull him close as she kissed him while they both fell back on the bed.

Then it was her turn. She knelt beside him, trailing kisses down over his chest, his nipples and then over his flat belly. He closed his eyes, his hands roaming over her as she caressed his thick erection, leaning down to kiss and stroke him until he rolled her over on her back on the bed.

His weight came down on her as he kissed her passionately, another possessive kiss that made her feel the bond between them more strongly than ever, making her want a union, want him totally.

While he had become important to her, this night he became necessary. They belonged together. She couldn't turn back now. She felt as if she had been moving toward this point since the moment she met him. On this night he was the most important man in her life and she desired him with all her being.

She spread her legs, opening for him, wrapping her

long legs around him. With a groan he stepped away, getting his trousers, hunting for protection.

"Ryan, I'm on the Pill," she whispered, and he returned, moving between her legs, poised while his gaze trailed over her with the effect of a caress.

"Ryan," she whispered again, grazing his hard thighs. He knelt, wrapping his arm around her, holding his weight slightly off her as he entered her slowly, tantalizingly, a torment that made her arch beneath him and cry out.

He thrust slowly, deeply entering, withdrawing as deliberately. Need drove her while she moved wildly. Her head thrashed back and forth as her hips gyrated, urgency building with pleasure pouring over her in a burst of release. His control shattered then and his thrusts were rapid, unleashed passion while he climaxed.

Ecstasy exploded, but she was deaf to all sounds except the drumming of her own pulse.

She gasped for breath, turning to kiss him while he gradually slowed, finally letting his weight down. It felt heavy, warm and solid pressing on her.

He showered light kisses on her temple, down over her ear and cheek, down along her throat and then her breasts. "Jessie, you're perfect, fantastic," he whispered. He held her tightly and let his weight down a bit more.

Aware of holding Ryan in her arms, she refused to think beyond the present moment. Their passionate lovemaking suddenly had seemed necessary to her.

His breathing returned to normal while hers did the same. He rolled to his side, taking her with him, and pushed hair away from her face, ran his hand down over her shoulder.

He kissed and caressed her lightly, holding her close

to him. She could feel his heart pounding with hers, both finally slowing.

"Jessie, I've wanted you more than I can ever tell you or you can ever know. This is perfect. I don't want to let you go."

"You don't have to yet," she whispered with her eyes closed, feeling a storm brewing within her.

"I didn't expect this tonight," he said, shifting to look at her.

"I didn't expect this either. I guess I'm not ready for dinner and dancing," she said.

"Don't be sorry. You're wonderful, beautiful, so special." His words wrapped her in a warm feeling that made her want to kiss him again, a sweet, slow kiss that reflected how much she liked him.

"I wanted this tonight. I wanted to make love, but now I'm not ready emotionally."

"Don't have regrets. We can back off—go back like we were."

She guessed he was trying to help, but she couldn't keep from feeling a tiny burst of disappointment. Was he having second thoughts? Was he having real regrets? She searched his dark eyes. Did he mean what he said? He kissed her temple while his fingers combed through her hair. He was so gentle when he wanted to be.

"You're special, Ryan. You've sort of given me life back. It's been so long since there was excitement or fun or joy like I've known here with you. Those things are very special. At the same time, I'm not ready for intimacy. I don't think I can handle this," she said.

He kissed her temple gently. "You'll get over all the hurts, Jessie. It'll all be in the past."

"You do all the right things," she said, pushing his hair from his forehead.

"Take it a day at a time. It'll work out. Don't worry about it tonight. No worries or concerns tonight. This is a special time now, so shut down thoughts about the past or the future."

"I'll try," she said. "Ryan, I wanted to make love."

"I'm glad you did. You know I did, heart and soul," he said, his brown gaze steady. He sounded as if he meant what he said. She began to feel better.

"And yet you never pushed me. That just makes me want you more." She smiled at him. "If you were pushing me, I could say no so easily."

"Contrary woman," he teased, returning her smile.

"I am filled with contrary thoughts and feelings. Tonight has been marvelous. Dancing, eating out at a fancy place—things I haven't done in so long and wanted to do," she whispered. "Maybe some things I desperately needed. At the same time, I just can't cope with the emotional side of becoming intimate."

"I told you, you don't have to cope," he whispered, kissing her temple lightly again, but this time he had a slight frown. "I don't want you hurt or worrying. Just accept tonight and we'll go from there. Actually, we can be more conservative. Just say no and I'll accept it."

"I know you will," she said, still wondering if he harbored regrets. She couldn't imagine he would, unless he felt she was taking everything too seriously.

Much later he carried her to the shower and then back to bed to make love again. Afterward she was in his arms, close against him with her head on his chest. "Ryan, tonight is an exception."

"I know and I understand. I hope you don't have regrets. I couldn't possibly, but I understand why you want it to be an exception. Hopefully, sometime you'll feel differently about it."

"I feel rocky and uncertain, vulnerable. At this point I could fall in love so easily, but it might be a reaction to all that has happened and not be my true feelings at all. I can't trust my own feelings."

"Yes, you can," he said, wrapping her in his arms. "Just take things one day at a time," he said. "Time will pass and you'll be more confident in your feelings and reactions."

"You're so positive."

"Tonight has been fabulous, Jessie. Every second of it. Do you mind if I call you Jessie? Would you rather be called Jessica?"

"Jessie is fine. You're the only person who has ever called me that."

"That surprises me. Jeb calls me Ry and has for as long as I can remember."

He rolled over to kiss her and talk ended.

The next Saturday, Ryan drove into town with her to get things he needed. As he drove back to the ranch that afternoon, her cell phone beeped and she pulled it out to read a message. "Oh, my word," she said, feeling her stomach drop. She glanced at Ryan.

"Do I need to pull over? Do I need to turn around and go back to the hospital? You look pale, as if you'll faint. What's happened?"

"Nothing that drastic. My parents have just landed in Dallas and are driving out to Bywater. They found out where I'm staying. I'm calling my sister."

When Jessica called, Lydia answered and they talked

for almost fifteen minutes until Lydia ended the call. "My dad insisted Lydia tell him because he's worried about me. He thinks I should come home."

"Does he know you're all grown up?"

She smiled. "Yes, they know, but they can't keep from telling me what I should do. My parents will stay in the hotel in Bywater. I doubt if they will stay long. Neither one will like the hotel or the town. Ryan, I'll drive back to town to talk to them. They'll stop at the hotel and want me to come where they are. They won't drive out to the ranch."

"Let me talk to your dad and invite him out. They can come eat dinner with us. I'll grill steaks if they like steaks."

"You don't need to get involved. My dad can be difficult sometimes. You're not going to talk him into coming here."

Ryan gave her a look. "Where's your usual optimism?" He took her hand and gave her a squeeze. "Don't worry. I'll help you with them. I'll call when we get to the ranch."

She shook her head. "You don't know my parents."

"I grew up with a difficult dad. I know plenty about dealing with a parent, plus my older brothers."

When they reached the ranch, as they walked into the house, her cell phone rang. "It's my folks."

"After you talk to them, let me talk to your dad."

Jessica took the phone to say hello, listening to her mother talk and standing quietly. "I'll be happy to come into Bywater to see you both. Ryan would like to say a word to Dad. Would you put Dad on the line, please?"

She handed the phone to Ryan and shook her head. She doubted if Ryan would get anywhere with her father, who could turn a deaf ear to anyone when he wanted to.

She knew he'd decide he didn't like Ryan before ever meeting him.

"Mr. Upton. This is Ryan Delaney." She listened as Ryan chatted politely a moment about their flight to Dallas. "Sir, there is no way you'll be really comfortable in that old hotel. Be my guest here at the ranch. I'll send the limo to pick you up. I have far more room than the hotel. My home is more comfortable and you'll have more time with Jessica."

He paused, listening to her father, and she could imagine her father saying no.

"Don't worry about the hotel. I know George Gleason, who owns it, and I'll take care of everything. Just wait in the lobby. It shouldn't take the limo long to get there— I'd say ten minutes from now. My driver will bring you to the ranch and we'll have dinner and you can talk to your daughter all you want. I promise you, sir. You'll be far more comfortable. The food is better here anyway."

There was another brief lull and she was amazed because she guessed he'd convinced her parents to come to the ranch.

"Ten minutes. He'll find you. His name is Odell." Ryan paused again. "Yes, sir, that's great. I'm looking forward to meeting you both. I've heard a lot about you."

Astonished, Jessica had to laugh as she shook her head.

Ryan ended the call and made another to tell his limo driver to pick up her parents at the hotel. When he finished, he turned to Jessica.

"So I was wrong," she admitted. "I'm shocked. And how are you getting a limo from here to Bywater in ten minutes?" she asked.

"Odell is in Bywater. He was having the limo serviced

and he would have hung around in town until after dinner and then driven back. He can get to the hotel in ten
minutes. Your folks will be waiting. Your dad said no
first, but then he said yes."

"I imagine you impressed him with the limo. I can
guess what he has been imagining about where I work.
Like some farm home out of an old silent movie."

"I'll unload the groceries and supplies and then shower.
They won't get here for a while, but Odell is speedy."

"I know that," she said, thinking about the few limo
rides she'd had with Ryan.

"I'll change, too," she added. She drew a deep breath.
"They'll want me to come home with them. I have no intention of doing that, but they will pressure me."

"I'll invite them to stay this week. They can see you're
in a good situation and getting along fine. That will probably help. I'll have to go to Houston on Wednesday, but
that will give you time alone with them, which will be
good."

"They won't stay that long, I don't think, but you just
worked a miracle, so who knows? Thanks, Ryan." He
crossed the room to her and her pulse began to drum,
beating faster while she watched him.

He stopped only inches away to place his hands on
her shoulders. Instead of being satiated from their night
of love, she wanted him more than ever. The slightest
glance, the slightest touch, pretty much anything involving him, drew her to him now. As she gazed up at him,
she felt breathless. She wanted to slip her arms around
his neck and kiss him. Temptation tore at her.

Temptation she couldn't ignore.

"Ryan," she whispered.

Seven

Ryan's arm circled her waist and he leaned down to kiss her. "Just one kiss," he whispered, and then covered her mouth again, drawing her tightly into his embrace.

After long moments Jessica finally shifted slightly to look at him. "We should get ready," she said breathlessly. His breathing was as ragged as hers and desire flamed in the depths of his dark eyes, making her want to step right back into his arms.

"Right. We better get busy. I'll grill steaks tonight. Can you toss a salad together?"

"Sure. Leave the rest to me."

When she came back to the kitchen after changing clothes, Ryan was there waiting. He'd already changed into navy slacks, a pale blue dress shirt open at the throat and his black boots, and once again he looked more like the Houston businessman than the West Texas cowboy.

He stood when she entered the room and his gaze drifted over her. "You look great," he said.

She looked down at her pale yellow sleeveless linen dress, which was tailored with a straight skirt ending at her knees. A string of pearls was around her neck. "Thank you."

"Odell just called. He's turned onto the ranch, so they'll be here in minutes."

"Let's go out front and wait."

When the limo stopped and the driver held the door for her parents, she hurried to hug her mother and father, giving each of them a light kiss on the cheek. "Mom, Dad, this is Ryan Delaney. Ryan, meet my parents, Charles and Mildred Upton."

"Mrs. Upton, Mr. Upton," Ryan said, extending his hand to her dad. "I'm happy to meet you. Welcome to the RD Ranch. Odell will bring your things in and put them in one of the guest suites on this floor, since Jessica is staying on the first floor also. Unless you'd rather be in a guest house off by yourselves...."

At the same time, they both answered that they'd prefer the suite in his home.

Ryan turned to give brief instructions to Odell. As soon as he turned back, he waved his hand toward the front door. "Come inside where it's comfortable. We can sit out on the patio. If you folks are ready for a drink, we have everything from iced tea to bar drinks. I'll show you the way through the house to the family room and the patio and then to your suite if you'd like to freshen up before we have a drink."

As they entered, Ryan held the door for her and then her parents and then led them through the house, chatting with them about their flight and about Memphis, remarking about his stays in the city. When they reached the family room, he pointed to the patio just beyond it. But her dad was more interested in one item in the room.

"And what's this?" he said, crossing the room to look at the framed Colt revolver Ryan had mounted there.

While Ryan followed to tell her dad about the revolver, Jessica turned to her mother. "I hope you're not fretting. I'm doing fine, Mom."

"We just wish you would come home. I've been so worried about you. We all have."

Jessica held out her hands and smiled. "I'm doing great. I feel better and it's been good to get away. I needed this."

When Ryan and her dad joined them again, they were still talking about antique revolvers. She guessed that topic of conversation would continue for some time.

She followed Ryan as he led them to a suite toward the front of the house, to the east. It held dark cherrywood furniture and had an Oriental rug centered in the sitting area on the polished oak floor. "Just join us on the patio when you're ready," Ryan said as he walked out, leaving Jessica in the room.

She smiled at her mother. "I'll wait and walk back with you."

Both her parents were looking at their tasteful surroundings and she suspected her dad had already mellowed some toward Ryan.

"I know you have questions, but I told you I wanted to get away where I could sort things out. It's very quiet here. Ryan works in Houston and is in and out. I got a job cooking for him."

"Is he married?" her mother asked.

"No." She knew what her mother was thinking and hurried to fill the silence. "He comes from a good family, a big family. I got to meet his siblings when he had a Delaney Foundation meeting in Dallas."

"Are they all ranchers? Why is he working in Houston? Isn't he a rancher?" her dad asked.

Patiently, Jessica explained. "He's got an energy company. He said it was a drilling business until a year ago and now they have natural-gas wells. I don't know too much about that. He loves the ranch, though, and this is where he spends part of his time. His brothers are in different businesses, as is his married half sister. Why don't we join him and he can tell you himself much better than I can about his family."

"We didn't come all this way to talk to a stranger. We'd like to sit down with you, Jessica," her dad said.

"Certainly. Let's join Ryan now, and after dinner this evening, I think he'll leave us alone to talk."

"That's reasonable, Charles," her mother said. "Let's go get to know Ryan Delaney."

Jessica laughed. "Mom, before you quiz Ryan to pieces, remember that I merely work for him and I will return to Tennessee in due time."

"I just want to know this man you work for. You haven't known him long, but you're working for him and living in his house. You're out here in the middle of nowhere, alone with him."

"Not exactly alone. Maybe tomorrow he can give you a brief tour, but he has houses nearby that he's built and people live there who work for him. The woman in charge of his cleaning staff is here most days of the week. The chauffeur you met, Odell, lives here and he's usually nearby, too. Ryan has a string of men who live in a bunkhouse and work here. It's almost a small town in and of itself."

"When he goes to Houston, you're in this palatial mansion all by yourself?" her mother asked, looking at her surroundings.

"Yes. He has a gym where I can exercise. There's plenty for me to do. I have speed dial to connect me with his foreman. And I have Gwen's phone number—she is the woman who cleans. I don't feel alone and there is a very good security system in the house."

Maybe she had done too good a job selling the ranch, because her mother seemed nervous when she said, "Jessica, I don't want you to fall in love and live out here at the end of the earth."

Jessica bit back a laugh. "Never fear. I'll come home to Tennessee. I have my plans and I told him when he hired me that this is temporary. I plan to go home. My family is there and my home is there. I love Tennessee. Besides, I don't think my new employer is thinking of marriage," she remarked.

"Well, thank heavens. I'm glad to hear you say that," her mother said. "Is there a woman in his life?"

"I think there are several of them, but none constantly on the scene right now. Shall we go?"

She led them to the patio, and Ryan stood the moment they stepped outside. He asked what they'd like to drink and took orders. Her dad trailed after Ryan to the nearby bar. "I hear you like to play golf, Mr. Upton," she heard Ryan say.

Thirty minutes after the arrival of her parents, Ryan was like an old friend. All through dinner and afterward Ryan and her parents chatted. He and her dad exchanged stories, laughing, with Ryan making sure to include her mother in the fun.

She realized Ryan was totally at ease charming them. He was entertaining and an excellent listener. Her dad sat back on a chaise lounge, looking as if he was enjoying the evening. Ryan already had a golf game scheduled with him for the next afternoon and they were all going to church together in the morning. At one point Ryan started to leave so she and her parents could talk alone, but her dad drew him back into the conversation and he didn't try to go again.

By ten her parents had said good-night, gone to their suite and left her with Ryan.

"You worked a miracle. I am impressed," she admitted when they were alone. "And my parents are very impressed. They flew out here to talk to me and now I don't think they care." She smiled at him with gratitude, pride and a hefty dose of surprise in the mix. "And thank you, but you didn't have to offer to fly them home in your plane."

He shrugged, returning her smile while he reached over to hold her hand. "I can have them flown back to Memphis easily, and frankly, I want them to like me so they don't worry about you being here."

"I think you've succeeded beyond your wildest dreams," she remarked with amusement. "My dad is so eager to play golf tomorrow. He's good, but I suspect you are good, too, and you're younger. Yet why do I think my dad will win tomorrow?"

Ryan merely grinned.

"He can't wait. You made this course sound like the best ever. My dad really loves golf and he's always interested in a course that's top-notch."

"Even though Lubbock isn't the biggest city, this is a fine course. It's a new country club and they really made an effort to have a world-class course. Wait until he comes back."

She shook her head. "I still can't believe they don't even care to talk to me. I owe you for that."

"Ahh, I intend to collect."

She looked at him, realizing he was no longer restraining himself from flirting with her—a plus and a minus, depending on what she wanted. At this point she liked being with him and he could flirt if he wanted to. It surprised her how much she had already mended in the short time she had been in Texas. She was finding the quiet that she had needed and her hurts were beginning to fade.

"So just how do you expect to collect?"

"I'll tell you when your folks have packed and gone and no one catches me doing something they think I shouldn't. Notice I said 'they think.'"

"I noticed. Ryan, this is good. I'm doing better in the short time I've been here. I've changed. This place is good for me."

"That it is. It's good for me, too. Maybe now you can see why I love it so."

"I can and I can't. I can't seem to get my mind around the fact that you could sink down and never leave the ranch and still be happy. I couldn't do that."

"I certainly could. This is fantastic. Peaceful, quiet, yet I have friends here and I have things to do, challenges, fun. It's beautiful. It's relaxing. It's quiet. No traffic. This is paradise."

"Not for everyone," she said. "Paradise is—"

"Tennessee," he said before she could. "To each his own," he added. "I'll tell you what paradise is right now—you in my lap. But we won't do that tonight."

"I don't think so," she said, smiling at him, still aware of his hand holding hers. "Because of you, this has all turned out fine and I don't have to worry about my parents. They haven't said one word to me about coming home and they don't seem to want to get me off alone to talk to me. I think you've wowed them."

"That's nice, but it's their daughter I want to wow."

"You've already done that," she remarked, and he grinned.

They sat and talked until she realized it was two in the morning. She told him good-night and went to her suite to climb into bed and fall asleep.

Sunday evening after dinner as they moved to the patio, her dad asked if he could talk to her a few minutes and Ryan told her to take his study. Her spirits dropped because she had thought they had completely changed their feelings about both Carlton and Ryan. Her dad had returned from the golf game raving about the course and how great everything had been. He had barely beaten Ryan, but he had won and he was filled with excitement, talking all through dinner about the game and the course.

As she closed the study door, she steeled herself, then turned to face him. He had changed to tan slacks and a dark brown sport shirt. His skin was ruddy from the afternoon in the sun and he looked robust and healthy. She loved him, but she also wanted him to stop meddling in her life.

"Jessica, sit down. I think we need to talk briefly. This won't take long."

She sat facing him, smoothing her cream-colored slacks over her knees and waiting in silence.

"I want you to know that your mother and I feel you're all right here. Ryan seems like a fine fellow and you seem happy working here."

"I am. I told Ryan this job would be only for a year. Then I'll go home, Dad."

"The main thing is that you're happy here. I want to tell you something. In hindsight, I should have let you handle your problems on your own, but I was less than happy with Carlton and the way he had treated you."

Surprised, she said nothing, waiting. This was not what she had expected.

"I had a talk with Carlton right after you left him. I have a lot of influence in Memphis because we're an old Memphis family and have roots since the earliest days."

"Dad, what on earth...?"

"I told Carlton if he didn't get you back and keep you happy, straighten up his act, he would have all sorts of financial difficulties at the bank. He's got most of his loans and money in my bank. I can cause Carlton all kinds of financial woes."

"Dad, how could you do that? Carlton could sue you."

"Oh, no. I kept within the law."

"I don't want Carlton to try to get me back. I'll never go back to him," she said, horrified by her dad's admission. "Go home and tell him you've changed your mind. No wonder he was so determined."

"No, I think he truly wants you back. He told me you were the perfect wife for him. I don't think I really had an influence, but I regret what I did. I was angry with him for being so damn stupid. I'm sorry, Jessica. I'm glad you're working things out and I hope you'll forgive me."

She took a deep breath. "Of course I forgive you. I love you, Dad, but please just leave Carlton alone. Except tell him you won't do anything so he'll stop pursuing me."

"I'll do that the minute I get home. And I won't let him know where you are."

She nodded. "Dad, I never want to go back to him. I would never again trust him."

Her father nodded. "Sorry, Jessica."

She stood. "Let's join Mom and Ryan. You forget it except for talking to Carlton when you get home. I know you meant well because you love me."

"I was angry with him."

She shook her head. "C'mon. It's over. It's passed and let's forget it," she said, thinking about Ryan giving her the same advice.

Her father walked up to hug her lightly. "You're being good about this, honey."

"I love you."

He brushed a kiss on her cheek. "You're a great daughter, Jessica. You're our baby. And you selected the right place to settle," he said, looking at his surroundings. "Ryan is a great guy."

She didn't want to remind him that not too long ago he would have said the same thing about Carlton.

"Did Mom know about your…talk with Carlton?"

"Eventually. She was a little upset with me, but on the other hand, she was as angry with Carlton as I was. I don't think she would have objected if I had started carrying out my threats."

"Oh, my. I suppose she knows why you're talking to me now."

"Of course. We just thought if Carlton straightened up and did what he should, you would have a happy marriage again."

"No. That is definitely over forever."

"Then this is a good place to be. Ryan has invited us back whenever we can come, so we'll come back in a month or so."

"Ryan is friendly. I'm sure he'll welcome both of you anytime you want to come visit."

They walked outside and Ryan gazed at her briefly. Her dad sat by Ryan and instantly started talking about the golf game.

Her mother turned to her. "Your dad told you about what he said to Carlton? Are you okay with your father?"

"Oh, yes. I wish he hadn't done that, but it's over and doesn't matter now. Don't worry about it."

"Good. He's had a wonderful time, so now neither of us is so worried about you. We miss you, but we know you found a good place and good people to be with, so we feel better."

"I'm glad. Tell Lydia. Actually, tell the rest of the family in case my brothers treat Carlton the way Dad did."

"We will, but your brothers are pretty close friends with Carlton. Jason, not so much, but Dillon and your brother-in-law have always been close with Carlton. Derek has been close the past few years. Dad will talk to all of them and tell them you're doing well here."

"Fine."

Her mother sat back in her padded chair and looked around. "I'm surprised you can take this quiet. I'm glad I brought a book."

Jessica smiled. "I think I needed this quiet."

"It's nice of Ryan to fly us home."

"He's a nice guy, Mom," she said, glancing at Ryan and meeting his gaze, looking into his brown eyes for seconds before she turned back to her mother.

If her mother saw the look that passed between them, she never commented. But Jessica had her suspicions.

* * *

Midmorning Monday she stood on the tarmac and watched Ryan's jet lift into the sky.

"Thanks to you, they went home happy and there is no danger of them telling Carlton where I am," Jessica said with a smile to Ryan. "And thanks to you, they've decided everything is fine for me to stay here. They'll do what I want now. They said very little to me about coming home. Thank you very much."

"I think you said you owe me one."

"So I did."

"I'll collect tonight at home," he said, gazing at her and letting his eyes convey what he wanted.

They climbed into his car for the drive back to the ranch. She turned in the seat to watch him drive and talk to him. She told him briefly what her father admitted he had done.

"I'm sure Daddy would have stayed within the law, but he is influential and he's wealthier than Carlton, plus he has a lot of older friends who could cause Carlton financial difficulties. I just can't imagine my dad doing that, but I suppose he was really angry with Carlton. Anyway, he said he would tell Carlton that I'm happy and I'm not coming back, so that's the end of that. I can see why Carlton has been so persistent. Maybe this will be the end of his interest in getting back together."

"I can understand why he would be angry. Your folks are nice, Jessica. But that's no surprise."

"Ryan, have you ever met anyone you didn't like?" she asked, thinking he had to be the friendliest person she had ever known.

"Oh, yes," he said. "Indeed I have, but rarely. People are nice. And Texans are friendly."

"So are Tennesseans," she said.

"I know they are. I've been there and they're very friendly."

As he drove down the wide stretch of asphalt that was the county road, he glanced at her and back to the road. "Thanks to Jeb, word has gotten around to my family about your cooking. They are asking pointed questions and I think every one of them wants to try your cooking and especially your rolls."

"Invite them over and I'll cook. I don't mind cooking for them."

"We'll pick a date. Trouble ahead," he said as they approached a faded, dented car pulled off to one side of the empty stretch of road. A young couple stood by the car.

Ryan pulled to a stop thirty yards behind them. "You stay here. Just being on the safe side. You don't know what they want."

"They look like two kids with car trouble," she said, her hand on the door handle.

"Yes, they do, but there have been some very hurt people who thought they would stop to help a stranger." Ryan jotted a number on a small sticky note to hand to her. "Now, stay here and if you need help, call the Bywater sheriff. His name is Sam and this is his number."

"I don't think I'll need help. They need help," she said, nodding out the windshield at the couple.

"I'll see. If you go talk to them, they'll be living with me in my house."

She wrinkled her nose at him. "I saw you playing with one of those pups in the barn this morning."

He shut the car door and walked to the couple. She watched him, to all appearances a tall, handsome cowboy with a purposeful walk who would jump in and do something about the situation. He had been perfect with her parents, saving her so much hassle with them. Ryan could be impressive. Sexy, quick-thinking, reliable. When she thought about how she had almost driven on and not stopped to apply for the job with him, she cringed. What a mistake that would have been. Then she thought about his kindness toward her and his leap of faith in giving her the job. But it was her thoughts about their lovemaking that made her heart race. Suddenly she wanted him to come back to the car.

Would he kiss her tonight? She felt certain he would. And she was looking forward to being kissed by the sexy, appealing, marvelous man.

Was she falling in love with him? She knew she shouldn't be, but even as she searched her heart and her head, she couldn't answer the question.

She looked out the windshield as Ryan joined the couple. She watched them talking and then Ryan made a phone call. Shortly, he returned to the car.

"I got help for them. Official help. They're from a town near the state line in East Texas. They ran away and got married because she's pregnant. Their folks are frantic and went to the police about an hour ago."

"Can you get them to call their folks?"

"Jessica, you didn't call your folks."

"I didn't do anything like this, Ryan. First of all, I'm not a kid. Second, I'm not without means. And lastly, I know what I'm doing and why. My situation is entirely different."

"I know. I'm teasing. The police are notifying their families. By now they probably already have. Those two have forty dollars between them. I gave them a hundred dollars, called the Bywater Hotel and booked them a room for tonight. I called Willie, my mechanic in Bywater, and he's coming in his tow truck to get their car. He will give them a ride back to Bywater and drop them off at the hotel. I told Willie I would pay for their car to be repaired and they can go back home. So now you can relax."

"And you accuse me of being softhearted."

"If I hadn't done all that, you wouldn't want to leave them."

"You're right there. You're a nice guy, Ryan. Even if you did that because of me. I think you would have done it even if this had happened before you met me. I think you would have taken care of them."

"Maybe," he said. They drove past the couple and they all waved.

"That's very nice," she repeated, squeezing his wrist lightly. "I am impressed by your care for others."

"Don't lay it on too thickly, Jessica."

"I mean what I say. You were nice back there." She shot him a smile. "Maybe we can check on them tomorrow."

"We don't need to check on them. They have $140 now and their car will be fixed and they are going home tomorrow. They really are okay, so forget them."

"Maybe I was hasty in my compliments."

He gave her a look and they both laughed. Despite the levity of the moment now, she knew Ryan was a caring person. He was certainly caring in so many ways with her.

He shot her a sideways look. "You know, you've turned my life topsy-turvy," he said.

"Me? I think it's the other way around. I just came and got a job as a cook."

"Sure, Jessica."

* * *

When they arrived at home, Ryan left her to attend to ranch work.

As he took samples to get a well tested, he moved automatically, his thoughts on the weekend and today. Jessica was right. He probably would have helped the stranded couple, but maybe not as much as he did. He would have called a wrecker for them and let the sheriff know about them so he could call their parents, but giving them money and putting them up in a hotel—that was Jessica's influence. If knowing her was changing him, how big was she becoming in his life? How important to him? He couldn't answer his own questions, but he worried because his relationship with her seemed different from any other he had ever had.

That night before dinner they sat on the patio to watch the sun go down. When darkness fell, he held her hand. "This is what it's all about," he whispered. "I don't want you to worry about your folks or your ex or even me. I want you to enjoy living here and get over what you've been through."

"I'm getting over it. You've changed my dad's view of Texas cowboys completely."

"I hope for the good," he said. "Your parents were nice, Jessica. I'm surprised they'd want you to go back to a man who wasn't honest with you."

"He's great in so many other ways."

"Maybe so, but honesty is the bedrock of a relationship. Without that, you don't have anything solid."

"Unfortunately, Carlton didn't see it that way. Actually, my parents seem to have a close, good relationship, so that makes their feelings for Carlton even more puzzling. I think Mom was happy with my life while I was married to him. I saw a lot of my folks because we all moved in the same circles. I don't know. At least they went home feeling differently, thanks to you."

They sat talking as darkness fell and the landscape lights came on.

"Ryan, this is so great. No wonder I'm doing better. At this ranch there's all the peace you need. You feel as if you're in another world of your own. This is one place where I can recuperate. There's no pressure, no stress. I'll always remember it."

"Well, for now, this is a beautiful evening, but I can think of a few things that would make it a degree better," he said, standing, picking her up and sitting back with her on his lap.

She had to laugh. "Not too subtle, are you? I thought we weren't doing this."

"We're just sitting and enjoying the evening. I sort of remember something about how you owe me one."

"Uh-huh. One what?"

"I think one kiss would be a good return."

The moment seemed light, not serious, not steaming with desire. One kiss, Jessica thought, shouldn't draw them into another seduction.

"One kiss," she repeated, only this time her voice was a whisper, the words drawn out, and she breathed heavily between the words as she looked at his mouth. "You started this. Just one short kiss," she continued. He inhaled deeply, his arm tightening around her waist. Shifting her, he cradled her against his shoulder.

She wound her arm around his neck, looked at his mouth while she ran the tip of her tongue over her lips. She leaned closer to touch his lips so lightly. She grazed his throat with a kiss and then kissed his ear, circling it with the tip of her tongue. She brushed a feathery kiss on the corner of his mouth and then another on the other side.

"Jessica," he said, grinding out her name as he drew her to him to kiss her.

The kiss deepened, became passionate. He shifted, leaning over her, kissing her hard and long. In a short time, he started to pull her T-shirt over her head. She caught his fingers and looked at him as she shook her head.

"Don't go so fast. I'm getting in too deep again. We've gone from teasing fun to something seriously hot and seductive. I'm on a rebound, Ryan. I don't want to go from one bad relationship to another one. One between us might not be bad, but I'm not emotionally ready."

"I know that, but we're only kissing."

"We *were* only kissing. Now you're about to change it to something else, something that's a bigger deal and could make a difference in our relationship. Just wait."

He raked his fingers slowly through her hair. "All right. We'll do what you want because I don't want to hurt you in any way."

She hugged him and leaned down to kiss him again, wondering how long she herself could stick by what she had asked him to do.

Moving back to her chair, she fanned herself. "It suddenly is ten degrees hotter than it was."

"If you're hot, get your suit on and we'll swim. A little exercise to work up an appetite."

She smiled and stood. "You don't have to ask twice," she said, starting toward the house. He caught up to hold the door for her.

"Race you out there."

She smiled again. "You've got a deal," she said, walking faster and turning to head to her suite.

She showered quickly and pulled on a new suit she had bought in Dallas because she had known of the availability of a pool at the ranch. She left her hair falling free, pulled a T-shirt over her suit and stepped into flip-flops to head to the pool.

She hurried out and then slowed to walk toward the pool when she saw Ryan bob up and swim to the edge to fold his arms and watch her, waiting quietly. His gaze was blatantly hot, intense and lusty.

Eight

Aware of his eyes steadily on her, she shed the T-shirt and kicked off her flip-flops after dropping a towel on her chair. She walked toward him, conscious of her bright blue one-piece swimsuit. It was skimpy, but it covered more than some of the suits she owned. Still, she had no intention of flaunting a nearly bare body in front of Ryan any more than she had to for swimming.

She suddenly hurried and jumped in the pool, swimming away from him farther into the deep end. He was instantly beside her. At the end of the pool he treaded water to face her. "Beat you once. Want to race?"

"Sure. What—to the other end and back here?"

"Yes. First one to touch this end of the pool wins."

It meant swimming around a fountain, but she was game. "You can say go."

"Oh, no. You say go. It'll give you a tiny edge that you'll need because I'm going to beat you."

"I don't think so," she said.

"One of us is wrong. If I win, I want a kiss. If you win, what would you like?"

She thought a moment and shrugged. "A back rub would be nice."

"Agreed. Say go when you're ready. I'll even give you five seconds."

"Don't be silly. Okay, let's go," she said, splashing into the water and swimming hard. They stayed together until they turned and started back and then he pulled ahead so easily she wondered if he had really tried before. She put all her effort into it, but there was no hope of catching him.

Bobbing up at the end, she shook her head and raked her hair back away from her face. "You win."

"You're good."

"Not good enough."

"You're definitely good enough," he said with innuendo. He moved closer while he treaded water. "I want my prize."

"Sure," she said, brushing his cheek with a kiss. "How's that?"

His arm banded her waist and he pulled her tightly against him. He was warm, wet, and they had almost nothing between them. One look at him and she closed her eyes as his mouth covered hers.

Instantly desire blazed, causing her to want to hold him. She wrapped her arms around his neck, tugging him more tightly to her while she kissed him in return. Their legs were brushing together, entangled, his leg slipping between hers while he pulled her against him and cupped her bottom to hold her close.

Her heart pounded. She lost awareness of everything except Ryan, his body, his mouth on hers, his hand moving on her. He leaned back and her top went down. He pulled her close, kissing away any protest.

His arm around her waist loosened and then she felt his hand on her bare breast, stroking her. Streaks of pleasure followed each touch and her hips thrust against him.

She wanted him. Need ignited into a raging fire, consuming her. His muscled leg was between hers, a warm, insistent pressure that added to desire. With a swift movement he pushed down her suit until it was caught around her legs. His hands seemed to be everywhere, caressing her, exciting her, driving her to want more, a steady demand that was sweet torment.

His erection was hard against her, hot, an indication of his hunger. She couldn't resist running her hands over his muscled shoulders, his chest and thick biceps. She trailed her fingers down his smooth back and then her hands slid over his firm buttocks down to his strong thighs.

She moaned with pleasure, a sound muffled by their kisses. He leaned away a fraction, cupping her breast and circling the tip with his thumb, causing her to gasp and cling more tightly to him.

She finally twisted away from him, treading water while she pulled her suit up again and tied it at the back of her neck. "Ryan, slow down," she said breathlessly. "We're once again headed where I can't go. I'm just not ready."

Treading water, he watched her in silence. Suddenly he pulled her to him and held her. "I'm more than ready. I'll do what you want, but I want you, Jessie, and someday again you won't say no. Someday you'll be as ready as I am because you have been and you're fighting yourself on this."

She started to answer, but his kiss took her reply and she was lost, kissing him back, knowing she was falling in love with this tall, wonderful Texas rancher. Her mind told her she shouldn't, because they had no future, but she couldn't stop what her heart felt.

Momentarily, she was tempted to yield to passion and stop worrying about falling in love with him and getting hurt again.

Instead, she wriggled out of his embrace. "Ryan, we swim or go in. Which is it?"

They both were breathing heavily. His expression proclaimed his desire, and his dark-eyed gaze devoured her. Silence stretched while she waited for his reply.

"We swim," he said, releasing her completely and swimming away as if he were in a race for his life. She let him get a bigger distance ahead and then swam after him, working as hard as he had to try to let swimming take all her attention and ignore the clamoring of her body and her heart.

They swam laps but kept a distance from each other, and gradually she cooled and then she began to have an appetite for dinner. She climbed out, picked up her towel and wrapped herself in it. She stepped into her flip-flops and headed toward the house, hearing him splash behind her. She didn't look back but went inside to shower and blow-dry her hair before dressing for dinner.

She wore red slacks and a matching blouse. She was covered from head to toe except for her exposed forearms in the short sleeves. Too clearly the moments in the pool stayed with her, the memory of his wet body against hers, their wet legs entangled in the water. She ached to kiss him, to make love with him, to toss all caution aside.

Even with the swim and shower, she was hot with wanting Ryan. She was falling in love. She hoped not too deeply or too lastingly.

She returned to the kitchen to find him already there.

He was dressed in jeans, a plaid shirt and brown boots. The ends of his hair were still wet. She drew a deep breath. Just the sight of him stirred her libido and she longed to be back in his arms. She wanted to walk up to him and wrap her arms around his waist and stand on tiptoe to kiss him.

Instead, she talked about dinner. "I can grill trout, make a tossed salad and green beans. How's that for dinner?"

"Sounds fabulous."

He walked to her and her heartbeat accelerated. "I'll tell you what's even more fabulous," he said in a husky voice, resting his hands lightly on her shoulders. "You are, Jessie. Whether you're in the pool or in my arms or just standing here talking to me about ordinary things like dinner. I want to make love to you again and sometime you'll want to, too."

She couldn't answer. She did want to make love to him. Too much. That was the problem. But if she did, soon she would be deeply in love with him and that would be disastrous. The ranch was wonderful for recovery. But not for a lifetime, not for her, and Ryan wasn't about to get serious anyway. He never had been and she didn't think he was close to becoming serious now.

She shook her head. "I can't afford to, Ryan," she answered solemnly, being truthful in that answer. "I don't want to fall in love. It's too soon and I'm too uncertain in everything involving my heart. You won't fall in love. You're lusty. You want seduction and an affair. I'm trying to get over a relationship, not get into another one I'll have to get over. No, I have to step away. As appealing and sexy as you are, I can't get involved."

"Appealing and sexy? You call me that and then you

want me to ignore you and you want me to walk away? That becomes impossible."

"You can. You have to." She moved past him. "I've got to tend to dinner. You can help if you like," she added briskly, getting things ready.

In minutes they were working together and it was as if the past hour hadn't happened and she relaxed a degree. But she couldn't shake her awareness of him moving around her, not totally. Finally, she had to get a cold drink on ice.

Throughout dinner they sat and talked and she thought everything seemed all right, but she could feel an undercurrent of tension and desire that remained constant.

It was one in the morning before she finally told him good-night. He walked her to the door of her suite. He didn't touch her or kiss her, which was what she had asked, but all the time, she felt tingly, expecting him to. Even though she knew it was for the best, she couldn't help feeling disappointed.

The next morning she was waiting when Ryan came downstairs for breakfast. As he strolled into the kitchen, his gaze ran over her jeans, the pale blue knit shirt with a collar. Her hair was in a thick braid. The sight of her accelerated his heartbeat, as it always did. He wanted to walk up, pull her into his arms and kiss her, but he would honor her wishes and try to avoid touching her.

She said she wasn't ready to become emotionally involved, yet she wanted to kiss. She had wanted to make love the night they had done so. Thinking about loving her, kissing her, he was hot again. He wiped his brow. He wanted her, but he didn't want her hurt.

She was so worried about falling in love—something

that never concerned him. He would not fall in love. She was another beautiful, fun woman in his life, although he had to admit she was special to him in some ways. She was different because he knew she would be unforgettable and because she was living in his house, but otherwise, he didn't worry about a broken heart. While he didn't worry about himself, he didn't want to hurt her. He had always remained friends with the women he had broken things off with and he didn't want that to change.

Convincing himself to sidestep her, he helped himself to fruit and cereal, orange juice and coffee and sat at the table.

As she got her breakfast and sat across from him, he raised a quizzical eyebrow.

"To what do I owe this honor? You haven't eaten with me for quite some time."

"I have a better grip on my emotions and I wanted to eat with you."

"Great. I'll go for that," he said, thinking she had the biggest and most beautiful blue eyes he had ever seen. How easy it would be to sit here and look at her for the next hour. He could allow himself to sit back and remember her soft, warm body pressed against him in the pool last night. He didn't figure he'd convince her to swim with him again. He knew that would be playing with fire.

As they finished breakfast, he sat back in his chair. "I have a feeling when you move on, Jessie, you will leave me with this ranch filled with animals that I will have to care for."

"Of course not. Just one yellow cat—Sunshine. I'll tell Gwen to feed Sunshine. You'll never even know any of them are here and this way you will have saved some animals and given them a home." She sat back, smiling at him. "You're a good person, maybe too appealing."

"Don't tell me things like that if you want me to leave you alone."

She gave him a dimpled smile and then they both sat quietly.

"Penny for your thoughts," he said, finally breaking the silence.

"That's about all my thoughts just then would be worth. Just thinking again how poor my judgment has been."

"That's in the past. Let it go, Jessie. It's over if you want it to be over. Walk away and don't look back."

"It's not that easy."

"Let me show you a way to forget." He got up and picked her up, sitting back down with her on his lap.

"Ryan, Gwen should be in anytime now and we weren't going to do this and get into these situations."

"I don't exactly remember promising that. And you can move if we hear Gwen coming in. This is better. Jessie, we're not getting into anything serious. I'm just holding you. I still say, when you want, try a few kisses for fun—and they are definitely fun. That's not going to hurt. Kisses should help."

She smiled, shaking her head. "Kisses are intimate and they involve the heart and feelings. This is exactly what I'm talking about."

She scooted away, shaking her head as she began to clear the table.

When she spoke a few moments later, he could tell she was aiming for aloof and professional. "So what's your schedule today?"

"When I get to Dallas I'm meeting a friend for lunch,

Jared Weston. I haven't seen him for a while. His dad worked for mine and our families are close. I'll be in Dallas the rest of this week."

"I'll miss you, Ryan," she said quietly, turning to walk away.

His heart skipped with her statement, so uncustomary for her. He watched her walk away from him in her tight jeans and desire stirred. He wanted her as much as ever, but he was trying to do what she wanted and keep his hands to himself.

He stood and left the kitchen. Knowing she would miss him, he needed to put space between them or he would be trying to kiss her.

He was flown to Dallas in the small jet he kept in Bywater. At lunch he waved when he spotted Jared entering the restaurant. His friend approached his table and Ryan rose to shake his hand.

"How's the old married man?" Ryan asked, eliciting a grin from Jared.

"Doing great. You need to come see us. Allison is redoing the Dallas house, which is a hassle. But hey, you've had a great shot at the rodeos because I've been too busy to deal with them."

"The last time I rode was in New Mexico, in April."

"I hear you have a new cook. I ran into Will. He said only you could come up with a cook who has drop-dead-gorgeous looks and can cook better than ninety-nine percent of the professional chefs in the state."

Ryan laughed. "My brother. I'll have to tell her. She is gorgeous and she can cook better than ninety-nine percent of the chefs in Texas or any other state, for that matter. I should have taken Jeb up when he offered to bet me she couldn't make toast, but at the time, I figured he was right. No one this pretty should be able to cook this well."

"Well, what do you know? You sound like you are headed for the altar."

"No. Not at all. She has plans. I am just a stop on her agenda. She is here for a year. Then she will return home to Tennessee and open her own restaurant. I think she is practicing recipes and trying them on me. I am a mere guinea pig."

"Why did she come all the way to Texas to try cooking?"

"She had a rotten marriage and a bad divorce. Her ex didn't want to let her go and her parents didn't want her to go. She needed to get away from them."

"That makes sense. Out on the RD Ranch, she's away. Far, far away from Tennessee, especially any of the cities."

"That's right. She'll go home when a year's up. Besides, you know I'm not interested in marriage. And neither is she."

"That's what I thought and look at me."

"Allison is a good-looking woman and you've known each other all your lives and you've worked together. For you, love just happened. Besides, you probably got married to get out of rodeo competition with me and save face since I beat you most of the time," Ryan said with good-natured teasing.

"Oh, sure. I'm so scared of you and your super talent for bull riding," Jared remarked drily. "If you end up married to your cook, I'll remind you of this conversation."

"Like I said, she's going back to Tennessee. She has no interest in the ranch," Ryan said, having a hollow feeling at the thought of the ranch without Jessica.

"Too bad. Will said Jeb has told him about her cooking. If he's gushy about how great it is, it really is. Jeb doesn't come out with praise for anything."

"Amen to that one. Jeb was in shock. Jessica and her fire-engine-red sports car."

"You better try to hang on to her."

"I'll hang on as long as I can," he said, clapping his good friend on the back. "By the way, I heard you sold the Houston mansion. I'm happy for you."

"It was beautiful and I'll always be grateful for the inheritance from your dad."

"He was always grateful to your dad for saving his life. He never forgot."

"I appreciate it and Dad would have had he lived to know. It just wasn't the place for me and I didn't need it."

"None of us wanted it, so it's just as well. I'm not sorry it's gone from the family. It got you and Allison together, so that was good."

They ordered burgers and after lunch as they stood on the sidewalk, Ryan shook hands with Jared. "Come see me soon," Ryan said. "You'll have a delicious dinner."

"I'm having some pretty good ones at home now."

He laughed. "Take care."

The two men parted and Ryan headed to the small office he kept in Dallas. His thoughts were on Jessica. He needed to go out with someone else and get his mind off her—get involved with someone who could distract him from Jessica. Right now the idea of taking someone else out held no appeal for him. He wanted to go dancing again with Jessica. He wanted it all with Jessica… and that wasn't going to happen. He couldn't imagine a year like the past week, trying to keep his hands to himself and avoid kissing her.

Was he falling in love?

He wasn't, and *if* it ever happened, he probably wouldn't realize it until she was gone out of his life.

Thinking about her, he was anxious to see her and be with her. He would be in Dallas until the weekend. If he had good sense, he would get busy and find something to keep him away on the weekend, too. On impulse, he called Jeb and asked him if everything was okay.

"If you mean Jessica, she's fine," Jeb replied.

"I thought I'd check and see."

"Another dog wandered up and of course she took it in and called me. I took it to the vet and had it dipped and cleaned up and now it's staying with the rest of the dogs."

"I'm sure that made Jessica happy."

"Yeah. She cooked some kind of chicken casserole for us. I picked it up and we had it for supper. I've never been as wrong about anyone in my life as I was about her and her cooking. That woman is the best cook I've ever known."

"That's rather high praise coming from you," Ryan said. "I wanted to let you know I'll be home late Friday afternoon. See you then or on Saturday." Actually, he wanted to go to the ranch now. He missed being with Jessica. She had become a part of the ranch life he loved, and he missed it. But most of all he missed her. He gave in to temptation and called her.

The moment he heard her voice, he felt a pang of longing. He wanted to get his plane and fly home in the next hour. He couldn't tell her he missed her, but he did. He missed her more than he would have imagined possible. When had she become so much a part of his life that he missed her when he was away from her?

"What's been happening?" he asked casually, though

her activities were the last thing on his mind. All he could think about was holding her and kissing her. He longed to ask her to go to dinner and dancing, but that wouldn't be what she wanted, so he bit back the invitation.

He listened while she told him about the new dog. "Another dog to add to the collection?" he said. "Jessica, word will get out and people will start dropping their animals at the RD Ranch."

She laughed as if he had made up the most ridiculous idea.

I miss you. He mouthed the words, wanting to say them but knowing the sentiment would not make her happy. He settled back to talk, listening to her argue that people couldn't possibly find out that they have new strays at the ranch and the strays now had a home and the RD Ranch would take any and all stray animals.

He didn't want to break the connection and end the call. It went on for the next half hour and he still wanted to continue talking to her, but she said she needed to go get something out of the oven and she cheerfully told him goodbye as if she didn't care whether or not they talked.

Even though he wanted to go to the ranch, Friday night Ryan accepted an invitation to go see Will and his family. He had dinner with them and stayed at the condo he kept in Dallas for occasions when he had to stay in the city on business. Saturday morning he flew back to the ranch early.

He called Jessica to tell her he was on his way back and when he entered the house, he found her in the kitchen. He felt as if he had been away from her for weeks instead of days. She turned to smile at him when he entered the room. Dressed in jeans and a V-necked red knit shirt, she looked breathtaking. He wanted to cross the room, take her into his arms and kiss her, but he knew better than to do so. He felt a tightness inside him and his voice developed a rasp he couldn't control.

"Hi. I missed you and you look great," he said, crossing the room but standing several feet away. He got down a glass to get a drink of water just to keep from reaching for her.

"Thank you. I hope you had a good week. Would you like some breakfast?"

"Thanks. I ate before I left Dallas. What's been happening here with you?"

"I'm trying new recipes. By the time I'm ready to open a restaurant, I want some new recipes that are uniquely my own. Maybe we'll have one tonight."

"Sounds good to me," he said, wanting to take her out dancing again but certain she would refuse.

"I'll have a cookie and a glass of milk," he said, pouring the milk and then getting one of her chocolate-chip almond cookies from the cookie jar. He sat at the table to talk to her while she moved around the kitchen.

"Let's drive to Lubbock to eat dinner tonight, Jessica. No dancing, just a nice dinner if you'd like that best. Want to?"

She turned again while she thought it over. "Yes, thank you. Dinner out should be fine. But that's a long drive."

"Not out in these parts. I'll get reservations."

The doorbell rang and Jessica headed for the front entrance. "I'll answer the door. You and I are the only ones here at the house today. It's probably a delivery," she said.

Ryan followed her to see who was there. It was so unusual to have someone come unannounced to the front door that he was curious about it.

She glanced out and looked over her shoulder at Ryan. "It's not a delivery. It's a new four-door white sedan."

"Wait a minute and let me see," he said, moving quicker as she looked out a window, peering around to see the front of the house.

Her face paled and she turned to look at Ryan. "I don't believe it. It's Carlton."

Nine

"Jessica, wait," Ryan said. "Let me go. You don't even have to talk to him unless you particularly want to. Just wait in the kitchen and I'll take care of this. Do you want to talk to him?"

The door chimes sounded again. She shook her head. "No, I don't. But I don't mind dealing with him, because you shouldn't have to. He is definitely not your problem."

"No, he sure as hell is not, so I'll talk to him. You go on. Don't give it another thought." Staring at him, she remained immobile as if caught in indecision.

"Go on, Jessie. I'll handle this. I don't mind," he said.

She nodded and passed him. He reached the door, taking the knob in his hand and pausing to glance over his shoulder. Jessica was nowhere to be seen, so Ryan swung open the door. A brown-haired man in a charcoal suit paced the porch and whipped around to face Ryan, striding toward him.

"I'm Carlton Thorpe. I'd like to see my wife, Jessica Thorpe."

"I'm Ryan Delaney and this is the Delaney ranch, Mr. Thorpe. And Jessica is no longer your wife. She's Jessica Upton now and she said she doesn't care to see you. You've had a trip for nothing."

"Look, she's my ex-wife. I came from Tennessee to see her and I'm not going back without doing so. One way or another."

Ryan tilted his head to look at Thorpe. He had looked up Carlton Thorpe and knew a bit about him—that he was wealthy and from a prominent Memphis family. His light brown hair and light brown eyes were like the picture of him on the computer. The man should have no trouble finding women who were attracted to him.

"You won't see Jessica if she doesn't want to talk to you. You don't have rights to force her to and you're not going to try, not on my ranch."

"I love her and I want her to come home."

Ryan still stood relaxed, watching Thorpe carefully. "She told me clearly that she doesn't want to talk with you. So that's that. Now, I can call Sheriff Rickle and have you removed from my property if I have to, but I don't think that will be necessary."

"Dammit. I need to see her," Carlton said, doubling his fists and moving toward Ryan.

"Thorpe, as far as her ever coming home to you again, it's not going to happen. I'm in love with Jessica and hope to marry her, so you might as well give up talking to her and go on your way."

Carlton Thorpe's mouth dropped open. With a flushed face and clenched fists, he stood there gulping for air. "You can't keep me from seeing her. And she can't marry you."

"Yes, she can. She is legally divorced. Like I said, you've had a long trip for nothing."

The two men faced each other. Carlton clamped his

mouth closed, standing with his fists still balled. Ryan faced him, waiting, watching for Carlton to swing at him. He kept his stance relaxed, but he was ready.

Suddenly Carlton turned and went down the steps. He strode to the car, climbing in and switching on the engine. With a squeal of tires, he pulled away. The car shot down the road, leaving a plume of dust rising behind it.

Ryan watched until the car was out of sight. He pulled out his phone to call Jeb.

"Hey, Jessica's ex, Carlton Thorpe, was just here." He filled his foreman in on the conversation. "I want you to get some guys to watch in case he comes back. He doesn't belong on the ranch. He's not welcome here, so just tell him to get off our property. Anything else he wants, he can try a phone."

"Sure. I'll pass the word and we'll watch for him. What's he driving?" Jeb asked.

Ryan gave him a description of the car.

"We'll watch. Don't worry about it."

"Thanks." He ended the call, pocketed his phone and went inside, pausing to lock the front storm door and then the inside door before heading back to the kitchen.

I'm in love with Jessica and hope to marry her.

The statement reverberated in his thoughts. A declaration that he loved Jessica. He stopped in his tracks to think about it. He had declared that strongly and with sincerity.

How much of that statement was true?

How easily the words had rolled off his tongue. He had told Carlton that to send him on his way back to Tennessee, but had there been any truth to it? What did he feel for Jessica?

Lost in thought, Ryan stood in his front hall. Was he

falling in love for the first time in his life? Was it real love, or did he feel so strongly about her because he wanted her back in his bed to make love to her again? He had never had a woman decline his offer to make love again. Was that what made him want her so badly? Or was it because she was living in his home, in his life regularly?

Was what he felt infatuation? Lust? Or real love? He had never been in love, so he couldn't answer his own questions.

Ryan frowned. Jessica was upsetting his usually happy-go-lucky life and for the first time he wasn't sure how deep his feelings went.

In the kitchen he found her stirring a mixture in a bowl. She looked up, put down the bowl and washed her hands, drying them and turning to him. He saw the concern on her face, though she obviously tried to hide it.

"Thank you. I take it he's gone."

"For now."

"He doesn't give up easily," she said. "I called home to see if either of my parents had let him know where to find me. My dad talked to him when they returned home, but he didn't tell him where I am. I also talked to Lydia, who had talked to my brother Derek." She shook her head. "I think it was through my brother-in-law or my brother. They're close with Carlton."

"It doesn't matter now. Hopefully, that's the last you'll see of Carlton unless you want to see him again."

"I don't know why he persists. Maybe it's his ego."

"I think he'll give up this time."

She shot him a concerned look. "You didn't threaten him, did you?"

"No. I didn't."

She crossed the room to hug him. "Thank you, Ryan. This has been the best possible place for me to find work and live. Thank you for hiring me and for talking to Carlton."

She hugged him lightly, but Ryan's heart thudded at her first touch. He was so glad to hold her. His arms tightened around her waist and he pulled her closer against him. He had longed for her all week. His mouth covered hers and he kissed her hard, his other hand winding in her silky hair. Everything inside him heated. He was instantly aroused, wanting her with a desperation that he had to bank.

He leaned over her. She was soft, tantalizing, gorgeous, and he was burning with desire. He had to back off, to go at her pace when all he wanted to do was carry her to bed and make love to her all weekend long. He raised his head. Her eyes were closed, her lips parted. She opened her eyes to look at him.

"I've missed you, Jessie. I want you," he whispered, and lowered his head to kiss her again.

She slipped an arm around his neck, holding him while she kissed him in return. In seconds her arm tightened. He picked her up, carrying her to a sofa, where he sat and cradled her head against his shoulder while he leaned over her to continue kissing her. He didn't want to stop or let her go. He was afraid to touch her elsewhere because it might break the spell, cause her to make him stop kissing her. He would take a chance later, but right now he couldn't bear to release her.

He had missed her, longed for her, dreamed of her, but he hadn't realized how much until she'd touched him and then he'd come apart with need. He held her as if she was necessary for his existence.

He kissed her passionately, letting go all his pent-up need. He poured into the kiss all the hunger for her he had tried to ignore all week while he was in Dallas. How many times had he reached for a phone and then pulled away, trying to give her space and peace of mind?

Now she was in his arms, warm, soft, sexy, making him hard with desire. Erotic visions of her from the time they had made love danced in his thoughts. He wanted all barriers of clothing gone between them. He wanted her bare body in his arms, held close against him, there for him to touch and kiss and fondle.

Her beauty took his breath away and made his heart pound. Her kisses set him on fire. He grazed her smooth throat, sliding his hand lower, so slowly, moving down beneath her knit shirt to caress her. With a moan she twisted slightly and her breast filled his hand, her softness making him want more. He ached to make love to her, to thrust himself into her softness, to become intimate, as close as possible to her, to pleasure her until she couldn't bear more.

Was this love? Was he really in love? He raised his head to look at her and he paused to pull her knit shirt slowly over her head. Next he unfastened her bra and pushed it off. He cupped both breasts.

He couldn't tell her his feelings, because it would upset her. She didn't want his love, didn't want a serious relationship or any kind of intimate relationship. Nothing beyond kisses and caresses. And he had to honor her wishes.

How could he be in love with someone who didn't love him in return? Was he totally wrapped up in lust, wanting her for hot sex and nothing else?

He shifted, moving her onto her back on the sofa while

he hovered over her. He continued kissing her as his hand slid down the length of her.

He yanked off his shirt to toss it aside, returning to kissing her because he was afraid she would make him stop at any moment.

Instead, she unfastened his jeans, freeing him, an indication that she wasn't going to stop. His heart pounded with excitement. Desire mushroomed, building until he was burning with need. For a fleeting moment the thought crossed his mind that he was getting involved with a woman who would want a total lasting commitment, something he wasn't into. Could he deal with that—or with the hurt he would cause by not making that kind of commitment?

Ignoring the thought, he stood up to step out of his clothes. He pulled her into his embrace, his hands peeling away her jeans and lacy panties, the bra having already fallen away. Kissing her, he picked her up and carried her to the nearest bed.

He flung away the covers and placed her on the bed. When he climbed onto the mattress, she rolled over so he was beneath her. She leaned down to him, her blond hair a curtain falling over her shoulders.

While she kissed him, he placed his hands on her waist and entered her, filling her slowly, trying to maintain control so he could pleasure her as long as possible.

She threw her head back, moving on him, wild and fast, and he pumped with her until his control shattered and he climaxed. She sprawled over him and he held her close, wanting to keep her in his arms against his heart.

"I missed you," he whispered, stroking her back lightly.

She turned to look up at him and then she shifted beside him. He turned onto his side to face her, still with his arm around her tiny waist.

"I want to stay here with you in my arms," he confessed. "I know we weren't going to do this, but I'm glad we did. I've been trying to do what you want, Jessie, but I missed you so damn much while I was in Dallas."

Her eyes widened slightly as if he had surprised her. Was she so wrapped up in her future plans that he meant nothing to her?

She squeezed him, hugging him tightly while she raised her head to brush a kiss on his shoulder, but she kept an uncustomary silence as she laid her head back on his shoulder. Had he angered her? Disappointed her? It wasn't like her to be so quiet.

Even as he worried, he couldn't keep from relishing the moment because she was in his arms and he didn't want to let her go.

Was he in love?

The question constantly plagued him now. If he was in love, he had fallen in love with the wrong woman. He didn't think she would move in with him or have even a brief affair. He wasn't ready for a lifetime commitment. Not at this point. He didn't even know if what he felt was truly love.

He combed his fingers gently through her hair, wishing she would stay in bed with him for hours.

"Jessica, are you unhappy?" he asked.

She shifted slightly to look up at him. "I'm worried because I wasn't going to do this again. Each time I make love to you, a chunk of my heart becomes yours and the bond between us grows stronger for me. I was a virgin when I married. I know, that doesn't fit with my looks and my social life. I've always drawn boys and been friends with them, but intimacy holds a deep meaning for me, physically and emotionally. That's why this divorce has been so upsetting. It tore up all my faith in myself and my judgment. I'm scared of doing that again."

"Ahh, I don't want to ever hurt you."

She shifted, scrambling to grab the sheet and tug it around her and beneath her arms. Getting aroused again, he watched her, thinking she had to be the most gorgeous woman he had ever known, and the sexiest. He reached out to toy with her soft hair. "You don't need that sheet."

"Yes, I do," she said, beginning to sound more brusque, as if she was throwing up a wall between them. It was his fault. Because of his actions he had brought on unhappiness for her and he'd never intended that. His hand stilled while he studied her.

"I shouldn't have let this happen," she said as if thinking aloud. He had never heard a woman say that to him before and it was like getting stabbed in his heart to hear it come from Jessica.

"Jessica, you were a willing, eager participant. I didn't force anything."

"Of course not. I didn't mean that. It's just that you're irresistible to me—"

He groaned. "When you say something like that, how can I keep from reaching for you? Irresistible? That makes me want you in my arms with all my being."

"It's just a fact. Now let me finish."

He inhaled and stared at her. "You're a complicated woman."

"We're all complicated, Ryan. Well, maybe you're less so because you don't take life too seriously. Look, you're not the marrying type. I have a feeling you've had a string of relationships that simply meant a good time to you.

I think you've left some broken hearts behind because I've seen local women look at you the way a hungry dog looks at a bone."

"Jessica—"

"Wait and listen to me," she said, frowning slightly. "Even if you fell madly in love with me and I fell in love with you, we couldn't possibly marry and I would get hurt badly again."

"I can think of reasons for us to avoid marriage, but I want to hear your theories on this," he said, scooting up in bed so he faced her and tossing the tail of the sheet across himself.

"I promise you that I'm going home to Tennessee," she declared firmly, giving him a steady, intense look. "You are going to retire in a few years and become a full-time rancher. We would not fly back and forth and see each other on weekends or anything else. I'm not giving up going home to Tennessee. I've told you before that your ranch has been perfect for me to have a quiet, secluded life, but for a lifelong commitment, I couldn't possibly live here.

"All of your relationships have been short, not serious. I don't care to stay in Texas for a fling and then watch you walk away. I'm really not the type for you. I'm way too earnest about life and relationships." She shook her head, as if to rid herself of her thoughts. "It's a moot point right now because we're not deeply in love. But if we keep making love like this—and I'm including dinner and dancing as well as making love—we might be in love. Real love."

"I think you're conjuring up something you don't need to worry about," he said quietly. "I don't mean to hurt

your feelings, but I'm not remotely ready for marriage. I
know you're not either at this point in your life."

"No, I'm not, but I don't want to fall in love with you.
We get along. We have fun together and you're incred-
ibly sexy. You're also incredibly kind and understanding.
More so than anyone else has ever been."

Leaning forward, he inhaled deeply as he slid his arm
around her waist. "Jessica—"

"Ryan, are you listening to me?"

"Absolutely."

"No, you're not or you wouldn't have put your arm
around me. That's exactly what I think I should avoid
and I've been telling you why." She wriggled away and
stood, sweeping the sheet around her and leaving him
and her clothes, which were scattered about the room.

"Way to go, Delaney," he whispered to himself. Now
he would have to keep his distance. Yet Jessica had been
ready and willing to make love. All the worries and cool-
ness had come afterward. She had been an eager partner.
Telling him that he was "irresistible" to her just made
him want her more than ever.

Even so, she was unhappy and he had caused it and it
made him feel terrible. He wanted her happy and filled
with her usual smiles. This wasn't like her.

"Dammit," he said, standing to gather his clothes. He
placed hers in a heap on a chair where she could find
them and then left for his suite to shower and change.

All the time he showered, he tried to think of ways
to make amends to her. The best way would be to stay
in Dallas or work in Houston. If he gave her time and
distance, she might cheer up and feel better again. He
would accompany her to church Sunday morning and
then leave for Houston.

He needed to treat her as his cook and nothing else. No taking her out again. It was what she wanted and he was making her miserable this way. Besides, he was beginning to feel too much, be too serious about her. He needed to distance himself for his own sake. He thought about the night, which had been perfect until after their lovemaking.

As he showered and dressed in jeans and a denim shirt, he continued to think about their lovemaking. She was exciting, fun, beautiful, sexy, hot and giving, totally responsive to him.

And now she was off-limits.

He sighed as he combed his hair. He hated to think about not being around her. He stared at his reflection, but instead of himself he was seeing Jessica's big blue eyes clouded with worry. He shook his head and left. He'd head out to find Jeb and some work to do. He had to keep busy if he wanted to keep out of Jessica's way.

He worked with his hands all day, ate at the bunkhouse with the men and then went back to the house, going to his suite without seeing her. He worked on his computer—he kept the same records at home as he did at his office. Finally, he showered and crawled into bed, but sleep wouldn't come.

He gave up and dressed again to go to the rec room connected to the bunkhouse. There were always guys still up and often a poker game he might watch. He never played at the ranch, because he didn't want to win and take money from guys who worked for him. Jeb was a poor sleeper, so he might still be up and around.

When he stepped outside, the yellow tabby was curled up in a padded chair. The cat raised its head to look at him with big cat eyes. He walked over to pet it. "Sunshine, right now you're making her a lot happier than I am. I hate to envy a cat, but I think I do. I hope you like your new home. You came to the right place, just please don't put out the word about the ranch." He went down the porch steps and stopped in the barn to look at the new dog and pups, but they were nowhere to be found and he guessed they must be at the bunkhouse.

"Ry?"

He heard Jeb and turned around. "Yeah."

"I saw the light come on up here and couldn't imagine who was in here. Most of the guys are in town. The few that are left are either sacked out or in a poker game."

"Where's the mama and her pups?"

"They're with the guys. The pups are getting cuter and everyone wanted them around, so they've moved her. Jessica seems happy and for sure the pups are. C'mon. We can sit on the porch."

Ryan went with him, switching off the lights and walking in an easy silence beside Jeb. They climbed the wooden steps and sat in tall rockers. Ryan propped his feet on the porch rail. "I've made her unhappy, Jeb. I think I need to stay out of her way. I'll go to Houston or Dallas and give her some space. I don't want her to quit, because she's mending. She keeps saying the ranch is a good place for her."

"Might be, but if you go to Houston or Dallas, there's no reason for her to stay and cook, because there's no one to cook for half the time. There's staff, but they eat here or elsewhere a lot of the time."

Ryan thought about Jeb's statement and they sat in silence. "She'll stay because she volunteers in town. When I'm here I have to stay out of her way and treat her the same way I do Gwen and the others," Ryan said finally.

"I expect that's right. I'm sure you never intended to make her unhappy. She understands that, doesn't she?"

"Yes. I think she's a little unhappy with herself. She thinks we shouldn't go out together. That's worrying her. She's still unsure of herself from what's happened and she doesn't want to get involved with anyone."

"So give her time alone. That's simple."

"Yeah," Ryan said. "I'm going to have to do that."

"You sound like you are declaring you're going to have to jump off Lonesome Peak."

"Yeah. I feel kinda like it," he admitted. "She's good company and if she leaves, I sure will miss her cooking," he said. He would miss more than her cooking, but he couldn't make that admission to Jeb. His private life had always been private. He was as close to Jeb as he was to Zach, maybe closer, but there were a lot of things he didn't care to put into words or try to explain or even share with anyone else.

"I figured this day would come sometime," Jeb said, "but I didn't expect it with her. When she drove up in that red car of hers, she looked like the party girl deluxe."

"Far from it. Jeb, she takes life seriously. She's fun when we're out, but she's not a party girl."

"Just goes to show you can't make rash judgments. I know she's tenderhearted. Just look at the dogs and the cat she took in. I'll tell you, if the animal kingdom can communicate, you're going to have a flood of homeless pets."

"I know. Let's just hope they don't communicate."

"We have a hound hanging around that she hasn't spotted yet and it's skittish with the guys, but I figure sooner or later, it'll drift up to your house and have a home. Then there was an old cat that Theo shot."

"Oh, hell. If she gets word of that, she'll pack and go."

"It wasn't like Theo did it for no reason. That cat was rabid for sure. It was an old fighter alley cat that lived its nine lives years ago. It had a stump of a tail, one ear slightly gone and one eye gone. It was killing chickens and kind of loony. It would hiss at anyone who came close."

"Nothing on this earth would hiss at Jessica. If it had rabies, it had to go. But please don't even mention it to Jessica."

They sat in another easy silence and Ryan thought about Jessica. He wanted to be with her now, to hold her. He should have just kept quiet and held her close and at least he would have had more time with her.

He sighed, hating that she was hurt or worried, missing her, wishing he'd done more to try to ease her concerns.

"Want a beer?"

"Sure."

Jeb got up and went inside to return in minutes with two beers, handing one to Ryan.

"Thanks."

They sat and sipped their beer and Ryan was lost in thoughts about Jessica again. Finally, he rose. "I'll head home. See you tomorrow, Jeb."

"Sure, Ry."

He walked back through the darkness, his thoughts on Jessica. Was she able to sleep? He didn't want her to quit or leave. He would have to avoid her and personal contact and when he was around her, treat her just as he did Gwen.

He wasn't certain that was possible. And it hadn't really helped that she'd told him that he was "irresistible" to her. He groaned aloud as he climbed the steps and crossed the porch to go inside. He locked the door and went to his gym. The door was closed, but he heard the treadmill running. He debated whether to go in or stay away. Maybe it was Gwen on the treadmill. If it was, he would go ahead with his exercise. But if it was Jessica... He thought he'd better leave her alone, so he turned around and went to his room.

Before he entered, he stopped and thought about her walking on the treadmill. She obviously couldn't sleep either. He swore softly and turned around to head back to his gym. He went inside and made his way to the elliptical machine with just a wave at Jessica.

She smiled, which made him feel a tiny degree better. At least she would smile at him.

Ignoring her, he adjusted the machine and began to work out. She wore earbuds and had a radio in her pocket. He worked up a sweat, which she had already done when he'd entered. Her hair was in a ponytail, bouncing as she ran, with tendrils falling free around her face.

She wore shorts and it took an effort to keep from looking at her long bare legs. When had she gotten so important to him? Whatever happened between them, he didn't want her to leave. That would make him feel terrible, besides missing her.

He'd worked out for twenty-five minutes when he heard the treadmill slow. He watched her stop and turn off the machine, then switched his off and stepped away.

"Jessica," he said, picking up his towel to wipe his forehead and drape it around his neck. "Wait up." He caught up with her. "You look like you've had a good workout."

"Yes," she answered, still waiting.

"Let's go get ice water and talk just a minute. We can sit in the kitchen. I want to talk to you."

For a moment he thought she was going to say no, but then she nodded. "For a short time, Ryan. It's late and church is tomorrow."

"Thanks. Also, I'd like to go to church with you—for the same reason I've gone before."

"Sure, thanks."

He walked beside her in silence, fighting the urge to touch her. He wanted to place his arm across her shoulders, an innocuous gesture, but he resisted and kept his hands to himself. She was uncharacteristically quiet with him, which also made him feel bad.

In the kitchen he switched on lights. "You have a seat. I'll get drinks or anything else you want. What would you like?" Ryan asked.

"A glass of water is good," she said as she headed for the kitchen table in the adjoining area.

Ryan got ice and filled glasses with cold water, then carried one to her before pulling out a chair across from her.

Jessica watched him in silence. She was torn with mixed emotions. She had said what she needed to and gotten away from him, something else that needed to be done. She should just quit and move on, but the place was absolutely perfect for what she wanted. She was already better, far more relaxed, stronger, healthier, more able to cope. She hadn't meant to sound so harsh and she could admit to herself that a good part of her anger and impatience was at herself and not at Ryan.

She hadn't meant for the lovemaking to happen today. Yet his slightest touch, his kisses, his being gone all week—it had all built to exactly what had happened. He was irresistible to her. She shouldn't have told him that, but he was. She should have discouraged him, avoided seduction.

She didn't want to quit and move on, but if she had to, she would. This had been the haven she wanted. On a temporary basis, she loved everything about the ranch and also about Bywater—the people she had met and friends she was beginning to make. No matter how great it all was, she couldn't deal with it and have an affair with Ryan at the same time. She would be in love with him and that would be a major disaster. He should understand, but she suspected he had never taken an affair seriously and he couldn't begin to grasp why she was so upset.

She faced him as she sipped her water and wondered why he wanted to talk. She wouldn't change her mind.

"Jessie, I didn't want to hurt or upset you today," he said solemnly, and she drew a deep breath. Now she felt she had been hurtful to him and that wasn't what she had intended.

"I know you didn't. We made love. We shouldn't have. I'm the one who should have prevented it. I'm the one who didn't want to while at the same time, you know I wanted to. That's the problem. I do want to, but I'll get hurt badly if I continue an intimate relationship with you."

"We won't, because you don't want to. Don't quit your job. You like it here and I like your cooking. I can work with you as employer and cook. I do need a cook. If that's what you want, that's what we'll do."

Wondering if he would do exactly what he said, she gazed at him. She finally nodded. "Very well. That would be good. This is a wonderful job."

"Fine. That's settled and we can let everything else go. Don't worry or concern yourself about what's happened between us. I'll still go to church with you, for the same reason I told you the first time, unless you definitely don't want me to go."

"Oh, no. I'll be glad for you to go with me. I don't want men asking me out."

"Good. I don't either," he said, smiling at her, and she smiled in return. Ryan was being kind, understanding and cooperative again—all the more reason she needed to keep a distance from him. Everything he did drew her to him. All her anger tonight—she had to admit that most of it had been directed at herself. She was the one who should have said no and walked away from making love, but she had wanted him with all her being.

"That's better," Ryan said, sounding genuinely relieved. "I don't want to hurt or worry you. I want to see you smile. We've got that settled. That's all I wanted. I'll go back to my workout unless you want to sit and talk for a few minutes."

For a moment she debated asking him to stay, which was what she'd have liked, but then wisdom said to let him go. She had to start keeping a distance from him.

"I suppose you should return to your workout and I have to get some sleep. I'll see you tomorrow about time to leave for church."

"Sure, Jessie. Tonight was special, but I'm sorry if it upset you."

"I'm okay and we're working it out where everything will be better," she replied, knowing it wouldn't seem better, but in the long run, it had to be better for her. Ryan could have an affair and walk away, but she couldn't, so that was that.

She watched him leave the room, her gaze running over him while her insides felt squeezed by an invisible fist. It was for the best, she reminded herself, trying to ignore the hurt and the forlorn feeling she had and the longing to be in his arms again.

Ryan left, heading back for his gym, but his thoughts were still on Jessica. She had hesitated for only a few seconds, but it was long enough that for an instant he'd thought she was going to ask him to stay. Instead, when she had merely nodded, he had risen, pushed his chair back to the table and left the room. He was disappointed she hadn't wanted him to stay and talk, but at least she had looked happier, relieved, and they were on better footing.

In the gym, he got on a treadmill to run, hoping to wear himself out so he could sleep and to run off the great longing he felt for Jessica. He had to forget her. The idea was ludicrous. He was about as likely to forget Jessica as he was to forget his identity.

It was less than two hours away from dawn when he finally sprawled in his bed, alone, and fell asleep.

The next morning he showered, shaved and dressed in his navy suit. Even knowing he had to stay professional and impersonal and keep his hands to himself, he couldn't wait to see her. When she walked into the informal living area that overlooked the pool and patio, Ryan turned, his attention caught by Jessie.

Dressed in a hot-pink suit, she looked ready for a photo shoot. Her hair was piled on her head, a far more formal look. She wore diamond studs in her ears.

He stood the moment she came through the door. "You

look nice and you don't look as if you missed five minutes' sleep."

"Thank you. I'm ready for church."

"Then we might as well go," he said, thinking he was making a monumental effort to remain polite and remote, to keep his remarks professional. He had a lot of other things he would far prefer to say and do. She walked out at his side and soon they drove away from the ranch.

It was a strain, but he spent the morning keeping his distance in every way. After church they did not remain in town to eat. The more he was with her, the more he wanted to let go and be himself, say what he wanted to her, touch her. Tomorrow morning he was heading to Houston to work for a few days. But in the meantime, he could foresee another sleepless night. How long before he began to get over her and forget about her?

He knew what he needed to do. He had to go out with someone else and try to get Jessica out of his system in every way. There was definitely no future with her.

At the ranch, he went to his suite to work on his computer while she got Sunday supper on the table. After she called him, he ate in a silent informal dining area. He was alone and didn't even see her. After dinner he left for the study to get out things he could work on, but after an hour he pushed the papers aside and decided to head for the bunkhouse and see what was happening there.

As he glanced outside, he saw Jessica bob up in the pool, which shocked him. He had guessed she would avoid any spot where she might encounter him, especially the pool. As if he were a puppet on a string with no control over his limbs, he headed outside for the pool.

He walked to the edge and waited until she surfaced.

She broke through the water, her wet blond hair swinging behind her face. He smiled at her. "How's the water?"

"Quite warm and pleasant. I'll be out in a minute if you're coming in."

His pool was definitely big enough for the both of them. He pulled a chair over and sat. She went under and shortly bobbed up farther away to swim to the deep end. It would make her happier if he left. Following his resolution and statements to her, he got up and returned to the house, going to his room to change into jeans, and then headed to the bunkhouse to see what the men were doing.

Jessica came up for air and saw Ryan going back into the house. As with everything involving him now, she felt both disappointed and relieved. She missed him constantly being with her. She missed his touches, his humor, his companionship. She had to admit she missed his lovemaking, too, but logically, this had to be better for her, so she was grateful to him again.

She swam for another half hour, climbed out and went in to shower and dress in jeans and her red T-shirt. She went to the kitchen to try a new recipe for next week's dinner.

Monday Ryan left for Houston and said he would be back on Thursday. She spent the days trying new recipes and cooking casseroles to put in the freezer for whenever Ryan would want them.

With each day, she missed him more instead of less and she missed the closeness they'd had. She hoped with a little more time, she would get over wanting to be with Ryan.

What she had gotten over faster than she had dreamed

would be possible was her failed marriage. That was one more thing that she had to be grateful to Ryan for. Because he was the biggest reason. All he had meant to her, and the quiet and solitude of his ranch.

She looked out the kitchen window at the land he loved so much. All around the house and the ranch were reminders of Ryan. Nowhere could she escape thoughts of him.

Did he care that they no longer shared the closeness they'd had? She wondered how much it had meant to Ryan. Did he even think about her when he was in Houston?

Did he miss her the way she missed him?

Ten

Ryan stood in his Houston office and looked out over the rooftops without seeing any of them. Instead he saw big blue eyes and a dimpled smile. He missed Jessie more than he had thought possible. She was right that they had no future together, so this was the way it had to be, and the sooner the better for both of them.

It all made sense when he thought it through, but it wasn't what he wanted. He wanted a full-blown affair and then he could let go. Deep down, each time he thought that, he suspected he was not being honest with himself. He wanted Jessie in his life—period. All the time. He thought about her constantly and he wanted to go back to the ranch to be with her. He missed her. He wanted to hold her, kiss her, make her laugh, make love to her, do whatever he could to keep her happy.

Unfortunately, the way to keep her happy was to stay away from her.

He hated not seeing her. He had never felt this way about someone before. Never. He called Jeb every day and asked about her. He hadn't gone home on Thursday as he'd planned and had been away from the ranch all of last week and most of this week. Today was Thursday, the second week of July, and he planned to spend another weekend in Houston, which was beginning to get him down.

He paced his office, circling back to the window as if he could look out and see his ranch, which was absolutely impossible. He felt caged in. He could not think of a single woman he knew that he wanted to go out with or even talk to. None but one.

Jessie.

In the afternoon he left his office to go shopping. Whether she went out of his life soon or next year, he wanted to get her something. She was important to him. He went to a jeweler he dealt with and spent the next two hours looking at necklaces and bracelets, finally deciding on a gold filigree necklace sprinkled with diamonds. In the center of the necklace sat a six-carat diamond encircled by smaller diamonds. He didn't know whether she would accept it or not, but he wanted to give her something lasting.

Anytime he thought about life without Jessie and contemplated the time when, in a year, she would pack and go forever, he hurt. He thought about his brother Zach, who had spent his adult life in demolition, getting so good at it that he was in demand worldwide. Zach had had wanderlust and had seldom been in the U.S., even less often at home in Texas. That was until he met Emma. Zach had tossed aside his whole way of life for her. He had settled down; he lived in Dallas and worked in an office that he went to daily.

Ryan thought about Jessie having to go home to Tennessee. Was Tennessee something she absolutely would not give up? Was living on the ranch something he wouldn't give up if it meant losing her?

Was that love?

He rubbed his head, which was beginning to hurt. Was he really in love enough to want to get married? It had happened too fast, too out of the blue.

On an impulse, he called Zach and made an appointment to have lunch with him the next day. He needed his brother.

Friday afternoon he flew to Dallas to meet Zach. At the restaurant as he sat across from his brother and ate a few bites of his burger, he told Zach about Jessie's father being so impressed by the Colt revolver. They talked about work and family throughout lunch and when they were finished, Ryan paid the check.

"It was good to see you," Ryan said.

Zach leaned forward and placed his arms on the table, pushing his plate aside. "Ryan, why the hell did you call me for lunch? What's wrong?"

"Nothing's wrong," he said, suddenly unable to tell his brother his problem.

They stared at each other and Ryan clamped his mouth closed tightly. "I'm fine, Zach."

"No, you're not. I'm trying to figure out what it is. Is your health okay?"

"Yes," he said, letting out his breath. "There's nothing wrong with me."

"I know it isn't money—unless you've taken up gambling."

Ryan had to laugh and shake his head. "Zach, how'd you make the transition from traveling all over the world to becoming a homebody?"

Zach's eyes narrowed and he studied his younger brother.

"Don't you dare laugh."

Zach couldn't hold it in. "Sorry, Ryan. This day has been a long time coming. Good grief. Propose to her. You'll survive getting married. It's a lot better than being single if you really love each other."

"How do you know if you really love each other?"

Zach laughed again. "I think you can answer your own question. That's probably why you didn't even bring this up after calling me." He sat up as if about to leave, but then his eyes narrowed again. "There must be a problem.... She doesn't like the ranch."

"Jessie loves the ranch."

"She can't gripe about your family. None of us meddle in each other's lives."

"She won't leave Tennessee."

"She's left it now."

"She's going back. She wants to live there and open her own restaurant and she's determined to do so."

"Ahh, I see." Zach stood and Ryan followed. "You'll work it out some way," Zach said as they walked out of the restaurant and paused in the parking lot. "I didn't think this day would ever come. I never thought it would happen to me. It does, bro, and if you can work it all out, it's great. Emma is my life. I wouldn't trade traveling everywhere for being with her for anything." He thumped his brother's shoulder lightly with his fist. "Cheer up, Ryan. You'll figure something out. And if it's not the real thing, you'll figure that out, too."

"Oh, thanks. I figured I'd get great words of wisdom from you," Ryan snapped, annoyed he had called Zach in the first place. "I don't want to hear anything about this at family gatherings."

Zach grinned. "Sure thing. Your secret is my secret. Why do I think everyone can guess just about as easily as I did?"

"Dammit, Zach—"

Zach laughed. "I'll see you, little brother. Take care of yourself and thanks for the lunch." He turned to head for his car.

"Dammit," Ryan repeated, wishing he had never had lunch with Zach. He wasn't one bit closer to getting answers to the questions he had and now Zach would torment him about being in love with Jessie.

In love with Jessie. How deep did his feelings really run? He was beginning to think really deep because the more he thought about it, the more he wanted her. He wanted her in his life all the time. He wanted to know she would be there when he came home.

He pulled out his phone to call his pilot. He was going home to the ranch and to Jessie. To hell with staying away. He wanted to be with her, even if he had to sit across a room and keep his conversation politely impersonal.

Jessica wondered about Ryan. He had told her he wouldn't be home again this weekend. She was convinced she had run him off. He was doing everything she had asked him to do—he no longer stayed at the ranch. She didn't hear from him and had no contact with him. He'd stayed away on the Fourth of July and she'd sat alone on the porch to watch the fireworks the ranch hands shot off. Jeb had politely invited her to join all the families at

the pond where they were picnicking and lighting fireworks, but she had thanked him and declined.

She missed Ryan, more than she had ever thought she
would. Had she gone from one problem to another one?

She was over her problems at home, but now she had
replaced them with new hurts.

How could she have fallen in love with Ryan so
swiftly? If it was because she was on the rebound, which
she had first thought, it seemed as if it would pass. The
longing for him, the feelings she had for him—nothing
had diminished in his absence. Far from it. She felt as if
she missed him more than ever. Each day seemed worse
and it seemed as if he had been gone much longer.

The ranch was quiet, solitary, empty without him.
She had asked Jeb to let her get a pup and bring it to the
house so she would have some company. He had come
up to meet her and walked with her, introducing her to
anyone they encountered that she hadn't already met.
She had sat on the floor of the porch of the bunkhouse
and played with the pups, finally picking a furry brown-
and-white one.

That had been two days ago. Now the pup lived in a
little area fenced by chicken wire that Jeb had made in
the yard and another dog pen in the kitchen with a small
crate and a soft pillow for a bed. Even though the pup was
cute and was fun, it couldn't replace Ryan. She missed
him and longed for him. She had fallen in love with him.
There wasn't a question in her mind whether or not she
loved him. It was a matter of how long it would take her
to get over him.

She had never intended for this to happen. She sat in
the grass in the yard, playing with the pup, wondering
how she had gone from hurting over one problem to hurt-

ing over another when she had come out here to recover and stop hurting.

She heard a car but didn't glance around, because cowboys came and went all hours of the day and night.

When the car stopped close to the house, she did look up...and she froze. She blinked as if she were imagining what she was seeing, because she recognized Ryan's black car. He was already out, striding toward the back gate.

She set the pup in the grass, stepped over the chicken wire and turned to watch Ryan approach in long strides. Her heart pounded and she wanted to run to him and throw her arms around his neck. She tucked back a lock of her hair that blew across her cheek. Ryan was in jeans and a navy knit shirt and he looked more handsome than ever. She became aware of her dusty cutoffs, her red T-shirt, her hair swiftly pulled back in a ponytail. And then she forgot everything else except Ryan.

She stood there, still fighting the impulse to go hug him, telling herself to remember what she should do.

Her heart thudded as he walked directly toward her. She wondered whether he would hug her, but then he stopped only feet away. "Hi," he said.

She couldn't get her voice, and the longing to throw her arms around his neck intensified.

"You decided to come home," she finally managed to say.

"Yeah, I did. I wanted to see you. I've missed you."

They stared at each other and her heartbeat raced.

"Oh, hell, Jessie," he said. "I know I promised I wouldn't touch you." He stepped forward and wrapped her in his embrace. "But I missed you so damn much."

She closed her eyes and hugged him. "I missed you, too, Ryan."

Her heart continued to pound, and longing made her cling tightly to him in spite of all the times she had said to herself that she wouldn't again. He felt so good, smelled so good. How was she going to resist him, even if he only wanted an affair and then he would be gone?

"Ryan." She leaned away to look up at him.

"Let's go into the house."

He slid an arm across her shoulders and walked with her into the house, closing the door behind them. When he lowered his arm from her shoulders, she walked away, turning to look at him.

"Let's go in the family room, where it's comfortable," he said. She still wanted to walk back into his arms. She loved him and couldn't keep from being glad to see him, happy to be with him again.

"I didn't know you were coming home," she said, smoothing her cutoffs. "I would have dressed better," she added, not even thinking about what she was saying to him.

"I don't care what you're wearing. You look gorgeous to me," he said. His voice was a deep rasp and desire burned in the depths of his dark eyes. Her heartbeat hadn't slowed. Resisting the urge to hug him continued to be an inner battle for her.

They entered the family room and he turned to her. "I wasn't coming home this weekend, but then I missed you. I had to see you."

"I'm glad you did. I've missed you, Ryan."

"Do you want me to go back to Houston next week?"

His question hung in the air. She knew he was asking about more than Houston.

"Ryan, I can't have an affair. I just can't do it." She couldn't keep the tears from spilling over and running down her cheeks. "I'm in love with you. I'll get over it because people do, but—"

He stepped close to slip an arm around her waist while he put his finger gently on her mouth. "Shh. Don't. Just let me talk a minute. I've been thinking about us."

"Ryan, there isn't an 'us.'"

"I think there is. Or at least there can be." He tilted her chin up so he could look into her eyes. "I missed you every day, every hour I've been gone. I want you in my life, Jessie. All the time. I want to come home to you. I don't think it'll be home without you."

"Oh, Ryan," she said, her heart breaking because his words were wonderful but what he was saying couldn't be. "I can't do it, Ryan. I've told you, I cannot have an affair."

"Jessie, let me talk. I've missed you more than I thought possible. And I've given a lot of thought to us." He framed her face with his hands. "I have never told a woman 'I love you.' Those words are for you. This is a first. I love you."

"Ryan," she whispered, hurting more than ever. His declaration made her heart ache, when she had wanted to avoid this and thought she was going to. "Ryan, we just can't."

"I love you," he repeated, gazing into her eyes. "Will you marry me?"

Startled, she stared at him. Never had she expected or thought about a proposal from Ryan. He had been so happy-go-lucky about everyone in his life.

"Marry you?"

"I want you to be my wife. I don't know how we'll

work it out, but if we love each other, there should be a way."

She blinked, still unable to fathom a proposal. "You want to marry me?" she whispered again. "But you're not the marrying type."

"You're not getting it. I love you. I have never been in love before," he said, slowly and distinctly.

She blinked as she stared at him. Suddenly, she hurt more than she ever thought possible. "And I love you. I've been in love with you almost since that first week. But we can't marry. I'm going home to Tennessee and you're going to live out here. I can't live on this ranch the rest of my life."

A muscle worked in his jaw and he stared at her. Suddenly, he wrapped his arms around her and drew her to him. "Dammit, I love you and I want to marry you. We've got to be able to work something out if you love me."

"We can't," she cried, swiping her hand at her eyes, hot tears still running down her cheeks.

He leaned down to kiss her. She could taste the salty tears, his mouth on hers. Her heart slammed against her ribs. She clung to him, tossing aside the worries for the moment while she kissed him hungrily, pouring out the love and longing she had for him.

Ryan was in her arms, holding her, telling her he loved her. She held him tightly, as if she knew she would lose him when she let him go. For right now he was in her arms for her to love and be loved by. At the moment that was all she wanted. The problems were insurmountable as far as she could see, but she wanted his kisses right now.

Finally, she pushed slightly against his chest to lean away and look up at him. "Ryan, we can't marry."

"We love each other. That's what's important. That's the most important thing. The other we should be able to work out some way. You want to live in Tennessee. I want to live here. Can we compromise some way? Let's think of possibilities. Can we live part of the time one place, part another?"

She shook her head, tears starting again. "We can't do this. You won't be happy away from your ranch. When the honeymoon is over and real life sets in, you'll want—you'll need—this ranch. And I'm that way about Tennessee."

"Jessie, I don't want to lose you. You're more important than this ranch," he said solemnly, his words bringing a fresh burst of tears to her eyes.

She swiped at them. "I can't keep from crying. I love you, but I don't see how we can work this out."

"I've been thinking about it," he said. "What if I open an office in Dallas and you open your restaurant there?"

When she started to speak, he held up his hand for her to wait. "I can get to the ranch from Dallas and we could spend some time here off and on. If I retire here, I can commute to Dallas. What if we build a home in Memphis or Nashville, whichever you prefer, and have it like a summer home or a vacation home and just live there some of the time? I know that's not exactly what you planned on, but could you live with that, Jess? I just can't see moving my office to Tennessee."

She stared at him while she thought about what he proposed. Live in Dallas most of the time. Open a restaurant there. A summer home in Tennessee.

How deeply did she love Ryan?

She looked into his dark brown eyes and had no doubt about the love he had declared for her, because it showed in his expression. Right now she felt his love enveloping her.

"I'm thinking about this, Ryan. That's a huge change. I've just always thought I'd spend my life in Tennessee."

"You can still spend some of it there and I'll spend some of mine there, too."

She thought about his proposal. Could she give up living all her life in Nashville? Would she be happy with what he suggested? She gazed into his eyes and considered his declaration of love. So many things all at once.

He leaned forward to wrap his arms around her. "I love you, Jessie. Really love you. I want to marry you. I want to be with you. This won't work if you don't want the same thing and if you don't love me, too."

"Ryan, I love you. I've been miserable without you." She gazed at him intently. "Yes, I'll marry you and we'll work it out and live in Dallas and sometimes here and sometimes in Tennessee. How's that?"

He swept her into his embrace to kiss her hard. She felt his heart pounding with hers. She wrapped her arms around his neck to kiss him as deeply as she could.

"I love you so," she whispered, crying and kissing him at the same time.

"I love you, darlin'. With all my heart."

She leaned back. "Ryan, the doctor said he thought I can have children, but he didn't give me a guarantee."

"If you can't, it sounds as if we have enough nieces and nephews between us that we can find some kid substitutes."

"You really can live with it if I can't give you a baby?"

"I can live with it. Ah, darlin', I want you. You're just right for me the way you are. We'll be together on this, whatever happens."

"You have to be the greatest, sexiest, most handsome guy ever," she said before she kissed him.

After a few minutes he stopped. "We have a lot of family to tell between yours and mine, but there's one call I have to make first. I need to call your dad and ask for your hand in marriage."

She giggled. "That seems incredibly old-fashioned."

"So do your folks, if you don't mind my saying so. I'm asking him before we call anyone else. Then you can tell your mom. Ah, Jessie," he said, "wait a minute. Don't go anywhere."

He left and came back shortly. He had his phone in hand and two small boxes.

"We can call in just a minute. First, this is for you." He handed her the larger of the two boxes. "I got it before I decided to propose marriage to you," he said, handing her a plain box tied with a pink silk ribbon.

She looked at him and then back at the box, taking it and untying the ribbon to open it. The diamonds dazzled her and she lifted out the necklace with the gold filigree and the diamonds.

"Ryan, this is gorgeous. This is too beautiful to wear."

"Well, I hope you'll wear it, because that's why I bought it. It's because I love you and you mean everything to me."

She held the necklace in her hand, turning it so light caught the diamonds and they sparkled. "Thank you." She threw her arms around his neck to hug and kiss him. His arm went around her waist and he pulled her tightly to him to kiss her in return.

She finally moved away to look at the necklace again. "This is so beautiful. Thank you."

"This is what I got after I decided to propose to you."

He handed her the smaller box tied with a yellow silk ribbon. She opened the box to remove another black velvet box and opened it. The ring—an eight-carat diamond surrounded by smaller diamonds—glittered in the light. She gasped, looking up at him in surprise and flung her arms around his neck again. He held her close while they kissed.

When she raised her head, they both gasped for breath. "I love you, Ryan, with all my heart."

He took the ring from her and held her hand, slipping the ring on her finger. "This is forever, Jessie. As long as we both live."

They kissed, another long kiss that left them breathless.

"Let's have this wedding soon."

"I don't want a giant wedding, Ryan, because I had one. And no destination wedding. I just want a small ceremony, just us. Will that upset you?"

He grinned as he shook his head. "Not at all. We don't have to have anyone except immediate family. Of course, that's still a lot of people on both sides. And we can have the wedding wherever you want. Let's let the family know. I want to call your dad."

She took the phone to put in the number and call. She talked briefly to her mother, then asked for her dad and told him that Ryan wanted to talk to him.

Looking at her ring, she listened to him ask to marry her. A silly tradition, but it would please her parents. And she felt sure that they liked Ryan and their only worry would be her living in Texas.

"Yes, sir," Ryan said. "We plan to live in Dallas. I'll open an office there or move the whole thing. Whatever I do, I'll work in Dallas. We'll build a home in Tennessee so we can live there part of the year and we'll stay on the ranch part of the time."

She listened while Ryan continued to talk and finally gave the phone to her to speak to her mother, who had listened to the conversation on her end of the line while the men had talked.

It was another ten minutes before she finally told her mother goodbye, promising to call back later in the evening after they had told the rest of the family.

"They're happy, Ryan. You impressed them, which I knew the minute you met them and invited them to the ranch."

He smiled. "Before we tell one more person, there's something else we've got to do. Come here. I've waited long enough." Then he picked her up and carried her to her bedroom.

Epilogue

They married in a chapel in Dallas with only relatives and close friends present. Will, Garrett and Jared were groomsmen, and Zach was the best man.

She wore a floor-length ice-blue dress with spaghetti straps, a straight skirt and plain lines. Her veil was suspended from a glittery headband. Around her neck she wore the necklace Ryan had given her.

As she started down the aisle on her father's arm, she felt overwhelmed with happiness. Her handsome fiancé waited, his gaze locked with hers. She couldn't see anyone else for looking at Ryan.

She repeated vows that she meant with all her heart and intended to keep the rest of her life. The love she had for Ryan seemed limitless and she just prayed they could have a baby.

They were pronounced husband and wife and introduced as Mr. and Mrs. Ryan Delaney.

They had pictures taken and finally were at a Dallas country club for the reception, to which many more guests had been invited.

The first dance was with Ryan and she stepped into his arms, smiling at him.

"You take my breath, you're so gorgeous, Jessie."

"You take my breath, as well, you handsome man."

He grinned. "The limo is ready. The plane is ready and we'll be in a New York penthouse tonight and Switzerland tomorrow."

"I don't care where I am if I'm with you," she said, squeezing his hand.

"Can the groom kiss the bride while we dance?"

"Why don't you save that for when we're alone?"

"I'll try, but I won't like it," he said. "This is wonderful, Jessie. You've made me the happiest man on this earth today."

She laughed. "A big Texas exaggeration."

"I'm the happiest and I've married the most beautiful woman."

"Whoo, that is a whopper," she said, smiling at him. "I can't wait until we're alone."

"Then let's escape this shindig soon. All these people know how to party."

"I have to dance with all the brothers—my brothers, your brothers, my brother-in-law, your brother-in-law. That's going to take a while."

"Wave at me when you're ready to go. I told you, the limo is ready."

It was three hours later when she waved across the room at him. In less than two minutes he was at her side, getting her out of a conversation with a group of her relatives.

They slipped out and dashed for the limo. As they turned onto the highway for the airport, Ryan pulled her into his arms. "I love you, darlin'. I'm the luckiest man ever."

"I love you, Ryan. I am so happy."

"I want to always keep you that way," he said, drawing her into his embrace as he leaned forward to kiss her.

Jessie wrapped her arms around his neck and kissed him in return. Her heart was filled to overflowing with joy and love for this tall man who was her wonderful Texas cowboy.

* * * * *

A sneaky peek at next month...

Desire™

PASSIONATE AND DRAMATIC LOVE STORIES

My wish list for next month's titles...

In stores from 21st February 2014:

❏ The Texas Renegade Returns – Charlene Sands

& Double the Trouble – Maureen Child

❏ Seducing His Princess – Olivia Gates

& Suddenly Expecting – Paula Roe

❏ The Real Thing – Brenda Jackson

& One Night, Second Chance – Robyn Grady

2 stories in each book - only £5.49!

Available at WHSmith, Tesco, Asda, Eason, Amazon and Apple

Just can't wait?

Visit us Online

You can buy our books online a month before they hit the shops!

Special Offers

Every month we put together collections and longer reads written by your favourite authors.

Here are some of next month's highlights— and don't miss our fabulous discount online!

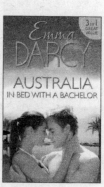

On sale 21st February   On sale 28th February   On sale 21st February

Save 20%
on all Special Releases

Join the Mills & Boon Book Club

Want to read more **Desire**™ books?
We're offering you **2 more** absolutely **FREE!**

We'll also treat you to these fabulous extras:

- Exclusive offers and much more!
- FREE home delivery
- FREE books and gifts with our special rewards scheme

Get your free books now!

visit www.millsandboon.co.uk/bookclub
or call Customer Relations on 020 8288 2888

Discover more romance at

www.millsandboon.co.uk

- ♥ WIN great prizes in our exclusive competitions

- ♥ BUY new titles before they hit the shops

- ♥ BROWSE new books and REVIEW your favourites

- ♥ SAVE on new books with the Mills & Boon® Bookclub™

- ♥ DISCOVER new authors

PLUS, to chat about your favourite reads, get the latest news and find special offers:

- 🔲 Find us on facebook.com/millsandboon
- 🐦 Follow us on twitter.com/millsandboonuk
- ♥ Sign up to our newsletter at millsandboon.co.uk

The World of Mills & Boon®

There's a Mills & Boon® series that's perfect for you. We publish ten series and, with new titles every month, you never have to wait long for your favourite to come along.

By Request

Relive the romance with the best of the best
12 stories every month

Cherish™

Experience the ultimate rush of falling in love
12 new stories every month

Desire™

Passionate and dramatic love stories
6 new stories every month

nocturne™

An exhilarating underworld of dark desires
Up to 3 new stories every month

M&B/WORLD4a

What will you treat yourself to next?

INTRIGUE...
A seductive combination of danger and desire...
6 new stories every month

Awaken the romance of the past...
6 new stories every month

The ultimate in romantic medical drama
6 new stories every month

MODERN™
Power, passion and irresistible temptation
8 new stories every month

True love and temptation!
4 new stories every month